9 780425 135273

50550>

NORMA BEISHIR

LUCK
OF
THE
DRAW

Behind
every great
fortune
is a
crime.

Behind
every great
love is
a lie.

Praise for
NORMA BEISHIR
and Her Bestselling Novels

Solitaire

"A dazzler! A fast-paced novel of passion and intrigue. . . . Don't miss this one!"
— SUSAN ELIZABETH PHILLIPS, *New York Times* bestselling author of *Fancy Pants*

"A classy novel . . . glamour, greed and glory-seekers—an explosive combination . . . I loved it!"
— SANDRA BROWN, *New York Times* bestselling author of *Mirror Image*

A Time for Legends

"Beishir pens a winner with this gripping thriller!"
— *Publishers Weekly*

Angels at Midnight

"Rife with sizzling sex . . . compulsive reading!"
— *Publishers Weekly*

Dance of the Gods

"*Dance of the Gods* has got it all—mystery and megabucks, thrills and chills, sex and romance. . . . Buckle your seatbelt. This is a runaway roller coaster ride that grips you from page one and races to its explosive climax!"

— JUDITH GOULD, *New York Times* bestselling author of *Sins*

"This is hot!" — *New York Daily News*

LUCK
OF THE
DRAW

NORMA BEISHIR

BERKLEY BOOKS, NEW YORK

LUCK OF THE DRAW

A Berkley Book / published by arrangement with
Moonstone-Solitaire, Inc.

PRINTING HISTORY
Berkley edition / March 1994

ISBN: 0-425-13527-6

BERKLEY®
Berkley Books are published by The Berkley Publishing Group,
200 Madison Avenue, New York, New York 10016.
BERKLEY and the "B" design
are trademarks belonging to Berkley Publishing Corporation.

PRINTED IN THE UNITED STATES OF AMERICA

10 9 8 7 6 5 4 3 2 1

When the chips are down, you find
out who your real friends are. With
that in mind, this book is dedicated to
Anna Eberhardt, Donna Julian and Mary
Martin . . .

. . . and a caring family helps, too,
so special thanks are also due
Sharon McCance, Norma Stockero,
Bert Correnti and Bessie Nelson.

Behind every great fortune is a crime.

—**BALZAC**

A man who strives after goodness
in all that he does will come to ruin;
therefore a prince who will survive
must learn to be other than good.

The man who would be prince
must be unencumbered by morals and ethics;
he must be part lion and part fox.

—**MACHIAVELLI,**
The Prince

LUCK
OF THE
DRAW

1

She was dead. He had killed her.

The reality of it hit him like a spray of bullets, tearing into his soul just as the hard, driving rain was hitting his face, plastering his bloodstained clothing to his body. A body too numb with shock to feel either the rain or the cold wind that slashed like a bullwhip between the skyscrapers vying for dominance on the Manhattan skyline. He wasn't wearing a coat. He'd had one, he vaguely remembered having worn one, but he had no idea where he'd left it. Not that he cared. He didn't care about anyone or anything. Not now, not anymore. In one instant he had destroyed everyone and everything that had mattered to him. No . . . he was better off not caring.

Unconsciously, he ran a hand through his thick, unruly gray hair. The weathered face that even in his youth had always been too hardened with bitterness to be considered truly handsome was now void of any emotion. Even pain. He was beyond pain. Beyond rage.

Beyond hope.

Looking up, he found himself standing in front of St. Patrick's Cathedral. The yellow police lines were still up, but the crowd that had gathered at the entrance was gone now. It was over, and all those who had come to see what had taken place there, what he had done, had put it behind them and gone back to whatever they had been doing before. Their lives had returned to normal when they left the cathedral.

His would never be the same again.

It occurred to him then, somewhere in the back of his mind, that he must have been walking in circles to have ended up back there, but he had no idea how long he might have been walking or where he had been up until that moment. He was sure it was late, very late. It was so dark. But as far as he knew, it could be midnight—or it could be four in the morning. He had lost all sense of time after he had left the cathedral. Time. It didn't matter.

Nothing mattered.

He stood there for what seemed to be an eternity, staring up at the cathedral, the all-too-vivid images of what had taken place inside flashing through his mind. With them came the renewed pain, rushing back like an emotional flash flood, engulfing him. "No!" he roared, his anguished cry that of a mortally wounded animal. "No!"

The streets were deserted. No one was around to hear his tortured scream, to witness his pain. No one was there to witness his guilt.

There was no sound in the hospital room except the steady whirring and hissing of the respirator, the reassuring beep of the cardiac monitor. The woman in the bed was pale, lifeless. She was motionless except for the shallow breathing made possible by the machines. At her bedside stood a man and a woman. Neither of them spoke or even looked at each other. They stood silent, unmoving, the man's arm around the woman protectively, looking on as a nurse checked her patient and made sure all of the equipment was properly connected and working as it should be.

They glanced up, surprised to see him there, standing in the doorway, covered with blood and drenched from the downpour. He was one of the richest men in the world, but right now he looked like a vagrant.

"What are you doing here?" the woman asked finally, not bothering to even try to hide her contempt.

"You think I wouldn't come?" He stepped forward. "I had to know if she was—you know—" He gestured helplessly.

"Dead?" The woman glared at him. "No—she's not. Not yet. The doctors aren't hopeful. But you shouldn't be surprised. You've never done anything halfway in your life, have you?"

"Go ahead. Take your best shot," he said wearily. "I deserved that."

"This is your fault!"

"You think I don't know that?" he replied savagely. "Do you think you could possibly hate me any more than I hate myself right now? No way."

The other man cleared his throat. "I don't think this is a good idea—"

"I don't give a goddamn what you think!" he snapped as he approached the bed. He frowned as he looked down at her, lying there, fighting for her life. He wanted to cry, but he didn't have that right. God, it *was* his fault: Her life was hanging by a thread now because of him. He'd pulled the trigger.

Now, as he fixed his gaze on her, willing her to fight, to pull through, the ghosts returned, surrounding him. Ghosts of a past he'd never been able to escape, no matter to what lengths he'd gone. No matter what he'd done. Maybe even because of what he'd done.

The truth shall set you free. Where had he heard that? he wondered as he continued to watch her, to pray silently for her as he'd never prayed for anything before. The truth had always been important to her, so important, in fact, that it had come between them in the end. It was kind of ironic that he'd fallen so hard for a woman who was so unlike him in almost every way. *Now,* he thought, looking up at the other woman, *it's coming between us, too.* With that realization came the decision he'd refused to make, the decision he'd always avoided in the past.

"We've got to talk," he said.

She avoided his eyes. "What is there to talk about now?" she asked coldly.

"More than you think," he said quietly. "I think you've got the right to know *why* this happened . . . "

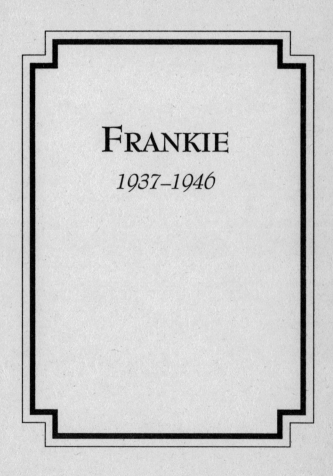

FRANKIE

1937–1946

2

"Stop! Thief!"

The boy couldn't have been more than twelve or thirteen years old, tall for his age and shabbily dressed. He'd been startled by the owner of the produce market, who caught him red-handed as he was stuffing fresh fruit into his partially zipped jacket. When the boy realized he'd been discovered, he ran out of the store, the heavy, red-faced man in hot pursuit. An orange fell from the boy's pocket as he fled the scene of the crime. His pursuer, in his rage, didn't see it, and the moment his foot hit it, he lost his balance and fell to the sidewalk.

"Stop him!" the man yelled as he struggled to his feet. "Stop that little thief!"

The boy ran swiftly, maneuvering easily through the crowds of Friday morning shoppers, clutching his jacket about his waist against the blasting March wind. In his desperation to get away, he knocked down a small woman carrying two heavy shopping bags, but he never stopped moving as the woman screamed at him, the contents of both bags spilling onto the sidewalk.

"Stop that little thief!"

The store owner had resumed the chase. Now he was joined by a uniformed policeman whose shrill whistle cut through the din of excited voices in the street. The boy didn't stop running. He ducked into a dark, cluttered alley between two tall, run-down brick buildings and found himself facing a dead end. He could hear the two men approaching, whistle blowing, voices raised in anger. Looking around wildly, he could see only one possible chance of escape. He jumped up onto the garbage cans clustered against the high fence at the far end of the alley, hoisted himself to the top of the fence—with one arm still clutching the bounty inside his coat—and leaped easily to the ground on the other side. Beyond the fence, he could hear the two men cursing loudly. Smiling to himself, he pulled an apple from his coat and took a bite.

Home free, he thought with satisfaction as he strolled away.

"I stopped at the market on my way home, Ma," he told his mother as she inspected the selection of produce on the small, badly scarred kitchen table. He'd had to think fast. She'd walked in on him before he'd had a chance to put it all away.

Kathleen Granelli, a slim, dark woman who looked older than her thirty-two years, eyed her young son suspiciously. "Mr. Jarvis pays you this much to deliver newspapers?" she asked.

He gave a shrug but deliberately avoided her eyes as he put a loaf of bread in the breadbox. "I don't make that much, Ma," he said quietly. "This stuff took everything I made this week."

She studied him for a long moment, not quite convinced. "All of it?"

"We have to eat, Ma," he said simply.

"I take care of us the best I can, Frankie," she said then.

He didn't look at her. "I know that, Ma," he said with a tightness in his voice that couldn't be missed. "I just keep hopin' one of these days I'll be makin' enough so you won't have to—do what you're doin' now." How his mother earned a living was a sore subject for young Frankie Granelli.

She gave a deep sigh as she came closer. "I know how you feel, Frankie. I feel the same way myself." She came up behind him, placing her hands on his shoulders. "But times are tough. With your father in jail, we have to get by the best we can. I don't have much education. No skills to get a decent job. This is the only way."

Frankie frowned. "For now, Ma," he said in a faltering voice that betrayed what he was feeling.

Only for now.

*   *   *

Frankie Granelli lay awake in the darkness in his small bedroom, unable to sleep, unable to escape the sounds coming from the next room. His mother's bedroom. She was in there now, with one of her "customers." Customers! Frankie knew what was going on in his mother's bedroom, knew what his mother did for a living. And though they never talked about it, though neither of them ever spoke the words, they both knew the truth.

Frankie's mother was a whore.

Frankie knew all about whores. He would have known even if his own mother weren't one of them. He'd learned all about such things on the back streets of Chicago when most boys his age were learning about baseball and building tree houses. He knew that there were women who were willing to sell sex to any man for money and that men were willing to pay for it. But Frankie had learned many of life's harsh realities at an age at which most boys would have been too young to understand.

Frankie Granelli had been forced to grow up fast. It had been only a few years since his father went to prison, leaving him, not quite ten years old at the time, as the man of the house. Years that had seemed like a lifetime. Years of struggles and setbacks and learning to survive under the most adverse conditions imaginable. Years of facing a reality he still found impossible to accept. *Damn you, Pa,* he thought bitterly. *Damn you to hell for doin' this to us!*

As a small boy, Frankie had worshipped his father. In his eyes, Joey Granelli had been a gentle giant of a man who took him for rides around the living room on his broad shoulders, played games with him, and taught him a philosophy he'd never learn in school: "There's a sucker born every minute," Joey often quoted, "and two to take him. The trick is to take the other guy before he takes you."

Frankie was eight years old when he discovered his father was a bootlegger, that what Joey did for a living was illegal. That was the first time Joey went to jail. It had been his first offense, so the judge sentenced him to sixty days in jail or the payment of a one-hundred-dollar fine. Joey Granelli, a small-time lawbreaker, didn't have a hundred dollars, he didn't need to take care of his family, so he got the sixty days.

That had been the beginning. Even after Joey went to jail that first time, Frankie hadn't suspected the truth. Not until the rumors started. Not until he got into a fight with a boy at his school who'd taunted him, saying his father was a criminal who associated with other criminals. He'd come home with a black eye, a bloodied nose, and his clothes torn. His father had demanded to know the truth when he hesitated to give an explanation for his fighting, and finally Frankie had obeyed.

And that night, Joey had told him the truth.

The sounds coming from his mother's room cut through Frankie's thoughts. Animal sounds. Frankie knew about whores and he knew about sex, but the sex act itself was still somewhat of a mystery to him. He'd seen dogs mating once or twice. Could a man coupling with a woman really be much different? In his mind, he saw the man who'd turned up at their door an hour earlier, the same big, dark, ugly man who came every week, same time, same day, to go into the bedroom with his mother for a couple of hours. He saw that man riding his mother like a male dog rode a bitch in heat, and it nauseated him. Yet, in ways that made him feel guilty and ashamed, it also fascinated him.

Frankie lay there in the darkness, listening to the sounds they were making, thinking about it, visualizing it. Finally, he got out of bed, drawn by something he couldn't identify and couldn't resist, and crept quietly out of his own room and down the short hallway to his mother's door. He opened it slowly, silently, just enough to look inside.

The lights were on. His mother lay sprawled on the bed. She appeared to be completely undressed, but from where he stood, Frankie couldn't see all of her. The man was also naked. He was hunched over her, and he was even uglier without his clothes. His fat, bucking body was covered with hair. *He looks like a gorilla,* Frankie thought with disgust. *A big, ugly gorilla. He has more hair on his body than he has on his head.*

He was riding her furiously, and her body seemed to convulse as he pounded himself into her, his big hands grabbing her breasts, squeezing them hard. She was moaning, and Frankie could tell the big man was hurting her, but she never once tried to fight him. She never even tried to push him away. Was it okay for a man to do whatever he wanted with a woman as long as he was paying for it? Frankie wondered as he watched them, mesmerized, wanting to turn away yet inexplicably unable to do so.

When the big man was finished, he got up on his knees near her head and grabbed her by the hair, pulling her face to his groin. "Suck it," he growled. She didn't protest. She took his sausagelike organ into her mouth and started to suck at it noisily.

Feeling the bile rise in his throat, Frankie closed the door quietly, crept across the hall to the bathroom, locked himself inside, and got down on his knees in front of the toilet.

Then he threw up.

While other boys his age spent their after-school hours playing ball or just hanging around the neighborhood, young Frankie Granelli had other, more important things on his mind. Once a week, and never on the same day, lest the shopkeepers become aware of any pattern to his activities and be ready for him, he made the rounds of the local grocery stores and produce markets, stealing whatever he could lay his hands on. He always told his mother he earned the money to buy the things he brought home. She thought he delivered newspapers. Had she known the truth, she would never have approved. *It's okay for her to sell her body to make a buck, but stealing's a sin in her book,* he thought resentfully. But he never said anything to her face about it because he knew it would do no good.

Frankie was a loner—not out of desire but out of necessity. Forming friendships meant visiting those friends at their homes, with reciprocal visits from time to time. Frankie could never allow anyone to come to his home, because if they did, they might learn the truth he'd struggled so hard to hide. They might find out his mother was a whore.

The closest thing Frankie Granelli had to real friends were his father's old cronies. There was Vinnie, the bookmaker, with whom Joey had grown up, right there on the South Side.

There were Alphonse and Lonny, who made their living as gamblers and had mastered every method of cheating known to man. And there was Billie, who sang in a speakeasy and was, she claimed, a former mistress to one of Capone's lieutenants, though she never said, specifically, which one. They had known his father, and they knew all about his mother—and they were the only ones he could turn to. The only ones he could trust.

Alphonse taught Frankie to play poker; Lonny taught him to shoot craps. "Do you ever make money at this?" Frankie asked them one day. "I mean *a lot* of money?"

Alphonse only laughed. "A gambler's money ain't got no real home, Frankie," he told the boy. "One day it's with you, the next day it can be with the other guy."

"But what if you're real good at it?" Frankie pursued. "What if you're the best?"

"There's no such thing as a 'best' gambler, kid," Alphonse told him, lighting one of those cheap, fat, smelly cigars he always smoked. "There's just good gamblers and bad gamblers. Bad gamblers are just fools. They gamble for the sake of gambling. They bet on anything and everything."

"And a good gambler?" the boy asked, genuinely interested.

Lonny grinned and poured himself a drink. "Being a good gambler just means knowing when to take risks," he said, taking a long swallow of the undiluted bootleg whiskey.

Frankie smiled, and his blue eyes lit up the way most childrens' eyes did only on Christmas morning. "That's all there is to it?" he asked, clearly amazed.

"Whoa!" Alphonse roared with laughter. "It ain't as easy as it sounds, kid. A big part of it's instinct—and that you gotta be born with. You got it or you ain't. You can't learn it."

"Teach me what I *can* learn," Frankie said promptly.

And they did.

"Watch real close now, kid." Alphonse sat at the round, wobbly kitchen table in his rooms overlooking one of the seedier South Side neighborhoods. He held the deck of playing cards in his left hand, the top of the middle finger of his right hand pressed against those cards at the top edge of the deck that were held in place by his left index finger. "You ever see somebody holdin' the cards this way, it might look weird, but it ain't no accident." He pressed his right thumb along the bottom edge of the deck. "Keepin' the pressure steady, you move all but that top card by slidin' the rest of the cards with the right hand." He demonstrated by easily moving the cards—except that top card—onto the four fingers of his left hand.

Frankie noted with amazement that Alphonse never lost control of that top card. "Show me again, Al," he urged.

Alphonse repeated the maneuver again and again until Frankie was convinced he could do it himself. The boy found the grip awkward and uncomfortable, and the first time he attempted to manipulate the cards, he only succeeded in flipping them clumsily, scattering them across the table.

"Damn!"

"Patience, Frankie," Lonny told him as they picked up the cards together. "You got to be patient if you want to be a gambler. And don't look so damn hungry!" He passed the cards to Alphonse.

Alphonse reshuffled the deck in an easy overhand motion, then handed it back to Frankie. "Try it again," he instructed with a nod.

The boy hesitated momentarily, then took the cards. In the hours that followed, he repeated the mechanic's grip again and again until he could do it smoothly and flawlessly.

"Now I'm going to show you how to hold on to the top and bottom cards," Alphonse told him. He took the cards in hand as he'd done before, but this time he pressed down with not only his left thumb, but the ring and index fingers as well, exerting pressure against the bottom card. He removed the pack with his right hand, and the top card fell gently onto the bottom card resting in his left hand.

Alphonse looked at Frankie questioningly. "Notice anything different?" he asked.

Frankie paused, frowning. "No."

"I'll do it again. This time, you pay attention, okay?" He repeated the maneuver. "Now—anything different to you?"

Frankie thought about it for a moment. "The cards—they

was makin' a kind of slappin' sound.''

Alphonse nodded, grinning. "Right. And that sound's a dead giveaway whenever the grip's bein' used,'' he pointed out.

"Except you can't always hear it,'' Lonny put in as he pulled up a chair. "Some games get pretty noisy—and some mechanics are good enough to do it without makin' a sound.''

Frankie paused for a moment, then reached out to take the cards. "I wanna learn to do it right,'' he announced.

"You ain't gonna master it overnight,'' Lonny warned.

Frankie shrugged. "I got time,'' he said. "I ain't got much else, but I got plenty of time.''

Besides, it gave him an excuse to stay away from home.

He could hear his mother moaning the minute he opened the front door. He closed the door and looked up at the old clock on the wall. For some reason, the broken hour hand, the one that had been broken for as long as he could remember, caught his attention now. He paused, staring at it, subconsciously trying to shut out the sounds coming from the bedroom. Half past midnight. It was Tuesday night. That meant *he* had been there. Was he still there? Was that why his mother was moaning? He was rough, that one; he'd hurt her more than once. Frankie had seen the bruises, the cuts.

He'd seen his mother cry after that animal had beaten her up.

Taking a deep breath, he withdrew his gaze from the clock and made his way to the bedroom. He opened the door, at first just enough to peek into the darkness. He could barely see her lying on the bed, the sheet tangled around her, covering her nakedness.

She was alone, so he went into the room and switched on the small lamp on the bedside table. Frankie gasped at the sight of her cut, swollen lip and blackened right eye. That bastard had really worked her over this time.

"Ma?'' he asked softly. "You okay, Ma?'' He knew it was a stupid thing to ask—of course she wasn't—but he didn't know what else to say.

She opened her left eye. "Frankie . . . you should be in bed . . . '' she whispered.

"And you should be in a hospital, Ma."

"Don't talk foolishness, boy." Her voice was weak. "You know we can't afford no hospital."

"He was here again, wasn't he? He did this to you, didn't he?"

"It don't matter."

"It *does* matter, Ma." He reached out and took her hand. It was trembling. "He belongs in jail. You should call the police—"

She barely managed to shake her head. "Can't do that, Frankie," she told him. "They'd ask questions. They'd find out about what I do—"

"So what're you gonna do?" Frankie demanded. "Just let that bastard keep beatin' you up?"

She shut her eyes, her face contorted with pain. "We talked about this before," she said. "We need the money."

"Not that bad, Ma."

"Yeah, Frankie. That bad."

He shook his head. "There must be something else, Ma, some other kind of work," he insisted stubbornly. "There has to be."

"Been through all this before, too," she said, her breathing labored. "You know and I know there's no other way. This is the only way . . . for both of us."

He fought back tears. "Gotta be a better way," he said in a barely audible voice.

Her expression was sad. "If there was, don't you think I'd have found it by now?" she asked wearily. "Frankie, this is how it is. Times are tough. Your papa's not here to look after us, so we make do the best we can with what we got. These men pay to spend an hour or two with me. That money—it puts food on our table and clothes on our backs."

"But what about Papa?" He didn't understand.

"It's got nothin' to do with your papa," she told him. "What I do with these men—it's not love, it's not even pleasure. It's just a way to survive."

"You don't like what you're doin', then?"

"What's to like about it?" She sighed deeply. "There are times I'd rather be dead, but then I look at you, and I know you need me. And the money."

*   *   *

So it was his fault.

His fault his mother allowed those men to do all of those terrible things to her. His fault she was subjected to so much pain and humiliation night after night. She was doing it for him. She was doing it because she loved him, because she was trying to take care of him the only way she knew how.

Because she loved him.

He thought about it now as he lay on his back in bed in the darkness, staring at a large crack in the ceiling illuminated by the light coming through the window from a neon sign on a building across the street. The bad things that were happening to her—they were happening because of him. If she didn't have him, if she didn't love him as she did—maybe then she wouldn't have to do these things. Maybe then she'd have a normal life. Her words echoed through his head: *There are times I'd rather be dead . . . rather be dead . . . rather be dead . . . .*

Frankie couldn't help wondering if perhaps she wouldn't be better off dead.

From that night on, there was a part of Frankie that would always feel responsible for his mother's predicament, and it made the reality of their circumstances even harder to live with. He found himself making a concerted effort to stay away from home when he knew one of *them* would be around. He spent more and more time with Alphonse and Lonny, learning everything they could teach him, and a great deal more besides.

"Could I move in with you guys?" he asked one night after a game of craps.

Lonny looked surprised. "Why would you wanna do a thing like that?" he asked.

Frankie shrugged. "Why not?" he asked casually, not wanting them to know just how anxious he was to leave home—or why.

"What about your mama?" Lonny wanted to know.

"She'd be better off without me," Frankie said, looking down at the dice he'd been shifting absently from one hand to another. "She can't afford to keep me."

Alphonse looked at him, silent for a moment. "She say that?" he asked finally.

Frankie shook his head, still looking down at the dice in his hand. "No. She wouldn't. But I know."

"So you think she'd let you just pick up and go," Lonny concluded. "Just like that."

"I don't think she'll mind, no."

"I think you might be wrong about that, kid," Lonny disagreed.

"She'll get by cheaper without me," Frankie said stubbornly. Finally, he looked up at the two men. "I can pay my way here, guys. Honest."

"How?" Lonny asked.

" 'How' probably ain't as honest as he claims," Alphonse put in.

"I can hustle," Frankie told them.

"You sure you're ready for that?" Lonny asked slowly.

"Damn sure. I had the two best teachers in town, didn't I?"

Alphonse poured himself a drink and turned to Lonny. "I got a feeling he's doin' a number on us right now."

Lonny looked at Alphonse, then back at Frankie again. "If you can pay your way with us, why can't you do it with your ma?"

Frankie's face was serious. "She'd never let me do it," he said quietly. "She don't like me to do those things. Don't want me to end up like my pa. I ain't even told her what you guys been teachin' me."

"Not a good idea," Alphonse agreed, taking a long swallow of his whiskey.

"She'd be real mad," Frankie said.

"I can imagine," Lonny said, looking at his partner out of the corner of his eye.

"So what's it gonna be, guys?" Frankie asked. "Can I move in with you or not?"

"Well," Lonny began with uncertainty in his voice, "I guess it'd be okay. If your ma don't mind."

"She won't," Frankie said quickly.

He knew she wouldn't object. She wouldn't have the opportunity—because he didn't plan to tell her.

He was going to run away from home.

Frankie dreaded going home. *He* was going to be there again, and Frankie hated being around when *he* was there. Frankie hated him more than the others because he was meaner than the others. *He* was the one who beat her so badly, who made her do all those terrible things, things no woman, Frankie reasoned, could possibly want to do. Things that made Frankie physically sick just thinking about them.

With any luck he'll be gone, Frankie thought as he reached inside his shirt and drew out the string knotted around his neck on which his house key hung. He paused at the front door and closed his eyes, drawing in a deep breath. *Here goes nothing,* he thought dismally. He slipped the key into the lock and turned it slowly, pushing the door open.

At first he didn't hear anything. He crept into the apartment and closed the door. Nothing. Not a sound. Thank God, he thought.

But his relief was short-lived. The sound of his mother's tormented scream pierced the silence. He jumped involuntarily, startled, then pulled himself together and swallowed hard. *God, that monster is still here.*

Frankie went straight to his room and closed the door, but it didn't help. It didn't block out the horrible sounds coming from the other side of the wall, from his mother's bedroom—the moaning, the periodic screams, the coarse language *he* was using. The coarse language he always used. Frankie threw himself down on the bed and covered his head with his pillow, but it didn't help. Nothing helped. He could block out the sounds, but he couldn't block out the knowledge of what was happening in there. What his mother was doing and why she was doing it. Why she'd been doing it all along.

She did it for him.

Frankie opened his eyes and lay still for a moment, not sure at first where he was. He wasn't sure when he'd drifted off or how long he'd been asleep. Then, as his mind began to focus, it came to him. He sat up on the bed, still fully clothed, and listened for a moment. It was quiet now. *He* must have left.

Finally, Frankie thought, getting to his feet. He crossed the small, cluttered room to the door, pausing to take a few deep breaths before opening it. *Better look in on Ma,* he thought. *Make sure he didn't hurt her too badly.*

He went to his mother's bedroom and opened the door. She was lying on her back on the rumpled bed, the sheet tangled around the lower half of her body. As he moved closer, he could see that she'd been badly beaten, more severely than usual. Her face was swollen and bruised. Her nose had been bleeding; there was dried blood on the lower half of her face and neck. Her arms and breasts were covered with scratches and bruises. Hesitantly, Frankie reached out and placed his hand on her chest. She was barely breathing.

She needed a doctor, no doubt about that. But Frankie knew that was out of the question. He couldn't call a doctor, couldn't have her taken to a hospital. If he called anyone, they'd ask questions. Questions he couldn't answer. No, all he could do for her now was tend to her bruises and hope for the best.

But would that be enough this time?

Looking down at her now, he was again faced with the painful knowledge of what his mother was—and why she was what she was. She was a whore. And it was because of him. She had taken the beatings, the degradation, because of him. It was *all* because of him.

His mother was the only person left in the world whom he still loved. The only person left who still loved him—and this was what that love had done to her. It had cost her her pride, her dignity, and nearly her life. It was his fault, all his fault.

Suddenly, he knew what he had to do.

He had to free her. He had to save her from herself, from the pain he had caused her. He left the bedroom and went into the kitchen. He rummaged through the utensil drawer until he found what he was looking for: a large ice pick, old, slightly rusty, discolored. He held it in his hands, staring at it for a long time, contemplating what he was about to do, unsure he had the nerve to carry it out. A tear escaped from the corner of one eye and slid down his cheek. Could he do it?

He had to do it. For her. For himself.

He cleaned the ice pick carefully. It had to be clean. He didn't know why, but it did. His mother was funny about things like that. She'd never use utensils—any utensils—that weren't spotlessly clean. When he was satisfied that it was clean enough, he took it with him back into the bedroom. His mother was still unconscious. He looked at her for a few seconds, then bent down and kissed her good night one last time. "I love you, Ma," he whispered.

Then, using all of his strength, he plunged the ice pick into his mother's chest.

3

Chicago, November 1937.

Now he was alone. Really alone.

Frankie sat on the bed in his room, knees drawn up to his chest. He'd done it. He'd killed her, and now he didn't know what to do next. As the reality of what he'd done set in, the numbness gave way to fear and a deep sense of loss, and he became a child again. A lost, frightened child who suddenly realized he really was all alone in the world.

He started to cry. It came slowly at first, tears that came to his eyes in spite of his fierce attempt to prevent them, sliding down his cheeks as he swallowed hard and willed himself not to lose control. He failed miserably. His lower lip began to tremble as the tears flowed freely. He cried and cried, until his sobs came out in dry, choking gasps. Until there were no tears left to cry.

Finally, he went back into his mother's bedroom and stared at her still, lifeless body for a long time. Soon, there would be a lot of people around. He'd have to get the police. *You never had no dignity in life, Ma,* he thought as he withdrew the ice pick from her chest and dropped it to the floor. *I guess it's the only thing I can do for you now.*

He pulled the sheet up over her naked breasts, then went to find a policeman.

"He says he saw the guy leaving," Officer Joe Sullivan, a tall, stout man in his mid-fifties told the homicide detective called in to investigate the Granelli case. "He seemed to be in shock, but—"

"What, exactly, did he tell you?" Sergeant Tim Delancey, shorter than the uniformed officer by a good six inches and at least ten years younger, scribbled in a small notebook.

"He said he came home late. God knows why any decent mother would let a boy that young be roaming the streets at all hours." Sullivan glanced at Frankie, who sat silent and motionless on the couch, watching the coroner's men take away his mother's body. "He said he found her in bed like that. Pulled the ice pick out of her—he didn't know any better, after all. Told me this guy—he came here a lot, according to the kid—had just left."

"I'm not surprised the kid was out on the streets," Delancey said. "You could hardly call that gal a decent mother. She was a whore, Joe. She's got a record—been turnin' tricks ever since Joey Granelli got sent up."

Hearing the detective's comment, Frankie leaped off the couch and flew at the man. "Don't say that about my ma!" he shouted, enraged, pummeling Delancey with his balled-up fists. "She was a *good* mother!"

Sullivan grabbed him by the shoulders and pulled him off the other man. The boy's arms were still swinging wildly, and Sullivan found him surprisingly strong for his age. "Calm down, kid!" he shouted. "It's okay. He didn't mean it!"

"Yes, he did!" Frankie kept fighting. "He called my ma a whore!"

Sullivan wrapped both arms around him in an attempt to restrain him. It took all of his strength to hold Frankie still. "It don't matter, kid—it don't matter what anybody thinks!"

Frankie finally stopped struggling. "She *was* a good

mother!'' he snapped. ''She wouldn't have been doin' none of this if it wasn't for me. She did this for me! She's dead because of me!''

''What're you talkin' about, kid?'' Delancey asked. ''What do you mean, she's dead because of you?''

''None of your goddamned business!'' Frankie shouted at him.

''Take it easy, kid!'' Sullivan told him. ''He's only trying to find out as much as he can so we can find the person who did this and make sure he's punished.''

Frankie looked at him. ''Punished?''

Sullivan nodded. ''Of course the person who ki—did this to your mother will be punished,'' he said, ''if he's caught. You want that, don't you, Frankie?''

The boy nodded.

''Then you've got to tell us everything you know about this.''

Frankie frowned. ''But I don't know nothin'.''

''I know you said the man who killed your mother was leaving when you came home,'' Sullivan said. ''But surely you know some of the—people who came to see your mother.''

''You mean the men,'' Frankie said quietly.

Sullivan nodded. ''Yeah.''

''I knew some of 'em,'' Frankie told him. ''The ones who came a lot.''

''Like who?''

''Like him—he came every Tuesday, and sometimes on Thursdays, too,'' Frankie said, settling back down onto the worn couch. ''He was mean—he hit my ma a lot, made her do things—''

''What kind of things?''

Frankie shook his head. ''Bad things. Things she didn't never want to do.''

''Like what?''

Frankie shook his head. ''I can't. Can't say it.''

Sullivan nodded again. ''That's okay, kid. What else can you tell me about him? Did you know his name?''

''Yeah.'' Frankie paused. ''Leonard.''

''And his last name?''

"I think it was Richards or Roberts, something like that," he said, pretending to be uncertain. "No, it was Rogers. That's it—Leonard Rogers."

"Can you tell me what he looks like, Frankie?"

"Yeah. Big and ugly. He had a lot of hair, all over his body. Not much on his head, though," he said. "And a mustache. A big mustache."

"What color were his eyes?"

"I didn't get that close," Frankie told him.

Sullivan looked up at Delancey. "What do you think?"

The detective frowned. "I think we need a better description—unless the kid knows his address. Which I doubt."

Frankie looked up at the policeman, his face expressionless as he thought about the man who'd done those terrible things to his mother.

Maybe, he thought now, Rogers would pay for what he'd done after all.

Frankie was made a ward of the court and placed in a foster home—from which he ran away the first night. After two weeks, his foster parents gave up on him, and he was sent to a juvenile detention center. There, he underwent psychological testing and evaluation. It was determined that he was not only bright, but intelligent beyond his years. Unfortunately, he'd had little formal education. Even more unfortunate for the staff at the detention center, he was also undisciplined and, in their own words, "incorrigible."

At night, he lay on his cot in a large room filled with many such cots on which the other boys slept, and his mind was always on the same thing: how he was going to escape.

He hadn't bothered to tell anyone, but he'd never had any intention of staying there. They kept telling him he was smart, but they had no idea just how smart he really was. *Too smart for them,* he thought bitterly. *Too smart to stay in this hellhole.*

No . . . he was definitely not going to stay there. Even before his mother's death, he'd already made his plans. He was going to live with Alphonse and Lonny. He was going to make his own way in the only way he knew how—as a hustler. For now. Frankie had decided long ago that he did want an education, a real education.

He'd promised himself he was not going to end up like his parents.

The morning of his escape was one Frankie would never forget as long as he lived. The rest of the boys had gone off to breakfast. Frankie was allowed to stay behind because he was sick. He'd managed to put on a convincing performance by downing a mixture he'd made while no one was looking. The concoction made him vomit, as he'd known it would: He'd found the "recipe" written on the inside of the medicine chest door at home when he and his mother had moved into their apartment.

It was an antidote for poisoning.

He lay on his cot and waited until the housekeeping personnel came around to change the sheets. He watched, trying not to be too obvious about it, until all of the attendants were well away from the deep, wheeled cart in which the dirty laundry was placed to be taken to the truck waiting downstairs. When he was sure they were all busy with other things and wouldn't notice him, he climbed into the cart and buried himself at the bottom of the heap of sheets and linens.

Great, he thought as his arm came into contact with something wet. *Danny pissed in the bed again. I'm gonna die in here. If I don't suffocate, the smell'll do me in.*

To his relief, the cart was taken downstairs and loaded onto the truck much more quickly than he'd expected. He fought the urge to sneeze as the cart was jolted around the back of the truck and the doors slammed shut. *Not now,* he thought. *Not when I'm this close.*

Not until the truck started and he was certain that they were well on their way did Frankie finally emerge from his hiding place. *First stop we hit I'm outta here,* he thought.

Unfortunately, it turned out not to be that easy.

Frankie was positioned at the back of the truck, both hands clutching the door handle, ready to jump. When the vehicle finally came to a stop, he twisted the handle with all his strength—but the door wouldn't open! "Shit!" he muttered under his breath. "Locked! The goddamned thing's *locked*!"

He hit the door with his fist as hard as he could, and was barely able to stifle the resulting cry of pain. "Damn, damn, *damn!*" he snorted. Now what was he going to do?

The answer, of course, was simple. There was only one thing he could do: wait until the truck reached its destination.

When the carts were unloaded from the truck at the laundry, Frankie was back in his original hiding place, waiting for another opportunity to present itself.

"Goddamned thing sure is heavy," he heard a man's voice saying as the cart began to move. "They must've filled it with wet stuff this time."

"No tellin' what you'll get over at Juvenile," said another male voice. "Let's put it over here for now."

Frankie listened as the sound of their footsteps faded into the distance, then he raised his head slowly and lifted the pile of sheets covering him so he could look around. Nobody in sight. Good. He pushed the sheets aside and started to climb out.

"Hey—kid!"

Frankie jerked around. A man in what appeared to be a blue maintenance worker's uniform stood some twenty yards away. In that split second, Frankie decided that, given the distance and the man's size, he had a good chance at being able to outrun him, so he took it. He ran for the nearest open door as fast as his legs could carry him, with the big man lumbering behind, struggling to catch up. Without so much as a backward glance, he vaulted through the open door and into the alley outside. He didn't stop moving until he was sure he'd given the man the slip.

He didn't have to think about where he was going or what he would do next. He'd known all along. All he needed now was to find a bus to take him there. As he was crossing the street to the stop, he passed a newsstand. The headlines on the morning edition caught his eye: SUSPECT ARRESTED IN MURDER OF PROSTITUTE.

Frankie smiled. He'd get his revenge.

"Do the cops know where you are, kid?" Alphonse wanted to know.

"If they did, they'd be beatin' the door down," Frankie said as he bit into a thick sandwich with just about everything on it.

Lonny threw up his hands, his eyes rolled skyward. "Great! Just what we don't need!" he groaned. "Al, we're harborin' a goddamned fugitive from the law!"

Alphonse shifted in his chair and looked up at him. "I hate to be the one to break this to you, pal, but *we're* fugitives from the law, just in case you forgot."

"They're lookin' for him, Al!"

"They been lookin' for us, too, Lonny. At least six months now," Alphonse reminded him. "This is Joey's boy. No way I'd turn him away."

Frankie looked up anxiously, waiting to hear Lonny's response.

Lonny hesitated for a moment, then nodded. "Yeah, yeah—I know that," he said irritably. "It's just the idea of cops makes me real nervous, that's all."

"We been one step ahead of them all this time, we'll stay that way," Alphonse said confidently.

Frankie breathed an inward sigh of relief. He wasn't alone after all.

4

Chicago, February 1938.

"Softest touch I ever had," Frankie said cheerfully as he emptied the contents of his pockets onto the kitchen table. "Talk about a sucker!"

"How much did ya get?" Alphonse asked as he put the week's groceries away and closed their small icebox with his foot.

"Twenty-eight dollars, fifty-three cents." Frankie flipped a coin, watching it spin on the tabletop. "Pretty good, huh?"

Alphonse looked down, surprised, at the cash that lay crumpled on the table. "Damn good, kid," he said. "You're gonna be deadly when you grow up!"

Frankie laughed. "Comin' from you, Al, that sounds like praise."

"Close as you're ever gonna get, kid."

Frankie was stashing his winnings in an empty lard can in which he always kept his money, stored at the back of the icebox, when Lonny came in. He had a newspaper tucked under his arm. He wasn't smiling.

"What's the matter, Lonny?" Frankie asked. "You look like you lost your best friend."

"I got some news about the guy who killed your ma," Lonny said solemnly. "It's in today's paper. He's been convicted."

Frankie stopped what he was doing. "They're gonna kill him, ain't they?" he asked anxiously. "He's gotta die. They gotta give him the death penalty!"

Lonny nodded. "He's gonna hang."

Since they'd had no living relatives to help them out and no money for a proper burial, the City of Chicago had disposed of the body of Kathleen Granelli. It was a source of frustration for Frankie that he had never been able to visit his mother's grave or take her a flower—she'd always loved flowers but seldom received any when she was alive—and that added to his bitterness.

Now, alone in that small apartment—Alphonse and Lonny were God only knew where—Frankie lay on the couch, reading and rereading the front-page story in the newspaper Lonny had brought home. It was almost over, he realized with considerably less satisfaction than he'd expected to feel. Leonard Rogers was going to pay for the hell he had put Frankie's mother through. That man was finally going to pay for all the beatings, all the degradation. But somehow it wasn't enough. It didn't erase the pain his mother had suffered. It didn't change what had happened.

And it did nothing to ease Frankie's own guilt.

*   *   *

"Whaddya mean, I gotta go to school with you tomorrow?"
Alphonse asked, clearly annoyed, as he cut the deck and shuf-
fled the cards in a manner that suggested the movements were
second nature.

"Just what I said, Al." Frankie pulled up a chair and sat on
it backward, leaning over on his crossed arms atop the high
padded back. "They got to see one of my foster parents."

Alphonse looked at him, one thick eyebrow raised. "We
ain't exactly your legal guardians, kid," he reminded the boy.

"*They* don't know that," Frankie responded.

"What am I supposed to do? Put a dress on Lonny here
and try to pass him off as your foster mom?" Alphonse
wanted to know. "Look, kid—nobody in their right mind is
gonna believe any judge in the country would give a kid to
the likes of us. It could get all of us in a hell of a lot of
trouble."

"But I gotta have *somebody* there!"

"What for?" Lonny asked, lighting a cigarette. "Whaddya
in trouble for?"

Frankie fell silent for a moment as he picked at one of the
small tears in the vinyl covering the back of the chair. "Skippin' school," he said finally, his voice timid.

"Skippin' school!" Alphonse looked and sounded angry.
"Now what did I tell you about doin' what you're supposed
to be doin' and makin' sure not to get caught doin' the stuff
you ain't supposed to do?"

"I know, Al—"

"Don't look to me like you do." Alphonse dealt the cards.
"You know not to do nothin' to call attention to yourself—
but you done it anyway. You got any idea how much trouble
we're all gonna be in if the authorities get wise to you? They
find out you're not really my nephew, that you're Frankie
Granelli, and we're all in deep shit! You wanna get sent back
to Juvenile?"

"You know I don't!" Frankie snapped.

"Then don't do stupid things," Alphonse growled, con-
centrating on the cards in his hand.

"I won't do it no more," Frankie promised.

"Make sure you don't." Alphonse discarded two cards and
drew two more. After a long pause, he looked up at Frankie

again. "I'll see what I can do, okay?"

The boy brightened. "Thanks, Al."

Alphonse did go to the school, and Frankie never got in trouble in school again. It hadn't taken him long to realize that a good education was the key to his future, his ticket out of the world into which he'd been born.

And that, after all, had always been his ultimate goal.

The day Leonard Rogers was executed, Frankie went to school, but he found it impossible to concentrate on his classwork. He couldn't stop thinking about what was happening across town. In his mind, he could still picture Rogers the last time he had seen him: on top of his mother on the bed, naked, his fat, bucking body pounding her into the mattress while he slapped her and called her filthy names. Frankie still felt all of the rage he'd felt then. He'd wanted to kill Rogers that night. He'd wanted to make him pay for what he'd done.

And today, at last, he would pay.

"I thought you'd be real happy today, kid," Lonny commented, noticing the frown on Frankie's face as he picked at his dinner.

"I thought so, too," Frankie admitted, his appetite all but gone. "I thought Ma and me would be at peace once Rogers was punished."

"But you're not."

Frankie shook his head. "It ain't enough," he said. "It ain't gonna bring Ma back. It ain't gonna make me forget—" He stopped short.

Lonny looked at him, puzzled. "Forget what?"

"Forget what my ma went through—what he put her through." Frankie shook his head sadly. "He did awful things to her. He made her do awful things. And he beat her."

Lonny put a hand on Frankie's shoulder. "I'm sorry you had to see it, kid," he said, trying to be sympathetic. "You're too young to have to—"

"Did anybody see today's paper?" Alphonse called out, barging through the front door. He came through the living room into the kitchen, waving the newspaper as if to emphasize his point. "Rogers is plastered all over the front page."

"Yeah? What does it say?" Lonny asked.

"Read it for yourself." Alphonse held it out to him, but Frankie intercepted it. "The reporters must've had a field day. They got in a lot of details about the hanging—right down to the wife and baby." He paused. "Can you believe it? That bastard had a baby, too!"

"And I bet the wife didn't believe any of what he did," Lonny concluded.

"According to the paper, she didn't say much of anything," Alphonse said, pausing to light a cigarette. "Says here she hasn't been seen since the trial. Probably left town, d'ya think?" He looked down at Frankie, who hadn't heard a word he'd said.

He was preoccupied with the newspaper's account of the execution.

Late that night, after Lonny and Alphonse were gone—they were often gone all night, but Frankie had no idea where they went or what they did—Frankie read and reread the detailed newspaper story. The reporters described the execution and the events leading up to it in almost too much detail. He didn't quite understand some of the words, but he didn't have to. He *knew*.

Rogers's execution gave him little satisfaction. Yes, the man had paid for all the horrible things he'd done to Frankie's mother. Yes, he'd been punished for his sins.

But no, his execution did not—could not—ease Frankie's own guilt. It had done nothing to drive away the nightmares that haunted his sleep every night since that night, vivid images of him entering the bedroom with the ice pick . . . plunging it into his mother's bare breast . . . watching her blood spurt from the wound. . . .

He stared at the newspaper photo of Rogers's infant son for a long time. He felt sorry for the kid, having to grow up without a father.

He knew only too well what it felt like.

"Snake eyes," Frankie called.

Lonny looked down at the dice on the table. "What are the odds?" he asked.

"Thirty-five to one—but the house only gives thirty to one, giving them a thirteen percent edge," Frankie recited. "Same goes for boxcars."

"Good. Real good." Lonny nodded approvingly. The kid had a real head for the game. Hell, he had a real good head for *any* game. He had a fantastic memory; no wonder he was doing so well in school. Once he set his mind to it, the kid could master just about anything.

"The Big 6 and Big 8 pay even money," Frankie continued, rolling the dice again. "With odds at six to five, the house gets a nine percent advantage. More than nine percent, really."

"How do you make a pass?"

"A seven or eleven on the first roll. A four, five, six, eight, nine, or ten rolled twice before a seven comes up."

"And if you *do* get, say, a seven on the first roll?"

"I win the bet on the pass line," Frankie said promptly. "Then I start all over again with the next roll. If the first roll's a six, I got to roll six again before I roll seven or eleven."

"What if you roll, say, two fives?" Lonny asked, lighting a cigarette.

Frankie shook his head. "It don't count. First roll was a six, so I got to roll another six for it to count."

"Right," Lonny said with a nod. "Any questions?"

"Just one," Frankie said solemnly.

"Yeah?"

"How the hell do you *cheat* at craps?"

5

Chicago, March 1941.

The years had only hardened Frankie Granelli. At the age of sixteen, he was a tall, good-looking young man but far too solemn for one so young. He did well in school but had no friends. He liked it that way. The less one knew about you, he reasoned, the less likely they would ever get anything on you.

And Frankie had secrets, the kind of secrets he couldn't risk having revealed.

He didn't really mind being alone. There were times—most of the time, in fact—when he wanted to be alone. It gave him time to think, to make plans. Mostly he made plans for his future, a future that *had* to be better than his past. A future he'd make sure was better than his past. He'd already taken the first step, but he still had a long way to go. Knowing this didn't discourage him; on the contrary, it had only fueled his ambition, made him more determined than ever to make something of himself.

I'm not going to end up like my parents, he thought stubbornly.

When he did feel like being with other people, he had Alphonse and Lonny. They weren't always home, but when they were, the three of them were like one happy family.

The closest thing Frankie had to a family now.

Frankie's long legs took the steep flight of stairs two at a time. When he reached the top, he rounded the corner at a run and sprinted down the long, gloomy hallway with its dim lights and peeling, yellowed wallpaper to the apartment he shared with Lonny and Alphonse. Digging into the pocket of his charcoal-gray trousers, he pulled out his key and started to unlock the door—but before he could do so, the door squeaked open.

That's strange, Frankie thought as he entered the apartment cautiously and looked around. *They'd never go off and leave the door unlocked.* Lonny was always going on about not inviting trouble, and sometimes he even closed and locked the windows when all three of them were going to be away from the apartment for any length of time.

Frankie checked all of the drawers and closets. Nothing was missing—at least not that he could tell.

"They're gone."

Startled, Frankie spun around. Mrs. O'Hara, who lived across the hall, was standing in the doorway. She was a small, frail-looking woman who looked ten years older than her sixty-two years, with thinning gray hair and a narrow, wizened face.

Frankie looked at her for a moment, not sure he'd heard correctly. "Did you say—"

"They're gone," the woman repeated. "The police took 'em away this morning. Not long after you left, I don't think."

"What for?" Frankie asked. "I mean, why were they arrested?"

Mrs. O'Hara shrugged. "God only knows, boy. They was always doin' somethin' they wasn't supposed to do, those two. Bootleggin', illegal gamblin', you name it—but then, I guess you knew that."

Frankie nodded absently. "I guess they'll be back later—as soon as they can post bail."

"I hope so," said Mrs. O'Hara. "For your sake, I sure hope so."

By ten that night, they still weren't home. Mrs. O'Hara, concerned about Frankie, brought him dinner—a large bowl of beef stew and biscuits—which he devoured as though it were his first decent meal in weeks. "My Lord, child," she said with concern in her voice as she watched him eat, "you must be starving. Ain't those two been feedin' you?"

"Oh, sure," he said between bites. "I've been eatin'. Just not today."

"Never thought it was a good idea, a boy like you livin' with the likes of them," the woman said, shaking her head. "They ain't no kind of good influence."

"They're not bad," Frankie said in defense of Lonny and Alphonse. "They're all I've got."

"Where's your folks?"

"Dead."

"Both of 'em?"

He nodded. "My mother died four years ago," he said quietly. "I didn't have any other family, so Lonny and Al took me in. They were friends of my father's."

"Some friends." She passed him another biscuit.

"You don't think much of them, do you," Frankie said, more a statement than a question.

"I've lived across the hall from 'em goin' on eight years now," she told him. "I always figured they'd come to a no-good end. Appears now I was right."

"They'll be back. I know they will," Frankie said confidently.

Mrs. O'Hara frowned. "Maybe in ten to twenty."

They didn't come back.

It wasn't until the next day that Frankie learned just how much trouble Lonny and Alphonse were in. It seemed they'd been in the wrong place at the wrong time—as they often were—and had been in a car with two old cronies when that pair held up a bank across town.

Under the circumstances, Frankie doubted he'd ever see either of them again.

"You can't stay here alone," Mrs. O'Hara protested, concerned.

"Sure, I can," Frankie insisted. "It's my home." It had been two weeks since Lonny and Alphonse were arrested. The rent was due, and there was no food in the house.

"Not for long," she told him. "When McNally finds out you're here alone, you'll be out on your ear."

"I'm going to get a job," Frankie said stubbornly. "I'll be able to pay the rent."

"Within a week?" She looked skeptical. "I doubt McNally will wait any longer. He's not what I'd call a kind soul, boy."

Frankie nodded ruefully in agreement. "So what do I do now?" he asked, more to himself than to Mrs. O'Hara.

"You can move in with me," she answered promptly.

He looked up, unable to hide his surprise. "Oh, no—I couldn't—" he began.

She looked at him questioningly. "You've got someplace else you can go?"

"Well—no."

"Jobs are scarce, boy," she told him. "Better not count on finding something right away."

He took a deep breath and let it out slowly. "Great."

She smiled patiently. "Come on. I'll help you pack."

He thought about it for a moment, then nodded.

"I don't have much."

6

Chicago, September 1941.

"There's talk we'll be getting into the war soon."

"No way."

"Some of our boys are already over there, you know, flying with the RAF."

"Don't matter. It's not our war."

"It will be. Hitler's a goddamned maniac. He won't stop with Europe—he wants it all."

"He'll never get this far. The Nazis will never set foot on American soil."

"Maybe, maybe not."

"It'll never happen."

Frankie ignored the conversations taking place around him and concentrated on the horse he was tending. He'd been working as a groom at the Oak Brook Polo Club since late May, and it had given him access to a world to which he'd vowed he would one day belong. When time permitted, he would hang around the picket lines, picking up bits and pieces of conversations among the players. He often exercised the ponies. And there were days when one of the players, Archie Williams, a retired banker in his mid-sixties who'd been playing polo for more than forty years, would stick around the fields after a match and attempt to teach young Frankie the fundamentals of polo.

"You should take lessons, boy," he told Frankie. "You've got the makings of a fine player, I believe."

"Thank you, sir," Frankie said, properly grateful. "I'd like to."

"Last player I saw with that kind of potential was Tommy Hitchcock," Williams recalled, wiping the perspiration from his face with a damp towel.

Frankie instantly perked up. "*The* Tommy Hitchcock?"

Williams smiled. "I see you've heard of him."

"To spend any amount of time here and *not* know about Tommy Hitchcock, I'd have to be deaf," Frankie retorted.

"I think you could be a very good player," Williams said again. "That is, if you're willing to put forth the effort."

"I'm willing," Frankie assured him. And adding to himself, *But my wallet isn't.*

"What's wrong, boy?" Mrs. O'Hara asked, looking disapprovingly at Frankie's plate. He'd barely touched his dinner. "You not feelin' well?"

"I'm fine," he told her. "I'm just not hungry, that's all."

She wasn't convinced. Reaching out, she pressed her hand to his forehead. "You don't have a fever."

"I'm fine," he repeated. "I've just got things on my mind."

"Things? What things?" She took a bite of her stew.

He shrugged. "I've been hearing talk," he said slowly. "A lot of people seem to think we're on the brink of war."

"Nonsense!" the old woman scoffed. "This isn't our war, Frankie."

"They say it's just a matter of time."

"Well, they're wrong—whoever *they* are," she insisted. "Anyway, why should you be worried about that? You're not even seventeen yet and still in school. Too young for the draft."

"I was thinking of enlisting," Frankie admitted. "If it comes to that, I mean. If we do go to war."

"They won't take you, boy. You're too young."

"They would if you signed for me, Mary," he reminded her. "You're the closest thing I got to a relative."

She studied him for a moment with narrowed eyes, her lined face serious. "Why on earth would you want to enlist?"

"I don't make much at Oak Brook," he explained. "I'd get a lot more in the Navy. I could send you most of my allotment—"

"Hold it," she cut him off. "I don't need you to do that. We're doin' just fine here, just the way things are. I don't want you doin' nothin' like that for me."

"Come on, Mary. I'm not blind—or stupid. I can tell we're just barely making ends meet."

"Still—"

"You took care of me when I didn't have anyplace to go, Mary," he reminded her. "I always said I'd repay you for that one of these days. And I will."

Somehow, he thought, *I'll make sure you never have to worry about money again.*

Frankie lay awake that night, thinking. He'd never really had a family. His father had died in prison when he was young, and his mother—well, he tried not to think about his mother anymore. Then there were Lonny and Alphonse, but they weren't coming back for a long time. Mary was the closest thing he had to a mother now. The closest thing he'd had to a mother in a long time.

Mary O'Hara, he'd discovered, had once had a family of her own. Her husband had died of pneumonia ten years ago. Her son, Johnny, her only child, had been in the Army during World War I. He'd been reported missing in action somewhere in Europe. She didn't talk much about it.

Which explains why she feels the way she does about me enlisting, he thought.

"Do professional polo players make a lot of money?" Frankie wanted to know.

Archie Williams laughed. "Hardly. They generally make their money in some other way, then get into professional polo. Players have to pay all of their own expenses—which can run into a lot of money when you start traveling—and few tournaments offer any kind of money. Usually, winning a match means getting a trophy and, if you're lucky, a photo in the local newspaper."

"Then only a very rich man can afford to play," Frankie concluded.

"That's pretty much the way it is."

Frankie nodded, lifting the mallets he'd been carrying over his shoulder as they walked together across the polo field. "I see," he said quietly.

"Having second thoughts?" Williams asked.

"No way," Frankie responded.

I've got my work cut out for me, he was thinking.

"December seventh, 1941, a date which will live in infamy . . . " President Roosevelt's voice was grave as he addressed the nation via radio that Sunday morning. "The United States of America was suddenly and deliberately attacked by naval and air forces of the Empire of Japan."

Frankie leaned forward, turning up the volume on the old radio as the newscaster's voice came on again: "The details are not available—they will be in a few minutes. The White House is now giving out a statement. The attack apparently was made on all naval and military activities on the principal island of Oahu. A Japanese attack upon Pearl Harbor naturally would mean war. Such an attack would naturally bring a counterattack, and hostilities of this kind would naturally mean that the President would ask Congress for a declaration of war."

Frankie took a deep breath. War was inevitable now. He raked a hand through his dark hair as he recalled something

Archie Williams had said: *"It's a hell of a thing to say, Frankie, but a war is exactly what this country needs right now."*

"Why is that?" Frankie had asked.

"It's good for the economy," Archie explained. *"Defense plants mean jobs. And jobs mean money. The poor make ends meet, and the rich get richer."*

"And someone who's trying to get rich?"

"The timing couldn't be better."

From that moment on, Frankie had hoped there *would* be a war. Now he was getting his wish—and he wasn't sure it was what he wanted at all.

The next day, war was officially declared. The day after that, Frankie Granelli enlisted in the U.S. Navy.

7

The South Pacific, July 1945.

From the deck of the U.S.S. *Indianapolis,* Frankie saw water as far as the eye could see in every direction. It seemed to him now that it had been years, rather than days, since he'd seen land.

The *Indianapolis* had set out from Mare Island, near San Francisco, on Sunday, July 16, bound for an unknown destination. As the cruiser cast off and passed beneath the Golden Gate at eight that morning, rumors flew that they were off on some top-secret mission. There had been a universal concern that the ship was not up to the voyage that lay ahead of it. It had been severely damaged when a kamikaze plane smashed into it at Okinawa in April, and the ship had returned to Mare Island for repairs. Though those repairs had been completed and the *Indianapolis* had all-new instruments and a fresh complement of some thirty officers and two hundred and fifty enlisted men, most of those men lacked the necessary experience for the mission. The ship had completed only a one-day shakedown cruise, even though such testing normally took three, or, better yet, four days.

But it would have been impossible to postpone this trip. Though no one aboard the *Indianapolis* knew it at the time, there was too much at stake. Under direct orders from the President of the United States, they were en route to the tropical island of Tinian, near Guam, to deliver parts of a secret weapon that was believed capable of ending the war.

It was from Tinian that the *Enola Gay* would take off on its flight into history via Hiroshima.

Frankie Granelli had been a loner before the war, and that hadn't changed all that much since he'd enlisted. He played poker and craps with his shipmates, but he never got into the habit of sharing confidences with them. He'd grown up knowing that anything anybody knew about you could eventually be used against you, and this was the one aspect of his life in which he elected to play it safe.

The closest he came to making an exception to that rule involved one Spencer Randall, who occupied the bunk above his. Randall was a good kid, if a little straitlaced. He'd grown up a rich kid from Massachusetts whose family had lost everything through some bad investments, and had no immediate family living. He'd lost his parents two years earlier in a hotel fire in France, and his maternal grandparents had gone down with the *Titanic* in 1912. Had it not been such a touchy subject, Frankie might have kidded Randall about attracting personal disaster. But Spencer Randall was an okay sort, so he left it alone.

"I lost my folks, too," Frankie told him one day. "Both of 'em, when I was just a kid. I'd have been on the streets if it hadn't been for a couple of my old man's buddies and a nice neighbor lady who took me in."

"The one you send your allotment to?" Spencer asked.

"Yeah," Frankie said with a nod. "Got to repay the debt." He didn't like the idea of letting anyone, even Spencer, see the chinks in his armor, even where they concerned someone who'd been as good to him as Mary O'Hara had been.

"I guess I was lucky to have had mine as long as I did,"

Spencer decided. "At least Dad got to see me get through Yale and Wharton."

Frankie grinned. "Yale? You're a preppie?"

Spencer made a face. "Don't start that."

"You really went to Yale?"

"Had to. Dad was set on me following in his footsteps."

"What did your old man do?"

"Investment banker. What about yours?"

Frankie hesitated for a moment. "He was—ah—into high-risk ventures." In a way, it was true. Nothing was more high-risk than being a bootlegger during Prohibition. "He took one risk too many, and it killed him."

"Risk comes naturally, then," Spencer said with a twinkle in his eye, looking at the deck of cards in Frankie's hand.

"Yeah, I guess you could say that." *But I won't be as stupid as he was,* he was thinking.

Spencer talked often and at length about his life before the war. *He's an open book,* Frankie thought as he lay awake in his bunk one night after one of Spencer's long walks down memory lane. *What he appears to be is exactly what he is— a decent, uncomplicated kid.* They had little in common except that they both pretty much kept to themselves, though for different reasons.

For Spencer, it was just shyness. For Frankie, it was survival.

"You sure those dice ain't loaded, Granelli?"

The question came from one of the seven sailors who regularly shot craps or engaged in poker games with Frankie aboard the *Indianapolis*.

Frankie laughed. "If you can't take the heat, Johnny, keep your butt out of the kitchen," he told the other sailor. He counted his winnings for the evening, folded the bills, and stuck them in his shirt pocket. "Better luck next time."

"I don't think luck's got anything to do with it, Granelli."

"Sure it does. I can't help it if it's all mine."

I'm making a bigger killing in this war than the Japs are, Frankie thought with mild amusement. The skills Lonny and

Alphonse taught him had come in handy. There were a lot of pigeons in the Navy.

He went back to his quarters to stash his winnings with the rest of his nest egg. *By the time this war is over,* he thought, *I'm going to be a rich man. A very rich man.*

"Take 'em to the cleaners again, Frankie?" Spencer Randall asked.

"What?" Frankie asked, not hearing his friend the first time.

"I asked if you took them to the cleaners again." Spencer stretched out on his bunk, his arms folded behind his head.

"What do you think?" Frankie asked, grinning.

"I think I should have known better than to ask."

Frankie took off his shirt. "Yeah? How come you never play?"

"Because I know you, remember?"

"Would I do that to you?"

"I don't know," Spencer said with a laugh. "Would you?"

"Hell, no!"

"I'll bet! I always thought your philosophy would be all's fair in love, war, and craps."

"Even I have principles," Frankie insisted.

When they suit my purpose, he was thinking.

"Doesn't it ever bother you?" Frankie asked. "Knowing you had so much—but will be going home to almost nothing?"

Spencer shrugged. "Money's never meant that much to me," he answered simply.

Frankie laughed. "That's almost un-American," he said.

"Why are you so obsessed with money, Frankie?" Spencer asked.

"I guess maybe because I never had any," Frankie admitted. "Everybody always wants what they don't have. It's human nature."

The *Indianapolis* made only one stop en route to Tinian. That stop had been in Pearl Harbor, where the ship refueled and discharged military passengers. There had been no destroyer escort, as there normally would have been, because speed was of the utmost importance and a destroyer did not have the cruiser's capacity for speed. Captain McVay had been assured, however, that should the *Indianapolis* face an emergency while the precious cargo was aboard, help would arrive immediately.

As long as the weapons parts were aboard, the ship would be constantly tracked. So important was their cargo that McVay had been ordered to guard it, literally, with his own life. If the ship went down, he was to reserve a lifeboat for it at the expense of crew members' lives.

It was a warm, clear morning, July 26, when the *Indianapolis* reached its destination, the expansive B-29 airfields of Tinian. When the ship dropped anchor in the island's small harbor and the crew gathered along the railings on the main deck, not a man aboard had any doubt that this had not been a routine mission. The ship was met by a swarm of small boats carrying a variety of military brass and squads of heavily armed marines.

"Hardly a typical island welcome," Frankie observed.

The canisters containing the weapons parts were unloaded and taken ashore aboard two separate landing craft manned by marines. Then Captain McVay's voice came over the ship's loudspeaker: "You have done a great job. The material you have brought over, I believe, will shorten the war."

Frankie watched the landing craft for a moment, then turned to Spencer, who stood next to him at the rail. "What were we carrying, anyway—an atomic bomb?"

Even after the cargo had been taken from the ship, the crew was forbidden to leave the *Indianapolis* while it was taking on fuel. No one except the ship's brass knew where they would be going once they left Tinian, but the scuttlebutt was that they were headed for the action. Formosa, according to the most prevalent rumors. An invasion, possibly.

No one was looking forward to it.

"So where do you think they're sending us?" Spencer wondered aloud.

Frankie shrugged. "To hell, most likely. Without the hand-basket."

"I'm serious."

"So am I."

"Think we'll actually end up in battle?"

Frankie raised an eyebrow. "There *is* a war going on," he reminded his shipmate.

"Yeah."

Spencer was scared. Oh, he didn't say it, not in so many words, but then, he didn't have to. It was written all over his face. *I'm scared, too, pal,* he thought. *I'm so goddamned scared none of us will get out of this alive—but I'll be damned if I'll let it show.*

I'll be damned if anyone's ever going to know it.

About the same time the *Indianapolis* arrived at its next stop, Guam, the Japanese submarine *I-58* was on a course from Guam to Leyte. Its mission was to attack enemy vessels off the coast of the Philippines, where the American forces were building up their invasion fleet. Because fuel was scarce at that time, Commander Hashimoto was unable to cruise the sea in search of enemy ships as he normally would have done, so he stuck to the most frequented routes to the various Pacific crossroads.

One of those routes was the one the *Indianapolis* would soon be taking.

July 30, 11:45 P.M.

Some two hundred men who would be reporting for duty on the midnight-to-four A.M. watch, most of whom had been asleep, struggled into their uniforms and made their way to their respective posts.

An ensign called out to his men in the gun mounts. No one saw a thing on the dark, slightly choppy sea. Nothing to report, nothing to shoot at.

It looked to be a quiet, uneventful night.

* * *

"Put up or shut up," Frankie said with a chuckle.

"What's the use?" one of the men asked. "I think you've stacked the deck!"

"Come on, come on—pay up and be quick about it," Frankie urged. "I'm supposed to relieve Spence up on deck in five minutes."

"Hey, Granelli—how come you've never given Randall the shaft?" another of the men asked. "Why is he safe?"

"Spence? He's a babe in the woods as far as this sort of thing goes," Frankie explained. "There wouldn't be any sport in it."

He wasn't about to admit that he wouldn't shaft Spencer because he considered the man a friend and therefore off-limits. *It would be a sign of weakness,* he thought.

Their banter was interrupted by a loud roar overhead, as if the sky had exploded above them. In the next instant, all hell broke loose. Men were running in all directions as the ship's horns blared. Frankie pushed his way through the chaos, headed for the deck. *If Sergeant Perry finds out I wasn't there to relieve Spence,* he thought, *I won't be worth a damn for anything but fish food.*

As he headed off to the wardroom, the ship suddenly shook violently with the impact of the first torpedo fired by the Japanese submarine, though at the time no one was sure of exactly what had hit them. Moments later, a second torpedo slammed into the ship just forward of the head. *Jesus,* Frankie thought. *We've been hit by another kamikaze!*

No—not a kamikaze. Too far from Japan. A mine, maybe? Odds against it. Wouldn't give that much of a jolt.

Jeez—Perry's gonna kill me if he doesn't find me at my post. Got to get to my post.

Maybe in all the commotion, he won't notice. And maybe the sun won't rise tomorrow.

He climbed down to the main deck but found there was no way to pass. Flames raged through all the corridors. Men splashed frantically in ankle-deep seawater, desperate for some kind of guidance in their panic. Others emerged from a hatch that led to a lower deck, their faces and bodies terribly burned, skin hanging loosely from their arms and legs. Someone was helping pull them through the hatch. Through the

thickening haze, Frankie could hear the wailing and moaning
that mingled with other, disembodied voices.

"Don't light that match . . . "

" . . . Open a port . . . "

" . . . Torpedo . . . been hit . . . "

"Lost all communication . . . "

" . . . Badly damaged . . . "

"Going down rapidly . . . "

"Abandon ship? . . . No . . . "

"Been through this all before . . . "

"Can't make out anybody up on deck . . . "

" . . . Never got to the engine room . . . "

"Can't see anything . . . "

Good God, we're sinking! The realization hit him with as
much impact as the torpedoes had hit the *Indianapolis*. As he
absorbed the reality of what was happening around him, he
heard someone saying something about compartments up forward flooding and not being able to close the watertight
doors. *The goddamned ship's going down, and the captain's
not giving the abandon ship order? Why?*

"We need help over here!" someone called out.

"Right!" Still in a mental fog, he moved mechanically,
pulling the badly burned men through the hatch, his mind on
the time. On how much time they might or might not have
left.

Then he saw Spencer.

He was burned, almost beyond recognition. He tried to
speak as Frankie pulled him through the hatch, but his vocal
cords were gone, along with most of his flesh. Frankie knew
he was dying as he knelt beside his friend and tried not to
cry. He'd never cried for anyone but his mother, but the tears
came now.

It's my fault, he thought. *I was supposed to relieve him.*

Looking down, he saw Spence's dog tags and broken chain,
lying a few feet from the now lifeless body. He picked them
up and looked at them for a moment, then shoved them into
his pants pocket. Then, without even thinking about it, he
pulled off his shirt and draped it gently over Spencer's face.
'Bye, old pal, he thought.

He started to cough uncontrollably as he made a run for

the lifeboats. Where was all the smoke coming from? He couldn't see where he was going, and it threatened to overcome him. He stumbled on until he reached the lifeboats. *The goddamned ship's sinking,* he thought. *The boats . . . where are the boats? Oh, God—where are the boats?*

As he started to jump, a loud roar behind him caused the ship to lurch again, throwing him off-balance. He felt as if he were on fire as he plunged awkwardly into the ocean . . . and the last thing he remembered was the cold, dark water closing over his head. . . .

Frankie bobbed breathlessly to the surface. The first thing he saw was one of the ship's screw propellers, still turning, directly overhead. The ship's stern extended straight up from the water's surface, the only part of it still visible. Clusters of men clung to the lifelines, their only hope quite literally a very fine thread. Others, he could see now, stood precariously on the blades of a second, stilled propeller. Within the bowels of the sinking ship, he could hear the cries of the men trapped there over the repeated crashes of falling equipment. Frankie had the feeling that even though he'd managed to get off alive, it was only a matter of time.

It'd be a hell of a lot easier if I just let go now and got it over with, he thought. *It's going to fall on me. The goddamned ship's going to fall on me. I won't drown. I'll be dead before I go under.*

But he was driven by instinct, a deeply rooted survival instinct. He swam, swam away from the ship as fast as he could. Moments later, feeling a blast of water and hot oil at his back, he turned to look over his shoulder as the ship, picking up speed now in its final death plunge, disappeared into the ocean's depths with enough force to send tons of water washing over Frankie and hundreds of other stranded survivors in what now seemed an infinite ocean. *How many,* he wondered somewhere in the back of his mind, *went down with her?*

In the distance, there was a flash of light on the horizon. *A Japanese submarine, most likely,* Frankie thought. *Probably the one that torpedoed us.*

Are they coming back to finish the job?

*   *   *

"A ship? Sunk? Then where the hell's the SOS?"

It was early Monday morning, July 31. The men at the combat intelligence office—CINCPAC—on Guam were confused by the message they'd intercepted from the commander of a Japanese sub. The *I-58* had reported having sunk an enemy ship.

"What kind of ship?" the captain wanted to know. "Did they give the latitude and longitude where it went down?"

"We broke the code, sir, but not their grid," one of his men responded. "We do know the *I-58* was haunting the same general area where the *Indianapolis* would be right now."

"But there's been no SOS?"

"None, sir."

The captain sighed heavily. It had been a long weekend. At least five hundred reports had come their way, and he had only a staff of eight to analyze and evaluate them. "It wouldn't be the first time they reported a sinking that never took place," he said thoughtfully. "They'll do just about anything to make themselves look good to their higher-ups."

"Sir, does that mean we're not going to check this one out?"

The captain shook his head. "No. It would probably be a waste of time anyway."

And that was that. For the time being.

Does anyone even know we're missing?

Frankie wondered at first if he had been the only one to make it. After the ship went down, he didn't see anyone for a long time. Or it seemed like a long time to him, bobbing in the cold water under a black sky. Then a few men, trapped in the air bubbles created by the ship's downward plunge, began shooting back up to the surface, splashing about in the oily foam the dying ship had left in its wake.

Spotting a cluster of men, maybe a hundred or more, floating in life preservers several yards away, he swam over to join them. It was impossible to recognize any of them by sight alone; their faces were covered with fuel oil from the slick caused by the capsized ship. One of them was straddling an ammo can. About fifty yards away from that group, several men huddled together on a raft.

"I'm going to swim to that raft," the man perched on the ammo can announced.

"Too far—you'll never make it," another man called out. "Stay where you are—they're bound to find us by morning!"

He didn't listen. He pulled off his life preserver, passed it to someone not wearing one, and dove into the water, swimming underwater, under the oil slick. Each time he bobbed to the surface, the raft seemed ever farther away.

How long? Frankie wondered as he watched the man finally climb aboard the raft. *How long before they find us? How long can we hold out?*

Though the men were clustered together in relatively small groups, they all tried to stay as close together as possible. It seemed to keep up the overall morale, as well as warding off shark attacks. Within the first twenty-four hours, most of the men who'd been seriously injured during the attack died, either from their injuries or from shock. All the men were haunted by the fear that they would drift away from the group and die alone. *The odds are against me,* Frankie thought dismally.

And yet something deep within him refused to give up. . . .

There were times Frankie drifted in and out of consciousness as he floated in his life preserver. There were times he could feel death, almost like a physical presence, hovering over him, watching, waiting. Waiting for him to surrender. *You can wait till hell freezes over,* he thought, stubbornly clinging to life just as he clung to his life preserver.

I'm not giving up, dammit.

The oil and saltwater intensified the pain of the burns that covered most of his body, burns he'd sustained in the explosion that had thrown him from the ship. Still, he was grateful for the oil, as were all of the men. It made them sick and it blinded them, but it also repelled both the sharks and the intense rays of the sun.

The ship's doctor continually warned the men not to drink

the water, but more often than not, it was to no avail. They drank despite the warnings, bloating themselves with it. Delirium came quickly, and with it, a kind of hyperactivity, bordering on manic energy. Frankie didn't even have the strength to drink by now.

I'm not sure where I'm finding the energy just to stay alive.

Each night, dozens of men disappeared, having died from their injuries, been grabbed by sharks, or simply drifted away.

Why haven't they found us yet? Hadn't they been missed in Leyte? Frankie wondered before he lost consciousness again.

In the early morning hours of Thursday, August 2, a Ventura crew testing a new antenna happened to be in the vicinity of the *Indianapolis* survivors. They knew nothing of the ship or its ordeal, though they had been briefed on all other ships in the area. The brass at the base knew of the *Indianapolis* but saw no reason to tell their men. After all, it was unheard of that any cruiser would be without a destroyer escort. No . . . there was nothing to worry about.

Nor did the Ventura crew know that on the morning of July 31 a C-54 pilot flying from Manila to Guam had seen what he believed to be a naval battle "with lots of fireworks that filled the sky with flashes of light." The pilot hadn't realized that the lights were flares sent up by the *Indianapolis* survivors.

Now, as the Ventura crew, having problems with the new antenna, attempted to navigate without it, they spotted an oil slick on the surface of the water. Thinking the oil had been the result of a crash dive by a Japanese sub, the Ventura crew armed its depth charges and descended to attack.

8

Samar, August 1945.

So this is what hell is like. Not what I expected.

Everything was white. His vision was blurred, but there was no mistake about that. White, everywhere. He might have thought it was heaven had he not known with certainty that Frankie Granelli was not, by any stretch of the imagination, destined for the Pearly Gates. There had even been some doubt among his shipmates as to his eligibility for hell.

Hell . . . the images flashed through his mind like a newsreel. Delirious men . . . men without hope . . . being hauled off by sharks. No food . . . no water . . . no hope. He remembered, only vaguely, his willpower weakening . . . his survival instincts fading . . . the pain taking over . . . and now . . .

He looked around, trying to focus on something, anything. No good. *Where am I?* he wondered.

"Ah—you're awake," said a soft female voice from somewhere above him.

The voice of an angel, Frankie thought. *Maybe I did go to heaven after all. Maybe somebody made a mistake. Maybe St. Peter let me in without checking the records.*

"It's a miracle you're alive," the voice said.

Tell me about it.

"Can you speak?"

What're you talking about, lady? Sure I can speak. I just did.

"Try to talk," she urged. "Try to say something. Anything."

Are you hard of hearing? I've been talking to you!

"Blink twice if you can hear me, if you understand."

*Dammit, I am—*then he realized what was happening. He

was talking to her—or trying to, anyway—but she couldn't hear him. His brain was engaged, but for some reason his mouth wasn't kicking into gear. *I've lost my voice,* he thought.

He blinked twice to let her know he could hear her.

It was several days before Frankie realized he was in a military hospital in Samar—and remembered fully what had happened to him. He remembered in terrifyingly vivid nightmares . . . the death of his friend, the sinking of the *Indianapolis.* . . . But his voice had not yet returned.

"You're a lucky man, Randall," the doctor told him. "God alone knows how, but you survived quite an ordeal."

What're you talking about? I'm not Randall—Randall's dead!

"You were the only survivor, in fact."

Randall's dead . . . but no . . . not the only survivor . . . no . . .

"It won't happen overnight, of course—but I think I can safely predict you'll make a full recovery."

Want to give me that in writing, pal?

Why do they all think I'm Spencer Randall? Frankie wondered.

Then it came to him. The dog tags. He'd had Spence's dog tags in his pocket. *But what happened to mine?* he wondered. *Did I lose them in the water?*

How do I let them know I'm not Spence?

"I feel like a goddamned mummy," Frankie complained.

The doctor didn't laugh. He didn't even smile. "The bandages are quite necessary," he said gravely. "You've suffered burns over most of your face and body."

There was a long silence before Frankie asked, "How bad is it?"

"Bad. Very bad."

"You sure as hell don't sugarcoat it, do you?"

"What would be the point? You have the right to know."

"Am I—disfigured?" Frankie asked slowly.

"You were very badly burned."

Frankie drew in a deep breath. "In other words, when all of this crap comes off, I'm gonna look like Frankenstein's monster, right?"

"I wouldn't put it that way—"

"I would," Frankie snapped. "You tell me I've been burned over most of my face and body but I'm not gonna look like some kind of monster? Sounds like bullshit to me, Doc."

"The burns *are* severe," the doctor said, "but a great deal of the damage can be corrected with skin grafts."

"But not all of it."

"Not all of it, no."

"So, in other words, I'll never look completely normal again."

The doctor hesitated. "Well—"

"Forget it, Doc," Frankie said sullenly. "You just gave me my answer."

The days in the hospital seemed endless. Frankie was unable to do even the most simple things, like look at a magazine or hold a fork. He had nothing to do but ponder his fate, once he left there.

What was going to happen to him, to his big plans for the future? God, he couldn't even begin to imagine what his face must look like under the bandages. Grotesque, no doubt. Horribly disfigured. He'd probably have to spend the rest of his life in hiding. *Like the phantom of the opera,* he thought bitterly.

As the days passed, he grew increasingly depressed. The prospects for the future—his future, anyway—looked impossibly bleak. All the plans he'd made, everything he was going to do with his life, had gone down with the *Indianapolis.* The new life he'd mapped out for himself had gone up in smoke. He was stuck here in some goddamned military hospital—God only knew where—severely burned and bandaged from head to toe. No one even knew who he was. They all thought he was Spencer Randall.

What, he wondered now, had kept him from telling them the truth?

* * *

Something deep within Frankie, something he couldn't even give a name to, refused to let him give up. The same survival instinct that got him through his mother's death and through all of the years that followed, kept him going now, kept him fighting, looking for a solution. A way out.

He questioned everyone who came near him—doctors *and* nurses—about the latest techniques in plastic surgery, looking for even the faintest glimmer of hope. But there was none. No one he spoke to seemed even the least bit optimistic. There was, they told him, only so much that could be accomplished through the tried-and-tested procedures, although new techniques were constantly being discovered. Perhaps in a few years, they said.

They don't understand, he thought bitterly. *I don't have a few years to just sit around and wait and hope they come up with something.*

He'd played a lot of long shots in the past, and had no doubt he'd play many, many more in the future, but this was one long shot he just couldn't afford.

"I hear you've been asking questions about certain surgical procedures."

The man standing at the foot of Frankie's bed was obviously a doctor, if the white coat and stethoscope were any indication. Frankie didn't recognize him. He'd never seen that one before, he was sure of it.

"Who are you?" he wanted to know.

"I am Dr. Burke," the other man told him, seating himself on a corner of the bed. "I just arrived here a few days ago, and heard of your interest in plastic surgery, so, after having a look at your chart, I thought we might talk."

"You're a plastic surgeon?"

"I was, before the war—that is, I was in training," Burke said. "I was working with one of the world's foremost plastic surgeons in Switzerland."

Switzerland! For the first time since he was brought here, Frankie was truly hopeful. The Swiss were ahead of their time on everything. "You think you can help me?"

"No. But I think you can be helped."

"Meaning?"

"The chances are excellent that your former appearance can be completely restored—at the Clinic of Miracles in Neuchâtel," Burke explained. "There, many patients who were considered otherwise hopeless made total recoveries."

"Great batting average."

"The success rate is impressive, yes."

"Must be expensive as hell." The next major concern.

"You don't understand," Burke said then. "Because much of the work done at the clinic is considered experimental, patients there are accepted on a volunteer basis—"

"Guinea pigs," Frankie concluded.

"Well—yes." The doctor paused. "But most of them consider it a chance worth taking."

Taking a chance, Frankie thought. The name of the game as far as he was concerned. *What have I got to lose?* Aloud he said, "So how do I get myself into this place?"

The war had been over for weeks before Frankie was even aware of it.

"The bomb?" he asked. "They used the atomic bomb?"

"Twice," Burke told him. "Hiroshima, then Nagasaki."

"And that was that, huh?"

"More or less." There was a pause. "The *Indianapolis* was carrying parts for the bomb. You didn't know that, did you?"

"No." Mentally, Frankie recalled that morning in the harbor at Tinian, watching the brass come out to meet the ship, watching the mysterious cargo being taken ashore. He recalled what he'd said to Spencer as they stood on the deck, watching.

What were we carrying, anyway—an atomic bomb?

The letter arrived two months later. "You have been accepted," Burke said, as elated as if it had been himself. He read the letter aloud to Frankie. "Do you have any questions?"

"How soon can I go?"

"Soon, very soon. When you are allowed to leave here."

"How long will I have to stay there?"

Burke shrugged. "Impossible to predict. Several months at the very least."

"How many—operations?"

"Again, this is impossible to predict at this point."

"But they'll be able to make me look like I did—before?"

"The chances are excellent, yes."

Frankie thought about it for a moment. "Suppose I wanted to look different?"

The doctor looked puzzled. "I am afraid I don't understand."

"Simple. Suppose I'd like to improve on what Mother Nature gave me? Could that be done?"

"I suppose so. But why would you want to?"

"I don't know that I would. I'm just curious, that's all."

But in fact, he did have something very definite in mind.

It seemed to Frankie that he'd been in the hospital forever.

With nothing but time on his hands and nothing to do but think, he did a lot of thinking. He thought about Spencer and about his own feelings of guilt about his friend's death. He thought about the small nest egg he'd lost at sea and the even larger nest egg waiting for him in a bank back in Chicago. He thought about how he'd finally repaid Mary O'Hara's kindness by having his monthly allotment sent to her. She in turn had deposited his winnings from poker and craps in a savings account that would be waiting for him when the war was over. There was enough there right now to start over, to start a new life, when the war ended.

A new life. Ironic . . . everyone here thinks I'm Spencer Randall. Too bad I'm not. It sure as hell would solve a lot of my problems, but could I really fool anybody? What if I ran into people who knew Spence?

Still . . . I probably know as much about him as anybody. He was an open book. He never kept any secrets. He recalled all the long talks they'd had at sea, all the things Spencer had confided to him. Then it hit him. *Why not?* It was the perfect solution.

At that moment, Frankie Granelli died and Spencer Randall was resurrected. Once the decision was made, he knew there could be no turning back.

He was now Spencer Randall.

9

It seemed as if he'd been there forever.

The Clinic of Miracles was like nothing Frankie had ever seen before. It was one classy place, that was for sure. The rooms—all private rooms, not a ward in the place—looked more like luxury hotel suites than hospital rooms. The food was the best he'd ever tasted, but, he figured, he'd been at sea so long, and in that base hospital after that, he'd forgotten what real food tasted like. The view from his room was magnificent, an almost unobstructed view of Lake Neuchâtel that probably should have reminded him of home, of Lake Michigan, but didn't. Nothing reminded him of home. That sort of thing was for people who had fond memories to recall.

Not for me, he thought bitterly.

Besides, it was a waste of time, and time was more valuable to Frankie Granelli now than gold bullion. Time was too valuable to waste, so he didn't, not on foolish thoughts of the childhood he'd missed out on, and not on worthless activities like mingling with the other patients, many of whom were just as bad off as he was. He'd never even met most of them. He seldom left his room, doing so only when it was necessary, only when he was required to do so for medical reasons. He preferred being alone as much as possible, because he needed to think, to plan. He needed to contemplate the future he would have when he left the clinic.

Spencer Randall's future.

He mentally coached himself, hour after hour, day after day, recalling every detail Spencer had ever revealed about himself and his life before the war. He memorized even the most trivial facts, because he knew one slip-up could ruin

everything for him. Once he assumed Spencer's identity in
the outside world, he would, sooner or later, have to face
people from the real Spencer's past. He knew that he'd have
to deal with that, and he would have to be damn good at it.
Convincing. The world would have to believe he *was* Spencer
Randall.

He would have to believe it.

"How many more—operations—will I have to have?" he
asked the doctor who cautiously snipped away at the bandages covering his face.

"We will just have to wait and see," the doctor answered
patiently. "I will know more once the bandages are completely off."

"Do I get a mirror this time around?" Frankie wondered.

The doctor shook his head. "There is still much to be
done," he said seriously, for he never spoke in any other way,
"and I do not think you are psychologically prepared to see
yourself the way you look right now."

"Pretty bad, huh?"

"By conventional standards, yes." The doctor peeled away
a section of the bandage. "You were severely burned, Mon-
sieur Randall."

"It's been so long since I saw my own face, I've forgotten
what it looks like," Frankie said, attempting humor.

The doctor didn't smile. He never smiled. He never
laughed. Frankie found it odd that a man who was able to do
so much for other people's faces had one himself that was so
devoid of any real expression. "You will see it again soon
enough," he promised.

Alone in his room, Frankie would spend long hours poring
over photographs of himself and Spencer taken before they
left Mare Island on what was to be the final voyage of the
Indianapolis. Photos he'd sent to Mary O'Hara before they
left port. Photos she'd returned to him along with his savings
from the bank in Chicago, winnings from all of those ship-
board poker games, except the last. Money she'd deposited
for him so he could get a fresh start when the war was over.

He missed Spencer. Frankie hadn't had so many friends

that he could afford to lose one, and Spencer had been better to him than most. Spencer had accepted him unconditionally, for who and what he was. That made Frankie feel more than a little guilty about having assumed his friend's identity now that Spencer was dead. But that was exactly why it didn't matter anymore—because Spencer *was* dead. That was the reality. He'd assumed Spencer's identity because fate had presented him with the opportunity. *Fate and a Japanese sub,* he thought. *They gave me the chance. Why shouldn't I take it? Spencer's gone—and there's no going back for Frankie Granelli. No future there.*

He looked down at the photos spread out on the table. *Yeah . . . I am gonna miss you, pal,* he thought. *But when I leave this world, it's your name everybody's gonna remember.*

Spencer Randall will definitely have left his—our—mark.

He wrote to Mary O'Hara regularly. He told her he was in Switzerland, but he never told her why. He sure as hell couldn't tell her what he was planning to do.

I've decided to stay here, he wrote her. *There are opportunities here that are just too good to pass up.*

That should take care of any questions she might have about why he wouldn't be returning to Chicago.

> *The Navy thinks you're dead, Frankie.*
> *Since you've got no living relatives, and your*
> *allotment was sent to me, I got the notification.*
> *A telegram. Lost at sea, they said. Why do they think*
> *you're dead?*

He wrote back to Mary O'Hara the same day, chalking it up to the usual bureaucratic red tape. The ship had gone down, a lot of men had died, there was much confusion surrounding the incident. He wasn't sure she'd buy it, but he couldn't have her trying to set the record straight with the Pentagon.

To his relief, she seemed to accept that lame excuse, pursuing it no further. But it made Frankie realize that the problems arising from assuming another man's identity were neverending. *It's like the interest paid on a savings account,* he thought wryly. *Compounded daily.*

New York City.

That was where Spencer Randall was going to make a new life for himself. It was one decision Frankie had had no trouble in making. He'd always known he'd return to the States when his stay at the clinic was over, but he'd known all along that Chicago was out of the question. So was Boston, which was the real Spencer's hometown, and going there would be inviting trouble.

Los Angeles, San Francisco, Denver, Dallas, Miami, Washington, D.C.—they'd all been possibilities. But in the end, he'd chosen New York because, of all the cities he'd considered, it best suited his plans. It was as simple as that. It was a city pulsing with excitement, with endless opportunities for a man with his natural talents.

When he was through, Spencer Randall would be the most powerful man in New York. For starters.

"I can't believe this is really it."

Frankie felt the way he figured most kids must feel on Christmas morning. *The way I can't remember ever feeling,* he thought, *because Christmas was always just another day for the Granellis.*

The long, difficult road to recovery had finally come to an end. The bandages were about to come off—for the last time. *The unveiling. The rebirth, the resurrection of Spencer Randall.*

He tried to curb his impatience as the doctor snipped away at the bandages. *Seems like it's been forever since I've been able to look in the mirror.*

But the results will be worth waiting for, if this guy lives up to his reputation, he thought confidently.

Carefully, the doctor peeled away the last of the gauze and tape, then stood back to scrutinize his work. Frankie searched the other man's face for some clue as to what he was thinking of his own handiwork. There was none, just the same grave, detached expression he always wore.

"Well?" he asked aloud. "What's the verdict?"

The doctor studied him for a moment. "Why don't you judge for yourself?" he suggested finally, handing Frankie a large hand mirror.

All these months, Frankie thought, suddenly nervous, *I've waited for this—and now that it's finally happening, I'm not sure I want to see it.*

But see it he did, slowly, apprehensively raising the mirror to give him a full view of his new face. And what he saw was unbelievable.

He looked so much like the real Spencer Randall that even Spencer's own mother wouldn't have been able to tell the difference.

SPENCE

1946–1948

10

Now, this is my kind of town, Spencer Randall thought as he walked alone down Park Avenue, oblivious of the heavy pedestrian traffic around him. *The perfect place to start over—a new identity, a new life. Another chance.* He stopped at the curb as the traffic light at the intersection turned red. Looking up at one of the skyscrapers dominating the midtown skyline, he smiled to himself. *Yes, sir . . . one of these days, I'm going to own this town.*

He wasn't yet sure how it was going to happen, but he knew with certainty that it would happen, sooner or later.

Standing there at the curb, momentarily contemplating his future, he pulled his tan wool overcoat around himself and belted it to block out the frigid winter wind. *Winter is definitely here,* he thought. It reminded him of the winters in Chicago. It reminded him of one winter in particular, so many years ago. . . .

No! he thought stubbornly. *No good. Frankie Granelli's dead as far as the rest of the world is concerned. He's got to stay dead. I'm Spencer Randall now. And Spencer Randall's going to make his mark on this town.*

Trouble was, what he had in mind was going to take money. A lot of money. A lot more money, unfortunately, than he had at the moment. Even with all the money he'd taken from his shipmates during the war, he still didn't have enough. *Not by a long shot,* he thought grimly.

A long shot.

It gave him an idea.

He'd been in New York two months. So far, the women had all been anonymous; after he was finished with them, he usually didn't remember their names.

If he'd ever known them at all.

It was better that way. He couldn't afford to let anyone get too close. The closer anyone got, the more questions were asked. He didn't intend to answer any questions. He couldn't.

He turned over in bed and looked at the woman sleeping beside him. Blond, full-figured, young—early twenties tops— a real knockout. Her name was Peggy—or was it Pamela? *No matter. Names weren't important,* he thought, fumbling in the darkness for a cigarette. *Not when you're never going to see the other person again.*

He took a cigarette from the pack on the night table, held it between his lips, and lit it with a match from a matchbook he'd picked up at the Algonquin earlier that day. He smiled to himself, amused by the thought that suddenly occurred to him: *I can remember the name of the goddamned hotel where I had lunch today, but I can't remember the name of the woman I'm in bed with!*

He thought about it. He rarely tried to analyze himself because he wasn't sure he really wanted to know too much about his so-called "inner self." *Doesn't really matter, one way or the other,* he told himself. The past was over. He couldn't go back, even if he wanted to. Only the future mattered.

Spencer Randall's future.

"What can I do for you?" the man seated across the desk from him inquired.

Spencer smiled indulgently. He didn't like the man's patronizing attitude, but he'd put up with it. For now. "That should be obvious," he said in a cool voice. "I want to buy stock. That *is* what you do here, isn't it? Sell stock?"

The broker, a thin, pallid man with a long, narrow face and pale blue eyes looking at him through horn-rimmed glasses, nodded. "What I meant is, do you have any particular stock in mind?" he asked.

"Of course." Spencer took a folded piece of paper from his breast pocket and passed it across the desk to the other man. "I think you'll find this pretty complete."

The broker looked it over thoughtfully. "Are you sure

about this?'' he asked. ''Some of these stocks—''

''I'm sure,'' Spencer said with finality.

Spencer hated holidays in general and Christmas in particular. Christmas was a ''family'' holiday in his book, a time for unity, for sharing, for families being together. Mary O'Hara was the closest thing he'd had to a real family. It only reminded him of what he didn't have and hadn't had for a very long time.

It reminded him of what he'd done, what he'd been trying so hard to forget.

He viewed the festive mood and elaborate window displays on Fifth Avenue with cold disdain. To him, Christmas was a day like any other. A day to work, to make plans, to take one more step toward his ultimate goal.

He brushed past a sidewalk Santa Claus without so much as a smile, oblivious of the rotund, red-clad fellow's cheery laughter and enthusiastic bell ringing.

Idiot, he thought irritably. *Only a fool would dress up like that—especially in public.*

He couldn't remember ever believing in Santa Claus as a child. Santa Claus was, after all, a fantasy—and there had been no room for fantasy in young Frankie Granelli's life. Only the harsh realities.

He ignored the uniformed volunteer from the Salvation Army soliciting donations in front of one of the department stores. He never spent money foolishly. He knew he would need every dime he could hold on to in order to begin the quest to reach one single, all-important goal. Spencer Randall wanted to be the most powerful man in New York.

For starters.

The first broker he consulted was soon replaced by an energetic young man named Dan West who worked for the same firm. Though not nearly as experienced as his predecessor, West was bright, hungry, and knowledgeable about the market. He gave Randall inside information when he could get it and helped him to make wise investments.

This kid's going to go far, Randall thought with satisfaction.

Randall's gambling instincts proved to be as valuable in the stock market as they were at the crap table, and he never ignored those gut feelings that had served him so well in the past. The stocks in which he'd invested had shown varying degrees of profit, all of which went directly back into the market. *I'm definitely making a profit,* he thought as he contemplated his next move.

I'm just not making it fast enough.

She was tall for a woman, tall and dark, with lush, full breasts and soft, rounded hips, the kind of figure that couldn't be hidden, no matter what she was wearing.

At the moment, she wasn't wearing anything.

She was naked, straddling Randall on the bed. He reached up and grabbed her breasts in his hands, pulling her down to him. Taking one of the large, brown nipples between his lips, he worked it with his tongue until it was a hard little knot, then he drew it further into his mouth, sucking fiercely as she hovered over him, supporting her weight on her hands, moaning with pleasure.

He focused his attention first on one breast, then the other, kissing, licking, sucking as his hands moved over her flesh, down the length of her body, cupping and squeezing her buttocks. His fingers moved between her legs, touching, playing with her, exploring the dampness he found there. He slid two fingers up inside her, moving rhythmically as he continued to suck at her breasts. Finally, unable to take it any longer, the woman cried out.

"Please," she moaned. "Please, Spence . . . please . . . stop . . . "

"You love it, baby," he growled, releasing her breast. "You know you do."

"No . . . too much . . . "

"Maybe I ought to be on top for a while, then." He rolled her over on her back and mounted her, driving himself deep inside her, panting, gyrating, coming to a quick, explosive orgasm as she writhed and moaned beneath him.

"You're really something, baby," he gasped as he lay on top of her, catching his breath. "Really something."

"Then you *will* call me again?" she asked, wrapping her arms around his neck.

"Not a chance, baby."

None of them ever understood, Spence concluded as he walked alone down Fifth Avenue. It was early, just before dawn, and it was bitterly cold. It had snowed during the night, and there was a thick blanket of white, virtually unblemished, covering the city. There were few people on the streets at this unholy hour, and this was the way Spence liked it. He preferred being alone.

They never understood that he liked them, really liked them, and thoroughly enjoyed them in bed—but that anything long-term was out of the question. They couldn't understand. And he couldn't explain it to them because he didn't understand it himself.

He paused at the corner of Fifth and East Fifty-first. Across the street was St. Patrick's Cathedral. He stared up at it for a long time, inexplicably drawn to it. He'd never been religious, never really observed the Catholic faith into which he'd been born, and yet . . .

When the traffic light changed, he crossed the street and entered the cathedral on the Fifth Avenue side. He stood in the vestibule for a long time, staring at the altar and baldachin, beyond the pulpit and sanctuary. Beyond that, he could see the elaborate stained-glass windows in the Lady Chapel at the far end of the cathedral.

Me—in a church, he thought. *I hope the roof doesn't cave in.*

He walked down the right-hand aisle, lost in thought. There was no one else in sight. He wouldn't have stayed if there had been. But now, confident that he was alone here, he made his way to the back of the cathedral, to the altar of St. Andrew. None of the candles on the altar were lit, and the box appeared to be empty.

"Looks like you don't get too much business this time of morning, Andy, old pal," he whispered as he pulled a fifty-dollar bill from his pocket and stuffed it into the box. He lit all of the candles. "I'm not going to rehash why I'm here or what I did, since you already know all of that anyway, but I'm paying my dues, all right? So how about putting in a good word for me with the Man upstairs, huh?"

He made the sign of the cross, one of the few things he remembered from his childhood. He started to walk away, then stopped, pulled another twenty from his pocket, and put it in the box.

Then he left the cathedral quietly, hoping he hadn't been observed.

11

Saratoga, August 1947.

Located in upstate New York's Adirondack Mountains, Saratoga has often been described as "the track where time stands still." Indeed, the central structure of the racecourse dates from somewhere around the turn of the century, the wooden construction and distinctive cupolas already a part of the storied grandstand on that historic day in 1919 when the legendary Man o' War was defeated by an aptly named horse called Upset in the Sanford Stakes.

A colorful history, indeed. But history was the last thing on Spence Randall's mind on a hot summer afternoon in 1947 as he studied the racing form. Two good days—so far—at Saratoga, and last week at Aqueduct, and he'd more than doubled what remained of his earnings from all those crap games in the Navy.

Nothing like a good day at the track to put a guy in a higher tax bracket, he thought, rather pleased with himself. He'd always been lucky, no matter what the game, no matter what the stakes, but if anyone were to ask him to describe his system, he wouldn't be able to. His only "system" was instinct. As simple as that and as complicated as that. He understood it, but he could never explain it.

Not even to himself.

He studied the racing form thoughtfully and made his choices, then went to the window to place his bets. *This is it for the day,* he promised himself. *It's a long drive back to Manhattan.*

"You've been very lucky today."

He turned abruptly. The woman addressing him was small, slim, and blond, dressed entirely in red: a slim skirt and matching jacket, belted at the waist, with a peplum, and a wide-brimmed hat. *A knockout,* he thought.

Aloud he said, "Yeah, I guess you could call it that."

"I don't suppose you'd be willing to share your secret with me," he pursued.

He grinned. "I would, but it wouldn't do you much good," he told her. "My system consists of relying entirely on gut feelings."

She smiled. "It might," she said in a low, incredibly soft voice, "if I were to join you. If you wouldn't mind sharing your box, that is."

"There's not much I wouldn't be willing to share with you," Spence assured her.

Spence had determined, right from the beginning, that the stock market was the biggest crapshoot in town, and for someone like Spence Randall, with gambling in his blood, its allure was irresistible. He invested every dollar he could manage, choosing his stocks as carefully as he chose his horses, and relying just as much on his gut instincts. And he'd been just as successful on Wall Street as he was at the racetrack.

Even more so, financially.

The results come faster at the track, he decided, *but in the market, the returns are bigger.*

And it was the long-range payoff that mattered most now.

"Do you have any idea how many men work down here, round-the-clock, day in, day out?"

The man walking with Spence along the pier was trying to sell him on a partnership deal in which Spence would be putting up the money to launch a small fleet of "lunch wag-ons," specially outfitted trucks that would drive around the docks at scheduled times, selling sandwiches and coffee to the dockworkers.

"Doesn't seem like there would be a hell of a lot of profit," Spence said, lighting a cigarette.

"You'd be surprised." The other man, taller than Spence and built like a prizefighter, raked a hand through his curly brown hair. "These guys work hard—work up big appetites. They'll buy, all right—they'll buy a lot. We could get rich."

Spence fixed his gaze on a ship leaving New York Harbor. "I'm already rich, Mr.—" He stopped short, unable to re-member the other man's name.

"Lombardi. Nick Lombardi."

Spence nodded. "Mr. Lombardi. Like I said, I'm already rich."

"You could get richer," Lombardi suggested.

"I could also lose my shirt, Nick, old pal," Spence pointed out.

"Won't happen," Lombardi assured him. "We're gonna do a boomin' business here."

"I'll sleep on it, pal," Spence promised.

He talked it over with Dan West, who advised him against it. "It sounds like a promising venture," Dan told him, "but I know Lombardi's reputation. He's bad news."

"I can handle Lombardi, if the potential for profit's there," Spence said confidently. "You think it's a good deal, then?"

"Without Lombardi, yes."

Spence stood up. "Good enough." He started for the door, then turned to face West again. "Know what, Danny boy? You don't belong here. You ought to be working for me."

"Yeah, sure." Dan chuckled. "You say that every time I see you."

"I mean it, pal."

"Sure."

"You don't think I mean it?" Spence raised an eyebrow questioningly. "I'll show you how serious I am. You go give your notice to that SOB you're working for, and I'll pay you double what you're making now."

Dan studied him for a moment. "I should call your bluff for once."

Spence grinned. "Damn right you should."

"All right, Mr. Randall," he said as he got to his feet, "you've got yourself a deal."

"There is one thing," Spence began slowly.

"What?"

"Call me 'Mr. Randall' again, and you're fired."

"Tell me, Mr. Hartson, why would I want to invest in this project of yours?"

The other man looked puzzled. "Why not?"

"Not good enough, college boy," Spence said, shaking his head. "You give me a reason, and I'll tell you if it's a good one—or maybe I should say good enough."

He was standing in the middle of a vacant lot in midtown Manhattan where, four months earlier, a hundred-year-old building about to be condemned had been demolished. The man with him was Ray Hartson, a real estate developer with, as Spence put it, "big-time ideas and small-time capital."

"It should be obvious," Hartson told him. "Real estate. You can't lose with real estate. There's always going to be a demand for it, and it's always going to increase in value. Especially here in Manhattan."

"You mean since there's really no place to go but up." Spence gestured skyward.

"Exactly."

"I'll let you know." Spence started to walk away.

"Don't wait too long, Spence."

He glanced over his shoulder as he kept walking. "Mr. Randall to you, Hartson."

"There's a gentleman from *The Wall Street Journal* here to see you, Mr. Randall," his secretary told him.

Spence didn't look up from the reports he was reviewing. "Has he got an appointment?"

The young secretary looked surprised. "Well—no," she said carefully.

"Tell him to make one." Spence still didn't look up.

"Uh—yes, sir," she said, confused. "When shall I make it for?"

"How about sometime in June 1990?"

"You should consider relocating," Dan West told Spence.

He raised an eyebrow. "Why? Is the mayor giving me forty-eight hours to get out of town—again?"

"I'm serious, Spence," Dan said impatiently. "You're big time now, and our present quarters are entirely too small. Randall Inc. should have its own building."

Spence laughed. "I like you, kid," he said, tapping the eraser end of his pencil on the desk top. "You think big."

"There's a building on Wall Street—"

"Whoa!" Spence raised a hand to halt him. "You've already been shopping around?"

West shrugged. "That's what you pay me to do, Spence."

"Yeah, right. Like I move my operations every day." He shook a cigarette from the pack on his desk and lit up.

"If you'll just take a look at the building," Dan said carefully, "I'm sure you'll agree it's much more suitable than these offices."

Spence smiled, amused by Dan's eagerness. "What the hell? I'll take a look," he promised.

The press dubbed him the "shark of Wall Street," the man who seemingly came out of nowhere one day to take the stock market by storm. He'd made his fortune in the market and was now branching out into other areas: food service, real estate, pharmaceuticals, and, it was rumored, oil. His business ventures made headlines, but no one knew anything about the man himself. And everyone wanted to know.

That created a problem of another kind for Spence Randall.

Randall hired a team of public relations specialists to deal with the media. They were given free rein to release information concerning Randall Inc. business transactions or acquisitions or the many charitable contributions the corporation made, but they were not allowed to give out any information regarding Spence Randall's private life. Not that they had any to give. If anyone who knew the real Spencer Randall were to read about him in the newspapers—

I can't risk it, he thought.

He'd always known it could—and would—happen sooner or later, but the letter still came as a surprise.

The return address indicated it had come from Boston. It was marked "Personal," so his secretary hadn't opened it. He would have preferred not to open it at all, but he knew it was unavoidable. *Might as well get used to it,* he thought, reaching for his letter opener.

The letter was from someone named James McCarthy. Spence searched his memory, mentally scanning all the conversations he'd had with the real Randall for references to that name. James McCarthy. . . . Yes, it was coming to him now. Jimmy McCarthy had been Spencer Randall's closest childhood friend. They'd known each other forever. *Great,* Spence thought. *Just what I need.*

McCarthy, as it turned out, was himself a successful businessman. He'd married and had a couple of kids, according to the letter. He was also still living in Boston. He did travel to New York frequently on business, as he would be in the weeks to come, and was looking forward to seeing his old friend. *We have a lot of catching up to do,* he wrote.

Just what I don't need, Spence thought, staring at the letter in his hand for a long time. Taking a deep breath, he summoned up every bit of information the real Randall had ever revealed to him about his oldest and closest friend:

They were about the same age. Spencer was five years older than me. That would make McCarthy about twenty-seven now, wouldn't it?

They lived on the same street. Opposite ends of the block. Their families were good friends.

They went to the same school. What was the name of that goddamned school, anyway?

Oakland. That's it. The Oakland Primary School.

His parents' names. Kevin and Mary. Original.

If I make a mistake, I can always blame it on the war. War does strange things to men's minds. And the sinking was a traumatic experience, after all.

Good old Jimmy might even buy it. . . .

*   *   *

His palms were sweating.

Spence couldn't remember a time when he'd been so nervous. Even as a kid, hustling on the streets of Chicago, he'd always had a cool head. *I'm about to be put to the test,* he thought. *It's the devil testing me to see if I'm eligible for hell.*

He made sure he was the first to arrive. *I won't recognize him, but he'll know Spencer Randall. He'll have to come to me.*

They'd made a date to meet for drinks in the bar at the Plaza. Spence arrived a half hour ahead of the appointed time and sat alone at the bar, nursing a drink. He really wanted to get stinking drunk to ease his nervousness, but he knew that wouldn't be smart. *You're going to need a clear head for this,* he told himself.

"I'd have known you anywhere, Spencer Randall."

Startled, he jerked around. The man addressing him was tall, slim, and his coloring obviously black Irish.

"Jimmy?" he asked, forcing a smile he didn't really feel like. "Jimmy McCarthy?"

The other man laughed. "Don't tell me after all these years you don't recognize me!"

Spence laughed, too, and he could only hope it sounded genuine. "Me forget an ugly kisser like yours? No way!"

McCarthy looked at him oddly for a moment, then smiled. "I think you were at sea too long, friend," he said, seating himself. "You sound like a sailor."

Damn! I almost blew it on the first shot, he reprimanded himself. *Got to be more careful.* Aloud he said, "You should have met some of my shipmates—" He stopped short, realizing how that must have sounded.

McCarthy's smile vanished. "I'm sorry—about the *Indianapolis,* I mean," he said quietly.

Spence nodded. "I guess I'm lucky to be alive."

"Yeah."

"What're you having?" Spence asked.

"Scotch. Neat."

They talked about the war. That was easy. He'd been there, seen everything the real Spencer had seen, known all of the same people. *If only it could all be so easy,* Spence thought, knowing that was too much to hope for.

They talked about the "good old days." At least half a dozen times, Spence caught himself wiping his sweaty palms on his pants legs. *Three strikes and you're out,* he thought anxiously. *How many mistakes can you get away with before good old Jimmy starts getting suspicious?*

But oddly enough, McCarthy never seemed the least bit suspicious. *Guess he buys the idea that the war changed the men who fought it.*

Those of us who came back alive, anyway.

It wasn't until he left Jimmy McCarthy and the Plaza behind that Spence finally felt safe. Alone in the backseat of his Rolls en route to his apartment, he felt his entire body sag with relief. He felt as though an enormous burden had been lifted. It wasn't until then that he realized that the back of his shirt collar was soaked with perspiration.

And this is just the beginning, he reminded himself.

"You're beautiful, baby." Spence stood behind the woman in the darkness of her bedroom. They were both naked. His hands were on her breasts, his thumbs rubbing her nipples roughly. She moaned with pleasure as he fondled her.

"Let me turn around," she said softly. "Then I can—"

"No!" he cut her off sharply. "I want you right where you are—for now."

Releasing her breasts, his hands slid slowly downward, over her smooth white skin, her slightly rounded belly. His fingers lightly brushed the curly red hair covering her pubis as he parted her lower lips. He stroked her slowly but insistently with the tip of his index finger until she began to wriggle against him excitedly. Taking a few steps backward, he sat in a large armchair near the window and pulled her around to face him. He looked up at her, admiring her high, full breasts with their taut nipples for a moment before pulling her down to him, entering her as she straddled his lap.

He sucked at her breasts as she moved on top of him, arching her back, moaning, gripping his shoulders. He never uttered a word during the sex act itself, and when it was over, he left her just as silently as he'd taken her.

He didn't even say good-bye.

On his way home, he stopped at St. Patrick's Cathedral. It was late—he always went late at night or early in the morning—and there was no one else in sight when he entered the eerily silent cathedral. He made his way to the back, said a silent prayer, lit all of the candles on St. Andrew's altar, then put two fifty-dollar bills in the box.

When he emerged from the church, his driver was waiting for him at the curb, opening the back door of his Rolls-Royce for him. He got into the car without so much as a nod.

Alone in the backseat as the driver headed uptown, he thought about what had taken place just before. He enjoyed sex, and yet he always remained detached from it. It was always as if someone else were doing it and he was on the outside, watching, observing. Like a voyeur. The sex act gave him physical pleasure, but nothing else. Afterward, he always felt the need to purge himself, so he went to St. Patrick's.

Will the ghosts of the past—Frankie Granelli's past—ever go away? he asked himself.

12

New York City, January 1948.

As the Randall empire grew and expanded its horizons, so did the legend. That's what the media called him these days—a living legend. And as the legend grew, so did the public's hunger for information on the real man behind the legend. Not a day passed that the public relations department of Randall International—the company name had been changed to indicate its worldwide operations—did not receive at least one request for a detailed biography of or an in-depth interview with Spencer Randall. At Spence's insistence, those requests were always denied. He wasn't about to discuss his private life with the press.

He couldn't.

"I warned you about that man," Dan West told Spence, barely able to control the anger in his voice. "Lombardi's been stealing you blind."

Spence looked up from the figures he'd been checking. "Yeah? How so?"

Dan thrust a sheaf of papers onto the desk in front of him. "See for yourself."

Picking up the papers, Spence looked up at him. "Sit down, Danny boy," he said with a grin. "You're pacing a hole in the carpet."

West looked at him for a moment, then dropped into a nearby chair. "Aren't you the least bit concerned?" he asked, puzzled by Spence's nonchalance.

"Sure, I am. But frankly, I'm a little confused," Spence told him. "I've been keeping close watch on the operations down there myself, and we *are* making a profit."

"We'd be making a lot more profit if Lombardi weren't skimming off the top. Take a look at those." He gestured toward the papers in Spence's hand. "The ones on top I got from accounting. The others I lifted from Lombardi's books when I was down there this morning."

"I see." Spence studied the papers silently, thoughtfully.

"You want me to confront him?" Dan asked.

Spence shook his head. "Naw. I'll take care of it."

Dan West was confused by his employer's behavior. *He doesn't seem concerned at all*, Dan thought. *It's as if it doesn't matter to him. That's not like Spence. He doesn't usually let anybody get by with anything.*

What's gotten into him?

Randall International continued to expand, and Spence spent a great deal of time traveling. He bought a shipyard in England, a bank in Australia, and a newspaper in Ireland. He checked out a freight company in Canada and visited a mining operation he was considering in South Africa. His photograph appeared in the media all over the world; his business deals made headlines.

But no one, absolutely no one, knew anything at all about Spencer Randall the man.

The call was unexpected. It caught him off guard, something he knew must never happen again.

It was a Friday, the end of a particularly long and busy week. His secretary buzzed him as he was about to leave for a meeting uptown. "Call for you on line two, sir," she announced.

"Who is it?"

"A Mr. Terence Hadley, sir."

"Never heard of him. Did he say what he wanted?"

"He says it's personal. That he's an old friend of yours."

An old friend? Terence Hadley? The name didn't ring any bells. To cover himself, he said aloud, "That's what they all say."

"I beg your pardon, sir?"

"It's a damn good way for reporters or would-be wheeler-dealers to get a foot in the door," he told her. "They tell you it's personal. They're 'old buddies' of mine."

"This man said he went to Yale with you," the secretary offered helpfully.

"A lot of people went to Yale," he pointed out. "But I don't know any Terence Hadley."

"Yes, sir. What should I tell him, then?"

"Tell him I don't—" He stopped short. *Can't take any chances,* he thought. "Tell him I'll have to get back to him. Get a number."

"Yes, sir."

He leaned back in his chair and stared at the telephone for a long time. He thought about it. *Terence Hadley. Don't remember Spencer ever mentioning anyone by that name. Of course, that doesn't mean he didn't know him. It just means he didn't talk about him. At least not to me. Probably wasn't all that close to the guy.*

So how do I handle this one?

*   *   *

"I can't believe you haven't done anything at all about Lombardi," Dan West told Spence when he returned from a trip abroad. "Are you going to just sit back and let him go right on robbing the company?"

"Hardly." Spence leaned back in his high-backed leather chair and lit a cigarette. "But we've got to be careful how we handle the guy. He's got connections, if you know what I mean."

Dan looked at him as if he weren't sure he understood. "You mean the underworld?"

"You got it, pal."

Dan laughed nervously. "What would the mob want with a two-bit hustler like Nick Lombardi?" he asked, unconvinced.

Spence shrugged. "I guess even the lowest life form has its uses," he said indifferently.

"So what are you going to do about Lombardi?"

For the first time since West entered the office, Spence smiled. "Don't worry, Danny boy. Lombardi'll get what's coming to him."

Spencer Randall became widely known for his philanthropic good works. He gave large sums of money to a number of important charities, and his public relations staff made sure those donations got him—and Randall International—plenty of good press.

What he never made public, and never would, were the cash donations he made frequently, either late at night or in the early hours of the morning, at the altar of St. Andrew in St. Patrick's Cathedral.

"There's a gentleman from *The New York Times* here to see you, sir," Spence's secretary announced.

"A reporter?"

"I think so, yes."

"Does he have an appointment?" Spence already knew the answer. He never gave interviews; therefore, he never made appointments with the press.

"Uh, no, sir—he doesn't."

"Tell him he'll have to make one, then."

The secretary looked at him oddly for a moment. "June 1990, sir?" she asked.

Spence grinned. "Nah—make it '91."

"I'm embarrassed," Spence confided to Terence Hadley over drinks at the Algonquin. "When you called, I really didn't recognize your name at all."

"I'm not surprised." The other man was surprisingly understanding. "From what I've heard, you're lucky to be alive."

Spence gave him a puzzled look.

"The war, I mean."

Spence nodded. *The war. Of course he would know.* "Yeah."

"You were on the *Indianapolis,* right?"

"Yeah, but I prefer not to talk about that unless I absolutely have to." Spence polished off the last of his drink and ordered another.

"I can understand that. Must have been terrible."

"Yeah." He paused. "So what brings you to New York, Terry, old pal?"

"Business." And for the next two and a half hours, Hadley described in the most intricate detail the deals he was putting together. The projects showed incredible promise, he told Spence, if only he could line up the right backers. "The potential's unbelievable," he insisted.

Unbelievable's the right word, all right, Spence mused as he left the Algonquin later. Hadley had talked all evening about these business propositions of his, but had said very little about the so-called "good old days" at Yale. Of all the possible scenarios Spence had imagined involving his encounters with the real Randall's past, this was one—in spite of what he'd told his secretary—he hadn't expected. *Now I know why Spencer never mentioned Terence Hadley,* he thought angrily.

He never knew a Terence Hadley.

"The usual, Mr. Randall?" the bartender asked as Spence entered the small tavern.

"After all this time, you have to ask?" Spence seated himself on one of the empty stools at the bar.

"Silly of me." The bartender poured a scotch and soda and placed it on the bar in front of him.

Spence only smiled. *You'd think he'd know better by now,* he thought wryly as he picked up his glass and sipped thoughtfully. He'd found this place right after he moved the Randall International offices to the financial district. He'd been walking one evening—he often took long walks when he needed to think—and wandered into this place. He'd liked it right away. Most of the clientele were businessmen like himself, bankers and stockbrokers, but the atmosphere was casual. He liked that.

Sometimes he played darts with the regulars. Sometimes he just drank alone. Once in a while he carried on meaningless conversations with the bartender. He didn't have to be on guard here. It didn't matter if he was a high roller named Spencer Randall or a streetwise hustler called Frankie Granelli.

That was what he liked best.

"There's a gentleman here to see you, sir," Spence's secretary told him. "He says he's from *Time* magazine."

"He got an appointment?" Spence asked.

"No, sir." The secretary sighed heavily. He knew the man didn't have an appointment. None of the reporters who tried to get to him in this way ever had an appointment. It simply wasn't allowed.

"Tell him he'll have to make one." Spence lit a cigarette.

The secretary sighed again. "Yes, sir. When would be a good time for you?"

"Judgment Day looks open."

"I thought we were keeping this under wraps for the time being." Spence passed the folded newspaper across the desk to Dan West. On the first page of the business section was a story on the latest Randall takeover.

"There's a leak," West said with a shrug.

"That's all you've got to say? There's a leak?" Spence's annoyance was clear in his voice.

"I wasn't aware of it until now," West admitted, somewhat embarrassed, "but that's got to be it."

"Yeah?" Spence was angry. "So what do we do about it, Danny boy?"

"We find the leak."

"Sounds simple enough," Spence said with a nod, an unmistakable undercurrent of sarcasm in his tone. "So after that, what do we do for an encore—part the Red Sea?"

"Look, Spence—I know this has got you bugged, but it's not like we can't do anything about it," West maintained. "We can trace the leak, but until we do, I think it's best that all confidential info be confined to top-level management."

"Brilliant deduction, Sherlock." Spence flicked the ashes from his cigarette into the ashtray on his desk. "Okay, Danny boy—I'm dumping it in your lap. Find the leak. Get rid of it."

Dan West stared at him for a moment. He opened his mouth as if he wanted to say something, then changed his mind abruptly. He got to his feet and started for the door. "I'll get right on it."

He doesn't understand, Spence thought after he'd gone. *He can't.* No one would be able to understand why he would never be able to risk that one, seemingly unimportant flaw within his organization. He took a deep breath and went back to reading his newspaper.

Tucked away on page twelve was a small item concerning the "mysterious disappearance" of a local businessman, Nick Lombardi.

ANNE

1946–1948

13

"Honestly, Daddy, I don't know why you're so opposed to the idea of me going to law school." Anne Talbott sat across the breakfast table from her father, a stern-faced man with sagging jowls and thinning gray hair that made him look much older than his forty-seven years. By contrast, his twenty-year-old daughter was slim and beautiful, with soft features, a heart-shaped face, and long blond hair. Her hair was so pale it looked almost silver, and her blue eyes were equally pale. She wore little jewelry, but all of it was genuine and expensive. She was simply dressed in a pale gray wool skirt and white blouse.

"The bar is no place for a woman," her father said curtly, not bothering to put down his newspaper so they could make eye contact.

"And just what do you consider to be 'a woman's place'?" Anne challenged, unwilling to give up.

"Anne, we've been through this before—" her father began wearily.

"Yes, I know that, Daddy, but I'd like you to tell me again," she pressed on. "I still find it so hard to believe."

"You're making fun of me, Anne," he said gruffly, his tone holding a warning note. She was so infuriating sometimes, his beautiful, willful daughter. Still, Arthur Talbott found it difficult to be angry with her. *Not that it would do to let her know that,* he'd decided a long time ago. *No, that would be a mistake.*

"Of course I am." She took a crisp slice of bacon from her plate, broke it in half, and nibbled on one piece as she stared across the table at him. "Your old-fashioned ideas are, after all, quite amusing."

"Oh?" Finally, he put down the newspaper. "You think the idea of making a good marriage, of financial security amusing?"

"Not at all," Anne said promptly. "I fully expect to be married one day. As to my future husband's financial status, well, I haven't a clue. Perhaps he will be well-to-do, perhaps not."

"How can you even suggest—"

Anne laughed, a rich, husky laugh. "Really, Daddy—haven't you ever heard that love is blind? Even to the contents of a Dun and Bradstreet, I suspect."

"That's a foolish attitude, Anne," her father snorted.

Anne got to her feet and came around to embrace him affectionately. "Well, what do you expect, Daddy?" she asked cheerfully. "I'm just a foolish female."

Anne Talbott didn't understand her father any more than he understood her. She didn't understand why he felt it was beneath her station, the idea of her even wanting to be a lawyer. She didn't understand why he felt it was so wrong for women to have careers at all.

"Lots of women work, Daddy."

"You're talking about lower-class women. Shopgirls. Waitresses. Maids. Not our kind, Anne."

"What do you mean by 'our kind,' Daddy?"

"You know perfectly well what I mean."

And that, as always, was the end of that. He refused to give her a reason for the way he felt, refused to explain why it was wrong for a woman—at least for a woman of her "station"—to have a career, or even want one.

But Anne was determined, and she was ten times more stubborn than her father. He was not going to win this one. She wasn't going to let him. She wanted to be a lawyer, and she wanted it more than she'd ever wanted anything. And no one, not even the father she adored, was going to keep her from achieving her goal.

No one.

It was curious, she thought now, that no one took her seriously because she was a so-called blue blood. Or was it because she was beautiful? Either way, it was a curse. *She's beautiful, therefore she must be stupid,* Anne thought resentfully. *She's rich, so all she's good for is to become a rich man's wife.*

Well, they could just forget about that. The idea of being nothing more than some rich man's wife, devoting her time among worthwhile charities, the arts, and producing blue-blooded heirs, was something Anne Talbott viewed as a fate worse than death.

Much worse.

Unfortunately, Anne's experience with men had been limited to those of her own social class, men like her father who believed upper-class women did not work, did not have careers. Men who thought women had but one purpose in life: to create a satisfactory environment for their men. *Selfish, arrogant, narrow-minded bastards,* Anne thought resentfully.

Her father wanted her to marry Charles Hargrove IV. Charles's family was as affluent as her own. His father was the senior partner in one of New York's largest brokerage firms. Charles was the most blue-blooded blue blood she had ever met—attractive, but, to Anne, unbearably dull. The world didn't exist for him beyond the firm and his own circle of equally blue-blooded intimates.

Anne smiled to herself. *Charles would be horrified if he ever saw a real slum,* she thought, amused. *He'd die if he were ever faced with poverty or hunger. He wouldn't even allow his driver to take a route that would pass through a low-rent district.*

Just like Daddy.

Her father and Charles Hargrove IV would have been shocked if they had known that the time she gave to "worthwhile charities" was not spent at fund-raising luncheons for some museum or other arts-related project, but dishing out hot meals at a soup kitchen and volunteering in hospital wards taking patients on relief. Her "double life" would have shocked them both, not to mention her mother. Her mother, who thought Anne was a throwback to some maverick of an ancestor who rode with swashbucklers and highwaymen.

Misfits, Anne thought wryly.

But it was an accurate comparison. She'd been born into a world in which she would never be able to fit in.

"Will you be seeing Charles tonight, dear?" her mother asked. She sat on the edge of Anne's four-poster bed, attempting to speak to her daughter as she scanned the clothes in the walk-in closet in search of something suitable to wear.

"No, not tonight," Anne responded, her voice raised so her mother could hear her from inside the closet. "Sorry to disappoint you, Mother."

"Disappoint *me*?" Her mother seemed genuinely surprised. "I would think you'd be thrilled by the attentions of someone like Charles."

There was a pause. "He's okay, I guess."

"*Okay?* Anne Talbott, proper young women do not use words like *okay*," her mother reprimanded her. "They do not say things like *I guess*."

"Then I guess I'm just not a proper young woman," Anne said cheerfully as she emerged from the closet, dressed in a pair of gray men's slacks and a cranberry pullover sweater.

Her mother was horrified. "You can't be thinking of leaving the house looking like that!" she gasped.

"No, I'm not *thinking* of it—I'm *doing* it," Anne stated flatly. "Why? Is there a problem?"

"Is there a problem?" her mother echoed. "Look at yourself, Anne—my God, you look like a *man*!"

"Maybe that's not such a bad thing," Anne said as she bent to kiss her mother's cheek. "As they say, it *is* a man's world."

"Anne!" her mother called after her as she dashed out the door.

It wasn't that Anne enjoyed working in the soup kitchens and charity wards. She didn't. She'd readily admit she found it depressing as hell. But it made her feel as if she were doing something worthwhile. Making a difference. It was rewarding in ways the life her parents had planned for her could never be. Most of the people she met never knew her name, but that didn't matter. Names didn't matter.

Now, as she looked into the face of an elderly woman who

smiled up at her as she heaped food onto a plate, she felt a deep sense of satisfaction that didn't require any personal recognition.

"More?" Anne asked.

The woman hesitated. "Maybe just a little," she said, lowering her voice as though she thought she might get into trouble by asking for more.

Anne frowned. The old woman was painfully thin and looked sickly. Her shabby dress hung loosely on her bony frame, and her stringy gray hair was pinned back off her cadaverous face. She looked like walking death, Anne thought, yet she was smiling. She had nothing to smile about, but her smile lit up her face like lights on a Christmas tree.

"How about a *lot* more?" Anne offered.

"Oh, I wouldn't want you to get in trouble, dearie," the old woman said quickly.

Anne lowered her voice conspiratorially. "Don't worry, I won't," she said reassuringly, heaping more potatoes onto the plate. "The boss doesn't keep track."

The woman took her plate, then looked up at Anne again. "God bless you, honey."

Anne smiled. "I think He already has, ma'am."

"Louise," the woman told her.

Anne nodded. "Louise."

She watched the woman make her way to a table, hunched over and barely able to walk. Anne's eyes scanned the crowded cafeteria, which had been set up in an old warehouse in the Bronx. It was gloomy and painfully depressing. The people who depended on this place seemed so hopeless, but looking at them now, she saw smiling faces, she heard laughter.

"You gotta wonder sometimes what they could possibly have to smile about, don't you, kiddo?"

Anne turned. Standing behind her, her supervisor, Jack McCleary, a tall, sturdily built man in his mid-forties with thick dark hair just beginning to go gray, twinkling blue eyes, and a nose that betrayed his past life as a prizefighter, was surveying the crowd thoughtfully. "Yes, I suppose it has crossed my mind," she said.

"More than once, I'd wager."

Anne nodded.

"Maybe they figure they're lucky just to be alive," McCleary suggested.

"Are they?" Anne asked dubiously.

"You and I might wonder, but it seems to me that's the way they see it."

Anne paused for a moment. "You've worked here a long time, haven't you?" she asked finally.

He laughed. "Does it show?"

Realizing what her question must have sounded like, Anne's face flushed. "I'm sorry!" she gasped. "I didn't mean—"

"Relax, Annie," he chuckled. "I know what you meant, but it would seem that I can't say the same for you."

Anne gave him a questioning look.

"What I was asking," McCleary explained patiently, "was if it showed that I'd been working here a long time."

"Well," she began carefully this time, "you seem to know so much more about all of this—you seem to understand so much more—that is—" She hoped she didn't sound like an idiot, because she certainly felt like one.

He patted her shoulder, giving her an understanding smile. "I know what you meant, Annie—and yes, I've been here a long time. I started out doing the same thing you're doing now—volunteer work. I guess I was here so long, they figured I ought to be getting a paycheck. So they put me in charge."

"How long *have* you been here?" Anne asked.

"Thirteen years," he told her. "I started during the Depression. A lot of the soup kitchens shut down after the Depression, but I talked the powers that be into keeping this one open because there were a lot of people who still needed it."

"Doesn't it ever get you down?" she asked, genuinely interested.

"Sometimes," he admitted. "But I've learned to deal with that. It's a job, one where it's okay to let myself get emotionally involved, but still a job." He paused, glancing at his watch. "We'd better start cleaning up, kiddo. Almost closing time."

*   *   *

"You need a ride home, kiddo?" McCleary asked as they were leaving later that night.

"Oh—no. I wouldn't want to have you go out of your way," Anne said quickly. The offer was tempting, but she couldn't accept. No one at the kitchen knew about her. They thought her name was Annie Turner and that she worked as a salesgirl at Saks. They didn't know about the Talbotts, about their money or their Social Register background. To them she was just Annie, one of the people who dished out the food. She was just one of the group, a prelaw student who cared enough to give a couple of nights a week to a good cause. And that was the way she wanted it.

"It's no trouble," McCleary insisted. "Unless, of course, you live in Jersey."

"No," she said, shaking her head. "I definitely do not live in Jersey." She'd never even been to Jersey.

"So where *do* you live?"

She had to think fast. "Uptown," she told him. "Way uptown. On First Avenue."

"Then it's not out of my way at all," he said, locking the double doors. "I'm going that way anyway. Come on."

"I couldn't—"

"Why not?" he asked with a grin. "You don't think I'm going to attack you or anything like that, do you?"

"Oh, God, no!" Anne was embarrassed. "It's just that"— her mind was racing—"I don't have any food in the house. I haven't had time to shop. I—I was going to stop for a bite to eat before I go home." She gestured toward a small diner across the street.

"Excellent idea," he said cheerfully. "I haven't eaten myself. It'll be my treat."

Now there was no way she could refuse gracefully. She'd just have to find a way out of letting him take her home by the time they finished eating. "Be forewarned," she told him, "I'm a big eater."

"Really? It doesn't show."

It was the first time Anne thought maybe—just maybe— McCleary might have actually noticed her as a woman, might have noticed her as something other than one of his kitchen helpers. She was elated because she'd noticed him as a man right away. Jack McCleary was different from any man she'd ever known, certainly different from Charles Hargrove IV.

"Well, thank you," she said slowly, "but I thought you should be warned."

The brightly lit diner was deserted. McCleary steered Anne to one of the red vinyl–upholstered booths at the back of the room and waved to the waitress behind the counter. "Bring us a couple of menus, would you, Sandy?" he called out to her.

"Sure thing, Jack."

It was obvious that they knew each other. "Do you eat here often?" Anne asked as they seated themselves.

"More than I care to admit," he said with a mischievous wink.

She looked at him. "The food isn't good?"

"It's passable," he said charitably.

Anne smiled. "Am I going to regret eating here?"

"Not till morning," he assured her.

She stared at him for a moment. Most of the time she wasn't sure when McCleary was joking and when he wasn't. Finally, she smiled.

"You've eaten here before—what do you recommend?" she asked.

"Extreme caution," he deadpanned without a moment's hesitation.

"Seriously, McCleary!" Anne scolded.

"I *am* serious," he insisted, taking a quick glance at the menu the waitress brought. "Don't order the roast beef. They keep it till it's all gone, and they don't get that many orders—could be two, three weeks old."

"McCleary!"

"It's no joke. The owner of this place has redefined cheap," he told her. "Pass on the hamburgers, too—most of their ground round brought up the rear at Aqueduct last week."

Anne almost choked.

"The BLT's safe. So's the chili, most of the time," he went on. "The best thing on the menu, though, is the pie."

"Which kind?" she asked.

"Doesn't matter. They're all good," he said. "They're not made here."

"Oh, I see—that explains it."

He smiled. "It does. They buy all of their pies from a sweet old lady who lives a couple of blocks away. She makes the best pies you'll ever eat—entirely from scratch—and never even looks at a recipe."

Anne leaned forward, elbows on the table, cupping her chin in her hands. "You seem to know an awful lot about the people and the neighborhood," she said.

He shrugged. "I've spent a lot of time here."

"Thirteen years, right?"

"Longer than that," he said. "I grew up here."

I had no idea, Anne thought, glancing at McCleary's profile in the darkness. She sat next to him in the car as he drove uptown—taking her home. Or so he thought. *I certainly can't tell him the truth now—not knowing what kind of life he's had.* She recalled the conversation they'd had over soup and hot apple pie. . . .

"I grew up here. Lived in a fifth-floor walkup right around the corner."

"So you've known a lot of these people since—"

"Since I was a kid?"

"Well . . . yes."

"I knew them, all right. I was one of them."

"One of them?"

"Poor. Dirt poor. Most times there wasn't enough to eat and no money to pay the bills. My father couldn't always find work, but when it was available, he'd do just about anything. Then one night he was coming home—it was late, he'd just made a little money—and some guy pulled a knife on him. He tried to put up a fight, and the guy—the guy stabbed him. After that, my mother just gave up . . ."

Anne suddenly felt ashamed of her wealth, ashamed of the luxury in which she'd grown up. Telling him about herself now would be like flaunting it.

No, she thought, *I can't tell him the truth. Not now.*

"Here we are."

His words cut through her thoughts. It took her a moment

to realize they'd reached the First Avenue address she'd given him. She forced a smile. "Thanks, McCleary," she said as he opened the car door for her. Then, impulsively, she kissed his cheek. "Thanks."

He looked surprised but quickly tried to cover it. "See you next week," he said, somewhat uncomfortably.

"You bet."

"I'll walk you to your door," he offered.

"Oh, no—you don't have to do that!" she said quickly, too quickly. Glancing over at the building, she saw a brightly lit stairway leading to the second floor. "You've already done enough. I'll be fine, I swear it."

"I'll stay here till you're all the way up the stairs," he insisted.

Great, Anne thought, but aloud she said, "Fair enough."

She climbed the stairs, silently hoping no one would be at the top. When she was sure he was gone, she went back down to the street, hailed a cab, and went home.

14

Anne Talbott was in love.

She told herself she was being stupid, that a man like Jack McCleary wouldn't look twice at her, not in *that* way, anyway. He thought of her as a kid. A child. He'd probably laugh at her if she were to confess how she felt about him.

Daddy wouldn't laugh, she thought. *He'd be furious.*

Her mother would probably just faint. Both of her parents would be appalled if they knew how she felt about McCleary. He was everything they didn't want for their daughter. He was everything Charles Hargrove IV wasn't.

Thank God for that, Anne thought wryly.

Now, all she had to do was find a way to get him to see her as a woman instead of as a child.

I could seduce him, she told herself.

Easier said than done.

I've never done that sort of thing before. I've never even been with a man before.

What if he laughs at me?

No. He wouldn't do that. Not Jack. God, that's the first time I've called him Jack—even to myself.

Why am I so nervous?

That's easy. What girl—woman, I am a woman now— wouldn't be nervous? I've fallen in love with a man and don't have the faintest idea how he feels about me. He's always thought of me as a kid. He probably still does.

She studied her reflection in the full-length mirror. She knew she was beautiful. She'd always known it but it had never mattered to her one way or the other until now. She was glad she was beautiful now. Men noticed beautiful women, even men like Jack McCleary, who knew there was more to a woman than just a pretty face.

Now, she thought, *if I could just make myself look a few years older. Maybe he wouldn't feel he'd be robbing the cradle.*

She paused for a moment, then started taking off her clothes. When she was completely undressed, she stood in front of the mirror again. *That's the body of a woman—no doubt about that,* she thought, satisfied. *If only I could get Jack to see it.*

But then, I can't very well march into his office and strip. Or can I?

"Got a minute?"

McCleary was alone in his small office, seated at the scarred old desk he often joked was as old as the building and in just as bad shape. He looked up from the papers he'd been reviewing, smiling when he saw Anne. "For you, Annie, I've got all the time in the world," he told her.

I wish you really meant that, she thought as she entered the office and closed the door. "Thanks, Jack."

He raised an eyebrow. "We're finally on a first-name basis, are we?" he teased. "After all this time?"

"Don't make fun of me, Jack." *This is hard enough as it is.*

"Never. Sit down, Annie. Tell me what's bothering you."

She stiffened. "What makes you think something's bothering me?"

He laughed. "Well, if you'll pardon me for saying so, you're as jumpy as a turkey in November."

I can't do this, she thought, frustrated. *I'm making a fool of myself.* "It's nothing, really," she stammered. "I shouldn't have bothered you. Sorry." She turned and hurried out of the room before he could stop her.

Anne didn't feel comfortable discussing her feelings for McCleary with her mother, but now that she was in the position of needing someone to talk to, she realized there was no one else she could confide in. She didn't have any close girlfriends. She had nothing in common with the girls she'd grown up with, girls from the same social circles who'd attended the same élite boarding schools. No . . . there was only her mother now, and she had to talk to someone.

"Mother, have you ever been in love?" she asked, not knowing how else to begin. "I mean *really* in love?"

They were alone in the study at the time. Her mother looked shocked. "Now, what kind of question is that?"

"An honest one," Anne maintained. "I know you didn't love Daddy when you married him, and I know you've never been passionately in love with him—"

"Passion always cools, sooner or later," her mother told her. "What your father and I have—and what you and Charles will have—is much more enduring."

"I'm not talking about Charles," Anne said abruptly. "I don't even *like* Charles, much less love him."

Her mother gave her a quizzical look. "I'm afraid I don't understand—"

"I'm in love—but not with Charles. Someone else."

"I wasn't aware you'd been seeing anyone else," her mother said, clearly concerned.

"I haven't really been seeing him—at least not in the way you mean," Anne confessed. "I met him when I started doing volunteer work. We've been working together for the past year.''

"At the hospital?" her mother asked.

"In a way," Anne answered evasively. Her mother knew she'd been volunteering in a hospital; she just didn't know what kind of hospital.

"Is he a doctor?"

Anne almost laughed aloud at the thought. McCleary? A doctor? No, his business had been taking bodies apart, not putting them together.

"No, he's not a doctor," she said evenly.

"You've never mentioned him before," her mother said then. "I can't help but wonder why not."

"Really, Mother." Anne looked away, standing in front of the French doors, her hands shoved down into the pockets of her sweater. "I knew you and Daddy wouldn't approve."

"What's wrong with him that we wouldn't approve of?"

"As far as I'm concerned, nothing. But I'm sure you and Daddy would never stop finding fault with him," Anne said with certainty. "He's not rich, he's much older than I am, and he's an ex-prizefighter."

Her mother looked as if she might have a stroke. "How on earth could you ever become involved with a man like that?" she gasped.

"That's what I'd like to know," Anne muttered.

"What?"

"I said, that's what I'd like to know." Anne turned to face her mother. "That's what I'm asking you, Mother—how to get involved with him."

"Then you're not already?" Her mother breathed an undisguised sigh of relief.

"No, Mother, I'm not," Anne responded coldly.

"Well, at least you've had the good sense not to rush into anything."

"No, I haven't," Anne admitted. "He's the one who's holding back."

Her mother gave her a quizzical look.

"He hasn't made any—overtures," Anne said, "though God knows I've made it clear I'm interested in him."

"Perhaps he realizes there would be no future in it," her mother suggested.

"What makes you think there wouldn't?"

"Please, Anne—don't force me to be cruel," her mother said. "You've said it all yourself—he's a good deal older than you are and he's a onetime prizefighter, for God's sake!"

"What's wrong with that?" Anne demanded hotly.

"What could you possibly have in common with this man?"

Anne's eyes met hers. "You'd be surprised, Mother."

He won't make any advances toward me, Anne thought with certainty. *No matter how he feels—no matter what he feels— he won't do it. He's that kind of man—and that's why I love him.*

But it makes what I have to do all that much harder.

Bringing the mountain to Muhammad was every bit as impossible as it sounded. Almost as impossible as it was going to be to make Jack go from being her friend to being her lover. It was going to require drastic action on her part. *What do I have to do?* she wondered. *Strip and throw myself at him?*

It wasn't an altogether bad idea. But did she have the guts to pull it off?

"You never talk about yourself much, Jack," Anne observed. "Why is that?"

They were having lunch in his small office at the Community Care Center. The door was closed—Anne silently wished it were locked—and it was one of the rare times during the center's operating hours they were actually alone.

"There's not that much to tell," he said, taking a bite of his pastrami sandwich. "You know most of it already."

"Have you ever been married?" she asked, the question more direct than she'd intended.

If it surprised him, he was doing an excellent job of concealing it.

"Once," he answered, "a long time ago. It didn't work out."

"Did you have any children?" She tried to sound casual.

"One—a daughter," he said. "She's about your age now."

Anne was speechless. *Just what I needed to hear,* she thought, struggling to retain her composure. "You never talk about her," she said finally.

He frowned. "I haven't seen her since she was four years old."

She didn't know what to say. "I'm sorry," was all she could think of.

"When we divorced, Emily—my ex-wife—took Katie and moved to Ohio. It hurt like hell at first," he recalled. "Emily poisoned Katie's mind against me. My own daughter hated my guts. After a while, I got used to it, but . . ." His voice trailed off.

"I'm sorry," she said again. Impulsively, she reached across the desk and covered his hand with her own.

My God, she was thinking. *He does love me.*

Like a surrogate daughter.

It took Anne weeks to get up her courage again. She went to the center three afternoons a week, as she'd always done. Her relationship with Jack remained pretty much the same as it always had—on the surface, anyway—but her frustration was reaching gargantuan proportions. There were times she thought he cared about her in the way a man cared about a woman. And there were other times—most of the time, in fact—she was convinced he saw her as a replacement for the daughter he'd lost.

The last thing I want to be to him is a daughter, she thought angrily.

Finally, her frustration gave her the courage she'd lacked before. *There's no other way,* she told herself repeatedly as she stood outside his office with her hand on the doorknob, knowing it was up to her to make the first move. *It's up to me to take the first step.*

Hesitantly, she knocked on the door.

"It's open," he called out gruffly.

She opened the door enough to poke her head inside. "You busy, Jack?"

He smiled brightly when he saw her. "Never too busy to

talk to you, Annie,'' he assured her. "Come on in.''

She took a deep breath as she entered. *I wish I knew how he meant that,* she thought.

"What can I do for you, pretty lady?''

Anne tried not to blush. "You can let me cook dinner for you—tonight.''

He looked surprised, but pleasantly so. "Well, I'm touched—but why? What's this all about?''

"Does it require a reason?'' she asked. "Can't a friend make you dinner without some ulterior motive?''

He looked embarrassed. "Of course.''

"You've been such a good friend to me—and I don't have many friends—'' she started.

He raised a hand to silence her. "You don't have to explain,'' he told her. "I'd love to have you cook dinner for me. Your place? What time?''

"Uh—better make it your place,'' she said, thinking quickly. "My landlord's having the exterminator in today.''

He thought about it. "I usually get in around seven. Want to come around seven-thirty?''

She shook her head. "I want to have it ready when you get there,'' she said. "Give me your key.''

He dug into his pocket and pulled out a large ring holding at least a dozen keys. Removing two, he passed them to her.

"I'll be leaving around four,'' she told him, taking the keys. She started for the door. "See you at seven.''

"Don't you want the address?'' he asked.

"I already know the address.''

Now, she thought as she walked out, *all I have to do is learn to cook by four o'clock.*

She solved the problem by having her mother's cook prepare a meal and the chauffeur deliver it. *I hope no one sees me,* she thought as she waited for the limo in front of his apartment in lower Manhattan. And then: *No, that's too much to hope for. The limo's going to stand out like a nudist at a Sunday school picnic.*

As soon as the car arrived, she rushed everything upstairs and sent the driver on his way as quickly as possible. *With my luck, Jack'll come home early and catch me in the act,* she thought as she hurried to set the table. *It wouldn't do to have him find out "Annie" has a cook and a chauffeur.*

Not yet, anyway.

She surveyed the finished table with satisfaction. *When in doubt, call an expert,* she thought as she turned her attention to messing up the kitchen. She removed everything from the containers the cook had sent, putting the food into the pans and bowls she found in the cabinets. *I'll serve it up when he gets here,* she thought. *Make it look good.*

While she waited, she walked around the apartment taking in her surroundings. It was so different from where she lived, it might as well have been another planet. It was obvious that a man lived there and lived there alone. There were no feminine touches, nothing of a woman anywhere on the premises. There wasn't a single photograph of his daughter. *He probably doesn't even know what she looks like now,* Anne thought.

And she wondered if he ever thought about having another child.

"You never cease to amaze me," Jack told her after dinner. "A beautiful girl who can cook, too—you're going to make some lucky guy a wonderful wife, Annie."

"Is that a proposal, Jack?" She tried to sound casual.

There was a long pause Anne hoped was significant. "You can do a lot better than a guy like me, Annie," he said tightly. "You're young, you're beautiful—and I'm way too old for you."

"Age doesn't matter," she insisted stubbornly.

"Come on, Annie—I'm old enough to be your father!" he protested.

"I love you, Jack."

He looked at her for a moment. "You might think you do, but—" he started.

"I don't *think,* I *know,*" she argued. "I've loved you for a long time."

He shook his head. "You're just a baby."

"I haven't been a baby for a very long time," she shot back angrily. "That should be obvious, even to you!"

"Compared to me, honey, you're a baby," he maintained,

pushing himself away from the table.

"You're nervous, Jack—it's written all over you, no hiding it," she said. "It wouldn't bother you if you didn't feel something for me."

"Of course I feel something for you!" he snapped irritably. "I've always cared about you, Annie—I've never made any secret of that—"

"That's not what I meant!"

"I know what you meant, dammit!" He got to his feet in a sudden movement that was quick but awkward. "I can see now that this was a big mistake."

"Is there someone else?" Anne asked calmly.

"What? Jesus, Annie—this is crazy!"

She persisted. "Is there?"

"No, dammit, there isn't—but that doesn't change anything!"

"It's been a long time, hasn't it?" she asked. "Since there's been a woman in your life, I mean."

"It doesn't make any difference," he said gruffly.

"You must be lonely," she said softly.

"It's got nothing to do with you," he growled. "I think it would be better if you left now, Annie."

"Make love to me, Jack."

He stared at her incredulously. "You don't say that sort of thing to a man unless you mean it, Annie," he warned.

"I've never meant anything more sincerely in my life." Before he could respond, she started unbuttoning her blouse. She was determined not to let him stop her.

To her surprise, he didn't even try. He stood there, watching her in silence, as she removed all of her clothes. When she was finished, her eyes met his again.

"Make love to me, Jack," she said again.

Anne could tell he was aroused. She could tell by his labored breathing, by the look in his eyes as he stared at her, by the very obvious bulge in his pants. She could feel herself trembling inside as he came forward, no longer resisting. *This is it,* she thought as he took her in his arms and kissed her with a hunger that matched her own. *It's really happening.*

She tried to remember what little her mother had told her about sex. Proper ladies didn't enjoy sex; it was something they did to please their husbands. *I must not be a "proper lady,"* Anne thought, because she was thoroughly enjoying the way Jack was touching her as they continued to kiss.

"Take your clothes off," she whispered.

His voice was shaky when he finally spoke: "I don't think I'm going to have time, honey."

She unbuttoned his shirt. *A man never respects a woman who will sleep with him without marriage,* her mother had told her. *But Jack's not like other men,* Anne thought. *I have to believe that this will bring us closer together—maybe even make him love me.*

His hands were all over her—caressing her buttocks, stroking the length of her back, fingertips running over the swell of her breasts. But he avoided touching her *there* and wouldn't let her touch him below the belt. "If you do, I'll come too quick," he rasped. "I won't even get to put it in you."

It hurts the first time—sometimes quite a lot, her mother had said. *Especially if the woman is very small, like you, and the man's—organ—is very big.* Anne wondered, as he lowered her to his bed, if Jack was big, if it was going to hurt very much. *Sometimes the woman bleeds.* She hoped she didn't. It would be so embarrassing.

He doesn't know I'm a virgin.

She watched him undress. He was big. He was enormous— and fully erect. Anne had never seen a man's penis before, so she had no basis for comparison, but he looked so big, she couldn't imagine him putting *that* inside her without ripping her apart.

Should I tell him I've never done this before? she wondered.

He lay on top of her, supporting his weight on his elbows, kissing her lips, face, and neck. She could feel his erection pressing against her, and suddenly she was nervous. She didn't know what to do next, but she knew she couldn't just lie there. She started stroking his neck, shoulders, and back.

"Jack . . . the lights . . . " she breathed.

"Let's leave them on, okay?" he whispered between kisses. "You're so damn beautiful . . . even more so than I thought you'd be . . . I want to be able to look at you."

She decided not to make an issue of it. The lights would remain on.

He kissed and nuzzled her breasts. When he started sucking her nipples, she felt as though electricity were coursing through her whole body. She wasn't at all sure she liked the feeling, but he seemed to enjoy what he was doing to her. He was apparently fascinated by her breasts and in no hurry to turn his attention away from them. She stroked his hair and whispered words of endearment.

Finally, he withdrew from her breasts. Moving downward, he left a trail of kisses down her belly, over her hip— *My God, what's he doing?* Anne wondered, alarmed, as he parted her legs and started kissing the insides of her thighs. Nothing her mother had told her about sex had ever prepared her for this. Of course, she couldn't imagine her very proper mother ever allowing her father to do this, nor could she imagine her father wanting to.

She let out a shocked gasp as she felt his fingers parting her, felt him kissing, licking her. She moaned, gripping the mattress. She'd had no idea that men did this sort of thing to women. She would never have believed she would allow a man—any man—to do it to her. Or that she would actually *enjoy* it.

When she was moaning and begging him to stop, unable to take it any longer, he pulled away. In an instant he was on top of her again, trying to push himself into her. At first he didn't understand it. Then it hit him.

"Jesus—you're a virgin!"

She looked up at him, concerned. "Does it make a difference?"

"Of course it makes a difference! Jeez, I would never have touched you if—"

"If you'd known I was a virgin?"

"Yes, dammit!"

Abruptly, the mood was broken. He pulled away, running a hand through his hair in a frustrated gesture. "You should have told me."

"You make it sound like I've got a criminal record rather than being—inexperienced!" She knew she was going to cry, and she hated herself for it.

"Dammit, I don't go around bedding virgins!" he snapped.

"It's not a contagious disease, you know." She sat up behind him on the bed, placing a hand on his shoulder. "I thought you'd be pleased that I love you enough to want you to be the first."

He turned to look at her. "I *am*—I mean, I'm happy that you cared enough to—but goddamnit, Annie, I wouldn't have—don't you see?"

"No," she said, shaking her head, "I don't."

"I love you!"

"Then why is it so wrong for us to make love?" she demanded.

"I should never have touched you to start with."

"Why?"

"Oh, come on, Annie—look at us!" he said irritably. "I'm a burned-out ex-prizefighter running a charity operation. You're young, beautiful, well-bred. What chance do you think we've got of making this last?"

"We can make it last if we want it to!" Anne cried.

His smile was sad. "You're so young, you can still believe in happy endings and all that."

"And you don't?"

"Look around you, honey," he said with a wave of his hand. "This is my life. This is how I grew up. There's never been any room for fairy tales. I've had to deal with cold, hard reality since I was a kid."

She was silent for a moment. "I love you, Jack McCleary," she said finally. "I don't care if it lasts a week, a month, a year—or a lifetime. I only care about you, right now."

"You'll care about it later, when you marry some nice guy and it's all shot to hell when he finds out the girl he married isn't a virgin."

"I could always marry the guy I gave my virginity to," she said lightly.

"This is serious, Annie."

"Look at me, Jack."

"Annie—"

"Look at me," she insisted.

Slowly, reluctantly, he twisted around to face her. She was

sitting on the bed, still naked, not bothering to even try to cover herself. Her legs were parted, not consciously, but rather the result of the way she'd sat up when he pulled away from her.

"I'm not asking you to tell me you love me," she started evenly, "but can you tell me now you don't want me?"

"I'd have to be dead not to want you." He was clearly uncomfortable. "You're not making this any easier—"

Her eyes met his. "I intend to make it impossible," she said honestly.

He pushed the sheet at her. "Cover yourself," he said gruffly.

"No." Her voice was soft but firm. "Stop being so god-damned noble, McCleary. You're not taking advantage of me. I came here of my own free will. I made the first move—and I knew exactly what I was doing." She wrapped her arms around his neck and pressed herself against him as she nuzzled his neck. "Just like I know what I'm doing right now."

He groaned, and she knew he wasn't going to have the willpower to turn away from her.

"Make love to me, Jack," she breathed, stroking his shoulder lightly with her fingertips.

"Dammit, Annie!" He was definitely weakening.

"I've never done this before. Sure, I'm nervous—but isn't it all the more reason why my first time should be with someone like you, someone who'll be gentle—"

At that moment, the last of his self-control evaporated. He took her in his arms and kissed her long and hard as they fell back onto the bed. "Damn you for doing this to me," he murmured as he started kissing her breasts again. "Damn you for making me want you so much."

His mouth closed over her nipple, and she moaned with pleasure. She stroked his head, holding him to her, silently hoping he wouldn't stop this time.

He didn't, and when he finally thrust himself into her, when she cried out in response to the sudden stab of pain that ripped between her legs, the thought that was pushed to the back of her mind was that neither of them had taken any precautions.

What if I get pregnant?

*   *   *

I wonder if sex changes everyone this much? Anne asked herself as she half ran along Central Park South, headed for the Plaza Hotel. She could have sworn she even *looked* different when she looked in the mirror this morning.

I look like a woman in love, she thought with deep satisfaction.

And Jack loved her. How many times had he said so when they made love? He hadn't said it as other men might, just to get her into his bed, either. Even if he hadn't tried so hard not to get involved with her, she would have known that. Jack McCleary just wasn't that kind of man.

He may have been a prizefighter, Anne thought now, *but he has a romantic nature.*

I've got to be the luckiest girl—woman—alive.

"Your father and I would like to meet your young man, Anne," her mother told her over lunch at the Oyster Bar.

Anne smiled. "My 'young man,' as you call him, is almost Daddy's age," she said without hesitation, "and I don't think an introduction would be a very good idea."

"As long as you insist upon seeing him, I think it's only proper," her mother pressured her.

"What's the use?" Anne asked with a heavy sigh. "I think we already know there's no chance either of you would ever accept Jack or our relationship, so why should I subject him to that kind of unpleasantness?"

"Because you're our daughter," her mother said promptly. "We're entitled to know what kind of man our daughter is involved with."

"I love him, Mother," Anne told her. "He's a wonderful man—ten times the man you would have had me marry—"

"Charles was the ideal man for you," her mother said.

"In whose opinion?" Anne asked sharply. "Jack's more of a man than Charles will ever be, even if he's not the man you would have chosen for me."

Her mother didn't bring it up again, but Anne had a feeling it was far from over.

Jack seemed to have come to grips with his guilt.

Anne lay contentedly in his arms one night after they'd

made love, her head on his shoulder, reflecting on how good it was between them now as compared to that near disaster the first time. It scared her now to think of how close she'd come to losing him.

"You're awfully quiet tonight," she said finally.

He was lying on his back, staring up at the ceiling. "Just thinking," he answered vaguely.

She hesitated. "Do I dare ask about what?"

"About what this has to be doing to you."

"I *like* what it's doing to me," she assured him.

"You know what I'm talking about," he said tightly.

She raised her head to look at him. "No, I don't," she said softly. "I really don't."

"Are you telling me it doesn't bother you, being torn between me and your family?" he asked, his tone skeptical. She hadn't told him *who* her parents were, only that she hadn't taken him to meet them because they didn't approve of the relationship.

"I've already taken sides, if that's what you mean," she said, stroking his chest, fingering the thick, curly hair.

"You shouldn't have to take sides, Annie."

She gave a little laugh. "You don't know my parents, Jack," she said. "No matter who I fell in love with, I'd have to take sides—unless it was someone they chose for me. And the man they chose for me was someone I knew was all wrong for me from the day we met. We had nothing in common."

"Except having grown up together and sharing a history," he concluded.

"That's not enough," Anne insisted.

"It's more than we've got," he pointed out.

"Jack, you and I have much more in common than I could ever have with Charles. We share the same views. We care about the same things." She kissed his shoulder. "We care about each other."

"Sometimes loving someone just isn't enough, honey," he said with a twinge of sadness in his voice.

"It is for me," she said simply.

"You're still young."

She raised herself up on one elbow. "Why do you keep saying that?"

"Maybe I think you need to be reminded."

"Maybe I'd rather forget."

He brushed his knuckles lightly against her cheek. "Honey, just what do you think it would be like for us twenty years from now—when you're forty and I'm sixty-five?"

"Jack—"

"I'm old enough to be your father, sweetheart," he told her, as if she needed to be reminded again. "Sooner or later, you're going to want kids, and you've got every right to want them, but if I were to become a daddy again now, at my age, they'd be more like my grandchildren. I'm too old, Annie."

She was silent for a moment. "Neither of us has been using anything," she said finally. "All these times we've made love—what if I'm already pregnant?"

He was suddenly concerned. "Are you?"

"I don't know. I could be," she said.

"Do you think you are?"

"I don't think so, no." Anne paused. "But I could be. As often as we make love—"

"I'll have to start using rubbers," he decided.

"What if I *am* pregnant? Now, I mean."

"I'd marry you."

She sat up in bed, not bothering to cover herself. "You'd only marry me if I got pregnant?"

"I love you," he told her. "I love you so much it hurts. It hurts because I know, rationally, that it can't last—and even knowing that, I can't bring myself to give you up. Every day, I tell myself that's going to be it, that I'm going to end it with you, that I'm not going to make love with you, then I take one look at you and there goes my willpower."

"You didn't answer my question, Jack."

"I've always thought of myself as a strong man—but not where you're concerned," he confessed. "But because I love you, I won't marry you. I won't compound the mistake. It wouldn't be fair to you. But if you were pregnant, I'd have a responsibility to you, to the baby."

She pressed a finger to his lips. "Ssh," she hushed him. "I don't want to talk about this anymore. I don't want to talk at all. I want you to make love to me.''

I want to make a baby.

As weeks passed and no symptoms appeared, Anne grew discouraged. *Why did I have to fall in love with such a noble idiot?* she asked herself, frustrated, as she marked off days on the calendar. *He loves me. He admits he loves me. And yet he claims he won't marry me because I'm young and have my whole life ahead of me. Dammit, McCleary, what's the real reason?*

More than once she'd asked herself if it could be just an excuse on his part, a way he could keep going to bed with her without making a commitment. But she knew Jack McCleary too well to really believe that. She'd had to throw herself at him to get him to touch her at all, and even then he'd resisted.

He loves me, all right, she thought. *He just doesn't love me enough to marry me.*

Jack McCleary was a tormented man.

He did love Anne. He didn't want to, he hadn't planned it that way, but there it was, an undeniable reality. *Damn, she's younger than my daughter!* he mentally reprimanded himself. *I should never have allowed it to happen in the first place.*

But it had happened. It had happened because Annie was persistent—and because he was weak. Because he loved her too much to turn away from her. *You're a fool,* he thought, looking at a photograph of Annie he'd taken one day in Central Park. *You're a stupid goddamned fool to think you could have any kind of a future with her. She's just a girl, a child. What do you think you're doing, anyway—recapturing your youth?*

That's a laugh.

He couldn't remember ever having a "youth." Circumstances had made it necessary for him to grow up fast. He'd had to become a man before he'd even had a chance to be a boy.

Is that why I'm so drawn to Annie? he wondered. *Does she represent everything I missed out on?*

15

"You can't be serious!"

"I'm afraid I am," Caroline Talbott said quietly, looking at her husband. "Our daughter seems to be quite infatuated with this man."

"And he's a—a prizefighter?" he asked incredulously.

"Ex-prizefighter," Caroline corrected.

"It doesn't matter whether he is or was," her husband said irritably. "I'll not have my daughter—our daughter—involved with that sort of man. And certainly not one old enough to be her father."

"I think it's too late."

He looked at her. "Meaning what?"

"I think Anne may be involved in an intimate relationship with this man." She put it as delicately as she could.

Her husband was appalled. "You've discussed this with her?" he asked.

Caroline nodded. "She came to me for advice."

"And you tried to dissuade her, of course."

She sighed heavily. "I tried, yes—but I'm afraid I accomplished nothing."

"You think she's having an affair with him, then," he concluded.

"I think she's definitely made overtures—and I can't imagine he would have turned her down," Caroline said.

"Then perhaps it's time I had a talk with her," Talbott decided.

Anne had never wished anyone ill, but right now, more than anything, she wanted the rabbit to die.

It's the only way, she told herself. *No matter how much he loves me, he won't marry me—unless I get pregnant. I'm trapping him—but there's no other way.*

And he does love me.

It wasn't as if she were trying to trap a man who didn't want her. *I'm just persuading a man who's having a little trouble making up his mind,* she told herself. *I'm just doing what's necessary to hold on to a man who keeps saying he loves me.*

So why do I feel so rotten about it?

"I wish it could always be like this," Anne said.

It was cold, unseasonably cold even for November in New York. She and Jack were walking in Central Park as they often did, arm in arm.

"Wishing doesn't make it so," he said tightly. *If only it did.*

"Effort can make it so," she said.

"Annie, you're incredible," he said. He was smiling, but there was sadness in his eyes. "You have this unshakable faith in the future. You never give up hope, do you?"

"I love you too much to give up," she said simply.

"You'd end up regretting it," he told her. "You'd be tied down to an old man, and you'd come to resent me. I couldn't live with that."

"No, I wouldn't," she insisted. "I know it wouldn't be a bed of roses, but I'm willing to take my chances."

"Annie—"

"I take the marriage vows very seriously," she told him. "You know, for better or worse—"

"Right." His expression was grim. "I couldn't do any better, and you couldn't do any worse."

"Make jokes if you want," she said indignantly, "but you'll never convince me it won't work."

"You've got your whole life ahead of you—" he began.

She stopped in her tracks and faced him squarely. "You know, I'm really sick of that speech of yours, McCleary," she told him. "Yes, I *do* have my whole life ahead of me— and I know *exactly* what I want to do with it. I want to go to law school. I want to become a criminal lawyer. I want to help some of those people who wouldn't be helped otherwise. But most of all, I want to marry you and have a family.''

He frowned. ''Has it ever once occurred to you that if we were to have children, I'd be more like their grandfather than their father?'' he asked. ''Have you ever stopped to think what it would be like for them? I'm too old, Annie—I'm too damn old for this!''

She studied him for a moment. This had come up before, more than once. ''Is that what's bothering you?'' she asked, her voice softer now. ''You really don't want children?''

''I'm too old to start a new family,'' he reminded her.

''So we won't have children,'' she said promptly.

He shook his head. ''That wouldn't be fair to you,'' he said. ''I know you want kids—''

''I want *you*,'' she told him. ''More than I want children, more than I want anything else.''

''You do now, but later on, it'll be a different story,'' he predicted.

''No, it won't,'' Anne insisted. ''You'll always be enough for me. More than enough.''

He took her in his arms and held her close. *If only I could believe it,* he was thinking.

''Whatever possessed you to do such a thing?''

Anne looked at her father, smiling. ''You make it sound as if I've gotten a parking ticket or was caught shoplifting,'' she said calmly.

''This is far more serious than that,'' her father replied. ''Your mother has told me about this man you've involved yourself with.''

''Involved myself with?'' Anne couldn't help laughing. ''Daddy, I'm in *love* with him!''

''You don't even know what love is!''

''I know what it isn't,'' she told him. ''I know it's not marrying someone you don't even like just because they're 'your kind'!''

''Charles is a fine young man,'' her father maintained.

''He's a dreadful bore!''

''He'll make a fine husband.''

''For someone else, perhaps. Not for me.''

"You've grown up with all of the advantages," her father reminded her. "Do you seriously believe you could learn to live on what this man most likely earns?"

"How would you know what he earns?" Anne challenged him angrily.

"I wouldn't—but I *would* know that he couldn't possibly earn enough to support you in the manner to which you're accustomed," he said. "You've never had to do without, Anne. Just how long would you stay with him if you had to do without for a while?"

"This is all pointless, you know," she said, turning to face him. "You don't have to worry about me running off to marry him: He won't marry me. He's already made that clear."

"He sounds like an intelligent man, I'll give him that," her father said. "He realizes it wouldn't work."

"It *would* work!" she snapped. "It would work if you and Mother would stay out of it and let me live my own life!" She started to leave the room.

"Don't you walk out on me, young lady!" he called after her.

But it was too late. Anne had already slammed the door.

"I want to move in here with you," Anne told Jack.

He laughed, thinking it was a joke. "Just when I start to think nothing you could say or do could possibly surprise me, you always manage to prove me wrong."

"I'm serious, Jack," she said. "I want to live here, with you."

"No decent woman lives with a man she's not married to—or so most people think, anyway."

"Well, you won't marry me, so I guess I can't be decent in the eyes of God and the neighborhood gossips," she said promptly.

"I'm serious, Annie."

"So am I," she assured him. "I want to move in with you."

"People will talk," he reminded her.

"Let them," she responded. "I don't care."

"Or so you think—now."

"Jack, we've been lovers for months now. I've shared your bed more nights than I've slept in my own," she reminded him. "I might as well be living here with you."

"What goes on between us in the privacy of my bedroom is nobody's business but ours," he said quietly. "But if you were living here, everyone would know it. You'd be the target of every gossip in the neighborhood."

"As I've already said, I don't care."

"I do."

She sat up and looked at him, clearly not understanding. "You can't mean that," she said.

"Damn right I mean that," he said gruffly. "I care if people are talking about you. I care what they're saying about you. You're no tramp, but that's what everyone will think if they find out about us."

"Let them talk," Anne said, unconcerned.

At three in the morning Jack was still awake. He lay in bed, watching Annie sleep, and he was filled with deep sadness. He was sad because he loved her, because now things were so good between them—and because he didn't believe for a minute that it would last. Oh, there were times he told himself it didn't matter, but even in his most romantic moments, Jack McCleary was, above all, a realist, and the realist in him knew the odds were against them ever celebrating a silver wedding anniversary. He was deeply in love with her, but she was young and, he suspected, more in love with the idea of being in love than she was with him. In time, she'd get bored with the idea of being tied down with a man who worked too many hours and always came home too tired for much of anything else. She'd want more from life than he could give her. Eventually, she'd leave, just as Emily had.

I won't go through that again, he promised himself.

"Mr. McCleary, I'm Arthur Talbott," the aristocratic, expensively dressed man who'd just entered Jack's office introduced himself. "I presume you know why I'm here."

Jack shook his head, a slightly embarrassed look on his face. "No, I'm afraid you've got me at a disadvantage there, Mr. Talbott," he admitted.

"I want to talk to you about my daughter, of course."
There was unmasked impatience in Talbott's voice.

"Your daughter?" Jack asked. "I'm afraid I still don't—"

"Anne. The young woman you've been—involved—
with."

Jack stiffened. *So someone does know,* he thought. *But Annie's name isn't Talbott. This doesn't make any sense.* "Look,
Mr. Talbott," he said evenly, "I don't know where you get
your information, but you've got it wrong—"

"No, I haven't," Talbott responded coldly. "You've been
seeing my daughter for several months now. She told me
herself."

"I have a young woman working for me, Annie Turner—"

"It doesn't surprise me that she's chosen not to reveal her
identity while working here," Talbott said disdainfully. "It
does, however, surprise me that she's kept it from you."

A faint sense of unease brushed Jack. "Suppose you tell
me exactly what you're talking about," he said carefully.

"It's really quite simple, Mr. McCleary," Talbott told him.
"My daughter, Anne Talbott—the young woman you apparently know as Annie Turner—has been working for you for
some time, and from what she tells me, she thinks she's in
love with you."

"Just how much has Annie—Anne—told you about that?"
Jack asked slowly.

"Not enough, I'm sure," Talbott said. "My daughter is a
rather rebellious young woman, Mr. McCleary. I had to have
her followed to find this place. Since she's an only child, I'm
afraid my wife and I have always spoiled her terribly, but for
Anne, nothing we did was ever enough. As she grew older,
she railed against the family wealth. She denounced all that
the Talbotts have ever stood for.

"I suspect this is just a phase she's going through. My
wife and I have tried to be patient. Even Charles has been
tolerant, but—"

"Charles?" Jack asked. The name did sound familiar,
but—

"Charles is Anne's fiancé," Talbott explained. "They've
known each other since childhood."

Her fiancé!

"We're all certain that once she gets all of this nonsense out of her system, everything will be fine," Talbott continued, "but we *are* quite concerned about her infatuation with you . . . "

It's all got to be a lie, Jack was thinking. *A lie. . . .*

"I'm going to have a baby."

Anne had to say the words aloud to believe them, and even then she wasn't one hundred percent certain. Even hearing them from the doctor who'd given her the news only an hour earlier had seemed more like a dream than reality.

I'm pregnant, she thought. *I'm really pregnant. I can't wait to tell Jack.*

Now he'd marry her.

Her parents wouldn't attend the wedding, of course. They'd probably disown her. Not that she cared. As long as she and Jack were together, that was all she cared about.

That's all that matters, she told herself.

She searched the contents of her walk-in closet. *No dressing down tonight,* she thought. *No more secrets. Tonight, I tell him everything—all of the things I should have told him a long time ago.*

She tried to tell herself it didn't matter, that she'd make it up to him. But Anne knew that it *did* matter. It would matter to Jack. Honesty had always been extremely important to him. She'd known, right from the beginning, that the longer she waited to tell him the truth about herself, the harder it would be to make him understand why she'd done it. But now . . . the baby was going to make everything all right.

At least she hoped it would.

On impulse, she made a reservation for two at one of her mother's favorite restaurants. After all, this was going to be a celebration. *I can only hope Jack feels that way,* she thought.

She stared at the phone for a long moment, finally picking it up and dialing Jack's number at the center. He answered on the second ring. "McCleary."

"Hi, darling. It's Annie."

There was an unexpected silence on the other end. "Yes, Annie," he said finally.

He doesn't sound like himself. "Is something wrong?" she asked.

"I'm just busy, that's all," he insisted.

"Well, I hope you're not too busy to have dinner with me tonight," she said. "I have a surprise for you."

"You're full of surprises, aren't you?" His tone was strangely flat.

"I hope this is one you'll like," she told him. "Seven-thirty?"

"That'll be fine."

"I'll pick you up at your place."

"Pick me up?"

"Don't ask." She laughed. "I'll see you tonight."

"Yeah." The receiver clicked in her ear.

She hung up slowly. *He sounded so strange,* she thought, concerned. She told herself not to worry. *After tonight, everything's going to be all right.*

She suddenly realized she had to get moving. She had to get Jack a tux.

All these months . . . it's all been a game for her, Jack thought as he left the center and locked up that night. *She's just a poor little rich girl out for some laughs. Trying to see how the other half lives.*

Trying to defy her parents, no matter what she had to do, no matter how extreme she had to be.

It seemed so impossible. The beautiful young woman he'd known as Annie Turner had been so warm and caring, so concerned about the people at the center. So concerned about him. She was in love with him, for God's sake!

Or had that been a lie too?

My daughter is a rather rebellious young woman, her father had said. *She's an only child. . . . My wife and I have always spoiled her. . . . Even Charles has been tolerant. . . . Charles is Anne's fiancé. . . . Once she gets all of this nonsense out of her system, everything will be fine. . . . This is just a phase she's going through . . . .*

Just a phase she's going through!

He didn't know what to think. *What am I supposed to think?* he asked himself. Her father had painted an image of Anne Talbott as a spoiled rich girl who went out of her way to denounce the affluence that was her birthright. A spoiled, willful child-woman whose fiancé was patiently waiting in the wings while she indulged her latest whim.

Not a pretty picture at all.

Is that all I am to her? Jack asked himself as he walked the darkened streets, headed for home. *A whim? A way to rile her upper-crust parents? What better way to get to them than letting them think she was seriously involved with a middle-aged ex-prizefighter from the wrong part of town?*

He'd been so deeply in love with her, but he'd never been completely convinced of *her* love. Now he knew why.

He'd been so preoccupied with his thoughts—with his pain—that he hadn't noticed the black limo parked across the street in front of his building. He hadn't seen Anne, looking like a princess who'd just stepped out of a fairy tale, standing on the curb, waiting for him. And he hadn't seen the headlights of the truck speeding toward him as he stepped out into the street.

Until it was too late.

16

It's all just a bad dream. It has to be.

But when Anne opened her eyes, she knew that it wasn't. She was in the hospital, and she was in a great deal of pain. The pain made her remember what she desperately wanted to forget.

Jack, her mind cried out in agony. *Why, Jack?*

The images that came rushing through her thoughts were all too vivid. She tried—unsuccessfully—to block them out. She could see herself, as if she were observing the scene from somewhere outside her own body, standing on the curb, waving to him. Calling his name. But he did not seem to see her or hear her. *Why? Why can't he hear me?*

He started to cross the street . . . and then she saw the truck. The driver was speeding. Why wasn't he slowing down? Everything was happening so fast, yet seemed to move so slowly, as if in slow motion. Jack was crossing the street . . . the truck was coming . . . she could hear a loud scream, but didn't realize at first that it was coming from her own mouth. In the next instant, the truck had come to a screeching halt, Jack was lying facedown on the pavement, and she was running toward him, screaming.

She remembered kneeling on the ground, cradling his head in her lap, trying to see his face through her own tears as she begged him not to die.

"*Please don't die, Jack. Please don't leave me!*"

"*I . . . I think it's out . . . of my hands now.*"

"*I love you, Jack.*"

"*I've always loved you, Anne . . . from the first, I think. . . .*"

He closed his eyes. She remembered the panic that had set in.

"*Jack! Jack! Don't die, Jack—oh, God, Jack—don't die!*"

"*I'm sorry, miss . . .*"

Where had that other voice come from? There had been a man standing over her, but the voice sounded so far away, as if it were coming from some distant tunnel.

"*I'm   sorry,   miss . . . I'm   sorry . . . I'm   sorry . . . sorry . . . sorry . . . sorry . . . sorry . . .*"

"*No!*" she screamed. "*No!!!*"

Almost immediately, there was a nurse bending over her, attempting to restrain her. Then she felt the prick of a needle in her arm and a fog descended over her within what seemed like seconds. But the pain didn't go away.

He's dead. Jack's dead.

"You've lost the baby. I'm sorry."

Sorry. I've lost everything that mattered to me and you're sorry. "How?" she managed to ask. Her mouth felt as if it were full of cotton.

"Sometimes these things happen without any apparent

rhyme or reason,'' the doctor told her.

There was a reason, all right. It was my fault.

"Physically, you're fine," the doctor went on. "No problems. You're young, healthy. No reason why you can't have children in the future."

No reason but one. I can't have a child by myself, and Jack's dead.

"I would suggest that you abstain from sexual relations for the next six weeks," the doctor was saying.

Six weeks, six months, six years . . . what difference does it make?

"I think you should be able to go home in a few days."

Go home, she thought. *To what?*

"I would have thought you'd be happy to be going home," her father said, genuinely surprised by her lack of enthusiasm. "Being confined to this room has to be terribly depressing."

"No more so than anywhere else," Anne said absently, leafing through a magazine for the third time without ever having read even a single line.

He looked at her. "I realize you're not feeling well—"

"Not feeling well," she repeated bitterly. "I just lost a baby. The man I loved, the man I wanted to marry, is dead. I saw him killed by a truck driver who'd had too much to drink. And all you can say is that I'm not feeling well."

"You aren't married," he pointed out coldly. "Perhaps this is all for the best. No one even knew you were pregnant."

Her head jerked up. "*I* knew."

"You know what I mean."

"Yes, I do know what you mean," she said quietly. "You're concerned about what people will think."

"You may not think it matters, but it does," he told her.

"To whom?"

"Anne," he said with a deep sigh, "I know this hasn't been easy for you. I know you were infatuated with that man—"

"I was in love with him," she snapped. "I wanted to marry him."

"Yes, I know." He paused for a long moment. "I went to see him that day."

Now he had her attention. "What for?"

"I didn't know you were pregnant, but I did know you fancied yourself in love with him," her father said. "I suspected you had been intimate with him, and I wanted to put a stop to it."

"What did you say to him?" she asked cautiously.

"I told him the truth," Talbott answered. "I told him we'd always spoiled you, that you were a willful, defiant girl who had most likely chosen to involve yourself with him out of rebellion."

"I've always loved you, Anne . . . from the first, I think . . . "

She remembered the look on his face just before he died, the way he'd walked out into the street without even looking up. He hadn't seen her, hadn't heard her call out to him. He hadn't seen the truck.

He thought I didn't love him. My God, he died thinking I didn't love him! She looked up at her father. "Get out," was all she said.

It's my fault.

They had given her something to make her sleep, but it hadn't been strong enough. It hadn't been stronger than the pain of her guilt.

Jack knew about me. He knew the truth, she thought. *Oh, God . . . he died thinking I deceived him . . . that I was just some spoiled rich girl using him to defy her parents.*

He died thinking I didn't really love him!

Her tears came freely now, and once she started to cry she wasn't sure she'd be able to stop. She didn't care if she did or not. *It doesn't matter. Nothing matters anymore.*

Her father had been right about one thing: She *was* spoiled. She had gotten involved with the center more as an act of defiance than out of some deep, altruistic motivation. *In the beginning,* she thought. *Only in the beginning. I did care about those people. I did care about what the center was doing for them. And I did love Jack.*

I loved him more than I thought I could love anyone.

I should never have lied to him. I should have told him the truth about me, right from the start. We probably never would have gotten together, but he'd still be alive. In her mind, she saw him crossing that street, obviously distracted by something. *His conversation with Daddy,* Anne concluded.

My lie killed him—and our baby.

Nothing will ever be the same again.

Physically, Anne made a rapid recovery. She was back on her feet within days and seemed to have made a full recovery within a few weeks. But emotionally . . . that was another story.

Emotionally, she wasn't sure she would ever be the same again. She didn't think she'd ever be able to care about anyone again, certainly not in the way she cared about Jack. *Never again,* she told herself. *I can't. I won't allow it.*

I can't.

Eventually, she did go back to work at the center. She told herself she was doing it for Jack, because it was what he would have wanted, but the truth was, she did it to ease her own deep feelings of guilt. Being there made her feel she was somehow making amends for her deception.

My penance, she thought.

Besides, it made her feel closer to Jack. There were memories of him everywhere. Sometimes, she would go into his old office and close the door, and the memories would be so vivid it was as if his spirit had materialized there. *I can almost reach out and touch you,* she thought with a deep, unbearable sadness. *It's as if you're still here with me.*

But then, you'll always be a part of me.

SPENCE
and
ANNE
1948–1955

17

"A New Year's Eve party?" Spence stared at Dan West incredulously. "That's what you're making such a fuss about? A goddamned New Year's Eve party?"

"It's a big deal, Spence," West maintained. "A lot of important people are going to be there."

"No shit." Spence reached for a cigarette. "In other words, I should be there because all of the so-called right people are going to be there."

"It can't hurt."

"Since when are we so damn worried about appearances?" Spence wanted to know.

"Since we need some of these people on our side," West said simply.

"I don't need anybody," Spence responded with finality.

"Did you take care of the charitable donations I'm supposed to have pledged?" Spence asked Dan West.

"I always do."

"And the check to the guys over at St. Patrick's?"

"Done." There was a pause. "If you don't mind my asking, why are you giving so much money to the church?"

"I do mind. It's none of your business," Spence said sharply. "What about the check to Mary O'Hara?"

West gave him a weary smile. "You ask me every month, and I always tell you the same thing," he said. "The check was mailed to Chicago right on schedule, just as it is every month."

"And there's no way it can be traced back to me?"

"Absolutely not. It's always a bank money order and always mailed in a plain envelope from a mailbox that isn't near the office. I think the people at the bank find it a little odd.'' He paused. ''What is this all about, Spence?''

''Just repaying a debt, pal.''

Spence contemplated the upcoming holidays wearily. A party—no, a social event—at the Waldorf-Astoria wasn't exactly his first choice as a place to spend New Year's Eve. He could think of at least a dozen places he'd rather be, but Danny boy had put up one hell of a convincing argument for this deal at the Waldorf, so he'd make the supreme sacrifice and play the wealthy philanthropist for one night. *It'll be a real pain in the ass,* he thought, *but what the hell? It's only one night.*

Not as if I'm going to make a habit of it.

He not only didn't know her name, he didn't know anything else about her. Except that she was great in bed.

Spence thought about it as he walked up Fifth Avenue, his white silk scarf drawn up over the lower half of his face to block out the bitterly cold winter wind. He stuffed his gloved hands into the pockets of his overcoat as he walked, his head bowed. The woman he'd just spent the night with had been good in bed, no doubt about that. Almost too good.

Everything she did—every move she made, everywhere she touched him, every technique—had been carefully orchestrated. He'd seen through that right away. *She operated like a pro,* he thought.

The sun was just beginning to rise on the eastern horizon when Spence entered St. Patrick's Cathedral and made his way back to the altar of St. Andrew. Automatically, he reached into his pocket, took out his gold money clip, and pulled a fifty-dollar bill from it. He put it in the box and lit all of the candles.

''You know what it's for, Andy, old pal,'' he said. Then he turned on his heel and walked away.

''Call for you on line one, Mr. Randall,'' his secretary announced. ''A Mr. George. Adam George.''

''He's got two first names? Sounds suspicious to me,''

Spence wisecracked. "He say what it's about?"

"He says it's personal."

Another of Spencer's old buddies from Boston? he wondered. *For a guy who claimed to be a loner, he's sure got a lot of "close personal friends" turning up. Could it be they smell money?*

"Put him on hold," Spence instructed. "Tell him I'll be with him in a minute."

"Yes, sir."

He pulled a handkerchief from his pocket and wiped the sweat from his palms, then took a few deep breaths before picking up the phone.

Am I ever really going to get used to this? he asked himself.

Everyone who knew Anne Talbott agreed that she had undergone a dramatic personality change since her hospitalization, though, to this day, no one knew exactly what she'd been hospitalized for. Oh, there had been rumors—everything from various forms of surgery to a nervous breakdown—but nothing had ever been confirmed.

Now, in the elegant ballroom of the Waldorf-Astoria, Anne Talbott was every inch the "ice princess" she'd been dubbed, cool and aloof in her simple, strapless black gown as she mingled, but only on the most superficial level, with some of her so-called friends. *None of them are really my friends,* she thought coldly. *They're my social circle. There's a difference.*

"Hey, beautiful—do you believe in love at first sight?"

She looked at the man addressing her. He was tall, blond, and quite handsome. "I don't believe in love at all," she said simply.

And she walked away.

Anne had finally stopped wondering what might have been, where she would be now. She'd stopped living in the past, stopped using her memories of her time with Jack as a replacement for reality.

She'd also stopped feeling.

She focused all of her energy and concentration on her studies. Fortunately for her, her father still didn't take her seriously. He thought she'd attend law school for a while, then she'd eventually get bored and give it up. *If he thought I was serious, he'd disown me.*

She attended social gatherings like the one at the Waldorf-Astoria only rarely, and she never dated. She'd stopped seeing Charles when she became involved with Jack, and she never resumed that relationship, such as it was. Nor did she see anyone else, even casually. After a while, men stopped asking her out. After a while, her parents stopped asking why no one did. All she ever told them was that she hadn't met anyone who interested her.

She hadn't yet met Spencer Randall.

There are more diamonds here than in the display cases at Tiffany's, Spence thought as he entered the crowded ballroom at the Waldorf-Astoria. *A jewel thief would have a field day.*

He had come alone because there was no one he'd cared to bring. No regular woman in his life. But then, there never had been. He knew there had been talk, a lot of speculation about his private life, but he didn't give a damn about that. *Let them talk,* he thought. The women who had passed through his life had done so for one purpose and one purpose only, and he'd never seen any reason to go through any of the meaningless rituals of courtship.

"You're alone?"

He turned. Dan West had just come in behind him with a beautiful dark-haired woman on his arm. Without a moment's hesitation, he responded, "What did you expect? Do you think I should hire an escort or something?"

West gave him a disbelieving look. "Are you trying to tell me you don't know any available women?"

"I didn't say that." Spence's eyes scanned the room, looking for no one in particular.

"Well, then?"

"There was no one I cared to ask. End of discussion."

West, knowing how far he could push his employer, backed off. He and his companion disappeared into the crowd, leaving Spence to fend for himself.

Let's get this over with, he thought as he ventured forth himself. *Maybe I can get out of here and go somewhere where I can really have a good time. Before midnight.*

He'd been to these affairs before, two or three times in the past, and it was always the same. Boring. Boring as hell. He knew only too well what to expect: a lot of meaningless small talk and a lot of drinking that made the small talk bearable. Stuffy executives, dreary intellectuals, and patrons of the arts pretending to have a good time. Vapid-looking debutantes hunting for husbands. A few good-time Charlies.

Dan West thought he had a distorted view of such social events. *I call 'em like I see 'em,* he thought.

And then he saw her.

She was on the other side of the room, talking to two other young women. She would have stood out in any crowd, anywhere in the world. She was tall, but it wasn't just her bearing that set her apart from the other women in the room. She had long blond hair, so pale it appeared to be silver, which she wore hanging loosely around her shoulders, hardly in style, but she didn't appear to care much about that sort of thing, judging by the simple black gown she wore.

Impulsively, Spence made his way through the crowd, interrupting her conversation with the other two women without so much as an apology. "I have to talk to you," he said in a low voice, taking her by the arm and physically extracting her from the group of women.

She looked at him. "Do I *know* you?" she asked, bewildered.

"No, but I think you should," he told her. "That is, I think we should know each other."

She started to laugh. "Well, I have to admit that's the most original line I've ever heard."

"It's not a line, sweetheart. I mean it. Every word of it," he said, his tone and the expression on his face indicating his seriousness.

She studied him for a moment. "We haven't even been properly introduced," she pointed out.

"Easily remedied," he told her. "My name is Spencer Randall. And you are—"

"Anne Talbott," she said, smiling. "So you're the notorious Spencer Randall."

He cocked an eyebrow. "Notorious? Is that what they're calling me now?"

She laughed again. "You weren't aware of it?"

"I tend to ignore gossip."

"Is it only gossip?" Anne asked dubiously.

He grinned. "What do you think?"

"I don't know you well enough to have an opinion."

"Easily remedied," he said again.

"They're probably wondering where we went," Anne giggled.

Spence shook his head. "Nah. I'd bet nobody even knows we're gone."

"You'd lose," she insisted. "My father probably knew the minute we left. And he's probably wondering."

"Let him," Spence said simply.

She still wasn't sure why she'd let him talk her into leaving the Waldorf-Astoria with him. She wasn't sure why she was sitting here in this small Italian restaurant near Gramercy Park with him, feeling a bit uncomfortable in her formal attire.

I must be losing my mind, she concluded.

"Do you believe in love at first sight?" she asked aloud.

"I don't believe in love at all."

His words stunned her, not because of what he was telling her, but because she'd spoken the same words herself not two hours earlier. They were kindred spirits. She'd sensed right from the beginning that Spencer Randall was a man who truly lived by his own rules, refusing to conform to whatever might be expected of him. Perhaps that was the attraction he held for her, for a woman whose life had been so sharply defined—and restricted—by the rules and regulations of society.

He's all the things I wish I could be, she thought, entranced.

"But," he was saying now, "I do believe in destiny."

"Oh?" This intrigued her. "You believe our lives are pre-ordained at birth? That no matter what we do, our fates have already been determined for us?" Coming from a man like the notorious Spencer Randall, this came as a big surprise.

"I didn't say that," he responded with an easy grin. "What I meant, actually, is that fate presents us with certain opportunities. What we choose to do or not do with them is what makes all the difference."

"Interesting theory," she acknowledged with a slight nod.

"Like tonight," he went on. "You and I were thrown together at an event that bored the hell out of both of us, so here we are. Now, if we're smart, we'll make the best of this chance meeting."

She smiled, her eyes meeting his. "That certainly sounds like an interesting proposition to me."

He laughed. "One of the many things I like about you, Anne Talbott," he told her. "You're not coy. I hate coy women."

"I learned the hard way that deception accomplishes nothing," she said simply. And to herself, *It can cost you everything.*

They talked about everything. They talked about nothing. Anne hadn't felt this way about anyone since Jack. She was happy just being with him. If she believed in love at first sight, she'd think she was in love with him. *But I don't believe in love at first sight. I don't believe in love at all.*

"We've got an hour till midnight," he said, looking at his watch. "Think we ought to get back to the Waldorf?"

She let out an exaggerated groan. "Do you really want to ring in the New Year in that mob in the ballroom?"

He dropped a twenty-dollar bill on the table and winked. "I wasn't planning on going back to the ballroom."

"It's almost midnight," Anne whispered.

"Good," Spence muttered. "For once I'll be bringing the new year in right."

They were in a room at the Waldorf. The lights were out, and the drapes were drawn so the room was in total darkness. Spence was sitting on the edge of the bed, stripped to his shorts. Anne was standing in front of him, her hands on his shoulders as he reached around to unzip the back of her gown. It slid down easily, falling in a heap around her feet. Then he unhooked her bra and removed it, tossing it aside. He cupped her breasts in both hands and nuzzled them. "For a skinny gal, you're pretty big here," he growled, enjoying the silky feel of her nipples against his lips.

She trembled at his touch. "Spence ... I ... It's been a

long time since . . . '' she said softly.

He stopped what he was doing and looked up at her. "That's hard to believe."

She met his eyes. "But true."

This was a switch. The women he'd known had been around the track more than a few times. "I hope you're not having second thoughts," he said.

She shook her head. "I just wanted you to know. I don't do this sort of thing as a habit."

He nodded. He didn't know what to say. What could he say, after all? And what could he do, other than move slowly, try to make her relax—good God, when had he ever cared about such things before? When had the woman's feelings ever mattered to him before?

But then, when had any woman ever affected him the way she had?

He kissed her nipples, gently at first, in an effort to arouse her, as he pulled her slip down over her slim hips. Underneath, she wore black silk panties and a black garter belt with seamed stockings. The sight of her like that, so scantily clad, increased his excitement. *How long's my self-control going to hold out?* he asked himself.

He pulled her down on the bed beside him and kissed her hungrily as he caressed her breasts. "God, you're beautiful," he whispered, burying his face in her breasts. "Beautiful . . . "

She stroked his hair, offering herself to him, wanting him to kiss her breasts again but not knowing how to go about getting him to do so without just telling him what she wanted. Was that permitted? She had no way of knowing. With Jack she'd never had to. He'd always taken the lead, always known what to do. With Spence, though, it was bound to be different. He was the kind of man who'd want a woman to be more of a participant.

The things Spence was doing to her with his hands and his mouth felt good, and she didn't want him to stop. She let out a low moan. . . .

He tugged at her panties, working them free of the lacy garter belt, down her legs as far as he could before the narrow straps of the garter belt got in the way. The fine hair that covered her pubic mound was as pale as the hair on her head. His fingers expertly caressed her inner thighs as he bent his head to kiss her there. Anne jerked at his touch, but he kissed her again and again until finally she began to relax. Then he started licking her, wriggling his tongue as far as the position of her legs, bound at mid-thigh by her panties, would allow. Finally, impatiently, he ripped the panties from her legs and buried his head in her, exciting her until she started to writhe beneath him, trying to pull away from him.

He wouldn't let her. His hands on her hips, he held her down, still working at her with his tongue. Her hands were on his head now, pushing his face into her as she started to moan. He felt her reach a throbbing orgasm, shuddering violently against his mouth as the clock struck midnight.

He pulled himself up on his elbows and looked down at her in the darkness. "Happy New Year," he said softly.

"I think I've just made a New Year's resolution," she said, reaching out to finger a lock of his hair.

Covering her body with his own, he kissed her lips, then her neck. "Oh, baby," he whispered. "It is going to be a happy new year."

Finally, unable to wait any longer, he entered with one strong, final thrust. She cried out, gripping his shoulders as he moved deeper inside her, reaching his orgasm quickly.

"Happy New Year, baby," he gasped.

"I've never done this sort of thing before," Anne said as she snuggled against him in bed.

He gave her a lazy smile. "That was pretty obvious," he said, lighting a cigarette.

"I've never just left a party like that. I've never taken off impulsively with a man I just met. And I've certainly never—" She gestured with one hand.

"This is a first for me, too," he said after a long pause.

She looked at him. "Surely you don't mean—"

He chuckled softly. "No, not in that way," he assured her. "No . . . what I do mean is that I've never really made love to a woman before. I've had sex, sure—but I've never made love. I've never cared about the woman. Her pleasure's never mattered to me."

She raised her head to look at him. "Are you saying—"

"I'm saying I think we might have a future together."

"I'm never going to get married," she said promptly.

He laughed, rumpling her hair. "Well, baby, I'm not proposing. At least not yet," he told her. "But I'm sure as hell not about to settle for a one-night stand, either."

Spence had never believed in love at first sight—he'd never believed in love at all—but after tonight, he was beginning to wonder.

18

New York City, February 1949.

Spence was amazed.

The intensity of his feelings for Anne Talbott had taken him completely by surprise. He'd never felt this way about any woman before. He'd never believed he was capable of feeling this way at all. Anne had tapped into a wellspring of emotion buried deep within him, one he never knew existed until he met her.

It's like finding a piece of a puzzle that's been missing for years, he thought. *The piece that holds the whole damn thing together.*

And he was going to marry her.

How ironic, he thought now, that someone like him—a man who'd always been a loner, never needing anyone, never caring about anyone—had fallen so hard. How ironic and how unexpected.

The ghosts would have a good laugh over this one.

Anne couldn't believe it.

She couldn't believe how quickly, how deeply she'd fallen for Spencer Randall. She couldn't explain it, not even to herself. *Call it chemistry,* she thought, not really caring to analyze it, not caring *why* she felt the way she did. *I'm just happy to be feeling again.*

She told herself that this time it was going to be different. *No lies, no deceptions,* she vowed. *Lies don't protect a relationship.*

They destroy it.

This time, when he went to St. Patrick's, it was the middle of the day. There were people around. Some of them, sitting in the pews, looked up as he passed them. He tried to smile. Others milled around at the entrance, cameras in hand, engaged in hushed conversation. *Tourists,* he thought with disdain. It seemed sacrilegious somehow that a church, no matter how beautiful, should become a tourist attraction.

Shouldn't be allowed, he thought angrily.

He followed the aisle along the south side of the church to the altar of St. Andrew. "Hello again, Andy, old pal," he said in a low voice as he looked up at the marble statue. "Doesn't look like you're doing much business today. Maybe all the sinners are staying home for a change. That's good— good for your boss, anyway. Right? It's good for me, too. It means I've got your undivided attention."

He paused. "You've listened to all my sins, old pal, and I'm grateful for that. But now I'm doing something right, and I need your help. I'm going to marry a wonderful woman and settle down. I know it sounds like a miracle, but then you guys are used to that sort of thing, right? Anyway, I want to make this work. No more whores. No more one-night stands. I love this woman. She'll be enough for me. More than enough."

He reached into his pocket for his gold money clip. "You're a good listener, Andy, old pal. The best. I want you to know how much I appreciate it." He took a hundred-dollar bill from the money clip, stuffed it into the box, and lit all of the candles. "I came in here with a lot to say, but I guess the words just aren't there." He paused. "No matter. You know everything I think and do anyway, don't you? See you around, pal." With a mock salute, he turned and walked away.

He never saw the priest who'd been watching him.

                    *   *   *

The following week, the church received an anonymous do-
nation through a Manhattan bank. Church officials tried to
locate the donor to express appreciation but were informed
by the bank that he wished to remain anonymous. They were
justifiably perplexed.

He had given them half a million dollars.

"It's been good seeing you again, Adam," Spence said, smiling as he got to his feet. He reached out to shake the hand
of the man across the desk.

"Stay in touch—and stop by next time you're in town."

"I'll do that," the other man promised. "And you do the
same when you're in Boston."

Like I'd ever be stupid enough to show my face in Boston,
he thought. Aloud he said, "Next trip. You've got my word
on it."

After the other man was gone, Spence sank back into his
chair and breathed deeply. His hands were trembling. *If many
more of Spencer's old friends drop in,* he thought, *I'll end up
with either a straitjacket or an Academy Award.*

"Let's get married," Spence suggested casually.

He and Anne were walking together in Central Park, both
of them bundled up in their warmest winter attire. From the
path on which they were walking, they could see a group of
children skating on the frozen pond.

"I don't want to get married," she told him.

He looked at her. "Don't be silly. What kind of woman
doesn't want to get married?"

"This kind of woman," she answered.

"Don't you love me?"

She laughed. "I barely know you!"

"Doesn't answer my question," he said promptly.

"All right. So maybe I'm crazy. Maybe I do love you,"
she admitted reluctantly. "It doesn't change things at all."

Spence grinned. "I'd say it changes a hell of a lot."

She shook her head. "I love you, but I don't want to love
you."

"Now, *that* makes a lot of sense."

"You're too much like my father," she said.

He stopped in his tracks. "Why do I have the feeling I've just been insulted?"

"My father is a very ambitious man." She stopped and turned to face him. "He's also old-fashioned, stubborn, opinionated—"

"That's what you think of me?" he asked, feigning wounded pride.

"Come on, Spence, you know it's true," she maintained. "You're all of those things. You'll want a wife who's willing to make you her career—"

"I want you—for better or worse, if you'll pardon the expression," he said stubbornly.

"You'll want children. I'm right, aren't I?"

"One or two of the little creatures might be nice, sure."

"I don't want any kids."

He couldn't hide his surprise. "What normal woman doesn't want kids?"

Her eyes met his, her stare challenging. "I never said I was a 'normal' woman, Spence," she said.

"It's a damn good thing you didn't!"

"I want to be a lawyer," she told him. "I have to go to law school, and that takes a lot of time. A husband would only slow me down now."

"Don't you ever want children?" he asked.

"I don't know," Anne answered honestly.

He studied her for a moment. "Well," he started carefully, "you can fight it all you want, babe. You can keep right on saying you don't want to get married, but I'm giving you fair warning now: I'm not giving up."

"Spence—"

He took her in his arms and silenced her with a kiss. "I *am* going to marry you, Anne," he told her. "Sooner or later."

19

New York City, April 1949.

"You've been arguing with your old man again," Spence guessed.

Anne grimaced. "How can you tell?"

"I'm clairvoyant," Spence said with a grin, pointing to his temple. "Feel like talking about it?"

"Not really."

"Try," he urged. "It'll do you good."

They were alone in the study of his Park Avenue apartment, having a brandy as they watched the falling rain through the windows. It was definitely a man's room, dark and rustic, yet Anne had always seemed at home there. She'd been right when she said she wasn't a "normal" woman. *Or maybe "typical" or "average" would be better words,* he thought, studying her now. She looked deceptively fragile in her black wool skirt and cream-colored silk blouse. *Tough as nails, that one,* he reminded himself with a twinge of amusement.

"Come on, talk to me," he said aloud.

She drew in a deep breath and let it out again. "He's so unreasonable," she said finally. "He thinks he can run my life."

Spence poured himself another brandy. "I can't imagine anyone even trying," he said with a low chuckle.

"He's threatened to disinherit me."

He stopped what he was doing. "What?"

"He says he'll cut me off without a dime."

"Do you think he's serious?"

"I know he is," she said darkly. "He's already refused to pay my tuition for law school. Now I'll have to get a job and work my way through."

"I'll take care of it," he told her.

"Oh, no, you won't," she said quickly. "All my life, my father's taken care of me. He paid the bills, so he called the shots, and now that I'm daring to defy him, he's cutting me off without a dime."

"But—"

"No, Spence," she said emphatically. "I'm not about to go from being taken care of by one man to being taken care of by another!"

"Then what are you going to do?" He loved her, but she could really test his patience sometimes.

"I'm not sure yet," she admitted. "I've got to move out of the house, I know that much. I'm not going to stay there after what he's done to me. I'm thinking about moving into the Barbizon Hotel—"

"What the hell for?" he retorted. "You can move in here."

She shook her head. "I told you, Spence, I'm not going to be obligated. Not to my father and not to you."

"So who's talking about being obligated?" he asked. "We're already sleeping together. This will just make things easier."

"Just because I'm sleeping with you doesn't mean I'm going to let you support me!" she shot back at him.

"Far be it for me to try to take unfair advantage of you!" he responded sarcastically. "I only want to help—unless there's a law against it!"

Of all the women I could have fallen in love with, he thought, *it had to be this one.*

The next morning, a special messenger delivered a large brown envelope to Anne at her parents' home. Inside was a check for twenty-five thousand dollars and a note:

> *Consider this a loan, babe, if it makes you*
> *happy. You can pay me back when you set up*
> *that law practice. The other offer still*
> *stands, no strings attached. I love you.*
>
> *S.*

No strings attached, she thought. *Who is he trying to kid?*

Where Spencer Randall was concerned there were always strings attached. *Where any man is concerned there are strings attached.*

Even Jack.

Why, she wondered, was she thinking of Jack now? Why, when Spence was being most stubborn and obstinate, did she think of Jack? Why did Spence's attempts to control her make her think of Jack's futile attempts to keep her at arm's length?

Men, she thought, frustrated.

"You just won't take no for an answer, will you?" Anne asked as she entered the study and closed the door.

Spence was sitting on the couch, reading a book. He put it aside and looked up, smiling. "Am I supposed to know what you're talking about?" he asked.

"You know damn well what I'm talking about!"

He shook his head. "Like I said—it's a loan."

"Then I want to pay interest, like anybody else," she said promptly.

"No way," he told her. "In the first place, you're not like anybody else."

"Then here's your check back," she said, taking it from her handbag.

He stared at her for a moment. "You're serious, aren't you?"

Her gaze was level. "Very."

He frowned, shaking his head. "Okay," he said finally. "You win."

"Five percent," she said.

"What?"

"The interest," she offered in explanation. "I'll pay you five percent."

He shook his head. "Two."

"Three, or it's no deal."

He hesitated momentarily, then nodded. "All right. Three."

"In that case, I accept your very generous offer," she said, locking the door.

"What are you doing?" he asked, puzzled.

"Well, I really do want to thank you for the loan," she said with a sly smile, "and I don't want to be interrupted."

He smiled, knowing immediately what she had in mind. "Oh, yeah?"

"It's only proper, as my mother would say." She unbuttoned her blouse as she started toward him. Pulling it free from the waistband of her skirt, she let it slip off her shoulders and fall to the floor, then she unhooked her bra and pulled it off. She unzipped her skirt and let it slide down over her hips and legs to the carpet, then stepped out of her shoes and peeled off her slip. By the time she reached him, she wore only a lacy white garter belt and stockings.

He looked at her and grinned. "Didn't you forget something? I'll bet the wind whistling up your skirt was cold."

"I was in a taxi—and I kept my legs together."

He nodded. "Good idea."

"I thought I'd make things easier for you," she said with a knowing smile. "Do you mind?"

"What do you think?" Placing his hands on her waist, he pulled her closer. "God, baby . . . " he gasped as he nuzzled her breasts. He fastened his mouth on her right nipple. With one hand he unzipped his pants, freeing himself. He was already rock hard.

He pulled her down onto his lap so that she was straddling him, her legs spread wide. His hands gripping her buttocks, he guided her into a position at which he could enter her. Finally, he turned his attention to her other breast. Shivering with pleasure, she gripped his shoulders and arched her back.

Spence's last rational thought was, *If everyone handled loans this way, the default rate would be a hell of a lot lower.*

The following week, Anne moved into the Barbizon Hotel, despite protests from Spence, her mother—and even her father.

"My mind's made up," she told her father. "I am going to law school—whether you like it or not."

"Maybe I was a bit hasty," her father conceded, surprised by her decision more than he was willing to let on. "We should talk it over—"

Her eyes met his. "It's a little late for that, don't you think?"

"Your father means well, darling. He just doesn't understand that your needs are, well—different from other women's."

Anne and her mother were having lunch at the Russian Tea Room. So intense was their conversation that they were both oblivious of the shining samovars and chandeliers festooned with tinsel and Christmas balls that were part of the restaurant's striking decor.

"Mother, you're wasting your time," Anne said wearily. "What's done is done."

"Come home, Anne." Her mother's tone was almost pleading.

"It's too late," Anne maintained with a shake of her head. "He threatened to disinherit me—or have you forgotten?"

"I've forgotten nothing," her mother answered her. "But it might be nice if you—and your father—could forget for once."

Anne shook her head. "Some things can't be forgotten, no matter how hard one might try." She knew her life would be a lot easier if she were more like her mother. Caroline Merrick Talbott was a real blue-blooded socialite, from the top of her always perfectly coifed head to the tips of her pedicured toes. Even now, in her wide-brimmed royal blue hat and matching Dior suit, with a single strand of creamy white pearls around her neck, she looked every inch the society matron. The one thing Anne knew *she* would never be.

"He's your father, Anne," Caroline said, taking a bite of her salad. She never ate "substantial" meals, at least not that Anne could remember.

"He seems to remember that only when it's convenient."

"Then you won't talk to him?"

"Of course I'll talk to him," Anne told her. "I just won't come home."

"Let's get married, doll."

"Oh, Spence, we've been through all of this at least a dozen times," Anne sighed, snuggling against him in bed. "You know I don't want to get married."

He kissed her hair. "And you know I don't give up."

She stroked his chest. "Unfortunately," she said with mild amusement.

"Be realistic, babe," he told her. "We're together now more than most married couples are. We love each other— even you admit to that. It's just plain stupid for you to go on living in that fleabag of a women's residence. You belong here—with me."

"Marriage would ruin everything," she predicted with certainty.

He looked down at her in the darkness. "How do you figure?"

"I know you, Spencer Randall," she said. "You'd never be happy with a wife who had her own career and interests, who wasn't always at your beck and call. You—"

He put a finger to her lips and chuckled softly. "Why don't you let me be the one to determine what will or won't make me happy?" he suggested. "I want you—and whatever having you might involve."

"Spence—"

"You might as well give up," he said, kissing her forehead, "because I'm certainly not going to."

Anne thought about it. In fact, she thought about nothing else for days. She *did* love Spence. She *did* want to marry him. In fact, though she'd known him only a matter of months, she couldn't imagine a future for herself without him.

But could it work? she wondered. *Does it have any chance at all of working?*

She arrived at his office unexpectedly, barging in unannounced. He looked up from the reports he was reviewing and grinned. "Hi, doll," he greeted her. "Nice of you to drop in."

"Ask me again," she ordered him.

He put down his pen and leaned forward slightly. "Come again, sweetheart?"

"Ask me to marry you." She stood in the center of the room, hands on her hips in a combative stance.

"What is it with you?" he wanted to know. "Do you enjoy making me suffer, or what?"

"For God's sake, Randall—my mother's out planning the biggest wedding Manhattan society's ever seen," she told him, "so will you just ask me now?"

He stared at her for a moment, not sure he'd heard correctly. "Do you want me down on both knees, or can I get by with just one?" he asked finally.

"Oh, forget it!" she snapped impatiently, heading for the door.

He shot to his feet. "Not a chance!" he shouted. "Anne Talbott, will you marry me?"

She stopped in her tracks and swung around to face him. She was smiling.

"You bet I will, Spencer Randall!"

20

New York City, May 1949.

I can't believe I'm doing this.

This is insane, Anne thought, balancing herself on a stool in the fitting room at Saks while a seamstress made necessary adjustments on her wedding gown. *This is really insane. I've known him barely five months.*

That, to Anne, was the crazy part. She'd fallen in love with a man she'd known only a matter of months, a man who represented everything she was against. A man who felt he had to take care of her. She was marrying him when she swore she'd never marry. She—

"Ow!" she yelped, her thoughts interrupted by the pin the seamstress had accidentally stuck in her ankle.

"I'm so sorry, Miss Talbott," the woman apologized

quickly. "If you'll just hold still for a few more minutes—"

"Of course," Anne responded impatiently, glancing at her wristwatch. "God, have we really been here over an hour?"

Her mother was appalled. "Anne! Please—remember, you're a lady!" she gasped.

"Oh, Mother, this is such a bore!" Anne lamented. "Is all of this *really* necessary?"

"It is if you want a proper wedding," her mother maintained.

Anne made a face. "That was your idea, not mine."

"It's expected of someone of your station."

"I really don't give a damn what's expected of me!" Anne declared, bounding off the stool in spite of the seamstress's protests. "I don't see why I have to have a big formal wedding to please other people!"

And she stalked off to the dressing room to change her clothes, leaving her mother and the seamstress staring after her.

The fitting left Anne depressed. Before she returned to the Barbizon that afternoon, she tried to phone Spence from one of the pay phones at Walgreen's, a place where many aspiring actresses hung out to call and be called by their agents. As she jostled for a position in the waiting line, she felt the beginnings of a monumental headache. Then, when she finally did get to a phone, she was told by Spence's secretary that he was out of the office for the afternoon.

"Would you like to leave a message, Miss Talbott?" the secretary asked.

Anne thought for a moment. "No," she said finally. "Yes—tell him I'll call later."

When she got back to the Barbizon, she locked herself in her room and lay on the bed, wondering how she could love Spence as much as she did and still feel the way she did right now. *What's wrong with me?* she asked herself.

Finally, it came to her.

She went to the closet and took out a hatbox, from which she retrieved a large envelope filled with photographs. Photographs of herself and Jack. Photographs she hadn't been able to look at for a very long time but still hadn't been able to part with.

She spread them out on the bed and sat there looking at them for a long time. She knew now what was wrong. She loved Spence and did want to marry him, but she had never really said good-bye to Jack. *I am now,* she thought as she gave each photograph one last look before returning it to the envelope. By the time she'd filed the last one away, her headache was almost gone.

Good-bye, Jack, she thought as she sealed the envelope.

Spence also had reservations about the wedding.

Not about marrying Anne, just about the wedding. He disliked the idea of a big, formal affair every bit as much as Anne did. Probably more so. He disliked participating in any social event in which he might be calling attention to himself.

"We ought to just go get the license and blood tests and get married in the judge's chambers," he told her in bed one night, after they'd made love.

She smiled up at him in the darkness. "I feel the same way you do, sweetheart," she said, snuggling against him. "But my mother, well—she feels she has to put on a good show for all of her friends."

He gave a low chuckle, rumpling her hair as he kissed her forehead. "I wonder what your mother and her very proper friends would think if they could see us right now?"

She giggled. "They'd die. They'd all die of shock!"

"What do you think they'd say about this?" He pulled the sheet down to expose her naked breast. With one hand he caressed her, slowly, deliberately, teasing her nipple with his thumb and index finger.

"They really would die," she said with a breathy laugh. "You'd enjoy that, wouldn't you?"

He grinned. "Not as much as I'm enjoying this," he assured her, pulling gently at her nipple.

"You know what I mean." Her tone was mildly scolding. "Hmm?"

"You enjoy shocking people, don't you?"

He continued to concentrate on her breast. "I don't think about other people one way or the other, doll," he said indifferently. "I just do whatever I want—and the hell with anybody who doesn't like it."

We have that in common, he was thinking.

Spencer Randall and Anne Talbott were married ten days later in a civil ceremony in a judge's chambers downtown. They told no one of their plans, and there was no one either of them knew in attendance.

Even the press didn't get wind of it for almost a week.

21

New York City, September 1949.

"Mr. Randall, there's a gentleman from *The Wall Street Journal* here to see you," Spence's secretary announced.

"A reporter?" he asked.

"Yes, sir."

"He got an appointment?"

"No, sir, he hasn't." He always asked. And he always knew the answer before she gave it.

"Tell him he'll have to make one."

She sighed heavily. "Yes, sir. When?"

"The first Tuesday in December."

She looked at him, unable to hide her surprise.

"1969," he added.

"Mr. Randall, your wife is here to see you," his secretary told him.

"My wife?" This came as a surprise. "Send her in."

"Yes, sir."

A moment later, Anne came into the office and closed the door. She wasn't smiling. She didn't kiss him as she normally would have. She just took a seat across the desk from him and stared at him.

"I thought you'd be in class," Spence said lightly, sensing something was wrong.

"I would be—normally," she said quietly. "But it doesn't look like I'll be doing that for a while."

"Oh? Why not?"

"I'm pregnant, Spence."

At this news, he broke into a broad grin. "My God, that's great!" he declared.

"I'm glad it makes you happy," she said without much enthusiasm.

"But you're not," he concluded.

"No—oh, I don't know, Spence." She sighed. "It's just so—unexpected—"

He grinned. "Well, doll, it's not like we haven't been making an effort," he pointed out.

"The timing is terrible!" She spat it out. "I'm going to have to drop out of law school—"

"Not necessarily," he cut her off. "When's the baby due?"

She thought for a moment. "March. The end of March," she said finally.

"So you miss one semester. Is that the end of the world?"

"*One* semester? You have to be kidding!" She stared at him incredulously. "With a new baby—"

"With *our* baby, we can have nurses or nannies or whatever the hell it takes," he reminded her. "Our kid will be in the most capable hands we can buy while you're at class."

She looked at him. "You make it sound so simple."

"It's as simple as we choose to make it."

It wasn't simple at all.

Anne's pregnancy wasn't an easy one. She was sick most of the time and spent the last six weeks of her pregnancy confined to her bed. Sex had been taboo for the last four months, which caused a great deal of frustration and tension between Spence and his restless young wife.

Though Spence loved Anne deeply, he had needs of his own—physical needs—he wasn't accustomed to ignoring. Finally, the temptations of the flesh became too strong to ignore, and he sought sexual satisfaction elsewhere.

He stuck to prostitutes because they made no demands on him beyond the usual monetary payment for services rendered. Hookers weren't going to talk. Hookers wouldn't call his wife and blow the whistle on him. Hookers wouldn't have expectations about a "relationship."

He fell into a routine. He would leave Anne early in the evening, always offering a perfectly plausible excuse for doing so. He would go to Times Square in search of a whore, spend an hour or so in bed with her at a seedy hotel, and leave with no regrets—and no protests from the woman. Then he would go to St. Patrick's Cathedral, have his usual brief chat with St. Andrew, put a fifty—at least—in the box and light all the candles.

Then he would go home. By this time, Anne would almost always be asleep, but lying beside her in their bed, he found himself kept awake by guilt. *I wish that baby would hurry up and get here,* he thought, frustrated. *I don't know how much longer I can keep this up.*

Anne spent three days in the hospital before giving birth to a seven-pound baby girl on March 24, 1950. When the nurse placed the baby in Spence's arms for the first time, there was not even a trace of disappointment at not having gotten the son most men always wanted. For Spence, there was only an overwhelming sense of pride he'd never experienced. He named her Maria.

"You're my kid," he said, staring into the tiny face, "and the world's yours for the taking."

22

"Don't you think you've gone just a little overboard?" Anne asked. "After all, she's not even four years old yet."

"Nonsense." Spence struggled into the study with a stack of brightly wrapped Christmas packages, twelve in all, and placed them under the elaborately decorated tree. "My kid's going to have everything, and she might as well get used to having it now."

"You'll spoil her," Anne worried aloud.

"Damn right I will." He started arranging the packages under the tree.

"It's not good for her, Spence, growing up with everything handed to her, never having to work for anything," Anne told him. She remembered her own childhood and what it had done to her.

He stopped what he was doing and looked up at her. "That sounds a little odd, coming from someone who was born with a silver spoon in her mouth herself."

She nodded in agreement. "I've experienced it. I know what harm it can do," she said. "That's not what I want for my daughter."

"Well, I want *my* kid to have whatever she wants," he said stubbornly. "No matter what it is."

Anne frowned. Her husband's absorption in their small daughter concerned her. He bought her everything, every toy on the market, even things she wasn't old enough to play with. And there was no reasoning with him. This was what he wanted to do, and he did it.

"There are times I wonder if you love Maria more than

you love me," she said casually.

He grinned. "You're not jealous, are you?"

"Should I be?"

"No way." He got to his feet and took her in his arms. "I love you as much as I ever have. More, in fact. But she's my kid—the only one I've got, as far as I know."

"She's *our* child, Spence, and I want her to grow up right. I want her to have values."

But even as she spoke the words, she knew it would do no good. Spence would continue to indulge Maria because he wanted to show her his love.

And this seemed to be the only way he knew how.

Maria adored her father.

Her first word was "da-da," which Spence swore she first uttered at the tender age of six months. When she took her first steps, those steps were to him. As soon as she was fully mobile, she followed him everywhere. When she learned to talk, she carried on long conversations with him about anything and everything.

For her first birthday, he'd staged a circus for her at their country home in Connecticut. Not the average backyard type of event, but a scaled-down version of Barnum & Bailey, complete with clowns and animal acts.

For her second birthday, he brought in a magician—who'd been performing to standing-room-only audiences in London. It didn't matter that Maria wasn't old enough to understand any of it. It made her laugh, and making his daughter happy was all that mattered to Spence.

For her third birthday, he gave her an amusement park carousel, which still stood, fully operational, on their estate in Greenwich.

With Maria's fourth birthday only three months away, Anne's biggest worry was how Spence intended to top that.

It's so damn hard to believe, Spence thought as he watched his daughter sleeping soundly in her bed. *Hard to believe that anyone could mean so much to me—even my own kid.*

But Maria did. She and Anne meant more to him than

anything he owned, anything he'd accomplished. Looking down at his daughter now, he made himself a promise:

Maria's going to have the kind of life a kid named Frankie Granelli couldn't even dream about.

"There's a gentleman here to see you, Mr. Randall," his secretary told him. "He doesn't have an appointment, but—"

"A reporter?" Spence asked, ready to issue the standard brush-off.

"No, sir," she answered. "He says he's an old friend of yours."

A friend of mine? he thought. *I don't have any friends—at least not any "old" friends.* "What's his name?"

"Paul Johnston, sir."

"The name doesn't sound familiar."

"He says the two of you went to school together."

Somebody from the real Randall's past? Not that he recalled. "The name doesn't ring any bells," he said aloud. "He's probably another reporter trying to sneak in. Send him away."

"Sir?" She looked confused.

"You don't understand English?" he snapped irritably. "Get rid of him!"

He'd known right from the beginning he'd have to deal with it.

From time to time, someone from the real Spencer Randall's past was bound to surface, to try to make contact with him. Childhood chums, college classmates, long-lost "relatives" hoping to cash in on his success. *How long before the past really starts to crawl out of the woodwork?* he wondered. *How long before someone puts the pieces all together?*

He stood up and turned to the window, staring absently at the Manhattan skyline without really seeing anything. He always expected it, yet he'd never really been prepared for it.

How long, he asked himself now, *could the ghosts continue to be silenced?*

* * *

"I think maybe it's time we put together a personal bio for the press," Spence told Ralph Martin, head of public relations for Randall International.

Martin tried to hide his surprise. "You're going to release *personal* info?" he asked. Not even his employees knew anything personal about Spencer Randall.

"I think it's necessary," Spence explained. "The reporters are driving me crazy. I figure, throw them a bone and maybe they'll back off."

"For a little while, anyway," Martin agreed with a nod.

I've got to buy some time, Spence thought. "What I want is something fairly basic," he explained. "A little on my childhood and college years, the usual statistics—play up my stint in the Navy."

Martin gave him a quizzical look.

"Makes it all sound patriotic," Spence offered in explanation.

"I see. Yes, I think you're probably right," Martin said thoughtfully. "It will make good copy—and it will certainly create a positive public image."

"It'll also bring back some pretty unpleasant memories," Spence said, gazing out a window.

Martin looked at him with interest. "Oh?"

"Yeah," Spence said, nodding slowly. "I was on the U.S.S. *Indianapolis* in the South Pacific. We were attacked by a Jap sub one night. A good buddy of mine, a kid named Frankie Granelli, was killed." He paused, his expression grim. "Hell, all of my shipmates were killed—or so I was told."

"You were *told*?" Martin looked as if he didn't quite understand.

Spence nodded again. "The ship was sunk. I woke up one morning in some base hospital. I was pretty badly burned—had to have a lot of plastic surgery. I came out of it with a lot of blanks in my memory that are still blank."

"That's quite a story," Martin said.

"It's not a story," Spence told him. "It's true. All of it."

"That's not what I meant," Martin said quickly. "I meant

it's a great PR story. The press will eat it up.''

I hope so, Spence thought. Aloud he said, "How soon can you get this out?"

The other man stood up. "I'll get on it right away."

After Martin was gone, Spence thought about it. For the first time, he was optimistic.

I should've gotten an Oscar for that performance.

23

Greenwich, June 1955.

"There are two gentlemen here to see you, sir," the butler announced as he came into the library of the Randalls' country home.

Spence looked up from his brandy. "Did they give their names?" he asked automatically, his thoughts on something else entirely.

"They're reporters, sir. They said—"

"I don't care what they said," Spence responded sharply, suddenly alert. "Get rid of them."

The following week Spence summoned a security expert to the estate. "I want the best you've got," he instructed. "Electric fences, alarms, the works."

"Exactly what is it you want, sir?" the man asked.

"I just told you." There was impatience in Spence's voice. "I want to make sure nobody—and I mean *nobody*—can get in. Is there a problem with that?"

"Not at all, Mr. Randall."

"Good."

Two weeks after the installation of the new security system was completed, a photographer managed to get past the electric fence and made it all the way to the main house.

"Best dogs you'll find anywhere," the trainer said confidently.

Spence studied the two Dobermans on the other side of the fence thoughtfully. "They don't seem so mean right now," he observed with some concern.

"Don't let their demeanor fool you, Mr. Randall," the trainer said with a chuckle. "Turn these dogs loose on your property, and nobody'll ever get past them—alive, that is."

Spence thought about it for a moment. "You'll guarantee that, of course."

"Of course."

He nodded. "Sold."

"Why are you so concerned about security?" Anne asked one morning. "We're smack in the middle of God's country. As far as I know, there hasn't been a lot of criminal activity in the area."

"It's not crime I'm worried about," he told her.

"Then who are you trying to keep out?"

"The press, of course."

The day after the dogs were delivered to the estate, a reporter sneaked onto the grounds in a delivery truck, having paid off the driver.

He was caught in the kitchen by a member of the staff.

Spence hired round-the-clock security guards.

"At least one of you will be at the front gate at all times," he told them. "Check all visitors. Look at identification and clear everyone with me—or someone at the main house—before letting them past the gate."

"No one will get past my men," the security chief assured him.

Spence looked him in the eye. "They'd damn well better not."

*   *   *

He had the phone number at the estate changed four times within three weeks. "How do they keep getting it?" he demanded of his secretary, his anger barely controlled.

"I have no idea, sir," the poor woman stammered nervously.

Notoriety, he thought, annoyed.

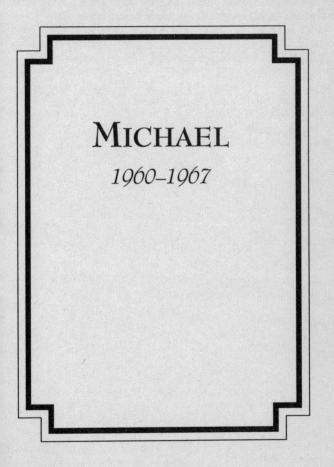

MICHAEL

1960–1967

24

I sweat through four years of college for this?

Michael Callahan ripped the sheet of paper from his typewriter with such force that it tore in half. Frustrated, he pulled the remainder of the sheet from the carriage and wadded all of it into a ball, then pitched it into the trash can beside his desk.

"Careful there, Callahan," one of his colleagues teased as he passed by. "Break that typewriter and Lawson'll make you pay for it, even if he has to deduct it from your paycheck."

"I don't think I make that much," Michael grumbled irritably, putting a clean sheet of paper in the typewriter.

In the four years he'd studied journalism at Northwestern, he'd envisioned his future as one of travel, chasing down stories on hot topics or people all over the globe. *A romantic's view of the business,* he thought as he stared at the blank page and tried, without much luck, to muster a little enthusiasm. In his first six months at the *Kansas City Sun-Times* he hadn't done any real reporting, and his writing skills had been limited to obituaries and wedding announcements.

Michael Callahan hadn't been in the business long enough to have completely lost his idealism. He was a month away from his twenty-second birthday, the youngest reporter on the *Sun-Times* staff. He looked even younger, slim, of average height, with dark hair and blue eyes behind tortoiseshell-framed glasses. The women in the office called him "Clark Kent."

He paid no attention to them. The attention was flattering, of course, but Michael already had a girlfriend. Actually, she was more than that. She was his fiancée. He and Janet Wilcox had met in college, and they became engaged just before his graduation. Much to Michael's relief, Janet had insisted they wait a year, until she graduated, to get married. He was relieved because he couldn't afford to get married yet. He could barely support himself, let alone a wife.

But that's all going to change, he promised himself. *Soon. Very soon now.*

"Hey, Callahan!" The gravelly voice of the managing editor, Grady Lawson, was yelling at him from the other side of the busy newsroom. "Get your ass in here—now!"

The chair squeaked as he pushed it back, away from the desk, and stood up. *Maybe,* he thought optimistically, *it's going to happen sooner than I expected.*

Maybe Lawson's finally going to let me do a real story.

"So what did Lawson want—besides your head?" asked Ben Tallman, one of the paper's news reporters, over drinks that evening at a bar near the newspaper's offices frequented by reporters and other newspaper people.

"He's letting me do soft features." Michael took a long swallow of his drink.

"Lawson's moving you to features already?" Tallman let out a low whistle. "Hey—I'm impressed!"

"Don't be," Michael said sullenly. "It's not as if he's suddenly realized that maybe I have talent or anything like that. He's just short-handed at the moment."

"What do you care?" Tallman asked. "A break's a break."

"Yeah, I guess you're right," Michael said with a nod. "I guess it was just my pride talking."

Tallman laughed aloud at the thought. "There's no room for pride in this business," he said bluntly. "You might as well learn that now."

"I think you're wrong," Michael replied. "I think integrity's important—*especially* in our business."

Tallman raised his glass in a mock toast. "As long as it doesn't get in the way of the story," he said.

Michael nodded. "As long as it doesn't get in the way of the story."

*   *   *

Michael lived in a rooming house in a quiet residential area. One room was all he needed, after all. When he was in it, he read or listened to the radio or wrote to Janet or slept. Nothing else. Never anything else.

Since moving to Kansas City, he'd resigned himself to the idea of carrying on his relationship with Janet by mail. There was no other way—at least not for the time being. If he couldn't afford to marry Janet now, he certainly couldn't afford to bring her to Kansas City, and even if he could, she wouldn't graduate for another five months.

My love life's at the mercy of the U.S. Postal Service, he thought miserably. *That's scary.*

He saw the other boarders at the rooming house only at mealtimes. His only friends in Kansas City were in the newspaper business, and what little socializing he did was with them. Not that he minded; he enjoyed talking shop with them. They'd been in the business longer than he had, and they all had stories to tell.

Besides, it took his mind off Janet and what he was missing by having to postpone their wedding plans, however temporarily.

Michael stared at the completed page still in the typewriter. Taking a deep breath, he removed it from the carriage. It was as good as he knew how to make it. Satisfied, he put it aside and put a fresh sheet in the typewriter. It was as if the dam had burst. His fingers flew across the keyboard, filling the page with words so quickly it made him wonder if he'd really written them. *If only they were all this easy,* he thought.

He filed the story and went to lunch early, confident it was the best work he'd ever done.

When his twenty-five-inch story ran the next day, it had been cut to eighteen.

"What do you think you're doing here, Callahan, writing books?" The managing editor, Grady Lawson, sat behind an enormous desk that almost filled the small office. "Three stories in the past three weeks, and every one of them had to be cut."

"I wrote them the way they had to be written," Michael defended himself.

"You've got a lot to learn, Callahan." Lawson lit a cigar.

"In journalism class—"

Lawson cut him off. "This isn't college anymore, Callahan, this is the real world," he said. "You can forget most of that classroom shit. It doesn't wash here."

"But—"

"You've got the makings of a damn good reporter," Lawson told him, "but as I said, you've got a lot to learn."

Michael thought about it as he walked back to his desk. *You've got the makings of a damn good reporter ... but you've got a lot to learn.* He sat down at the typewriter and finished the page he'd been working on when Lawson called him into the office.

At five that afternoon, he turned in another twenty-five-inch story.

It was late, almost midnight, when Michael sat down at the small rolltop desk in one corner of his room and took out a legal pad and ballpoint pen. In spite of the lateness of the hour and the fact that he had to be at work early the next morning, he needed to write to Janet, needed to share his thoughts with her. He looked at the small framed photograph of his fiancée on top of the desk. She was an attractive young woman, petite, with short blond hair, blue eyes, and a winning smile.

The girl next door, Michael thought affectionately. And he started to write:

January 10, 1960

Dear Janet,

God, I miss you!

I've been busy—you wouldn't believe how busy—but not so much so that I haven't thought about you or missed you, honey.

I'm finally getting a chance to be a real reporter. Not obits and wedding announcements, but real stories. Human interest–type stories. The one I'm working on right now is, well—I can't really explain what I'm doing, but I'm excited about it. It's a terrific break for me—for us. I'm moving up in the business now, honey. It won't be much longer. Then we can be together. We can get married. Maybe even start a family!

God, I miss you—

All my love always,

Michael

There was so much more he'd wanted to say, but he couldn't quite find the words. No matter. Janet would understand. She always understood. There were times he thought Janet understood him better than he understood himself.

He took out an envelope, scrawled her name and address on it, and licked a stamp, which he placed in the appropriate spot. Folding the yellow sheet carefully, he put it in the envelope and sealed it. He'd mail it first thing in the morning, on his way to work.

He took off his clothes and got into bed. Lying there in the darkness, he thought about Janet, so far away now, and about how long it might be before they could be together, before they could get married. He also thought about his own needs, because they couldn't—wouldn't—be ignored. He was a man. A young, healthy man with certain needs that had to be taken care of. Certain needs of a sexual nature. And he didn't know how much longer he could wait.

If only he could come up with a really big story. . . .

Spencer Randall.

That was the answer, Michael thought as he studied the photo layout in *Time*. The wunderkind of Wall Street. The man who seemed to have come out of nowhere one day to take the financial world by storm. He was an enigma if ever there was one. No one seemed to know much about him. He never talked to the press, never gave interviews. What was known about him was minimal. He'd been in the Navy during the war. Afterward, he'd turned up with a sizable amount of money he'd managed to parlay into an enormous fortune through a series of well-chosen investments. Now, he was the head of Randall International, a multinational conglomerate that was actually a holding company that had acquired a number of varied, profitable companies worldwide.

And that was all anyone seemed to know about him.

If I could get a story on him—the real story, the one nobody's been able to uncover yet— Michael dismissed the thought almost as quickly as it came to him. It was ridiculous. Even if he could somehow get to Randall, get an exclusive on him—and he was sure he could—there was no way Lawson was going to spring to send him to New York without a guarantee. *Hell, to convince Grady Lawson, it would probably have to be chiseled in stone.*

But if I could get a story. . . .

"Are you nuts?"

"If you'd just hear me out—" Michael started.

"I've already heard enough!" Grady Lawson snorted. "You want me—the paper—to send you all the way to New York to chase down a man nobody else has been able to get to. A man who doesn't give interviews. I repeat—in case your hearing's gone along with your sanity—are you nuts?"

"This could be a big story, Grady," Michael maintained.

"I agree. Spencer Randall is news, in any part of the country," Lawson said with a nod. "But what makes you think you can get to him when nobody else can?"

"I don't *think*, I *know*," Michael said confidently, pulling himself up straight.

"Pretty sure of yourself, aren't you, kid?"

"Send me to New York and I'll prove it."

Lawson shook his head. "Sorry, kid, no dice," he said almost regretfully. "Even if I were willing—and I'm not sure I would be—the guys upstairs wouldn't be. They don't like to throw money away. There's no way they'd go for this without a guarantee—and they'd probably want it signed in blood."

"I see."

Michael wasn't ready to give up. He returned to his desk, unable to get it out of his mind as he struggled to finish the story he had to file by five that afternoon. *Okay, so the paper won't send me,* he thought resentfully. *I can rule that out. They're not going to pick up the tab.*

I could go on my own, cover the expenses myself.

Sure, I could. On what? My looks? File that one under "dumb ideas." I barely make enough to pay my rent and eat here, let alone cover what could be a long stay in a hotel in New York.

There's no such thing as a cheap hotel in New York. Even their cheap hotels are expensive.

Maybe I could stay at the Y. . . .

He barely made his five o'clock deadline. He was still trying to come up with a solution to his problem as he drove back to the rooming house that night. Finally, it came to him.

There *was* a way. . . .

When the train bound for New York pulled into Union Station in St. Louis to pick up passengers, Michael almost got off. He felt guilty about doing this without talking it over with Janet first. It was going to take every dime of the nest egg they'd been saving—together—to make this trip. The money they'd been saving to get married, to get themselves off to a good start. He hadn't even talked to her about using the money. If this didn't pan out, what was he going to tell her? And what was he going to tell Lawson?

He'd called his managing editor from the train station that morning. His excuse for taking off had been a death in the family. He had to get to Minneapolis as soon as possible. Fortunately, Lawson had bought it without asking too many questions. Michael wasn't sure what he would have done if his boss had questioned him too carefully. He'd only come up with that excuse on his way to the train station.

But how long will it hold up? he asked himself. *How long can I stay away with such a lame excuse?*

25

New York City, February 1960.

Michael got off the train at Grand Central Station just before daybreak. Luggage in hand, he made his way through the main terminal to the doors leading to East Forty-second Street and climbed into one of the empty yellow taxis parked at the curb.

"Where to?" the cabbie asked.

"Good question," Michael said, feeling slightly embarrassed. He'd never been to New York before and knew practically nothing about the city, and because he couldn't tell anyone what he was doing or where he was going, he hadn't been able to ask those of his colleagues who had been there for information. "Can you recommend a decent but not-too-expensive hotel?"

The cabbie thought about it for a moment. "You gonna be in town long?" he asked.

"Possibly," Michael said. "Does it matter?"

"Sometimes," the cabbie told him. "There's a place over on Eighth Avenue, other side of Broadway. I take a lot of out-of-towners in town on business there."

That's me, Michael thought wryly. *An out-of-towner if ever there was one. Whether or not I do any business here remains to be seen though.* "Sounds good to me," he said aloud.

"Neighborhood ain't too good," the cabbie went on, "but the hotel's clean and the rates are reasonable—compared to the rest of the hotels in town, anyway."

"Good enough," Michael said promptly.

The cabdriver had been right about the hotel. It was indeed in a rather seedy neighborhood, one in which only the most courageous would dare venture out at night. *Speak softly and carry a baseball bat,* Michael thought as he looked down at Eighth Avenue from the only window of his tiny room. But the hotel was also immaculately clean, and the rates were more reasonable than he'd expected. *Too bad the rooms are so small,* he thought, glancing around. *It's like being trapped in a shoebox.*

Room service was a luxury he couldn't afford, so later in the day, after he'd had a chance to get some sleep and bathe, he ventured out to look for a cheap restaurant. He found a small sandwich shop on Broadway where the food was at least edible, if not great. He bought a copy of *The New York Times* and read while he ate.

Now, this is what it would be like to be a really top-flight reporter, he thought. *Working for the* Times. *Maybe one of these days. . . .*

He figured he'd be lucky to still have a job at the *Sun-Times* by the time he got back to Kansas City.

He got the address of Randall International from the Manhattan telephone directory. He was amused at the size of the book. *It's not just a joke,* he thought, *it really is that big.*

Every day for the next three days, Michael waited outside the Randall International building in the financial district. Whenever Randall left the building, Michael followed him. He followed him to meetings, to lunch, to his Sutton Place apartment. And every night, when Randall left his office at precisely six-thirty, Michael followed him—on foot—to a small bar six blocks from the Randall building. Michael sat alone at a corner table watching Randall, always parked on a stool at the bar, drinking and carrying on a dialogue with the bartender as if he'd known the other man all his life. *If only I could get even that close to him,* Michael thought as he observed them. *I need a reason to strike up a conversation with him.*

Next time, he promised himself. *Next time.*

Michael lay awake that night, trying to come up with a plan. He had to be careful in approaching Randall. One of the few things that *was* known about the man was that he was no fool. He didn't get where he was today by being easily taken in. *Those who know him say he has the instincts of a jungle cat—and is every bit as fierce*, Michael thought, recalling a passage from the *Time* magazine story.

Michael didn't doubt it for a moment.

Michael was waiting at his usual post when Randall left his office the following evening. He followed Spencer Randall to his regular watering hole, then, after waiting a short time, went inside and took one of the stools at the bar. As always, Randall was engaged in a lively conversation with the bartender.

Michael sat in silence, looking on while he nursed his drink. Randall wasn't what he'd expected. It was hard to believe that this man, who seemed so much at home among the odd assortment of regulars in the bar, was the same man who'd been dubbed "the shark of Wall Street," the same man who'd built a multimillion-dollar financial empire. But here, mingling with a group that included Wall Street underlings, office peons, and dockworkers, it was as if he were really one of them.

"Excuse me," Michael said finally, addressing the bartender as he withdrew a slip of paper from his pocket, "can you tell me how to get to this address?"

The bartender took the paper from him, looked at it for a moment, then handed it back, shaking his head. "Sorry. I know it's somewhere on the Upper East Side, but that's about it. That part of town's a little too rich for my blood."

Randall intercepted the paper before Michael could take it back—as Michael hoped he would. "I know the area," he said. "Let me have a look."

"Thanks."

Randall looked at it briefly, then gave it back to him. "That's not far from my place." He gave Michael directions. "You in a hurry?"

Michael hesitated for a moment, then shook his head.

"Good. Stick around until I'm ready to shove off, and I'll take you there," Randall offered.

"Thanks." Michael breathed an inward sigh of relief. *It worked,* he thought.

"I take it you're from out of town," Randall said then.

"Yeah," Michael said, nodding. "I'm here on business. The man I'm supposed to see—he lives at that address."

Randall grinned. "Well, I can't say that I know too many of my neighbors, but I *do* know that address."

"I'm afraid I don't know New York at all," Michael admitted.

"Where are you from?" Randall asked.

"Uh—Minneapolis." Michael hoped Randall hadn't picked up on his momentary hesitation.

"The Midwest."

Michael nodded.

"It's been a long time since I've been anywhere in the Midwest." Randall paused. "I travel a great deal on business."

"So do I," Michael said.

"Yeah?" Randall seemed genuinely interested. "What line of work are you in?"

"I'm a writer," Michael said carefully. "A novelist. I write mystery novels."

"Yeah? Like Sir Arthur Conan Doyle?"

Michael gave him a weary smile. "You might say that. My publisher wouldn't, but I certainly don't mind if you do."

"What's your name? Maybe I've read some of your stuff."

"James. Michael James. If you've read any of my books, that would make you part of a very exclusive group of three. My mother and girlfriend are the other two."

"Sales haven't been all that spectacular, I take it."

"You take it right. But I'm working on one now that I hope is going to be my big break." *I should get an Oscar for this,* Michael thought, really getting into the role now. *Good thing I've covered all the bases.*

"No kidding." Randall signaled the bartender. "Hey, Tommy—another round for my friend and me!"

"Oh, I couldn't—" Michael began.

"Sure you can, pal. My treat," Randall insisted. "Now, tell me about this book of yours . . . "

For the first time, Michael felt optimistic. He'd not only connected with the notorious Spencer Randall, he was pretty sure he'd made the man *like* him. *Getting him to trust me won't be so easy,* he thought as he crossed the hotel lobby and stepped into the elevator. *Unfortunately, time is a luxury I don't have.* He punched the button for the tenth floor. New

York was an expensive place to stay. And he didn't exactly have an unlimited budget.

He'd put off writing to Janet, letting her know what he'd done and what he was going to do, because he didn't know how to tell her. Worse yet, he didn't know how she was going to respond. If this thing didn't pan out . . . he didn't even want to think about that.

It had to work. Everything was at stake.

"So, how's the book coming along? You haven't mentioned it in a few days," Randall commented.

Michael sat with him at the bar. They'd met there, every night for the past week, always at the same time, spent a few hours shooting the breeze, then went their separate ways. But in all the time they'd spent talking, Randall hadn't said anything that was even remotely revealing. Still, Michael refused to give up.

"It's coming," he answered, somewhat evasively. "Slowly but surely."

"Well, you know what they say, pal—Rome wasn't built in a day." Randall pulled a cigar from his pocket and lit it with an engraved gold lighter.

Michael's laugh was hollow. "I have a feeling my career's not going to be built in ten years," he said sullenly. And to himself: *It just might be the truth.*

"I'll bet your girlfriend's not too crazy about you being here so long," Randall said then.

Michael downed the last of his drink. "I'd say that's a safe bet," he agreed with a slight nod. *She's probably going to kill me. It's a good thing we're not already married. Then she could divorce me too.*

When the train pulled out of Grand Central Station early on a Saturday morning, bound for Kansas City, Michael felt he was leaving empty-handed. In all the time he'd spent with Spencer Randall, he had not been able to uncover anything that could be considered sensational or newsworthy. *I don't know what I expected,* he thought miserably. *If he's been hiding any skeletons in his closets, why would he suddenly show them to me?*

Out of necessity, Michael turned his thoughts to what he was going to tell Grady Lawson. Had he been able to go home with a hot story on the enigmatic Spencer Randall, it would have been different, but now he was going to have some explaining to do. He was going to have to explain why he'd lied about where he'd gone. Where he'd been for the past two weeks. He would be damn lucky if Lawson didn't fire him on the spot. And if he *didn't,* Michael figured it was a safe bet that he was going to be back on obituaries and wedding announcements for at least the next five years.

And then there was Janet. She was going to be furious— and hurt. She'd contributed to that savings account too—not as much as he had, but still, she'd contributed. It belonged to both of them, and he'd taken it without even talking it over with her. They'd have to start all over again. It might be another five years before they could get married, if Janet was still willing to marry him at all after this.

Maybe Randall's got it right after all, he thought, recalling his last conversation with the man. *Now, there's a man who not only understands business, he understands people. He knows himself better than most of us ever will.* And then it hit him.

Maybe he *did* have a story, after all.

26

"I ought to fire you, Callahan. I could, you know. I'll bet you didn't think of that when you ran off half-cocked to New York, did you?"

Michael had only to look at Grady Lawson to know the man was barely controlling his rage. "Oh, I thought about it, all right," he said calmly. "I wondered if I'd even have a job when I got back."

"They why the hell did you do it?" Lawson demanded.

"To prove myself, Grady," he answered. "I knew I wasn't going to get any big stories here—probably not for a long, long time, anyway."

"And you thought you'd get your big story in New York," Lawson concluded.

"Not only *thought*," Michael announced with a grin, "I *did*."

Lawson gave him a disbelieving look. "You're telling me you actually got to Spencer Randall?"

"I sure did."

"How'd you get him to talk?"

"Simple. He didn't know I was a reporter," Michael explained. "I followed him for a few days, learned his routine. Then I started hanging out at his favorite watering hole when I knew he'd be there. Pretty soon, we struck up a conversation."

"And he never suspected? A man like Randall? That's hard to believe."

Michael shrugged. "He thought I was a down-on-my-luck mystery writer by the name of Mike James." He paused. "I was just a guy he met socially. There was no reason for him to be suspicious of me."

"So he just opened up and confided in you?" Lawson asked. "A guy he just met?"

Michael laughed. "Grady, I have a feeling Spencer Randall's a man who never really confides in anyone," he told his editor. "But I *did* get to see a side of him I'd be willing to bet few people ever get to see."

"And this is going to be your big story?"

"Don't condemn it until you've seen it," Michael urged.

"Which brings me to my next question," Lawson said, leaning forward on the desk. "When do I get to see this masterpiece?"

"As soon as it's finished."

If it's ever finished.

Michael drew in a deep breath as he pondered the half-completed page still in the typewriter. Something about it just didn't feel right. He couldn't pinpoint what was missing, but he knew deep in his gut that something was. He reread it twice. Still unable to target the problem, he reviewed his notes. Something was definitely missing.

But what the hell was it?

He recalled that last night in the bar with Randall, how candid he'd been, how much in touch with himself and his needs he was. How many people really knew themselves that well? *I sure don't,* he thought as he sat there, staring at the page he'd been working on.

And then it hit him. The angle he'd been looking for. He took the half-typed page out of the typewriter, put in a clean sheet, and started to type:

> He's been called ''the shark of Wall Street'' and ''the man with the Midas touch.'' He's been described as a living legend, a stock market wunderkind, and an assortment of other things—most of them quite unflattering. The truth is that little is known about the man who seemingly appeared out of nowhere at the end of the war to take Wall Street by storm. It is ironic that he probably knows himself far better than most of us ever will. . . .

That was *it*. The one element that had, up to now, been missing. The single most important part of his story, the angle that would set this story apart from everything else that had been written about the elusive, enigmatic Spencer Randall.

The story that was going to put his career—his life—on the right track.

His piece ran as a cover story in the paper's Sunday magazine section, with the headline ''Spencer Randall: A New Perspective'' emblazoned across the top of the first page. Michael would have preferred something a little more colorful, but he couldn't complain. The story had prominence, and it was proof, in black and white, of his journalistic ability. It had brought him to the attention of his bosses. With any luck, they'd realize they weren't taking full advantage of his skills. They'd see that he was ready for bigger and better things.

He hadn't told Janet about their savings yet, about what he'd done. He'd hoped to be able to give her good news with the bad. He'd hoped to be able to tell her it had been worth the gamble, that the story had gotten him a fat raise and better assignments.

But so far, it hadn't gotten him anything but praise, which was fine, but it wasn't going to pay the bills.

Right now, he needed money more than praise.

"I'm sending you to St. Louis, Callahan," Lawson told him.

"What's the story?" Michael was surprised but tried not to show it.

"An execution." Lawson filled him in on the details. "Take the train—and take a photographer with you."

"Right."

Better stories were definitely coming his way, he decided as he crossed the newsroom and headed back to his desk. It had been two weeks since the Randall story had run, and the quality of the assignments he'd been given in that time had decidedly improved.

If only the money would improve.

"Ever covered an execution before?" the photographer, Jimmy Washburn, asked as the train headed east, bound for St. Louis.

Michael shook his head. "First time," he admitted.

"It's no picnic."

"I can imagine." Michael forced a smile he didn't really feel. He had other things on his mind.

"I've done more than a few."

Michael looked at him, surprised. "I didn't think they allowed photographs."

"They don't," Washburn said quickly. "I get pictures of the family, if there is any—and the victim's family. I feel like a vulture circling a carcass, waiting to move in and feed."

"I've never done hard news reporting before," Michael told him. "I've been on features. Mostly soft features."

"I read your piece on Spencer Randall," Washburn said then. "You made him sound a hell of a lot more human than anything else that's been written about him so far."

Michael shrugged. "That's the way I saw him."

"You sound as if you really liked him."

He thought about it for a moment. "Yeah," he said finally. "I guess I did." *Had circumstances been different,* he thought now, *we might actually have become friends. It's possible.* Spencer Randall had made a strong, favorable impression on him. It was conceivable that they could have become friends.

Anything, he'd discovered, was possible.

Getting off the train at Union Station in St. Louis, Michael mailed a letter to Janet he'd written almost a week earlier.

27

Kansas City, October 1961.

Spencer Randall was a tough act to follow, no doubt about that.

But Michael had always known he would be. Only an exclusive interview with a president or a king could top his in-depth look at the enigmatic Spencer Randall—and how often did presidents or kings pass through Kansas City these days?

He stared at the blank page in the typewriter and willed the story to come, but it wouldn't. Nothing would come. *It's like going to the movies and staring at the blank screen when the film breaks,* he thought, frustrated. *Only there's nobody here to fix my broken reel.*

He reviewed his notes again, hoping something in his hasty scribblings would somehow miraculously kick the muse—or whatever magical being helped reporters to churn out their stories—into gear. *So this is writer's block. Terrific.*

"Hey, Callahan—Lawson wants to see you," one of his colleagues shouted across the busy newsroom. "Now."

Michael looked up from his notes. "Is he in his cage?"

The other reporter nodded. "Yeah—and he's rattling it. Hard."

"Wonderful," Michael muttered under his breath. He looked up as one of the office gofers passed by with sandwiches from the coffee shop across the street, en route to the feature editor's desk. "Hey—can't you read the sign?" Michael called out, pointing to a crudely lettered paper sign tacked to the wall over a row of four-drawer file cabinets: DON'T FEED THE EDITORS.

"Mind your own business, Callahan," the editor growled.

Michael laughed. He got to his feet and made his way through the maze of desks in the newsroom, headed for Grady Lawson's office. *What does he want now?* he wondered idly.

Lawson was on the phone when Michael reached his office. The editor waved him inside, then returned to his conversation. When he was finished, he replaced the receiver and turned to Michael, who'd taken a seat and used those few minutes to try to put his story together in his mind.

"I want you to go to Washington," Lawson announced without preamble.

Michael didn't bat an eye. "State or D.C.?"

"D.C. I want you to interview President Kennedy."

I was right, Michael thought as he packed that night. *Presidents and kings don't pass through Kansas City all that often. But reporters from all over the country go to Washington all the time.*

Some reporters do, anyway.

When he boarded the train bound for Washington, D.C., at five-thirty the next morning, Michael was fighting to keep his eyes open. *The downside of success,* he thought as he stowed his suitcase and found a seat near one of the windows. *When I'm as famous as Edward R. Murrow, then they'll spring for first-class accommodations,* he told himself. *Then I'll get a sleeper car and a suite in a good hotel.*

Until then, he'd just have to endure having to sleep on

crowded trains and in matchbox-sized rooms in fleabag hotels. *But one of these days, things will be different,* he promised himself. *A lot of things are going to be different.*

Michael had anticipated all kinds of problems. He'd imagined everything that could possibly go wrong during this interview. He'd even had nightmares about it.

"What paper do you write for, Mr. Callahan?" the press secretary asked.

"The Kansas City Sun-Times."

There was a long pause. "I'm afraid I don't have your name in the President's appointment book."

"There must be some mistake—"

"No mistake. It's not here. You'll have to make another appointment."

"Fine. What time?"

"How's three forty-five?"

He looked at his watch. One-thirty. "That'll be fine."

"On Wednesday, October seventeenth."

"But that's three weeks away!"

"The President will see you now," the secretary told him.

"Thank you."

He walked into the Oval Office, tripped on the carpet, and fell flat on his face.

Right at the President's feet.

"I'm sorry, Mr. Callahan, but you won't be able to see the President."

"May I ask why not?"

"You didn't pass our security check."

"What?"

"It seems someone by your name and fitting your description is wanted for armed robbery in Omaha."

"This is ridiculous! I want to talk to your security chief!"

"Of course. He's on his way."

He'd worried for nothing.

The interview had gone smoothly. No, it had been better

than that. Much better. In fact, he'd practically written the story in his head on the train going back to Kansas City.

Grady Lawson had been more than satisfied with the end result. It had resulted in a number of important assignments for Michael.

And a substantial raise.

That was, without a doubt, the best part of all. Though he was still a long way from being financially able to get married, there was something he did have to do now. Something he hadn't been able to do before.

On his lunch hour, he went to a jewelry store near the newspaper office and bought Janet an engagement ring.

28

Minneapolis, December 1961.

As the train pulled into the station, Michael felt pretty much like an actor about to make his debut. His hand was trembling as he reached into the pocket of his overcoat, took out a small black jeweler's box, and opened it slowly. The ring inside was hardly spectacular—a thin gold band with a diamond solitaire so small Janet would probably need a magnifying glass to find it—but it said everything he wanted to say.

Well, almost everything.

Janet was going to be surprised. She wasn't expecting him. He hadn't written or called. He hadn't told her about the ring. In fact, they were barely on speaking terms. She'd been furious with him when he told her that he'd used all of their joint savings to make an unauthorized trip to New York in pursuit of a story his editor hadn't even approved. He still remembered—verbatim—the angry phone call that followed her receipt of his written confession:

"How could you?" she demanded angrily. *"After all this*

time, all the scrimping and saving—God, Michael, you knew we couldn't get married until we saved—"

"That's why I did it, Jan," he cut her off. "I knew we'd be saving forever on my salary. I knew a big story—something really important—could get me a raise."

"So you risked everything we'd worked for to get that one big story," Janet concluded, barely managing to control the anger in her voice.

"There are times you can't go anywhere without taking risks," he reminded her.

"You know what I think, Michael? I think all you cared about was advancing your own career," she snapped bitterly. "I don't think you were thinking of us or our future at all!"

"How can you even say that, much less believe it?"

"I don't know, Michael," she answered truthfully. "I'm not sure of anything anymore."

"Not even us?"

"Especially not us."

At that moment, he'd been afraid the relationship was over, that the damage he'd done was irreparable. Janet no longer trusted him. No longer believed him. But in the end, she had come around.

She'd been able to forgive, if not forget.

She was very surprised to see him. "I thought you couldn't afford to come home for Christmas," she commented after giving him a most affectionate welcome.

"I couldn't stand the thought of spending another Christmas alone in Kansas City," he said lightly. "Besides, I have a present for you I figured ought to be delivered in person."

"Oh?" She raised an eyebrow questioningly.

He nodded. "Could we sit down?"

"Oh—of course." Slightly embarrassed, she led him to the couch in her parents' living room and sat beside him, smoothing her navy blue wool skirt over her knees.

Michael studied her for a moment. Janet wasn't a raving beauty, but she was pretty in an understated, natural kind of way. She wasn't the most exciting woman he'd ever met, but he wasn't looking for excitement. She was exactly the kind of girl he'd always expected to marry: a real, down-to-earth, girl-next-door type. And he did love her.

He took the box from his pocket and put it in her hand. "Merry Christmas, honey," he said softly.

She looked at him, then at the box, opening it slowly. "Oh, Michael!" she gasped. "I didn't expect—"

"I know you didn't," he said, "but after everything we've been through in the past two years, I figured there was only one thing I could spend my raise on."

She laughed and kissed him. "You're such a romantic."

He took the box from her and removed the ring. "Here— let me put it on you," he said, taking her left hand. He slipped the ring on the third finger and kissed her hand. "Now it's official," he said.

"It was always official," she told him. "This is just the icing on the cake."

How like her to say that, he thought, looking at her now, still amazed by her good-natured tolerance of their circumstances. How many women would be so patient? he asked himself.

Even as he spoke the words, he couldn't believe they were really coming from him: "Let's get married, sweetheart."

Janet couldn't hide her surprise. "Now?"

"Right now."

The wedding took place at City Hall two days before Christmas. Janet wasn't wearing the long white dress she'd always dreamed about, always talked about, but if she was disappointed, she was doing a first-rate job of concealing it. As he stood beside her during the simple, brief ceremony, Michael couldn't remember ever seeing her so happy. *I've done the right thing—for both of us,* he told himself, chalking up his nervousness to normal bridegroom's jitters.

But the truth was, he was worried about what he was going to do about their living arrangements once they got to Kansas City.

29

Dallas, November 1963.

"The President's been shot!"

Around him, Michael was acutely aware of a panic that spread like a brushfire. People began to move away from the motorcade at the sound of what was first believed to be a car backfiring, but was quickly identified as a gunshot. The presidential car broke from the motorcade and sped away, and moments later a motorcycle cop jumped the curb at the Dealey Plaza overpass, abandoned his bike, and scrambled up the grassy bank with his gun drawn.

Michael had come to Dallas with expectations—both Lawson's and his own—for a big story. Kennedy's visit to the Lone Star State had promised to be just that. Texas was a political hot spot for the Democrats, with all the bitter infighting within the party. Word had it that the President considered this visit to Dallas a necessary fence-mending mission, though he'd been advised by Adlai Stevenson not to make the trip at all. *Yes,* Michael thought, reacting automatically as the reporter in him took over and he moved to follow the presidential limousine. *I expected something big from Dallas.*

But I didn't expect this.

He called Lawson from Parkland Hospital.

"He's dead, Grady," Michael said, struggling to catch his breath. "Shot in the head." He gave the editor as many details as he could over the phone.

"They get the guy who did it?" Lawson wanted to know.

"I haven't been able to confirm yet, but there have been rumors," Michael told him.

"Check it out."

As if I need to be told, Michael thought wryly. But he didn't say that to Lawson.

"I'm on my way," was all he said.

Every reporter in town must've had the same idea, Michael thought.

Pandemonium erupted in the police station when Lee Harvey Oswald, the man who'd been arrested for the assassination of President Kennedy, was brought through the crowd of reporters who were waiting there for an official statement. At the sight of Oswald, there were angry shouts from the crowd. Flashbulbs popped.

Michael pushed his way through the mob to get a better look. He knew he was witnessing history. *But if I'd had a choice,* he thought, *I'd have chosen a different course of events.*

He looked up just as another man stepped forward from the crowd, produced a gun, and fired. In the next instant, Lee Harvey Oswald, the man who'd allegedly killed the President of the United States, was dead.

Killed by a man named Jack Ruby, Michael reported.

"I'm not going to be able to leave Dallas tomorrow after all," Michael told Janet when he called that night.

"I know. I've been watching on television." The words were there, but there was a total absence of either sympathy or understanding in her voice.

"Grady wants me to stay down here and cover the story for the paper." *This is silly,* he thought. *Why do I have to struggle for the words to make conversation with my own wife?* "Makes more sense than sending someone else down at this stage of the game."

I don't even know what to say to her, he was thinking. *What's happening to us, Janet?*

"I suppose," she said quietly.

"I'll be home as soon as I can," he promised.

"I know." Her tone was weary. "I'm sorry, Michael. I don't mean to complain so much. It's just that—" She started to cry.

"It's okay, honey," he said soothingly. "I know this hasn't been easy for you."

"It seems like you're never home anymore," Janet sobbed.

"I'm surprised Matthew even recognizes you!"

"It's not always going to be like this, Jan," he promised her. "I told you it would be tough in the beginning, that there would be times I'd have to do things I didn't want to do."

"It's been almost two years, Michael."

"Two years isn't a long time," he pointed out.

"It seems like an eternity," she said, frustrated.

"Have you talked to the doctor?" he asked then.

"My mood has nothing to do with my pregnancy, Michael," she insisted. "It has to do with not having a husband—or having one part-time at best."

"I have to take care of our family," he reminded her. "To do that, I have to work."

"I wish you'd chosen another profession," she admitted.

"I love my work, Janet," he said patiently.

"I don't doubt that for a moment," she responded without hesitation. "Sometimes I think you love it more than anyone or anything else."

Where did we go wrong? Michael wondered.

He thought about it as he lay awake that night, for some reason unable to sleep. *Things changed so quickly. I didn't think the honeymoon would end on the wedding night.*

Janet had been so patient, so tolerant in the beginning. There had been so much they'd had to do without, especially since she'd gotten pregnant with Matthew almost immediately, and they'd needed every cent they could scrape together to buy things for the baby. Her pregnancy hadn't been an easy one, but she'd never complained. This time around, however, had been a very different story.

The baby was due around Christmas, and the past seven months had been pure hell for Michael. Nothing he did or tried to do pleased Janet. She was irritable, impatient, and very quick to anger. She blamed it on his long absences, yet when he was home, they argued constantly. She was never happy, never satisfied.

What else can I do? he asked himself. *I'm running out of ideas.*

30

Kansas City, August 1966.

If Michael had his way, he'd dump both the typewriter and the telephone into the trash can.

The day had not gone well. Hell, the *week* had not gone well, as long as he was being brutally honest about it. He had three stories on deadline (one of which had turned out to be a real bitch to write, and he was convinced he would still be working on it at this time next year), was going out of town tomorrow to cover some civil rights–related story in Alabama, and Janet wasn't speaking to him again.

The story wasn't going well because his sources didn't want to cooperate. He was going out of town—a last-minute assignment, no less—because the reporter originally assigned to the story had broken his leg that morning and wasn't going anywhere anytime soon. And Janet wasn't speaking to him— again—because he was out of town more than he was home, worked long hours when he *was* in town, and on those rare occasions when he was actually at home, he was too exhausted to do anything but fall asleep on the couch after having eaten only half of his dinner.

The price of success, he reminded himself.

"Hey, Callahan!" someone called out to him. "You going to the staff meeting, or are you some kind of privileged character or something?"

Michael muttered an oath under his breath, then added, "Coming."

"Michael, we've got to talk."

"Sounds more like we're going to argue," he said calmly as he took his suitcase from the closet and put it on the bed, opening it.

Janet stood in the doorway, arms folded in a belligerent stance. "Call it whatever you like, but we do have to talk."

He opened the suitcase and started to pack. "Do I dare ask about what?"

"About this—this trip."

"We argue before every trip, Jan," he said wearily. "And I keep telling you, I don't have any choice. I *have* to go. It's part of the job."

"The job!" she echoed, her voice rising. "It's *always* 'the job'!"

He folded a shirt and placed it in the suitcase. "You knew what I did for a living before you married me."

"I didn't know your job was going to take *all* of your time," she shot back. "I didn't know your colleagues at the newspaper were going to be seeing more of you than I do, than your children do."

The children. She always used the children when she wanted to make him feel guilty, and he hated that. They'd had both boys right away, right after they were married. The rhythm method, he decided, certainly hadn't worked for them. *So much for Vatican roulette,* he thought. It had been a burden at first—an enormous financial burden—but he wouldn't trade his boys for anything on earth. Matthew turned four next month, Daniel would be three in December, and having a family was, without a doubt, the best thing that had ever happened to him.

"Don't drag the boys into this," he said.

"Why not?" she exploded. "Don't you think they're affected by all of this? God, Michael—I have to show them your picture every day so they won't forget what you look like!"

He stopped what he was doing and turned to face her. "Don't be ridiculous," he said tightly. Now he was more angry than battle-weary.

"It's not much of an exaggeration," she insisted. "Do you realize you were here only ten days out of thirty-one last month?"

"It couldn't be helped," he answered. "It's my job."

"*Damn* your job!" Janet snapped bitterly. Realizing she was wasting her time, she turned on her heel and walked away.

Michael continued his packing. *It's going to get worse before it gets better,* he thought ruefully.

He lay awake in the darkness, pondering their situation but unable to come up with a solution. In the beginning, Janet had been so patient; she'd understood the demands of his work and had handled it incredibly well. She hadn't been crazy about the idea of being without him so much, but at least she'd tolerated it. Her tolerance level had dropped dramatically, however, after the boys came along. Alone most of the time, the stress of having to deal with two children—two healthy, active boys—had drained and exhausted her.

He understood all of that. He even felt guilty about it. But he didn't know what to do about it. He had responsibilities too. And it was part of the job. Trouble was, she didn't understand his predicament.

I'll make it up to her, he vowed. *I'll make a concerted effort to make the best of the time we do have together. No more sleeping on the couch. No more excuses for not doing things with Janet and the boys.*

She came into the bedroom then, undressed quietly, and slipped into bed beside him. *No time like the present,* Michael thought. He rolled over on his side and started nuzzling her neck. She didn't respond. When he slid his hand under her nightgown and tried to touch her breasts, she pushed him away.

"That won't solve anything, Michael," she said tightly, turning away from him.

It was then that Michael realized his marriage was in real trouble.

31

Biloxi, Mississippi, December 1966.

It looked as if he wouldn't be going home for Christmas.

Michael dreaded having to call Janet to tell her that. He dreaded having to tell his sons he wouldn't be there on Christmas morning. It would be like telling them Santa Claus wasn't coming.

Now, that's ironic, he thought.

Janet was going to be furious, that much he knew for sure. She wouldn't understand that he wasn't stuck here in Biloxi by choice, that he was here because the interviews he'd been conducting couldn't be completed until the day after tomorrow, and there was no way the paper was going to pay for another round-trip airfare to send him back after Christmas. He could imagine Grady Lawson's reaction if he even asked.

Bah, humbug, and all that crap.

So here he was, stuck in Biloxi on Christmas Eve. *He'd be lucky if he had a home to go home to after Christmas,* he thought ruefully. There would be no family dinner with Janet and the kids tomorrow, no watching the boys' excitement when they got up Christmas morning and saw all of their toys under the tree for the first time. There would be only a dinner, either from room service or in the hotel restaurant, eaten alone, and a day spent in his hotel room because, being a holiday, there would be nothing else to do in town. Just about everything would be closed.

His resentment grew at the thought. *None of that will matter to her,* he told himself. *She doesn't care that this isn't easy for me, either.*

What's happening to us?

*   *   *

"You're not coming home?" Janet's voice rose several decibels. Even over the phone, her anger was only too clear. "May I ask *why* you're not coming home, or do I not have that right?"

"I haven't completed the interviews," he said quietly, knowing even as he spoke the words that she didn't really care what reason he had for not coming home. "I can't talk to these people until the day after tomorrow. There's no way the *Sun-Times* is going to spring for me to fly home, then back down here again on—"

"The boys have been waiting all day for you to come home!" Janet shouted. "They've been waiting for you to put up the Christmas tree and set up their train. Doesn't that matter to you at all?"

"Of course it matters!" he responded angrily. "You sound as if you think you're the only one who's having a rough time of it here! Dammit, do you think I *like* being stuck here over Christmas? Do you think I *like* not being able to spend Christmas morning with my kids? Believe me, this is no picnic for me, either! I'm not crazy about being alone on Christmas!"

"Is someone holding a gun to your head?" she asked coldly.

"Yeah. Grady Lawson."

And he hung up on her.

The waitress was pretty. Petite but full-figured, blond—natural, not a "bottle blonde"—pleasant, the way his wife used to be. And she'd noticed him, too. He could tell. One didn't have to be clairvoyant to know those things. He could tell by the way she looked at him, the way she brushed against him as she placed his plate in front of him.

"So, you're working on Christmas, too," he said in an attempt at idle conversation.

She smiled and nodded. "You're working?"

"You might say that. I'm a long way from home tonight."

"Oh?" She stopped what she was doing and looked at him. "Where are you from?"

"Kansas City."

"That's too bad." She paused. "I get off at nine. They couldn't get many volunteers to work tonight, but I got nobody waiting for me at home, and I need the money."

Bingo, he thought as he watched her walk away. In that one minute, she'd managed to let him know she was unattached and would be getting off work in a couple of hours.

He thought about it. He wondered what it would be like, taking her back to his room, having sex with her. It wasn't something he'd ever done before, or even thought about doing. He loved his wife. He'd never needed another woman.

Until now.

Things had been so bad between him and Janet lately, their sex life was virtually nonexistent. In fact, he couldn't remember the last time they'd made love. Either she was already asleep by the time he got home, he was too exhausted to make the effort, or they were fighting. He looked at the little blonde again.

It has been a long time. . . .

32

Kansas City, December 1966.

The offer from *The New York Times,* which Michael received upon his return, came as a complete surprise, though, reflecting on it as he drove home that night, he didn't know why it should. He'd spent the past six years working his butt off to make a name for himself in this business. Why shouldn't a big-time newspaper like the *Times* be interested in him?

The problem, he decided, *will be in telling Janet.*

To say she wouldn't be thrilled would be in the nature of a textbook understatement. It would mean having to relocate, moving to New York. He could imagine what she'd have to say about that.

He wasn't looking forward to telling her.

*   *   *

"New York?" She stared at him incredulously. "You're actually considering this? You're actually thinking about accepting this—offer?"

"It's a damn good offer," he replied.

"Then you *are* considering it!"

"Of course I am. I'd have to be crazy not to," he told her. "In this business, the *Times* is just about as good as it gets. Getting an offer from them—"

"If you go, you go alone," Janet said promptly.

He looked at her for a moment, not sure he'd heard correctly. "You can't be serious," he said finally.

"I can't take it anymore, Michael," she said gravely. "You're gone all the time, and on those rare occasions when you are around, you're either asleep on the couch or on the phone following up on some story or other. We don't have any kind of life together anymore—and don't think I don't realize that things would only be worse in New York."

"I have to work," he said sharply. "I'm the head of the household, the provider, remember? It's up to me to take care of this family. If I don't do it, it doesn't get done. If I don't work, the bills don't get paid. What do you expect me to do—sell shoes? I'm a journalist!"

Janet took a deep breath and let it out in a quick gasp. "You're a journalist who'll go to New York alone, if you go," she said with finality.

"We'll all miss you," Grady Lawson said, looking over Michael's letter of resignation. "You've become a damn good reporter."

"Thanks, Grady," Michael said, genuinely sorry to be leaving. "I'll miss everybody here, too, but as you've said yourself, this is an opportunity that's just too good to pass up."

"That it is," Lawson said with a nod. "I don't blame you at all for taking it."

Too bad Janet doesn't feel the same way, Michael thought as he walked back to his desk.

He understood how she felt. He'd certainly experienced

enough guilt over it these past few years. But she didn't understand his position. She didn't understand that he was just doing what he had to do.

As he passed a colleague's desk, he noticed a copy of *Time* magazine lying on top of a stack of unopened mail on the corner of the cluttered desk. On the cover was a photo of Spencer Randall. He stopped, picked it up, and looked at it for a long moment.

Brings back memories. . . .

"I've decided to accept the *Times*'s offer," he told Janet that night.

He expected her to be angry. He expected her to rant and rave. He expected her to accuse him of not caring about her feelings, about what she might or might not want. She didn't do any of those things. She just looked at him dispassionately.

"Your mind's made up, then?"

He nodded. "It's a good opportunity. Too good to pass up."

"I'm sure." She wasn't smiling.

"Try to understand, Jan."

"I do. Perfectly." Her eyes met his, and her gaze was ice-cold. "Will you file for the divorce, or shall I?"

33

New York City, April 1967.

Well, I didn't pick this place for the view, that's for sure.

Michael's apartment was on the fifteenth floor of a building on Manhattan's Upper West Side. From his kitchen window—there was only one window because the kitchen wasn't much bigger than his clothes closet—he could see the Hudson River, and beyond that, one of the less scenic areas of New

Jersey. *Bustling industry and floating garbage*, he thought
with mild amusement. *No matter. I won't be around enough
to have to look at it that often anyway.*

He wasn't finding it easy, adjusting to the single life again.
And that's what he was, like it or not. Single. He and Janet
were still legally married, but since he was in New York and
she and the kids were in Kansas City, the legalities of their
situation didn't make a hell of a lot of difference. And he
hated it. Michael was a man who genuinely liked being married, loved the idea of a home and family. He'd never quite
fit into the carefree bachelor lifestyle.

But Janet didn't give me much choice, he thought sadly.

If his life had been hectic in Kansas City, it was ten times
worse in New York. There were days he felt as if he didn't
even have the time to stop long enough to catch his breath.
There were times he didn't see the newspaper office for days,
as he raced from one interview to another. There were other
times he never left the office, times when he had four stories
on deadline and only a matter of days—or hours—to get them
finished and filed.

He was leaving the office late one Friday afternoon, having
survived a particularly grueling week. He'd promised himself
an entire weekend off, even if he had to take the phone off
the hook. He needed a break, a real break, and he was taking
one. No matter what. Or so he thought—until he passed the
newsstand on the corner near his office.

There he was, big as life, on the cover of one of the news
magazines: Spencer Randall.

He read the story over a TV dinner that night. Whoever came
up with that idea must have had him in mind, Michael mused.
He was certainly no cook—cold cereal and sandwiches were
just about the full extent of his culinary capabilities—and a
complete frozen meal he could just stick in the oven for half
an hour or so suited his hectic lifestyle perfectly.

But tonight, Michael imagined he could have been eating
dog food and wouldn't have known it, he was so absorbed in
his reading. Since his own story had appeared in 1960, countless articles had been written about Spencer Randall. They

had focused on various takeovers and business deals, his vic-
tories at polo all over the world, his philanthropy. Not one of
the stories he'd read, however, had ever focused on Randall
the man. Not one of the reporters who'd interviewed him had
ever gotten beneath the surface to the real man behind the
legend. Not that Michael was surprised. He remembered
clearly his own experiences with Randall, years ago, in that
little bar down in the financial district.

Suddenly, he wasn't hungry anymore.

He saw Randall as soon as he walked into the bar.

He was sitting at the bar alone, nursing his drink, just as
he had been that night seven years earlier when they'd first
met. *It's like it all happened yesterday,* Michael thought, *like
no time has passed at all.*

"I don't believe it!" he declared aloud, hoping Randall
would remember him. "My first night back in town, and I
run into a familiar face right off!"

Randall looked up, and smiled when he saw Michael.
"Mike, old pal—long time no see," he greeted the other man.

"I wasn't sure you'd remember me," he admitted, taking
a stool next to Randall. "It *has* been seven years."

Randall grinned. "I never forget a face or a name," he
said, signaling the bartender. "Bring a drink for my friend
here."

"Right," the bartender responded with a mock salute.
"What'll you have, buddy?"

"Scotch and soda."

"Comin' up."

Randall turned to Michael again. "Where've you been all
these years?"

"Freelancing," Michael replied with a shrug. "The books
weren't paying very well. Then I hit a long dry spell—writer's block, I guess you'd call it. I had bills to pay, so . . ."

Randall nodded. "Yeah, I get the picture." He picked up
his glass and took a long swallow. "Have you ever done
anything else? Besides writing, I mean?"

"Nope," Michael said, shaking his head. "I don't have
any other salable talents—at least none I'd want to use making a living."

"Too bad," Spence responded. "I was thinking you might come to work for Randall International."

"I'm not the executive type," Michael said with a laugh. "I'd never make it as a desk jockey." He certainly couldn't tell Randall the truth.

"It's your decision." Randall paused. "Tell me—you ever marry that girl next door?"

Michael stared at his drink. "Married, had two kids—and split," he said with a twinge of sadness.

"Sorry to hear it." Randall sounded genuinely sympathetic.

"What about you?"

"You had to ask." Spence pulled out some photos and proceeded to show off his daughter just as any proud father would. "Next weekend. Are you free?"

"I'm not sure," Michael responded, barely able to hide his surprise.

"Well, if you are, you should come to Greenwich with us . . ."

"You ever been on a horse?" Spence asked.

Michael grinned. "Only if you count the pony rides at a traveling carnival."

They were seated at the table in the elegant dining room of the Randalls' Connecticut home. Dinner was being served, though one member of the family was not yet present.

"That won't do you much good with my father's horses," Maria told him, picking up on the conversation as she came into the room. "They're polo ponies. They have a lot of spirit."

"Maria," Anne said coolly. "Where have you been?"

"Now, where do I look like I've been?" Maria replied cheerfully, calling attention to her snugly fitting riding attire.

"You're late," Anne pointed out.

"How can I be late?" Maria seated herself. "There's no food on the table."

Anne shot her a disapproving glance. "Michael, this is our daughter, Maria. Maria, this is your father's friend, Mr. James."

"Michael," he corrected.

"Michael," she repeated, smiling in a way that seemed beyond her teenage years.

Michael returned the smile, though a little self-consciously. Maria was a beautiful girl; she reminded him of the young Elizabeth Taylor in *National Velvet*. It was already apparent that she would be a stunning woman.

And he was embarrassed by his own thoughts.

"So, how long have you known my father?"

Michael hadn't heard her coming. He'd left Spence tied up with business calls in the library a half hour earlier and went for a walk on the grounds alone, winding up at the stables. The last person he'd expected to run into was Maria Randall, but here she was, facing him in the darkness, looking more like a woman than a teenage girl.

A man could get himself in deep trouble with a girl like that, he thought. *But not this man.*

"Off and on, for about six, seven years," he said aloud.

"Off and on?"

He nodded. "We actually met back in '60—but then we didn't have any contact for a lot of years," he explained.

"You're not married," she said then.

"Divorced. Why do you ask?"

She gave a little shrug. "I'm just curious, that's all."

He nodded, feeling more than a little ill at ease and not quite sure why. "I think I'll go back to the house," he excused himself clumsily.

"I'll go with you," she told him.

By the time he returned to New York, Michael had come to some conclusions about himself. One, he still had a conscience. He genuinely liked Randall and hated deceiving the man. Two, he'd been looking at Maria Randall the way a man looked at a *woman*, not a child. Even if she did have the body of a woman already, it wasn't right. It made Michael realize something he didn't want to face.

I've been without a woman too long.

34

New York City, June 1967.

"I was beginning to think you weren't coming," Spence greeted Michael as he approached the bar.

"I've got a new book idea," Michael said, taking a stool next to Spence. "I met with my old editor to talk about it."

"Yeah? What's it about?" Spence signaled the bartender.

Michael grinned. "Can't talk about it yet," he said. "It's an old writers' superstition." *I'm not that fast,* he thought, grateful for the excuse that popped into his head so quickly. *Who'd have thought he'd want to know what the "book" is about?*

"Sounds intriguing," Spence said as the bartender placed their drinks in front of them and retreated.

"I hope the publisher feels the same way," Michael said, reaching for his glass.

"Listen, pal—I'm going up to Saratoga to look at some real estate," Spence said then. "If you can tear yourself away from the Great American Mystery Novel for a while, I could use a second opinion."

"From *me*?" Michael laughed aloud at the thought. "What I know about real estate couldn't fill one page!"

"I'm not asking for expert advice," Spence said easily. "Just a second opinion."

"But why me?"

"Why not you?" Spence reached for his drink and took a long swallow. "There aren't many people I trust, Mike. You could count them on the fingers of one hand. But you're one of them."

"I'm touched."

"Don't get sickening on me, pal." Spence's tone held a

warning note; Michael wasn't sure if he was serious or not.

"Far be it for me—" Michael chuckled. "By the weekend, I'll be glad to get away from my manuscript. What the hell—count me in."

Michael was beginning to feel like the biggest louse on the face of the earth.

He felt like a louse because the book he was writing—and he was indeed writing a book—wasn't a mystery novel at all. It wasn't even fiction. It was a collection of biographical essays.

Biographies of the ten richest men in the United States—including Spencer Randall.

The idea had been easy to sell. Everybody—according to the editor at Howard House Publishing who'd signed the book before a word had been written—wanted to know what Wall Street's mystery man was really like. And a book written by a journalist of his caliber—one who knew Randall personally—was definitely going to be a hot seller.

"This could go to my head," he joked to his editor, Kate Rollins, *an attractive, dark-haired woman in her mid-forties.*

She laughed. "Where it's going to go, Mr. Callahan," she said confidently, "is straight to the top of the best-seller lists."

He smiled. "You're awfully sure of that."

"I've been in this business almost twenty years, Mr. Callahan. I know what sells and what doesn't," she said simply. "This book will sell."

"I don't want any advance publicity," he said then.

For the first time, she looked surprised. "May I ask why not?"

"Well, Kate, for one thing, there's my position at the paper. I've got obligations to them. I also wouldn't want somebody who could turn out a book faster than I can stealing my idea." He didn't want to tell her he didn't want Randall finding out because he'd know then who "Mike James" really was—and his book would be down the toilet.

"Fair enough," Kate Rollins agreed without further question.

*   *   *

Randall genuinely liked him. That's why Michael felt like a louse.

He thinks of me as a friend. He trusts me, Michael thought as he rode up alone in the elevator to his floor. He dug into his pocket for the key to his apartment. *But business is business.*

Or it's supposed to be, anyway.

SPENCE
and
ANNE
1965–1970

35

Vienna, March 1965.

Maria was a teenager, and Anne was more concerned about her now than she had been when her daughter was a small child. Perhaps, she thought now, she'd made a mistake in not spending more time with Maria while she was growing up, but her fledgling law practice had taken so much of her time. . . .

She was thinking about it now as she sat with Maria and Spence in the splendidly elegant Baroque riding hall of the Spanish Riding School, watching a breathtaking performance of the classical art of equitation by the world-renowned Lippizaner stallions. While Anne studied her daughter thoughtfully, Maria was absorbed in the flawless execution of a *manège,* as one of the white stallions leaped high into the air and kicked out with his hind legs in a movement similar to a dancer's.

Spence had chartered a plane to fly the three of them to Vienna to celebrate Maria's fifteenth birthday, for no reason other than a desire to see the horses perform, which Maria had casually expressed over dinner one night.

It was exactly that kind of behavior on Spence's part that worried Anne. The day Maria was born, Spence had promised her the world, but at the time, Anne hadn't thought he meant it literally. *Apparently, I was wrong,* Anne thought now. *He really does intend to give her the world—or at least as much of it as he'll be able to buy.*

It brought to mind memories of past birthdays. . . .

"Close your eyes, Pumpkin," Spence said.

The three of them were in an elevator in the Empire State Building.

"Where are we going, Daddy?"

"It wouldn't be a surprise if I told you, now, would it?" Spence asked, grinning. *"Now close those eyes, or all bets are off."*

"Oh, Daddy!"

They rode alone all the way up to the eighty-sixth-floor observation platform. As the door opened and they stepped out, a band set up on the platform launched into a lively rendition of *"Happy Birthday."*

"Her eyes are lit up like Rockefeller Center at Christmas," Spence told Anne. He scooped Maria up in his arms and carried her over to the waist-high wall surrounding the platform.

"How high up are we, Daddy?" the child asked, clearly in awe of the impressive Manhattan skyline.

"Higher than anybody else in the city," he told her. *"Look out there—there's the harbor and the ships—"*

"And the ocean?"

"And the ocean." He kissed her cheek. *"It's all yours, Pumpkin. Yours for the taking."*

Anne stood back, silently wishing he wouldn't put such ideas in her head.

Maria was ten. Spence took over Madison Square Garden for the evening.

His gift to her that year was her own private circus. A real circus, fresh from a twenty-five-city U.S. tour. There were clowns and animal acts and aerial performers, all of it playing to an audience of three. That was the year Spence gave Maria her first taste of champagne.

"Spence, she's too young," Anne protested.

"Nonsense." He chuckled. *"It's Dom Perignon. She might as well get used to it."*

"She's only ten years old!"

"She's my kid—that makes her different from other kids," he said promptly.

"That's what worries me."

It did worry her. Anne was also concerned about the striking difference in their roles in Maria's life. Anne was the disciplinarian, the one who made her go to school and do *her homework. It was Anne who enforced curfews and placed restrictions on her, while Spence gave her everything and denied her nothing.*

It worried her, all right.

She thought she'd gotten through to him when, on Maria's thirteenth birthday, he announced they would be having dinner at home, just the three of them.

The dinner was lavish, of course—Dom Perignon and beluga caviar for starters, followed by a four-course meal and Maria's favorite dessert, baked Alaska. Afterward, she blew out the candles on an elaborately decorated, three-tiered birthday cake. It was extravagant, yes—but not nearly as much so as Spence's past productions.

Anne was about to congratulate him on his restraint when he suggested they all adjourn to the terrace.

"I've got a surprise for Maria," he told her.

He led the way out onto the terrace, looking up at the star-filled sky as if he were searching for something. Then, suddenly, he grabbed Maria's hand and pointed skyward. "There it is," he told her, pointing. "Look."

Due east in the night sky, it was easy to spot: the Goodyear blimp, headed southward at a snail's pace, its lighted message board spelling out the greeting HAPPY BIRTHDAY, MARIA!"

Maria squealed with delight and hugged her father, kissing his cheek. Anne could only shake her head.

So much for restraint. . . .

"Aren't they magnificent, Mother?"

Maria's words cut through her mother's thoughts, bringing Anne abruptly back to the present. "What—oh, yes, darling, they are. Truly magnificent."

But she was thinking: *This one's going to be hard to top, Spence. What are you going to do next year?*

36

New York City, August 1967.

"For heaven's sake, Spence—stop playing God!"

He looked at Anne with a wry smile. "Who's playing God?" he asked, lighting a cigar.

"What would you call it?" she demanded.

"I'd call it business."

"You put a man out of business," she reminded him.

"I repeat, it was business," he responded calmly. "Everybody gets into this crapshoot with the same chances. Everybody takes risks—and deals with the consequences. That's the way it is—the law of the jungle and all that."

"What you did wasn't just business," Anne argued. "You didn't just take over a business—you ruined a man's life! You drove a man to suicide!"

"He knew the score," Spence maintained. "He knew if he put everything on the line, he could lose it. And he did."

Spence had backed a man named Alvin Harley, who was launching a chain of fast-food restaurants, a new concept that showed great promise. The plan was to offer a limited menu—mostly hamburgers—that would appeal to teenagers and families on the go. These restaurants, Harley had told him, would eventually replace the privately owned soda fountains as the after-school hangout of choice. The food would be cheap and the service fast, which would also appeal to families on weekend outings or busy moms in need of a break from cooking. Spence saw promise in the concept and provided the financial backing. The idea hadn't taken off as quickly as Harley expected—a lot of the kids still preferred the old ice cream parlors, where they could listen to the jukebox and dance if they wanted to—but Spence was still convinced it would. When the time came and Harley couldn't repay the loan, Spence foreclosed and took over the business completely.

Two days later, Alvin Harley shot himself.

Spence felt no remorse, no sense of responsibility for the man's death. This infuriated Anne, who'd never approved of the way her husband did business. "You said yourself it would succeed, given enough time," she told him. "If you'd given him an extension—"

"That would have been a pretty stupid thing for me to do, doll," he told her. "By owning the store myself, I stand to make a lot bigger profit."

"Profit?" She stared at him incredulously. "Is that all that matters to you? Profit?"

He shrugged. "That's why I'm playing the game," he said, puffing on the cigar.

"That's how you see it—as a game?"

"Doll, I love you—and you'll get away with a lot more with me than anybody else would," he said as he stood up. "But even you can't tell me how to conduct my business. Got it?"

She sat there on the couch, looking up at him, not saying a word.

"Joan of Arc was a do-gooder, too, doll—and look where it got her."

Anne had to admit—if only to herself—that she didn't understand her husband.

Spence, who was so warm and caring and generous with her, who was such an adoring father to their daughter, could be downright cold-blooded when it came to business. *Ruthless* was the word that came to mind. He could destroy men's lives without a second thought. That was the part Anne didn't understand.

It wasn't as if she wasn't accustomed to the cutthroat world of big business. Her father was a banker, after all, and he'd been ruthless himself at times. Many times, in fact.

But never could she recall him being as heartless and unfeeling in his business dealings as Spence had been.

She didn't understand it. She didn't understand it at all.

*   *   *

Spence knew his marriage had problems.

He knew Anne didn't approve of the way he did business. He should know. They'd argued about it enough. That had never made sense. *Why should she care?* he wondered. *What difference should it make to her? I don't tell her how to run her law practice!*

And he resented that. As much as he loved her, he deeply resented that. He wasn't about to let anyone—including his wife—tell him how to run Randall International. He loved Anne more than he'd ever believed he could love anyone. He'd loved her enough to overcome the deep-seated resentment he felt toward all women, to make a commitment. To marry her. *God, I'd kill for her,* he thought.

But she's got to understand that Randall International is off-limits. Even to her.

Anne was beginning to feel like one of the unlisted assets of Randall International.

She was Spence's wife—she had his name, she'd borne his daughter, she shared his bed—but he'd made it clear that their partnership ended there. He did not welcome her criticism of his business practices. In fact, she thought, he shuts me out completely when it comes to business.

"It's as if I suddenly cease to exist for you when some business-related problem comes up," she said angrily. "You just shut me out."

He lit a cigar. "Do I tell you how to run your law practice?" he asked. "God knows I'm not crazy about the idea of my wife playing storefront lawyer, setting up an office in a low-rent district and defending all kinds of questionable scum, but have I ever told you not to?"

"No—of course not," she conceded. "But I don't shut you out. I discuss my work with you."

"I don't interfere in your work."

She stared at him incredulously. "Is that what you think I'm doing?" she asked. "Interfering?"

"What would you call it?"

He sounds so cold! "I'd call it what it is—concern for my husband," she said carefully.

"Because you don't approve of the way I do business," he concluded.

"Because it scares me, Spence, the way you manipulate not just your business deals but people's lives. Because I don't understand how you can totally destroy someone and not give it a second thought."

"No—you don't understand," he said sharply.

She ignored his sarcasm. "And I can't understand your obsession with revenge," she said irritably.

"I doubt you ever will," he said, making it clear he didn't intend to discuss it further.

"Women," Spence lamented with disapproval in his voice. "If anybody ever figures them out, he'll make a fortune."

"I'd certainly pay for that kind of information," Michael said as the bartender placed their drinks in front of them. "Trouble on the home front, I take it."

"You might say that." Spence picked up his glass and took a long swallow.

"Want to talk about it?"

"Not particularly."

Michael knew better than to press him, even though he would have liked to know what was going on between Randall and his wife. *So he really is human,* Michael thought with mild amusement. *He's got human problems just like the rest of us.*

"How's the new mystery coming?" Spence asked then.

"Coming along," Michael said vaguely. He couldn't very well tell Randall that his first and only book—not a mystery at all—would be in the stores in just a few weeks. He certainly couldn't tell the man what the book was about. *But jeez, what do I say to him after the book does come out?* Michael wondered.

That would be the hard part. It would be a hell of a lot different if he didn't *like* Randall, if he hadn't come to think of him as a friend. . . . That was the trouble. He had let himself get personally involved. *If things were different, we could have been friends,* Michael thought. *It is conceivable that we could really be friends.*

"You don't sound too enthusiastic," Spence observed.

"What? Oh—yeah." Michael frowned. "I lose my optimism

at the start of a book. Beginnings don't come easily to me.''

"That's something I couldn't do," Spence said, shaking his head. "I could never write a book. I'm lucky if I have the time to read one once in a while.''

Will you be reading mine? Michael wondered.

Michael's advance copies of the book arrived, delivered by special messenger. He was surprised by the ambivalence he felt as he cut open the large cardboard carton and took out a copy. This was something he'd always wanted to do, something he'd given a lot of thought to, even back when he was studying journalism in college.

I should be thrilled, he thought. *How come I'm not?*

He had to admit they'd done a good job on it. The jacket was simple but eye-catching, in bold red and black, with the title and his name in block letters and, among the photos featured, a color photo of Randall that had originally run in one of the news magazines. Michael's own photograph, in black and white, plus a few lines about his background, was on the back flyleaf.

"This book is going to be a major best-seller," his editor had told him many times, right from the beginning. Until now, he'd found that hard to believe. But now . . . now, holding the finished book in his hands, seeing the reality, he suddenly felt as though it might actually be possible.

From the time he'd decided to study journalism, he'd always had two goals in mind, two objectives: a Pulitzer Prize and a best-selling book. Now, the latter seemed to be finally within his grasp. One of the dreams he and Janet had once shared was on the brink of becoming a reality.

It made him a little sad that Janet wasn't going to be around to share it with him. After all those years of struggling together, of scrimping and saving to make this possible, he had succeeded, but the marriage had failed.

He thought about it for a moment, then making his decision, picked up a pen and wrote on the title page: *To Janet— at least one of the old dreams survived. Michael.*

He'd wanted to sign it "Love, Michael." But it was too late for that.

37

"I've got something here you'd better look at," Dan West said as he barged into Spence's office unannounced.

Spence looked up from the reports he was reading and grinned. "Don't you believe in knocking?" he asked jokingly.

West's expression was grim. "This is important," he said, holding up a package wrapped in brown paper.

"Yeah? What is it?"

"See for yourself." He gave Spence the package.

Spence tore it open. It was a book. And his photo was among those on the cover. "An encyclopedia of tycoons?" he asked. Then he looked up at West and grinned. "Good photo of me, don't you think?"

West looked puzzled. "You're not upset?"

"I don't like it, if that's what you mean," he said indifferently. "But according to my lawyers, there's not a hell of a lot I can do about it unless they print something libelous."

"Do you intend to read it?" West wanted to know.

"Sure," Spence said. "I like good fiction every now and then."

"Glad to see you're taking it so well," West observed.

Spence studied the cover. "Who's this Michael Callahan?"

West shrugged. "Some reporter for the *Times,* I think."

"Figures," Spence said with a frown. He flipped the book over—and stopped cold when he saw the author's photograph on the flyleaf.

The author was his so-called friend, Mike James.

Michael was looking at the photo on the book jacket too. *I wonder if he's seen it yet.*

He put the book down and stared out the window at the
murky expanse of the Hudson River. *Of course he's seen it,*
he thought. *The first copy sold was probably bought by one
of his spies. I'm surprised it got to press without him finding
out about it.*

Instinct told him to avoid Randall at all costs. This was a
man who took the biblical "eye for an eye" literally. He'd
be out for blood now. Randall would want revenge, and God
only knew how he'd get it.

I don't even want to think about that.

Got to face the music sooner or later, Michael thought grimly
as he walked down the darkened street, approaching the tavern with all the enthusiasm of a condemned man headed for
the electric chair.

He paused at the entrance and drew in a deep breath. *Time
to face the firing squad,* he thought miserably.

He spotted Randall the minute he was inside the door.
There he was, sitting at the bar—there were times Michael
thought that damned stool had the man's name on it!—pol-
ishing off a scotch. He didn't look up, didn't smile. At first,
he didn't speak. Michael seated himself at the bar and signaled the bartender. Then he turned to Spence. He opened his
mouth to say something, then changed his mind.

Let him make the first move.

After a few minutes that seemed like an eternity, he did.
Spence ordered another drink, downed it quickly, then turned
to Michael, his eyes filled with cold contempt.

"You've got a lot of nerve showing your face around me,
you son of a bitch," he said in a low, deadly voice.

"Look, I never intended to—"

"Don't give me that crap," Spence growled, keeping his
voice so low that no one else in the bar could hear him. "You
did exactly what you intended to do. You wrote your goddamned book."

"I didn't write any lies."

"No? Saved 'em all for our conversations, did you?"
Spence ordered another drink.

"I knew you'd never talk to me if you knew what I did
for a living," Michael said quietly.

"Damn right I wouldn't have," Spence said. "And now that I *do* know, I don't intend to make that mistake again in the future."

"If you'd just read the book—" Michael began.

"I've read it," Spence said sharply. "Very entertaining." He waved to the bartender, pointing to his empty glass.

"Comin' up, Mr. Randall," the bartender promised.

"Did you find anything in it that wasn't true?"

"Nope."

"Anything damaging?"

"Not that I noticed."

Several moments of dead silence followed before Spence spoke again. When he did, his voice was low and unmistakably threatening. "Let me give you a bit of advice, *friend*," he said. "No matter where you go or what you do, make sure you never stop looking over your shoulder."

Michael gave him a quizzical look.

Spence frowned. "You'll never know when or how I'll turn up—*friend*."

38

New York City, February 1968.

"Mr. Randall, there's a gentleman here to see you," his secretary told him.

"Another reporter?" Spence asked. He'd already turned away two that week.

She shook her head. "He says he's an old friend of yours."

"Yeah? What's his name?"

"Michael Callahan."

"He's no goddamned friend of mine," Spence snorted angrily. "He's a fucking reporter."

"What should I tell him, sir?"

"Tell him I said he can—" He stopped short, slamming his fist against the desk, frustrated. "Tell him to go straight to hell."

The bastard, Spence thought, his mind still on Michael Callahan and his book as he sat alone in the back of his limousine headed for home that night.

The truth was, he was even angrier at himself than he was at Callahan. He was furious with himself for having fallen for Callahan's act. *A down-on-his-luck mystery writer—bullshit!* he thought, enraged. *A book in the works that could change everything—damn right it could, you bastard! You were writing about me! All that time . . . you were getting information for a book. You're good, Callahan—I'll give you that.*

Too damn good.

Michael was beginning to wish he'd never written the book.

It had been nothing but trouble, right from the start. He'd had to hide it from his colleagues at the *Times*. And thinking back now, recalling how he'd had to work on it at night—sometimes *all* night—he knew he would never have made it through the long months it had taken him to complete the manuscript if his publisher had not paid him so much money. He had to admit, if only to himself, that the money had definitely made a difference. A big difference. It had made him keep going no matter how difficult it became, no matter how many long, sleepless nights he'd endured.

It had also enabled him to double-cross a man he'd come to think of as a friend.

That was the worst part. He had come to think of Spencer Randall as a friend. He'd come to think of Randall in that way. He actually liked Spence Randall.

I feel like Judas, Michael thought. *Except I was paid a hell of a lot more than he was.*

Not that Randall was an innocent victim. He wasn't. Not by a long shot. His was a story that had demanded close scrutiny. It left a lot of unanswered questions in its wake, questions Michael fully intended to have answered one day.

And if he didn't genuinely like the man, he wouldn't feel the least bit guilty about it.

"I'm going to file for divorce."

Spence stared at Anne in disbelief. Finally, he started to chuckle. "Okay, okay—what's the joke?"

Her face was serious. "It's no joke, Spence," she said quietly. "I'm leaving. I want a divorce."

He poured himself a brandy, still unconvinced she was serious. "If you'll tell me what I'm guilty of, doll, I'll know how to plead."

"That's part of the problem," Anne told him, her tone grim. "You've never been able to acknowledge the fact that our marriage is in trouble."

"I can't see what isn't there," he stated flatly.

"You can't see it because you don't want to see it," Anne argued. "Or maybe there's just nothing for you to see because for you there's no problem."

"Damn right there isn't," Spence said. "I'm married to the only woman I ever loved, I've got a terrific kid, and the world is my oyster, if I may be allowed to be corny for a moment here. Yeah, I'm happy—is that some kind of god-damned crime?"

"And it's never occurred to you that I might not have been as happy with things as they are as you seem to be?"

"Oh, I think you've made your displeasure pretty clear on more than one occasion," he responded, taking a long swallow of his brandy. "But I've got to admit that I never thought you were unhappy enough to—leave."

"Maybe you never paid enough attention," she suggested.

For the first time, he realized that she was serious. "Look, don't make any rash decisions," he urged, his tone suddenly softer, more concerned. "Let's talk about it—"

"It's too late, Spence," Anne said quietly. "No matter what we do, it's not going to work."

"You've made up your mind about that, have you?"

She looked away. "I love you, but I can't live with you," she told him.

He drew in a deep breath and let it out slowly. "Some consolation," he said with a twinge of sarcasm in his voice.

"I'm sorry." She brought her gaze back to meet his. "I'm so sorry."

Long after Anne had gone, Spence sat alone in the study, nursing the same drink hour after hour, trying to figure out what had happened. He'd known they had problems, but he'd never suspected that Anne was so unhappy she'd actually leave him. *How couldn't I have known?* he asked himself now.

"Daddy?"

His head jerked up. Maria was standing in the doorway, looking at him with concern. "Hi, Princess," he said wearily.

"Is something wrong?" she asked quietly.

"Wrong? Why do you ask?"

She came forward. "Well, for one thing, you're sitting here alone in the dark," she pointed out.

He hesitated for a moment, tempted to lie. "Your mother's left," he said finally.

"Left?" She gave him a quizzical look.

He nodded. "Left. Moved out," he said. "As in divorce."

"Divorce?" Maria sat down beside him, her confusion apparent in the expression on her face. "You and Mother are getting a divorce?"

He nodded. "That's what she wants, apparently," he answered softly.

"But *why*?"

His smile was sad. "You don't know either?"

"No, of course I don't."

"Your mother, it seems, has been unhappy with me for a long time," he said, not knowing any other way to explain it to her. "She just decided to do something about it."

"I knew there were problems—I mean, I'd hear the two of you arguing sometimes—but I never thought—"

"Neither did I," he admitted.

It was the first time Spence had gone looking for a hooker in a long, long time.

Whores made him think of his mother.

But tonight, he wanted a whore. He wanted a woman who'd let him do whatever he wanted with her as long as the price was right. So here he was, walking alone down Broadway near Times Square in search of a prostitute to take care of his needs.

He ignored the first woman who approached him, an obviously dyed redhead with a pallid face, overly made-up eyes ringed in black and sea green, and thick lips painted bright red. She couldn't have been more than sixteen.

Bypassing a wino looking for a handout, he was immediately approached by a second woman. This one was a bleached blonde, an Amazon of a woman with teased hair that looked like straw, dressed in black leather. *Probably into whips and chains, too,* Spence thought.

"Want a good time, mister?" she called out to him.

He shook his head. "I have a feeling your idea of fun and mine aren't quite the same," he responded.

"Fifty bucks and anything goes," she offered.

"I don't think so." Spence kept walking.

After he'd walked another four blocks or so, he was approached again. "Fifty bucks for an hour in paradise, lover," she told him.

This time he stopped. The woman was a brunette: her dark hair, almost black, was pulled back and twisted into a knot at the back of her head. Eyes as dark as her hair. Not much makeup. Beneath her unbuttoned coat she wore a strapless rose pink dress and pearls. *She looks like a fucking prom queen,* he thought, intrigued.

"Fifty bucks," she said again, "and I've got a room."

He laughed. "What are you, a vice cop out for an evening of entrapment?"

Her expression was serious. "Hardly, lover," she said in a voice that held a faint trace of a southern accent.

Honey-dipped, he thought.

"Well—what's it going to be?" she wanted to know.

He thought about it for a moment, then nodded. "Sure—why not?"

The room she'd mentioned was on Eighth Avenue, not far from Times Square. It was in one of the older, seedier buildings favored by prostitutes and transients. It was a small, shabby room with only a bed and, in one corner, a sink. There was one window, with a shade but no curtains. The wallpaper was dirty and peeling. "I hope you weren't expecting the Waldorf," she said coolly.

The Waldorf, he thought. *The Waldorf-Astoria.* It brought images of Anne to mind. "I'm only expecting to get laid," he said dispassionately.

"Good. That's all you're going to get from me." She tossed the coat across the foot of the bed and stepped out of her high-heeled pumps, then unzipped the back of her dress and peeled it off. Underneath, she wore only a lacy white garter belt and stockings. "Want the stockings on or off?" she asked.

"Everything off," he said. "And let the hair down, too."

She shrugged. "It's your nickel."

He finished undressing and sat on the bed, watching, as she removed the stockings and garter belt. She really did have a spectacular figure. She was small, quite petite, but her curves were in all the right places. Her breasts were large for a woman so small. The nipples were dark and as big as half dollars. Watching her take down her long hair—it reached almost to her waist—he realized he was fully erect.

"Get over here," he growled.

She approached him obediently. When she was within his reach, he grabbed her and pulled her close, his hands on her buttocks, and buried his face in her breasts. He sucked her nipples fiercely, his fingers digging into her flesh as he gripped her bottom. Finally, he pulled her down onto the old bed. The springs creaked loudly, but he paid no attention. He fondled her breasts, but he was not gentle about it. This was not Anne. He was paying for this woman, and he'd do whatever he wished with her. He let one hand roam down over her flat belly. His fingers pulled at the thick, dark hair covering her pubis; he stroked her roughly, insistently; then, he put two fingers up inside her. She started to moan, but he didn't stop. He didn't let up at all. He just continued his rough, almost angry exploration of her.

"Hey, take it easy, lover," she gasped, struggling beneath him. "I've got to turn a few more tricks tonight—"

Suddenly, it was as if a thousand lights had exploded inside his head. Her words replayed over and over in his mind at a speed that made her voice sound like a frantic screech. He was on top of her, riding her, pounding into her with a fury he couldn't control. She begged him to stop, but she sounded so far away, as if she were off in a tunnel somewhere. Images—first of Anne, then of his mother— flashed through his head, and something snapped. Love and hate and rage merged, consuming him. His hand lashed out across her face. She fought him, but that only made matters worse. He hit her again . . . and again . . . and again. And he kept hitting her. . . .

Until he finally realized she was unconscious.

When he left her, Spence had no idea where he was going or what he was going to do. He just started walking, needing to get as far away from her as he could get.

Was she dead? He wasn't sure. He didn't think so. He'd checked her pulse; it was thready, but it was there. But would she still be alive by the time someone found her? That might not happen for several hours, possibly longer.

He decided not to leave it to chance. He stopped at the nearest phone booth. Fishing a coin from his pocket, he deposited it into the slot and dialed the operator. A woman's voice came on almost immediately. "Operator. May I help you?"

"Yeah, operator," he started, faking a Brooklyn accent. "Listen, I need ya to call the police—"

"I can connect you, sir—"

"No, no," he said quickly. "Just tell 'em there's a woman in a room at"—he fumbled with the address for a moment, not sure he remembered it correctly—"and I think she's dead. Looks like she got beat up pretty bad." Then, before the woman could ask him anything else, he hung up.

I hope they find the poor bitch before it's too late, he thought.

He started walking again, and this time he didn't stop until he reached St. Patrick's Cathedral. He didn't know what time it was. He didn't care. He walked fast, looking around to make sure he hadn't been seen before entering one of the confessionals. Once he was safely inside, he knelt.

"Yes, my child?"

Startled, he looked up. He didn't think there would be anyone around at this hour. He could barely see the shadowy
figure of the priest on the other side of the screen. *My child?*
Oh, yeah—I get it.

"I—ah, I—" he stammered.

"Yes, my son?"

"Forgive me, Father, for I have sinned. I—" His mouth
was open, but the words wouldn't come. "I, ah—I—" He
took a deep breath. He knew what he wanted to say, but the
words wouldn't come.

Finally, unable to make his confession, he broke down,
sobbing openly.

In the morning paper, he found a small item tucked away on
page ten about a woman found severely beaten in a fleabag
hotel on Eighth Avenue. She had a record of arrests on pros-
titution charges. She had been taken to the hospital and was
expected to make a full recovery.

She had refused to describe her assailant.

39

New York City, October 1968.

"I've accepted a position with the Justice Department. I'm
moving to Washington," Anne told Spence. She'd turned up
at his office unexpectedly that afternoon to tell him her plans.

He looked at her as if he thought it was a joke. "You can't
be serious," he said finally.

Anne wasn't sure whether to feel insulted or not. Didn't
he think the Justice Department would want her? Or didn't
he think she would ever really leave New York—or him?
"Of course I'm serious," she replied. "What makes you
think I'm not?"

"Come on, doll—"

"Don't you think the Justice Department would hire me?"

"You're a woman, for God's sake!"

At that last comment, she laughed aloud. "You're still living in the Dark Ages, Spencer," she accused. "Women are no longer expected to all be barefoot and pregnant. We do hold down, quote, real, unquote, jobs. Some of us even have real careers."

"And you want a real career with the Justice Department," Spence concluded, lighting a cigar.

"I do—and believe it or not, *they* want *me*," she added.

"Oh, I believe it," he assured her. "It's not hard at all for me because I've always wanted you."

"That's not what I mean—"

"I know what you mean, doll," he said. "And I think you know what I mean."

She nodded, frowning. "Only too well."

"You used to like it, you know," he reminded her. "That I wanted you so much. That I let you know it."

"A lot has happened since then, Spence."

"Too much," he agreed. "I never wanted the goddamned divorce in the first place."

She rolled her eyes skyward. "This is all pointless—"

"Yeah, I guess you're right," he said with a deep sigh, "but I never could give up on you. You know that, don't you?" He paused. "Okay—if that's what you want, I can't do a damn thing about it. But I *can* take you out to dinner—to celebrate."

She shook her head. "That's really not necessary—"

"Dammit, I know it's not necessary," he said crossly. "I just want to do it. Humor me, okay?"

She tried not to smile, but she couldn't help it. "Same old Spence," she said with a slight nod. "Times change, years pass, but Spencer Randall always stays the same." She looked up, her eyes meeting his. "All right. Dinner it is. Should be innocent enough."

He took her to the Waldorf-Astoria.

"Remember the first time we were here together?" he asked over dinner.

She nodded. "New Year's Eve 1948," she said quietly. "A lifetime ago."

He smiled. "Seems like it, doesn't it?"

"It really was, in a way," Anne said, taking a forkful of her salad. "We were little more than two reckless kids then."

"I was old enough to know what I wanted," he insisted, his expression very serious. "I wanted you."

"I remember," she said, her voice suddenly lower, softer. "I remember that night quite well."

"I didn't want to go to that party," Spence recalled. "I thought it was going to be a colossal waste of time."

Anne's smile was sad. "I didn't want to go either," she admitted. "I had better things to do than spend the evening in a fishbowl—being paraded around like some prize filly at auction in search of a husband." She paused. "Or so I thought."

"I never believed in fate," he said, "until that night."

Anne laughed aloud at the thought that Spence might suspect anyone or anything other than he himself could even remotely influence his destiny. "You believe in fate?" she asked.

"I believe something brought us together that night," he said seriously, reaching across the table to cover her hand with his own. "I believe we were meant to be together."

"I don't think this is a good idea, Spence," Anne said, still trying to figure out how he'd talked her into this.

"I think it's an excellent idea," he disagreed as he led her into the suite, then closed and locked the door.

"We're divorced—"

"Is that my fault?" he asked, pulling her into his arms. "You were the one who wanted the divorce, I believe." He kissed her long and hard.

"It's over," she murmured against his mouth. "Let it stay that way . . ."

"Just saying good-bye, doll." He kissed her again.

Her willpower dissolved under the heat of his kiss. She felt like an idiot, but he'd always had this effect on her. Even when their marriage was falling apart. Even after all these years. . . .

Spence didn't turn on any of the lights. There was no need. He scooped her up in his arms and carried her to one of the bedrooms, depositing her on the bed. After a long, intense kiss, he pulled away and started shedding his clothes hastily.

"You're so extravagant, Randall," she laughed, unbuttoning her own blouse. "You took an entire suite for—this?"

He grinned. "We had this suite that first night—remember?"

"Like it was yesterday." She lifted one leg, unfastened the garters from her stocking, and pulled the stocking from her long, shapely leg.

He stood back and watched her, aroused by the show she was putting on, as she removed the other stocking. "Should've left them on," he said hoarsely. "You were wearing them the first time."

"And you had a hell of a time getting my panties off," she recalled with amusement.

"I ripped them off," he reminded her. "As I recall, you didn't seem to mind it too much then."

"I had other things on my mind that night." She sat up and pulled off her blouse, then reached back to unhook her bra.

"We both did." He sat down beside her, cupping her breasts in his hands. "You still do it to me, you know," he whispered.

"Do what?" she asked, kissing the tip of his nose.

"Make me lose my head." He kissed her lips, her chin, her forehead. "You make me forget everything but how horny I am." His breathing became more labored. "Even after all these years . . . no other woman's ever gotten to me the way you have."

She stroked his thick, unruly hair as he bent his head to kiss her breasts. She moaned when he started to nuzzle her, lightly teasing her nipples with the tip of his tongue. Then he lowered her to the bed and started to kiss them, first one, then the other, first lightly, then fiercely. He unzipped her skirt and worked it down over her hips and legs, letting it fall off the bed and onto the floor.

"You bring out the worst in me, Spencer Randall," she

breathed as he caressed her nakedness, his fingers probing between her legs.

"Makes us even, I guess," he muttered against her breast. "You always brought out the best in me—and until I met you, I didn't know there was any best to bring out." He covered her body with his own. She parted her thighs willingly, even eagerly, as he entered her, taking her quickly, wordlessly.

Afterward, he lay in the darkness, holding her as she snuggled against him. He felt more content than he had since the day she left him.

So much for the Justice Department, he thought happily. *She'll never leave me now.*

Two days later, Anne left for Washington. But it was a week before Spence discovered she was gone.

40

New York City, December 1968.

Spence felt a lot like Ebenezer Scrooge.

The thought of Christmas this year filled him with bitterness. As he walked alone down Fifth Avenue, hands shoved deep into the pockets of his overcoat, head down in an attempt to block out the brisk, cold wind and falling snow, he made a deliberate attempt to block out all the sights and sounds of Christmas that were all around him: the shoppers carrying their brightly wrapped packages, the elaborate displays in the store windows, the Salvation Army Santas ringing their bells and calling out "Merry Christmas!" as they made their bid for donations on street corners.

All he could think about was the reality that Anne was gone.

He'd been so sure she wouldn't go. After that night at the Waldorf, he'd been positive she wouldn't leave. He'd been certain they were on their way to a reconciliation. It had come as a shock to discover she'd gone to Washington after all. He remembered what she'd said when he finally tracked her down:

"What we had that night, Spence, was wonderful," she told him. *"It brought back a lot of memories. But that's all. It wouldn't work. Surely you know that."*

"The hell it wouldn't!" he exploded. *"We belong together—we always have!"*

"I love you, Spence—a part of me always will," she admitted. *"But I could never live with you again. I know it, and I think you know it, too—even if you won't admit it."*

Spence could barely control his rage. *You're wrong, doll,* he thought. *Dead wrong. And one of these days I'll make you realize it.*

One way or another.

The woman was a redhead. He didn't know her name and didn't really care to know it. He didn't care who she was or where she'd come from. Nothing about her mattered except that she was a willing body at his disposal, there only to take care of his needs.

Now, lying on his back with his arms folded behind his head, completely naked, he was thinking about Anne, about that night at the Waldorf, while the redhead worked on him with her hands and her mouth. It was thoughts of Anne, not the redhead's considerable skills, that enabled Spence to achieve—and maintain—an erection.

It's always been Anne, he thought, frustrated.

It was still dark when he left her. Dawn, he calculated mentally, was at least an hour away. He didn't call for his car. After a few unsuccessful attempts at hailing a taxi, he started to walk, heading uptown on foot. It was bitterly cold, the wind was fierce, and snow was falling heavily. It was the kind of night when no one in his right mind was out on the streets unless it was really a matter of life and death, but Spence was out, and he was on foot.

He didn't stop walking until he reached St. Patrick's Cathedral.

Like a somnambulist, he entered the cathedral, made his way down the aisle to the altar of St. Andrew, and stood there for a long time, staring up at the marble statue as if it were a living, breathing, flesh-and-blood being. As if he didn't quite know where to begin or what to say.

"I guess you know why I'm here, don't you, Andy, old pal?" he said finally. "I guess you know everything there is to know about me by now, right?"

He paused. "I tried, Andy, old pal. I tried to make it work, even when she said it didn't, I kept trying. I loved that woman. I still love her, God help me. But I can't get her back when she doesn't want to come back to me, can I? Right—I just answered my own question. Why can't I do that anywhere but here?"

Automatically, he reached into his pocket and withdrew his money clip, pulling a fifty-dollar bill from it. He stuffed it into the box and lit all of the candles. Then he left the cathedral without looking back.

41

Greenwich, June 1970.

"Want to tell me something about her?" Maria asked.

Spence looked up from the newspaper he'd been reading. "Her who?" he asked, genuinely surprised.

"Whoever it is this weekend," Maria said in a teasing voice. "You bring your woman of the moment out here every weekend, but so far, you've never brought the same woman twice."

He shot her a disapproving look. "You're my daughter. You're not supposed to notice those things," he told her.

"I may be your daughter," she said, "but I'm hardly blind. And I'm not naive."

"Didn't anybody ever tell you you're supposed to look the other way when it comes to your old man?" he asked.

"Come on, Daddy—I'm no innocent. And you're entitled to your fun." She paused thoughtfully. "Though I will admit I've always hoped you and Mother would get back together."

He only half-smiled. "You're more of an optimist than you let on."

"It's not optimism," she said with a shake of her head. "Just wishful thinking."

Spence didn't comment. What could he say? That he wanted it too? That it was her mother's fault they weren't together? What would that do to Maria—and to her relationship with Anne?

There had been many women in Spence's life since Anne, but there had never been one special woman. There never would be because no one could ever take Anne's place. No one would ever measure up to her in his eyes.

Dolores had been the wife of a business associate of Spence's. He'd met her at a cocktail party. She was young— a good twenty years younger than her husband—blond, with a stunning figure and a face that belonged on a magazine cover. She'd also had a string of lovers that could have reached from one end of Manhattan to the other. Spence had just been one in a long line of many.

Not that it had mattered to him, one way or the other.

Melissa was a dancer in a Broadway show, tall and slender, with a dancer's body and the face of an angel. She was a redhead, with long, lush hair the color of autumn leaves. Spence spotted her during a performance one night and arranged an introduction backstage after the show.

She hadn't bothered to hide the fact that she was impressed with him. He'd made it clear that he was attracted to her. They'd spent an incredible weekend together in Connecticut.

He hadn't seen her since.

*   *   *

Annabeth was different from the others.

She was a real southern belle, a reincarnation of Scarlett O'Hara. In fact, she'd been told more than once that she bore a strong resemblance to Vivien Leigh. She had a fiery temper, but was not sexually aggressive. He had been the pursuer; she had been coy, playing hard to get. Of all the women who'd passed through his life since Anne, Annabeth was the one Spence had been most tempted to stick with.

For a while, anyway.

But in the end, none of them had ever lasted. Spence had never cared enough about any of those women to even attempt to sustain a relationship, even one that was entirely sexual.

None of them ever measured up to Anne.

MICHAEL
and
MARIA
1971–1974

42

He still didn't believe it.

Even when he received a copy of the final divorce decree, Michael was still having a hard time believing that Janet had actually gone through with the divorce. He'd never believed she'd do it, not really. Somewhere in the back of his mind, he'd always thought she'd have second thoughts about the split and eventually she and the boys would join him. At least that was what he'd always hoped would happen.

Now, there was no chance of it.

The marriage was over. It was all there in black and white, signed by the judge and sealed by the State of Missouri. She wanted to be free of him, and now she was. Michael wasn't sure how Janet was feeling, but he was hurting. He didn't want this divorce and never had. What he *did* want right now was to get roaring drunk.

I deserve at least that much, he thought sullenly.

"You here alone?"

The woman addressing him was quite attractive. Even in the dimly lit bar he could tell that much. He could also tell that she was slim and blond. *Blond like Janet,* he thought sadly. In the dim light he could almost believe she *was* Janet.

I really have had too much to drink.

Aloud he said, "Yeah, I'm alone."

That made her smile. "May I join you?"

He nodded. "Sure. Why not?"

She slid into the leather-upholstered booth beside him. "I've never seen you here before," she said in a low, soft voice.

Michael frowned. "I've never been in here before." *She looks like a debutante,* he decided upon closer inspection.

"I didn't think so," she said promptly. "I would have certainly remembered you."

"I'm flattered." *She doesn't belong here, in a place like this,* he thought. *My God, she dresses like a schoolteacher!* "Would you, ah, would you like a drink?"

She smiled demurely. "We haven't even been properly introduced," she reminded him.

He smiled too. "How rude of me. I'm Michael Callahan."

"Michael. That's a nice name," she said thoughtfully. "I'm Catherine. Catherine Nash."

"I'm very pleased to meet you, Catherine," he told her. "Now, would you like a drink?"

"A ginger ale would be very nice."

"One ginger ale, coming up."

She is attractive, he thought as they went through all the motions, engaging in the usual small talk over their drinks. *Very attractive. God, how long has it been since I've been with a woman? Could I get her into bed?* He dismissed the thought as quickly as it had entered his mind. *Nah—she's too much of a lady.*

Still, she did choose to spend the evening in a place like this, so maybe. . . .

She did go with him back to his apartment that night. They did end up in bed, and he was surprised at how uninhibited and even adventurous she was sexually.

"You're not what I expected," he admitted, lying on his back in bed, arms folded behind his head, watching her dress.

"Oh?" She paused in front of the mirror over the bureau, raking her hair into place with her fingers. "Why is that?"

"I don't know—you just seemed so prim and proper somehow—"

"Too proper for what we just did?" she asked.

"Well—yes."

She laughed. "It's all part of the game, honey," she told him.

"Game?" he asked, puzzled. "What game?"

"Oh, come on—don't tell me you didn't know." She approached the bed, extending her hand. "Don't play dumb, honey—you owe me fifty dollars."

"Fifty dollars?" And then it hit him. "Oh, God—you're a *pro*!"

She nodded.

He'd never felt so foolish in his life. She was a prostitute— a goddamned hooker! Worst of all, he'd never suspected a thing. She'd completely fooled him.

All he could think of to say was, "I want a refund."

43

Lausanne, January 1972.

Maria was definitely her father's daughter.

Spence would have been appalled by his daughter's conduct during her four years at the university in Switzerland, even if he couldn't honestly be surprised by it. That is, if he had known about it. He would not have approved of her exhausting social life, staying out until all hours of the night and sometimes getting quite drunk. Nor would Spence have been tolerant of his daughter's succession of lovers, some of the most attractive—if not always eligible—men in Lausanne. But Spence never found out because, to Maria's credit, she not only managed to stay out of trouble, but also maintained high grades.

A classic case of "do as I say, not as I do," if ever there was one, Maria thought, knowing how her father would react if he ever found out. *The notorious Spencer Randall—an outraged father!*

But that was exactly what he would be.

The skier's name was Jean-Paul.

Maria knew little more than that about him, other than the

obvious facts: that he was French, that he was older than she by at least ten years, that he was one of the best-looking men she'd ever met, that he was a onetime Olympic silver medalist, and that his skills in the bedroom surpassed his abilities on the slopes.

That affair had lasted almost four months, until his wife demanded he return home to Chamonix.

Charles was a writer for some magazine or other.

He was British, but Maria didn't hold that against him. The only Brits she'd known while she was growing up were the rather conservative businessmen with whom her father had had dealings from time to time. Charles was not like any of them. He wasn't conventionally handsome, but he was attractive to Maria in ways even she couldn't define. He was witty and fun and willing to experiment sexually.

He was also twenty years her senior.

Raul was thirty-nine. He was a stage actor from Barcelona with a hot-tempered wife who'd threatened to castrate him if she ever caught him cheating on her again. When he met Maria, he felt an involvement with her would be safe since he would see her only when he was in Lausanne.

He was wrong. When he returned home late one night after having spent a weekend with Maria, his wife shot him.

David was an American businessman who spent a great deal of time in Switzerland. Maria suspected that his business dealings weren't completely aboveboard, that he probably had more than one numbered Swiss bank account, but none of that mattered to her.

He had been a very good lover.

"Don't you ever date anyone your own age?" Anne asked when she visited Maria during her last year at the university.

"The men—boys, really—my own age are boring," Maria told her. "We usually have nothing in common."

"And you *do* have more in common with these older men?" Anne looked unconvinced. She'd been there herself.

"As a matter of fact, yes."

"Other than sex?"

"Yes!"

Anne frowned. "Are you sure you aren't just looking for a substitute for your father?" she asked carefully.

Maria laughed aloud at the thought. "Where on earth did you get an idea like that?"

"It's quite common in young women like yourself," her mother assured her. "Women who are very close to their fathers, women who . . . " Her voice trailed off.

"Idolize their fathers," Maria finished.

"Well, yes," Anne said uncomfortably.

"You can stop worrying," Maria reassured her. "There's no one like Daddy. I stopped looking a long time ago."

But Anne was worried.

Maria is her father's daughter, no doubt about that—and becoming more like him every day, Anne thought as she settled back in her seat and glanced out the window absently as the plane taxied down the runway. The flight was departing from the Cointrin Airport in Geneva an hour and a half behind schedule, but for once Anne hadn't minded. She'd been so preoccupied with thoughts of Maria and the direction in which she seemed to be heading that those ninety minutes had seemed to fly by.

She's headed for trouble. Anne was convinced of that. *She has her father's ambition and drive, but she also has his unforgiving nature, his disregard for rules, for the law. She has his hedonistic streak.*

God help her.

44

Spence sat alone in the VIP lounge at Kennedy Airport waiting for the arrival of Swissair flight 16. *Damn, it'll be good to have her back.* He'd never liked the idea of Maria going to school so far away, not really. But none of that mattered now. The only thing that was important was that she was finally coming home.

Spence ignored the overly accommodating attendant who was ready and more than willing to cater to his every need. He got to his feet and walked to the windows, where he could watch the planes coming and going. He looked at his watch. Swissair flight 16 was now twenty-two minutes late. *Why can't those goddamned planes ever be on time?* he thought, annoyed. Why couldn't they be on time—just once?

"Flight 16 just arrived," the attendant told him, as if reading his mind.

He forced a smile, his thoughts still elsewhere. "Thank you."

"Anytime."

He decided to walk down to the gate to meet her. Leaving the lounge—and the attendant—he made his way through the crowded terminal to the designated gate and waited just beyond the security checkpoint.

God, it was going to be good to have his little girl home again!

She's not really a little girl anymore, he thought when he saw her. That time in Europe had given her an elegance and sophistication beyond her twenty-two years. Now, watching her walk toward him, dressed in a royal blue suit and hat and carrying a silver fox coat over her arm, her dark hair worn in an elegant coil at the back of her head, he thought, *No, she's all grown up now.*

"Spence!"

In the next instant, she flew into his arms, and the sophisticated woman who'd returned from Switzerland became his little girl again, hugging and kissing him with the same enthusiasm she'd demonstrated as a child.

"It's good to have you home again, baby," he told her, somehow sensing she would not approve of being called "Princess" or "Pumpkin" anymore. "You look great."

"So do you," she said, drawing back to take a better look at him. "I really like the gray in your hair. It's sexy."

He laughed. "You're not supposed to see your old man as sexy."

"Oh, but you are," she insisted. "Just because I'm your daughter doesn't mean I'm blind, Spence!"

"Spence?" He looked at her disapprovingly. "What happened to 'Daddy'?"

"You're much too attractive to be called 'Daddy,' " she said with a sly smile. "Why, look at that woman over there." She nodded toward the attractive Swissair flight attendant who stood several yards away, smiling at him appreciatively. "You could probably have her if you made half an effort."

"Maria," he growled.

"Oh, come on—do you think I don't know?" she chided him. "You haven't exactly led a monk's existence. There's not a damn thing wrong with that."

"I think we'd better change the subject," he said sternly as he put one arm around her and they started to walk. "Have you given any thought to what you want to do with your life, now that you're out of school?"

"I certainly have," she assured him. "I want to work with you at Randall International. I do have a degree in business administration, after all, and—"

"Hold it!" Spence laughed, patting her shoulder affectionately. "You don't have to sell me on it—I'd be damn proud to have you." He paused. "There's just one thing that bothers me, though."

"And that is?"

"When are you going to settle down and get married—

and make me a proud grandpa?"

Maria smiled. "Just as soon as I find a man just like you."

Spence laughed aloud at the thought. "God help you if you do!"

"Well, what do you think?"

Maria walked to the center of the spacious corner office and paused to look around. "You can't be serious," she said finally.

Spence smiled. "Would I kid you about something as important as this?"

"This is my first job—I don't have any experience—"

"You're my daughter. Around here, that counts for more on the old résumé than anything else," he pointed out.

"Spence—"

"Hear me out, okay?" he suggested, raising a hand to silence her. "One of these days, when I'm gone, this is all going to be yours. The whole pie. It's best you learn the ropes now, while I'm here to teach you."

She looked at him suspiciously. "So what position did you have in mind for me?"

"Director of personnel."

Maria laughed aloud. "I can imagine what your executive staff will think of that!"

"What do you care?" he asked. "You're the boss's daughter."

"My point exactly," Maria said. "Put me in charge now, and everyone will say you did it only because I'm your daughter."

"So what?" He gave a halfhearted shrug. "You'll have plenty of opportunities to prove yourself."

"You'd let me run the department? Really run it?"

"That's what I said, didn't I?" He lit a cigar and paused thoughtfully. "I will give you some advice, though."

She smiled. "I'm all ears."

"Trust no one," he said. "Listen to what the so-called experts have to say, but don't let them make decisions for you. Everybody's out for number one, remember that. You've got a good head for business—use it. Don't let the bastards take advantage of you."

Maria only smiled. "Wish me luck?"

Spence laughed. It wasn't like his daughter at all. "Luck," he told her, "is nothing more than knowing when to take risks."

Nobody knew that better than he did.

45

New York City, December 1972.

Michael was intrigued.

How long had it been now? he wondered. How many years had passed since the first rumors surfaced that Spencer Randall was being pursued as a potential political candidate? How long since Randall's name was mentioned as a possible senatorial nominee?

Michael thought about it now as he walked alone along Central Park South, so deep in thought, in fact, that he was only dimly aware of the heavy pedestrian traffic around him. He was puzzled by Randall's consistent refusal to toss his hat in the ring. If ever there was a man meant for politics, it was Spencer Randall. He was smart and shrewd and charismatic. He also craved power. The man was a natural for the political life.

So why wouldn't he run?

The "official" reason he'd given was that he would have to relinquish control of Randall International, and he simply wasn't willing to do that. The press and the general public bought that explanation. Michael didn't. Spencer Randall had always shied away from the public eye, refusing to give interviews, never allowing the press access to his private life. Some of his colleagues attributed it to a Howard Hughes–type, reclusive-genius personality. Michael wasn't buying that, either.

There was more to it than that. He was sure of it.

He stopped at a hot dog vendor on the corner opposite the Plaza Hotel. "One, with everything on it," he told the vendor. "A Coke, too. And two pretzels." He was crazy about those pretzels the street vendors sold. They were having a slightly negative effect on his waistline, but he'd never been able to resist them. "By the time I retire, I'll probably weigh two or three hundred pounds," he said, raising his soda can to the vendor in a mock toast.

The man laughed. "If they ever come up with a nonfattening pretzel, we'll make a fortune."

Michael's thoughts turned to Spencer Randall again as he walked toward Fifth Avenue.

The man reminded him of a puzzle with a few missing pieces.

The incident with the hooker made him reluctant to approach women for a long time after that. Some of his colleagues had tried to fix him up with friends of their wives or girlfriends, but he always declined. His excuse was always the same: "I'm too busy to have a social life."

If Janet thought I was a workaholic before, she should see me now, he thought. *The only time I'm not working is when I'm sleeping.*

It's better this way.

"Hey, Callahan—you're still a celebrity!" one of his colleagues greeted him as he entered the newsroom. "Somebody called—said he was your publisher."

Just what I need, Michael thought. "Am I supposed to call him back?" he asked.

The other man grinned. "I think you'd better."

"Thanks." *It sure as hell took them long enough,* he thought as he crossed the busy newsroom to his own desk. His last book—focusing on a sensational murder case in New Orleans—had been published two years earlier. Of course, it had been nowhere near the success his first book had been. Neither of the books he'd written since—both of them nonfiction—had been as successful.

Now, with all the interest in Randall as a potential senatorial candidate, he had fully expected that the publisher would want another book. A book on Randall. A book Randall would do anything to stop from being written—or published.

Reaching his desk, he pushed aside a stack of papers and unopened mail and flipped through a half dozen telephone messages while he dialed his publisher's number.

"George Mason's office."

"Yeah—is he in?"

A pause. "Who may I say is calling?"

"Michael Callahan, returning his call."

"One moment, please."

A few moments later, Mason came on the line. "Michael, it's been a while."

"A long while," Michael said with a chuckle. "I figured my books weren't selling well enough to cover the cost of a phone call."

"Nonsense! As a matter of fact, I have good news for you."

"You want me to do a book on Spencer Randall." Michael leaned back in his chair and propped his feet up on the cluttered desk.

"Well, yes. How did you know?"

"A lucky guess," Michael told him. "Why not? I can use the money."

"This time, they're willing to pull out all the stops," Mason told him. "Promotion, publicity—you'll be doing interviews all over the country. TV, radio, you name it."

Publicity. Probably even before the contract was signed, for a book like this. Randall would have advance warning.

Why don't you just order a hit on me? Michael was thinking. Aloud he said, "Sounds good to me."

46

"Well, how do you like being a part of Randall International so far?"

"I love it," Maria told her mother. "I wouldn't want to be anywhere else. Working with Spence is a real experience."

"Mmm . . . I can imagine," Anne said, smiling as she raised her wineglass to her lips.

They were having dinner at La Ruche, a small, plant-filled French restaurant with cushioned wicker chairs, candlelit tables, and for atmosphere, background music by Piaf and Brassens and American music from the 1940s.

"You still love Spence, don't you?" Maria asked then.

Anne was genuinely surprised by her daughter's question. "Your father and I have been divorced for several years now," she pointed out.

Maria's eyes met hers. "That's not what I asked," she said. "And you do still love him. I can tell."

"It would be hard not to feel something for the father of one's child," Anne said evasively.

"I think there's more to it than that." Maria was unconvinced.

"I think you're seeing what you want to see," Anne said firmly.

"Come on," Maria pressed. "Are you going to sit there and tell me you don't still have strong feelings for him?"

"I'm going to tell you it doesn't matter what I do or don't feel," Anne said. "Our marriage didn't work. We couldn't live together."

"Can't live with him but can't live without him, is that it?" Maria asked with a nervous smile.

"We divorced."

"*You* divorced *him*," her daughter reminded her. "He didn't want it."

Anne frowned. "He told you that?"

"He didn't have to. I can tell."

"Your father was happy with things the way they were. I wasn't," Anne admitted. "I needed something more. Something he couldn't give me, something I couldn't get from our marriage. Surely you, of all people, can understand that."

"Why do you say that?" Maria wasn't quite sure she understood.

"You're a woman now, Maria. You have a life of your own, a career—"

"Yes, and I understand any woman's need for those things," Maria said quickly. "But quite honestly, I can't imagine any woman willingly walking away from Spence."

"You're his daughter. Of course you're going to feel that way." Their conversation was interrupted by the waiter, who brought dessert.

"If I weren't his daughter, I'd give you a run for your money," Maria said as soon as the waiter was out of earshot.

"You worry me when you say things like that," Anne said, taking a bite of her *gâteau amande chocolat,* which was layered with meringue and whipped cream. "I see it in the things you say, the goals you set for yourself, even in the men with whom you become involved. You're looking for someone just like Spence."

Maria laughed. "There is no one exactly like Spence."

"But you're looking."

"And you don't approve of that," Maria concluded.

"You've seen only one side of him, darling," Anne said patiently. "You've seen the doting father who gives you the world and thinks the sun rises and sets in you. You've never seen the *other* Spencer Randall—the one who's calculating and ruthless and plays God with other people's lives when it suits his purposes."

"Sometimes in business it's necessary to be ruthless," Maria offered in defense of her father.

Anne frowned. *She sounds—and acts—just like him,* she thought.

God help her.

47

Washington, D.C., December 1973.

I spoke too soon, Michael thought as the 727 touched down on the runway at National Airport.

His publisher had wanted him to write another book.

The question that had nagged him ever since his publisher had called was a valid one: Could he dig up enough material for another book? He'd tried—but Randall hadn't spoken to him in years—and had ordered his employees and associates to do likewise.

How, Michael wondered now, *am I supposed to come up with something new to write about?*

As soon as the plane came to a full stop and the FASTEN SEAT BELT sign went off, Michael collected his coat and brief-case and got to his feet, waiting impatiently for the passengers blocking the aisle ahead of him to collect their bags from the overhead compartments and start moving along.

It was a good fifteen minutes before he was finally off the plane and headed through the airport's main terminal en route to the baggage claim area. As he passed the airport news-stand, something caught his eye. He stopped to check it out.

On the cover of the current issue of *Newsweek* was a color photograph of a striking young woman—dark hair, a self-confident smile, and to Michael, a face all too familiar. He picked it up and read the cover copy accompanying the photo: *Her Father's Daughter: Maria Randall.*

Maria Randall, Michael thought, recalling the bright, beautiful girl he'd met once or twice in the company of her father. It was hard to believe that that precocious teenager was all grown up now and working with Spencer Randall. It made Michael think of his own sons. *How time flies,* Michael thought. He paid for the magazine, stuck it into his briefcase, and went on his way.

Maria Randall. It was a start, anyway.

Lying awake in his hotel room, Michael felt as if he were about to receive a visit from the Ghost of Christmas Past— or whichever of those darned ghosts came first. He hadn't read Dickens since his college days, which had been fourteen, fifteen years ago, but those years in between suddenly seemed like a lifetime.

His Christmas spirit had plummeted to an all-time low. He normally dreaded the holidays; they only served as a painful reminder of how little time he'd had with his sons while they were very young. He recalled the last time he'd seen them . . .

"Why don't we get to see you more, Dad?" Matthew wanted to know.

"I can't always get away," Michael began. *"New York's a long way from here, and I have to work. My work keeps me from coming to see you as much as I'd like to."*

"That's what Mom says."

Michael sighed. "Your mom was never real happy about my work."

There was a long pause. Finally, Matthew asked, "Was it really your work—I mean, is that really why you and Mom split up?"

Michael thought about it for a moment. "I think it was a big part of it," he said quietly. "I was away so much of the time, and there she was, a young mother with two small children, pretty much having to do it all alone. It wasn't fair to her, I know, but there wasn't much I could do about it. It was my job. I had to do it."

"We—Danny and me—really wished you were around more when we were real little," Matthew confessed then. "We didn't understand why you couldn't come home sometimes. We thought it was our fault—something we'd done. We thought you were mad at us."

Michael stared at him for a few seconds, not knowing what to say at first. Finally, he reached out and took his son in his arms. "*It never had anything to do with you or Danny,*" *he insisted.* "*I was never mad at you guys. It was between your mother and me.*"

"*Didn't you love each other?*"

The question took Michael by surprise. "*I think we did—in the beginning,*" *he said slowly.* "*Trouble was, we just didn't love each other enough.*"

His son looked at him, not quite understanding.

"*We were under a lot of pressure,*" *Michael explained.* "*We had a lot of problems. Right from the beginning. There was never enough money. I was traveling—I was on the road more than I was home. And your mother was stuck at home alone with two little boys. She loved you both very much but it was a lot of work for just her.*"

"*She used to cry a lot,*" *Matthew remembered.*

Michael nodded. "*She thought it wasn't fair—and she was right.*" *Looking at his son now, he could see in Matthew's eyes the pain the boy had carried within him all these years. And he wished he could somehow erase that pain. . . .*

Michael's thoughts returned to the present. He rolled over on his back, his arms folded behind his head, and stared up at the ceiling for a long time. He'd done a lot of things in his life he would have liked the chance to do all over again, but if he had the opportunity to change only one thing, it would be undoing the unhappiness he'd caused his children.

He looked at his watch. Two A.M. The Ghost of Christmas Present would be arriving soon. . . .

What's left to write about Spencer Randall that hasn't already been written? Michael wondered as he showered that night. *Probably plenty, but what would it take to unearth it?*

He'd always had the feeling there were a lot of skeletons in the Randall closets. Spence Randall had always been too reclusive, too obsessed with his privacy. A man like that had to be hiding something. Michael would have bet on it. *Finding it,* he thought. *That's going to be the problem.*

Most of Spencer Randall's life was a carefully guarded secret, and Randall meant to keep it that way.

Michael shut off the water and reached for a towel as he

stepped out of the shower. Wrapping it around his middle and tucking it in at his waist, he dried his hair with another towel. It had been a long day and he was exhausted, but, he suddenly realized, he was also hungry.

Famished, in fact.

He called room service to order a sandwich, then put on a pair of drawstring pajama bottoms and a robe. While he waited for room service to deliver, he glanced over the *Newsweek* cover story. He was impressed. For a woman who'd been an overindulged child and a rather wild teenager—he'd heard all the rumors over the years—she'd turned out to be quite a businesswoman. *If the reports are to be believed,* Michael thought.

It gave him an idea. *A new chapter in the Spencer Randall legend?*

48

New York City, January 1974.

"There's a gentleman here to see you, Miss Randall," her secretary announced.

Maria looked up from the reports she'd been reviewing. "Does he have an appointment?" she asked, sure she hadn't scheduled anything for the afternoon.

"No," the secretary said, somewhat hesitantly. "He's a reporter. A Mr. Callahan from the *Times.*"

Suddenly, Maria was interested. "*Michael* Callahan?" she asked.

"I believe so, yes."

"Send him in," Maria said promptly.

"Yes, Miss Randall."

Maria settled back in her chair and smiled to herself. *So,* she thought, *after all these years, the notorious Michael Callahan returns.*

She remembered having seen him at least once or twice when she was growing up—after all, he and her father had been friends—but that had been years ago. When she was older, she'd heard her father talk about him—many times, in fact—always in the most unflattering terms. And she'd always been curious, always wondered what he was really like.

Now she was about to find out.

"Thank you for seeing me, Miss Randall."

She looked up as he came into the office. Behind him, the secretary closed the door. "Mr. Callahan," she said with a slight nod. "Please, sit down."

"Thank you." He crossed the room and took a seat in front of her desk. "I wasn't sure you'd see me," he admitted.

Maria smiled. "You mean because of my father."

He nodded.

"I like to make up my own mind about things." She paused momentarily, and in those seconds, she made a quick appraisal. He was neatly dressed, a little on the conservative side, dark, but with blue eyes behind wire-rimmed aviator glasses—and one of the warmest smiles she'd ever seen. "Not what I expected," she told him.

Michael grinned. "Let me guess—you thought I'd have horns and a tail, a forked tongue, and cloven hooves."

"Something like that, yes."

"I'm not surprised," he said. "Your father wasn't too happy with me the last time I saw him."

"Do you blame him?"

Michael thought about it for a moment. "Not really. I wasn't straight with him." He paused. "But then, if I'd told him who I was, he would never have spoken to me in the first place."

"I'm sure." Maria leaned forward a little. "So, Mr. Callahan, what brings you here? Why do you want to see me—or shall I tell you?"

He gave her a quizzical look.

"You're doing a book."

Michael couldn't hide his surprise. "Well, yes—I am," he said carefully. "But how did you know?"

"Word gets around," she answered evasively. "Spence's people know everything. Tell me, do you expect me to give you information on my father?''

''I was hoping you would, yes.''

''You've got nerve, I'll give you that,'' she said with a cool smile. ''You really expect me to talk to you about my father?''

''Miss Randall, I would think you'd want anything written about your father to be as accurate as possible,'' he said evenly. ''I'm going to write this book with or without your cooperation. Wouldn't it be better if you did cooperate? It could only be to your advantage—and your father's.''

She studied him for a moment. ''That sounds like a threat,'' she said, her eyes meeting his.

''Not at all,'' he said quickly. ''I'm simply giving you the option of having at least some degree of control over the content of the book.''

Maria paused. ''I'll have to think about it.''

I'll have to do a lot of thinking about it, she told herself.

He really *wasn't* what she'd expected.

Maria was intrigued. Michael Callahan wasn't at all as she'd imagined. He'd been joking when he made that remark about horns and cloven hooves, but she'd had a mental picture of him as some kind of monster, a fiend who'd double-crossed her father.

She thought about it now, as she soaked in a tub full of fragrant bubbles, attempting, as she did every night, to wash away the day's stress. Michael Callahan had been direct, but not pushy, pleasant, but not overly so.

Not bad-looking, either, she thought as a slow smile came to her lips. Exactly the kind of man she'd always been attracted to. *Spence would have a stroke!*

It made her feel guilty, feeling an attraction, however casual, to a man her father hated. But Michael Callahan *was* an attractive man, there was no denying that. Had circumstances been different, she might have—no, she *would* have—acted on that attraction.

No doubt about it.

She's got a lot of her father in her, Michael concluded.

He was impressed with Maria Randall. She was young,

beautiful, intelligent, accomplished. The fact that she was Spencer Randall's daughter made all of that a hell of a lot easier to swallow. *It's in her blood,* he thought.

But she didn't get her looks from her father. Even in his prime, Randall never looked that good!

He felt more than a little guilty about some of the thoughts he'd had about her since meeting her that afternoon. After all, he was twelve years older than she was.

But he was still attracted to her. If she decided to give him her cooperation on the book, it promised to be interesting.

If not too comfortable.

49

Minneapolis, May 1974.

As the plane touched down on the runway, Michael closed the magazine he'd been reading and glanced out the window to his left. The sky was clear, the sun was shining, and, had he been driving down some Minnesota country road, he was sure he'd be able to hear birds singing.

Today, though, it wouldn't have mattered if he had been able to hear them.

His mother was dying.

He could still hear his father's voice on the telephone the night before: *It's cancer, Michael. They say it's spread so far already that radiation treatment would be pointless.''*

What about chemotherapy?

They think it's too late for that, too.

How . . . how far has it spread?

Lungs, liver, kidneys, bones. There's no telling how long she's had it. You know how your mother felt about going to the doctor.

Yeah. She had to feel like she was dying.

The trouble with the goddamned cancer is that it sneaks up on you. You don't feel a thing until it's too late.

Yeah.

She wants to see you, Michael.

I'll be on the first flight I can get, Dad.

Michael's thoughts returned to the present as the seat belt sign clicked off and the other passengers began filing into the aisle, pulling their carry-on luggage from the overhead compartments. He waited until the last of them were gone before disembarking. He wasn't in the mood to be jostled. Not today.

He thought about it as he walked to the baggage claim area, his carry-on bag slung over his left shoulder, his coat hanging on his arm. The thought of his mother dying . . . it was so damn hard to comprehend. When he thought about how little time he'd spent with her over the past fifteen years, he felt guilty. The logical, rational part of him knew it had been necessary, but he still felt guilty.

Maybe Janet was right, he told himself.

Maybe it's time to slow down.

"How is she?"

"About as well as can be expected." Michael's father, John Callahan, was in his late fifties, a man of average height and build to whom his son bore no resemblance beyond those two factors. "She's trying to be strong, but I can tell the damn illness is taking its toll on her. Her spirits are low."

"Not surprising," Michael said. "They're not going to keep her in the hospital, are they?"

"Not if I have anything to say about it," John said tightly. "She's been through enough. They've already said there's nothing they can do for her, so there's no point. She'll be better off at home when the time comes."

"Surely they can at least give her something for the pain—" Michael began.

"They can," John said darkly, "but after a while, even that won't help."

Michael hesitated. "How long—how long does she have?" he asked, his voice faltering.

"Two months. Or less." John paused. "Probably less."

"We're talking about *weeks*?"

"It's in the most advanced stages, Michael."

"I want to see her. Now."

"I always said I'd have to be at death's door to get you to come home."

His mother was smiling, but Michael could tell she was in a great deal of pain. "Don't even joke about such things," he said stiffly as he bent to kiss her cheek.

"If I don't laugh, Michael, I'll cry."

Mary Margaret Callahan, who had always, as long as her son could remember, been a strong, vital woman, now looked as though death had already claimed her. She was pale and drawn and had lost a great deal of weight. The luxuriant red hair that had gone white in recent years was now thin and stringy. The once sparkling eyes were now lifeless.

It was all Michael could do to keep from crying.

He took her hand. It was cold and limp, and he could feel every bone. "How are you feeling?"

"Better, now that you're here."

He could tell her smile was forced. "Seriously, Mom—are you in much pain?" he asked gently.

She took a deep breath. "I've learned to tolerate it."

He felt like an idiot. He didn't know what to say to his own mother! "How long have you—not been feeling well?" he finally asked. "The truth, I mean."

She thought about it for a moment. "A year, maybe," she said in a low voice.

He told her with a glance that he wasn't convinced.

"A year and a half," she admitted in a barely audible whisper.

"Why in heaven's name did you let it go on so long?" he asked, working to control his voice. "Why didn't you see a doctor?"

"She claimed she didn't have the time," John Callahan answered for her.

"I didn't think it was anything serious," Mary Margaret insisted. "Just old age creeping up on me."

"Listen, I could really use a cup of coffee," Michael said then, needing to get out of that room and feeling like a fool for it. "You want anything, Dad?"

The older man shook his head.

"I'll be right back, then." He gave his mother's hand a little squeeze before walking stiffly to the door. Once outside, with the door closed securely behind him, he sagged against the wall and did something he hadn't done since he was a child.

He cried.

It's funny, Michael thought as he walked around the living room, taking in everything, absently touching all the old, familiar objects. *It's like nothing's changed in thirty years.*

Almost nothing.

He paused at the window, staring for no particular reason at the St. Francis of Assisi birdbath. The bright morning sunlight filtered through the trees, creating a dreamlike effect. *That's it,* Michael thought. *I'm dreaming this. Yeah. This is all a dream.*

"You're up and about early."

Michael turned as his father came into the room. "I was up all night," he said honestly. "Couldn't sleep. I think I wore a hole in the carpet."

"I know, son," John said sympathetically. "I've had a lot of nights like that in the past couple of weeks."

Michael picked up a puffin figurine and fingered it absently. "How long?" he asked. "How long have you known about her?"

"A little over two weeks."

"Why did you wait so long to call me?"

"Your mother didn't want you to know—at first. She didn't want to burden you with it," his father said. "But then she started thinking about it. She knew she didn't have much time, and she was afraid if she didn't tell you, she might not see you again before . . . " His voice trailed off.

Michael nodded, putting the figurine back on the table. "I come home so often," he said with a twinge of sarcasm in his voice.

"She understands about your work, Michael."

"I'm not sure *I* would have understood, Dad," he said evenly, "if she'd died and I hadn't been able to see her again."

"She's always been proud of you."

That's not much consolation at the moment, he was thinking.

He couldn't remember the last time he'd visited the offices of his father's newspaper.

He'd spent his weekends and his afternoons after school there when he was a kid, and he'd always loved it. Watching his father struggle to get that small rural newspaper off the ground had been the root of Michael's own ambitions. It was his father who'd made Michael decide to become a reporter.

"Brings back memories." He sat in his father's chair behind the scarred oak desk that had been old twenty-five years ago when he used to spend most of his free time there.

His father gave him a tired smile. "I remember how you used to hammer out your stories on my old typewriter. You'd have page after page of typos, misspelled words, and lines crossed out, but you were really trying," John recalled. "I always thought when you got out of college, you'd come to work here, with me. This will all be yours one of these days anyway."

Michael nodded. "I thought so, too," he said, "but the more I thought about it, the more I realized I had to know if I could do it on my own, if I could get a paper to hire me even if my father wasn't the publisher and editor-in-chief," he admitted. "I always figured I'd end up coming back one day."

"It just didn't work out that way," John concluded, his disappointment apparent.

"It might still happen, Dad," Michael told him, rising from the chair. "I've been giving a lot of thought to it lately."

"It would certainly make your mother happy," John said. Then he added, "It would make us both happy."

Michael nodded. *He's going to need someone here . . . when it happens.*

Mary Margaret's condition deteriorated much more quickly than even her doctors could have predicted. By the end of that week, her doctors informed John and Michael that her days were numbered.

"It's going to happen," Dr. Webb, her primary physician, told them, "and it looks like it's going to be very soon. If there are other family members to be notified, I suggest you do so quickly."

"I want to take her home," John told him.

The doctor shook his head. "That wouldn't be a good idea—"

"I don't see why not," John said crossly. "You've already admitted there's nothing you can do for her."

"We can make her comfortable. We can give her medication for the pain," Dr. Webb reminded him.

"No matter what you do for her, she won't be as content as she'll be at home," John insisted. "When her time comes, she should have her family around her—not a bunch of anonymous nurses and lab technicians!"

In the end, even medical science couldn't argue with that.

Michael glanced at his watch as he climbed the stairs, a mug of hot chocolate in his hand. *Midnight. God, when was the last time I went to bed—and actually went to sleep—at midnight?* he asked himself.

He paused at the top of the stairs. The door was closed, but he could still hear voices coming from his parents' bedroom. He smiled to himself. *They've still got a great relationship,* he thought. *They still share the same bed.*

"What's the point?" his father was asking. "After all these years, wouldn't it be better not to tell him at all?"

"It's been a lie, John. I can't die with it on my conscience."

"What do you think it's going to do to him when he finds out?"

"He has the right to know the truth."

He who? Michael wondered. *And what does "he" have the right to know?*

"Can't they give her something for the pain?"

John Callahan shook his head. "They've given her all they can outside the hospital's supervision," he said quietly, avoiding his son's eyes.

"Then maybe we should take her back to the hospital," Michael said.

"That's not what she wants."

"Then maybe we should be thinking not about what she wants, but what's best for her," Michael responded sharply. There was a long silence before he said, "I can't stand seeing her like this, Dad."

His father's jaw tightened visibly. "It won't be for much longer."

"She's finally asleep," John announced as he came down the stairs.

Michael was clearing the dinner table. "I don't know how she stands it," he said tightly.

"She doesn't have a hell of a lot of choice." His father started to turn away.

Michael stopped him. "Dad—I overheard you and Mom talking the other night," he began. "I didn't mean to eavesdrop, but I heard her tell you something that didn't make any sense."

His father stiffened. "What did you hear?"

"She said something about telling him—whoever 'he' is— before it was too late. She said she didn't want it on her conscience." He paused. "I don't know why, I can't explain it, but I had this strange feeling it had something to do with me."

John turned to look at Michael. "Why would you think that?" he asked.

The look on his father's face, the sound of his voice told Michael he was on the right track, so he responded with a question of his own: "Does it?"

John was hesitant, and Michael could tell that he'd been tempted, at least for a moment, to lie. Finally he said, "Yes. It was you she was talking about."

Michael wasn't at all sure he wouldn't have preferred to hear a convincing lie. "So," he said, taking a deep breath, "are you going to let me in on it?"

His father nodded slowly. "I told Maggie I was against this," he said quietly, gesturing to Michael to sit down.

Michael pulled up a chair, saying nothing.

John sat down too. "All these years," he began nervously, "and I still don't know quite how to say it."

"The direct approach usually works best," Michael suggested.

"Easier in theory than in practice." John seemed to be considering his options. At last he said, "I'm not your father."

50

Michael felt as though he'd just been slapped. Hard.

"I don't understand," he managed.

"I'm not your father in the biological sense," John was trying to explain. "I've always thought of myself as your father in every other way."

Michael was having a hard time digesting this new reality. "If you're not, then who is?" he asked carefully.

"It's a long story."

"I've got the time."

John drew in a deep breath. "Before your mother and I knew each other, she lived in Chicago. She was married to someone else then—a man named Leonard Rogers who was abusive and drank too much and ran around on her. She was young and frightened—and she had you to think about," he said gravely. "You were just a baby when Rogers landed in some serious trouble—he killed a prostitute he'd been seeing on a regular basis. When he was sentenced to be executed, she took you and left town. She hadn't been in Minneapolis long when I met her, and you were only fourteen months old when we were married."

"My birth certificate says you're my father," Michael remembered.

"I adopted you. Getting a new birth certificate wasn't all that difficult," John said. "For what it's worth, I've always thought of you as my son."

Michael's eyes met his for the first time since the conversation began. "It's worth a lot," he said.

Some things never change.

As a boy, whenever he had a problem or just needed to be alone to think, sitting on the shores of Mille Lacs always seemed to help. Now, when he needed to be alone to think, to deal with this newest blow that had been dealt him in the wake of his mother's impending death, coming here had been an unconscious action.

My mother is dying. My father's not really my father. Amazing how much can happen in two weeks, he thought, staring out at the incredibly calm surface of the lake, illuminated by the bright afternoon sunlight. *In one instant, your life can be irrevocably changed.*

He picked up a small rock and fingered it absently for a moment, then threw it into the water, staring at the ripples it made on the surface of the water as he thought about the conversation he'd had with his father the night before. *My father,* he thought with a twinge of sadness. *Genetics aside, he is still my father. The only father I've ever known.*

So why do I feel such a need to know the truth about the other man my mother married?

"Where have you been?" John demanded the moment Michael walked through the front door. "I've been calling all over town!"

"I had some thinking to do, so I drove out to the lake," Michael said. "Why?"

"Your mother—she's taken a turn for the worse," John told him. "Dr. Webb is with her now."

Michael was suddenly alarmed. "She's not—" he began, unable to finish.

John shook his head. "Not yet," he answered, but the look on his face told Michael it probably wasn't going to be long. "She wants to see you."

Michael nodded. "Now?"

"I think you'd better hurry," his father said.

Michael was overcome by dread as he climbed the stairs. *Is this it?* he asked himself. *What do I do? What do I say?*

He paused outside the bedroom door, not at all sure he was

going to be able to deal with what he knew he would be facing in there. *You're going to be saying good-bye, and you're not going to get another chance.*

Taking a couple of deep breaths, he reached for the knob and opened the door. The first thought that hit him at the sight of his mother, lying there in bed, was that he was too late, that she was already dead. Dr. Webb, sitting in a chair beside the bed, looked up as he entered the room. "Is she—" Michael began hesitantly.

The doctor shook his head. "She's been slipping in and out of consciousness."

"Is she conscious now?" Michael asked.

Webb nodded. "I think she's been waiting for you."

Michael sat in the chair vacated by the doctor and took his mother's hand. It was ice cold. *The chill of death,* he thought. *It's already set in.* Her eyes were closed and she didn't appear to be breathing.

"Can she hear me?" he asked the doctor.

"I think so, yes."

He turned back to his mother. "I'm here, Mom," he said softly. "Can you hear me? Do you know I'm here?"

There was a faint movement of her eyelids, but nothing more. She never opened her eyes, never looked at him, never spoke. Michael refused to give up. He stayed with her, holding her hand, talking to her, driven by the hope that he was somehow reaching her. When her breathing ceased and her heart stopped beating, just after midnight, he was still with her, still holding her hand.

"It's over," the doctor said gently.

"I never got to say good-bye," was all Michael said in response.

The bright, sunny afternoon seemed to mock the group of mourners who had gathered at the small cemetery on the edge of town to say good-bye to Mary Margaret Callahan. Michael sat next to his father, with Janet and the boys behind him, staring in silence as the priest began to speak.

I never got to say good-bye.

Around him, the sounds of muffled sobs rose steadily.

I never got to tell you how much I love you.

His father struggled to maintain his composure.

I never got to tell you how sorry I was that I never got to come home as often as I would have liked.

A woman at the back of the group, someone he didn't even know, began to sob loudly.

Why did you wait so long?

His father's lower lip began to tremble.

Why didn't you tell me the truth before?

His father started to cry, unable to hold it back any longer.

Why did you bother to tell me at all? Wasn't I better off not knowing?

He reached out and took his father's hand.

He's my father. The only one I've ever known.

This is too much to have to deal with at one time.

My mother has just died. I've been told my father isn't really my father.

It makes me wonder who and what I really am.

Michael drove with no particular destination in mind, yet when he ended up at Mille Lacs, he was not surprised. He parked the car, got out, and started to walk, drawn to the lake and the positive memories it held for him. Memories of a happy childhood . . . of family picnics . . . of visits to the Indian reservation . . . of fishing with his father. . . .

My father, he thought sadly. *The only father I've ever known. Yet there are no blood ties between us.*

Does that really matter?

I'd like to think it doesn't.

Apparently it doesn't make any difference to him. He couldn't have been more of a father to me.

But what was my other father like?

What, after all, do I know about him?

He was a drunk. He ran around with whores.

He killed one of them.

He wanted to know the truth, yet he didn't.

He thought about it as he packed his suitcase. He wanted answers, he *needed* answers, but he wasn't sure how he was going to feel, how he was going to react, when he had those answers.

"What's this?"

At the sound of his father's voice, Michael looked up. "Packing," he answered solemnly.

"You're leaving?" John asked, concerned.

"I don't have much choice, Dad. I've already been here three weeks longer than expected," Michael reminded him. "If I stay any longer, I may not have a job to go back to when I get back."

"You could always stay here and work with me at the paper," his father suggested.

Michael hesitated. "Maybe one of these days," he said finally.

"But not now."

There was a long silence as Michael methodically folded his shirts. Finally, his father spoke. "I told her," John said, shaking his head. "I told her no good could possibly come from telling you now, after all these years. I told her it would change everything."

Michael's jaw tightened visibly. "Everything hasn't changed. Just me."

John sat down on the edge of the bed. "How do you figure?"

Michael's laugh was hollow. "Come on—I came here as Michael Callahan, son of the best newspaperman I know. Now, I'm Michael who? My father was a drunkard and—"

"You're a *Callahan*—legally and in every other way that counts," John insisted. "You're as much my son as you'd be if I'd performed the—bodily functions myself!"

Michael shook his head. "Look, Dad, I could never think of anyone but you as my father," he said quietly. "But the reality is there, and now that I know about it, I need answers."

"I understand that, Michael," John told him. "I understand your confusion—you've had a lot to digest all at one time. But do something for me—for yourself—will you?"

Michael looked at him questioningly.

"Don't do anything about it right away. Give yourself some time to think about it," John advised. "Before you go off in search of the truth, make sure you're prepared to accept whatever you might find."

Michael drew in a deep breath. ''Meaning the truth might be too hard to take?''

''Something like that.''

''Tell me, Dad—why didn't Mom ever tell me before?'' He had to know.

John gazed out a window. ''When I met your mother, she was running away,'' he remembered. ''She'd been to hell and back because of that man, and she was reluctant to let herself get involved with someone else. If I hadn't been so determined to win her over, well—'' He gave a little shrug. ''What Maggie wanted, more than anything, was to give you a better life than you would have had if—fate had not provided her with a second chance. When she realized I could not only be a good husband, but a good father as well, and that I loved you as much as if you'd been my own, she reconsidered her position.''

Michael said nothing, waiting for him to go on.

''When we were first married, we agreed we'd never tell you,'' John continued. ''I was your father, and there was no need for you to ever know otherwise.''

''Then she changed her mind,'' Michael concluded.

''When she found out she was dying, she had second thoughts,'' John said. ''She was afraid that, at some point, you might somehow stumble onto the truth. She didn't want to take that chance. She didn't want you to hear it that way. It had to come from us, but when it came right down to it, she couldn't go through with it, so the responsibility fell to me.''

''I wish it could have remained a secret,'' Michael admitted.

''Which is precisely why I'm urging you to not pursue this any further,'' John said, ''until you've given it a great deal of thought.''

Michael stared at him for a moment, then reached out to embrace his father. ''You *are* my father,'' he said, ''in all the ways that count.''

That afternoon, when Michael arrived at the airport, he'd already reached a decision: as much as he would have liked to, there was no way he could close the door on the past, *his* past. He'd been telling the truth when he said John Callahan had been his father in all the ways that mattered—but he also had a lot of questions that needed answers.

He switched his destination from New York to Chicago.

I know his name was Leonard Rogers. I know he was executed in 1937 or 1938. The case would certainly have made headlines.

Thank God for microfilm, he thought as he scanned the library's microfilm records of local newspapers from that time period. *If it was ever in the papers, it can be found at the local public library.*

It took him all morning and part of the afternoon, reviewing the microfilm records until he was bleary-eyed, but he finally found what he was looking for.

When he did, he wished he hadn't.

"Leonard Rogers . . . executed today . . . killed a known prostitute . . . Kathleen Granelli," he read aloud. "Body was found by her son, Frank . . . "

"Dear God," he said aloud, but in a very low voice. It was one thing to learn one's father was not one's *biological* father.

But his biological father was a murderer.

51

New York City, June 1974.

Maria hadn't seen or heard from Michael Callahan since he'd come to her office that January afternoon to talk to her about cooperating with him on that book of his. He'd never even called back to get her answer. She'd often wondered why. For a time she'd considered the possibility that Spence had found out about their meeting and had applied pressure in the appropriate places to make sure it never happened again. It had also occurred to her that the book itself had been scrapped. It had crossed her mind that he might have decided she would not be open enough—or objective enough—to suit his needs.

It hadn't once occurred to her that he hadn't contacted her again because he felt an attraction to her he didn't want to feel.

But that was precisely why he'd never called back.

He felt like an idiot. It had been a long time since he'd felt that kind of attraction to a woman. Under normal circumstances, he would have been thrilled. It had been a long time. Too many years had passed since his divorce. He wasn't, and never had been, a man who liked being alone. He'd always thought of himself as a family man, a husband and a father. In spite of what had happened with Janet, he'd remained optimistic, believing he would eventually remarry. As the years passed, his optimism had waned considerably. Now . . . now that he'd met someone he found attractive, now that he'd found someone he really wanted to get to know better, it was all wrong.

It was wrong because she was Spencer Randall's daughter. It was wrong for a lot of reasons and right for none. And still, the attraction was there. Even when she was a teenager, when he'd visited the Randalls in Connecticut, he'd thought her attractive.

That was why he'd never contacted her again. He figured he'd be pretty transparent, that what he was feeling would be obvious to her, and he didn't want her to see it. No . . . that was the last thing he wanted. He could imagine her reaction. She'd probably laugh. That wouldn't surprise him at all.

Yes, he thought, *she'd have a good laugh over that one.*

But their paths did cross again. It was inevitable.

"I was surprised to hear from you," Maria told him. "When you didn't call me again, I assumed you'd given up on the idea of doing the book."

Michael shook his head. "I've been out of town. Family matter." He didn't want to get into it further with her.

"You're aware, of course, that my father will do everything in his power to prevent anyone you might approach—including me—from giving you their cooperation," she reminded him.

"I first met your father almost fifteen years ago, Miss Randall," he said. "I'd think he was ill if he didn't put up a good fight." *Why did I say that?* he wondered, feeling like kicking himself. *Why the hell did I remind her I've known her father for almost fifteen years?*

"Please—call me Maria," she was saying.

"Only if you'll call me Michael."

"Of course." She paused thoughtfully. "I'll talk to you on one condition."

"And that is?"

"I want approval of anything you write."

He wasn't sure his publisher would agree, but he said, "You've got yourself a deal."

Maria called two days later and invited him to lunch.

At first he was going to refuse. He fumbled for an excuse but, unable to come up with a believable one, finally accepted her invitation.

"I'll have my secretary make a reservation," she told him. "Do you have a preference?"

"Someplace small and private." Realizing how that probably sounded to her, he was instantly embarrassed. "I meant only that—"

She laughed. "Don't qualify it. You'll ruin everything between us." She paused. "How's Pete's Tavern at twelve-thirty? We won't even need a reservation."

Maria Randall at Pete's Tavern? Michael laughed aloud at the thought. "You're full of surprises, lady," he told her. "I would never in a million years have imagined you among the regulars at Pete's."

"Why not?"

"Well, I don't know. I could see you at Lutèce or the Four Seasons or—"

She laughed again. "I think you're reading me all wrong, Callahan. We'll have to do something about that."

* * *

He hung up and went straight to the men's room.

Looking at himself in the mirror, he saw a man who still looked pretty good, still trim, fit, and in good health. He also saw a man who'd harbored many insecurities about his desirability to women.

He did not see a man who could attract a woman like Maria Randall.

Maria couldn't remember when she'd enjoyed being with anyone so much.

Michael made her laugh with amusing anecdotes about his experiences as a reporter. They shared an appetizer, a platter of potato skins loaded with cheese and sour cream, and they were so caught up in their conversation that they never got around to ordering a main course.

"Did you ever want to be anything but reporter?" she asked, licking melted cheese off her fingers.

"I suppose I did at some point in my life, but I can't remember what it was," he admitted, reaching for his drink. He talked about how much he enjoyed studying journalism, and about his first job in Kansas City on the *Sun-Times*.

It wasn't until they left the restaurant that either of them realized they hadn't discussed the book at all.

They fell into the habit of meeting for lunch two or three times a week, whenever they were both free. Michael and Maria were well aware that they came from different worlds, and were surprised and delighted that they could find so much to talk about.

When is he going to ask me out? Maria wondered.

So how do I make the first move? Michael asked himself. *What if she laughs? What do I do then?*

I think I'm falling in love with her, God help me.

"Just what the hell do you think you're doing?" Spence demanded angrily.

"Calm down, Spence—" Maria began.

"Calm down, my ass!" he snapped. "I just found out my daughter—the one person in the world I thought would always be loyal to me—has been seeing Michael Callahan! How do you expect me to calm down?''

"I'm not seeing him! He's writing another book, and—"

"And you're helping him with the goddamned book!"

"Isn't that better than having him talk to a lot of people who'd tell him God only knows what?" she asked.

"No, dammit, it's not!" he said crossly. "You're my daughter, and I don't want you to have anything to do with that man! Do you hear me?"

"Perfectly," Maria said calmly, "but I'm afraid that's not going to be possible."

He turned to face her. "What's that supposed to mean?"

"I like him, Spence," she confessed. "I've come to care a great deal for him."

His eyes narrowed suspiciously. "You're sleeping with him, aren't you?"

Now *she* was angry too. "That's none of your business!"

"The hell it isn't! I'm your father!"

"And I'm twenty-four years old—too old for you to be choosing the men in my life!"

"You *are* sleeping with him!"

"What if I am?" she shot back.

"You'd better understand now that you can't have it both ways," he warned. "Him or me—not both!" He turned and walked out of the office, slamming the door in his wake.

Not until he was gone did she begin to cry. She'd never gone against her father before, and it hurt. It hurt terribly.

But she was falling in love with Michael.

It took her two months to get him to come to her apartment. After dinner was prepared, she gave her maid the night off and made sure the woman was gone before Michael arrived.

It was a pleasant evening in spite of Michael's insistence that they discuss the book. "Wouldn't want you to waste an entire evening," he said half-jokingly.

"I don't consider it a waste at all," she said. But she was thinking, *Do you, Michael? Do you feel you're wasting the evening?*

After dinner, she suggested they have a drink in the library. He was visibly surprised when she settled down close to him on the midnight-blue velvet couch. "I've tried to be patient, Michael," she began, "but I'm not a patient woman by nature."

He gave her a quizzical look.

"How long have we been—well, seeing each other now?"

"Uh, since June. Why?"

"We seem to be hitting it off so well, and yet you've never asked me out. I can't help wondering why not."

He laughed nervously. "Come on, Maria—I'm too old for you!"

"Numbers are only important to me in the office," she said stubbornly. "I wouldn't care if you were two hundred."

"Compared to you, honey, I might as well be two hundred."

"Don't be silly." She kissed him long and hard—and though he tried not to, he felt himself responding.

"We shouldn't—"

"Make love to me, Michael," she whispered. "Please—"

As his hand moved down her arm, he suddenly realized she'd somehow managed to peel the top of her pine-green silk dress down to her waist while they were kissing. Now, the fullness of her exposed breast pressed against his hand.

I'm done for, he thought.

He lowered her to the couch, kissing her as he stroked her breasts. She pushed the dress down over her hips—he realized then she hadn't been wearing anything underneath—as he bent his head to kiss her breasts.

He ripped the dress in an attempt to get it out of the way and popped three buttons off his own shirt in his rush to get undressed. He took her swiftly, maybe too swiftly.

"I wanted to do this right," he told her, holding her close afterward. "I wanted it to be slow and sweet, but I thought I was going to explode."

She stroked his chest. "It's all right," she assured him. "Next time."

I am done for, he thought.

52

Maria had hoped her father would come around and accept her relationship with Michael, but so far he hadn't. He hadn't disowned her, as she'd once thought he might, but their relationship hadn't been the same since he found out about them.

She'd tried to convince her father that a book—an *authorized* biography—was really a good idea. But Spence had been stubborn about it.

It just doesn't make sense, she thought. *Why is he so obsessive about it?*

"Randall's managed to throw up a roadblock at every turn," Michael told his publisher. "Nobody who knows him will even take my calls."

"What about his daughter?"

He hesitated momentarily. "I've talked to her, yes."

"Rumor has it you've been doing more than talking."

"That's nobody's business," Michael said defensively.

"Do whatever you want with her, as long as you're doing what you've been paid to do. What else do you have on the agenda?"

"Possibly a trip to Boston," Michael suggested. "Nobody's ever done any real digging there. He was in the Navy during World War Two. I might look into that, too."

Unless Randall's got his roadblocks there as well, he thought.

"When are you going to make an honest woman of me?" Maria asked in bed one night.

He kissed her hair. "I thought the modern, liberated woman didn't need marriage to be fulfilled and happy."

"That's what I thought, too," she said, stroking his chest, "but I was wrong."

"Maria—"

Her eyes met his. "I love you, Michael."

"And I love you. But—"

"We're practically living together now. We might as well be married," she reasoned.

"There's a world of difference between being married and *practically* living together," he pointed out.

"I want to be married to you. I thought that's what you wanted, too." She sounded hurt.

"Maria, you only think you want to be married to me—now," he said gently. "But you're still young. I'm thirty-six. What happens when you wake up one morning and decide you don't want to be tied to an old man anymore?"

"You're not an old man—and I'll never get tired of you," she insisted, snuggling against him.

He held her close. *If only I could believe that,* he thought sadly. It wasn't the age difference that bothered him, not really. It was the fact that she was Randall's daughter, that she seemed to be rebelling against her father by seeing him. Would she still want him when she no longer felt a need to rebel?

He wondered.

SPENCE
and
MICHAEL
1974

53

Michael was no longer sure he wanted to do the book.

And it wasn't just because of Maria, because of his relationship with her. In more ways than one, he'd come back from Minnesota a different man. *I'm not Michael Callahan, he thought. I'm somebody named Michael Rogers, and I'm not at all sure who that man's father is. I just know Leonard Rogers was a man—but not much of a man—who drank too much and liked to beat up hookers. Liked it so much he killed one of them.*

Stop it! he ordered himself. *You can't change the reality, so you're just going to have to live with it.*

"What, exactly, is the problem, Michael?"

His publisher's voice brought him back to the present abruptly. "What?" he asked, slightly embarrassed that he hadn't heard what Mason had said the first time.

"I asked what the problem is with the book," George Mason repeated patiently, clearly puzzled by Michael's preoccupied state.

"The problem is the subject himself," Michael answered. "Trying to get information on Spencer Randall is like trying to get a bunch of two-bit hoods to blow the whistle on a Mafia kingpin. Nobody wants to talk. They're all scared to death of him."

Mason smiled. "Don't tell me you're getting cold feet—not you, of all people."

Michael hesitated. "It's been a bad year, George," he said evasively. *What else could I say?* "Well, George, it's like this: It's been a hell of a year. My mother died, and my* *father's not really my father—my father, it turns out, is some SOB who got the death penalty for having a little too much to drink and getting a little too rough with his favorite whore. Oh, and by the way—I'm sleeping with Randall's daughter. You understand how this could complicate things, don't you?"*

"Yes, of course," Mason was saying. "I'm sorry about your mother."

"Thanks." *We're saying all the right words, but do they really mean anything?* Michael suddenly found himself analyzing everything. *Why?* he wondered idly.

"I'm sure we could arrange an extension on your deadline—"

"That would help, yes," Michael heard himself saying. "I *have* been thinking about going back to the beginning—all the way back. Going back to his childhood, if I can . . ."

"The man is using you!" Spence roared. "Can't you see that?"

"You're so blinded by your hatred of his profession that you can't see what a truly fine man he is," Maria maintained. "As I recall, you thought a great deal of him when you thought he was a down-on-his-luck novelist."

"He couldn't even level with me about who he really was," Spence growled.

"Would you have given him the time of day if you had known he was a newspaper reporter?" Maria asked dubiously.

"Hell, no!"

"Then why does it surprise you that he kept it from you?"

"It doesn't—now that I know what his game really was," Spence responded without hesitation.

"And it's never occurred to you that, job or no job, he might have actually *liked* you?" she asked.

"No—and I doubt it ever occurred to him, either."

"Spencer Randall's the worst kind of SOB there is," Michael told Mason.

Mason grinned. "I take it this is the voice of experience speaking."

Michael nodded. "I'd say there's enough history between us to qualify me as an expert," he said.

"Which is exactly why you're the best man to do this book," Mason pointed out.

"And why Randall will stop at nothing to prevent this book from being written," Michael warned.

"I'm telling you, the bastard can't be trusted," Spence insisted, his irritation at his daughter increasing by the minute. "He'll stop at nothing to bury me."

"Including using your daughter?" Maria suggested.

"Yes. Including using my own daughter."

"So—you don't think it's possible he could be attracted to me for myself?" Maria asked, her own voice rising angrily.

"Callahan? Hell, no!"

"Well, thank you very much!" Maria snapped, her pride wounded. "That's just what a woman needs to hear from a man—especially her own father!"

"Oh, come on—you know I've never thought any man was good enough for you," he said in an attempt to cajole her. "Least of all a bum like Callahan—"

"Who couldn't possibly find me attractive," Maria cut him off crossly.

"I didn't say that!"

"You most certainly did!"

"Well, dammit, I didn't mean it!" he said, irritated. "I meant that Callahan isn't above using you to get to me—and that doesn't have a damn thing to do with your attractiveness."

"It just has to do with you, is that it?"

His eyes met hers. "It has to do with revenge."

"Revenge?" Mason asked.

Michael smiled wryly. "Right after the first book came out," he said, "he promised me he'd get me, one way or another. Told me I'd better keep looking over my shoulder. He's been out to nail my ass ever since."

"That worries you?"

"Hell, no," Michael replied with a chuckle. "But it has certainly made things interesting, especially since word got out that I've been signed to do this book."

"He's quite an interesting character, no doubt about that," Mason observed with mild amusement.

"Well, I'll soon find out if he was always such an interesting character," Michael said then. "I figured rather than get some more doors slammed in my face over at Randall International, I'd start at the logical place."

"Which is?"

"The beginning. Randall's beginning, that is."

"You're definitely going to Boston?" Mason asked.

Michael nodded. "It seems like a good place to start."

"Think you'll find anything worthwhile?"

"I think," Michael began carefully, "that going back to his roots will tell me why Randall's the man he is today."

Word has it Callahan's digging into my—Spencer's—background. The more he digs, the more likely he is to uncover things I can't afford to have uncovered.

Can't let that happen.

Spence was alone in his office overlooking lower Manhattan, pondering his situation with Callahan—and with Maria. He had a score to settle with Callahan, now more than ever.

The son of a bitch is coming between me and my daughter, he thought angrily.

That's the worst mistake he could have made.

So . . . do I tell Maria what I'm going to do, or not?

Michael thought about it as he stood on the corner of Thirty-sixth and Madison in the pouring rain, trying in vain to hail a taxi. *She knows I'm doing the book. It's not as though I've been trying to hide it from her.*

She knows about the book. We just don't talk about it.

Not anymore.

How do I stop him?

Spence thought about it. *What can I do to impede his progress that I haven't done already?*

Buy his publishing company?
Order a contract hit on him?

Then it came to him. He picked up the phone and dialed a number he'd memorized long ago. It was answered on the second ring.

"Yeah—it's me. I've got a job for you."

54

"I wish I knew what you're thinking right now."

Maria snuggled against Michael and drew the sheet up to cover both of them. He was lying on his back, one arm behind his head and the other around her. "What makes you think I'd be thinking about anything or anyone but you?" he asked, smiling contentedly.

"Call it a hunch." She stroked his chest, making small, circular movements with her fingertips.

"Men have hunches," he told her. "With women it's intuition."

"That's sexist!" she retorted in mock anger. Then she said, in a much more subdued tone, "I'm going to miss you."

"You think I won't miss you?"

She kissed his chin. "Will you?"

"Of course."

"How long are you going to be away?" she asked then.

"I don't know exactly," he answered honestly. "A week, maybe a little longer."

"Must be a big story."

"It is." He paused for a long moment. "But it's not for the *Times*."

Maria stopped what she was doing. "The book?" she asked hesitantly.

He nodded.

"You're going to Boston to look into my father's background.'' She sat up in bed, pushing her long hair back off her face with one hand. ''I should have realized when you said you were going to Boston—''

''I thought you'd accepted the idea of me doing this book.'' He wished she'd cover herself. She was making it hard for him to think clearly.

''I've accepted it,'' she said quietly. ''Accepting it doesn't mean I like it.''

''Maria, I signed a contract. I have to write the book,'' he reminded her.

''I hate being caught in the middle,'' she complained. ''I hate being torn between you and my father.''

''Maybe you're going to have to choose between us,'' he said, thinking: *Better now than later, after we're married.*

''My father thinks you're out to get him,'' Maria said then, ignoring his suggestion.

''Your father thinks everyone's out to get him—every reporter, that is.'' He switched on the bedside lamp.

''He thinks you're only doing this for revenge,'' Maria said.

''Revenge?'' Michael laughed aloud at the thought. ''Look, I know you love your father, but the man is paranoid! He's the one who's been out for revenge. Ever since I wrote that first book, he's been out to nail my ass. I'm not out to get him—he's the one who's after me!''

''Then why the book—'' Maria began.

''My publisher came to me—I didn't propose it to him,'' he told her. ''It was the publisher's idea, not mine.''

''You're telling me you wouldn't have done this book on your own?'' she asked.

''No,'' he answered honestly. *I have enough problems.*

The ship was sinking.

The light from the fires burning aboard the cruiser seemed more brilliant somehow against the black night sky. He could hear the voices crying for help, but there was nothing he could do . . . nothing. . . .

Then he was back in that dreary little apartment in Chicago, standing by the bed, staring down at his mother. Only it was Spencer Randall looking back at him, burned almost beyond recognition, looking up at him as the last breath slipped from his body. . . .

He was looking in a mirror, only it was Spencer's face looking back at him, and then the mirror shattered into a million pieces. Beyond it, he could see his mother's face as it had looked that night, pale and bruised. Lifeless. He could hear her voice saying, "There are times I wish I were dead . . . wish I were dead . . . wish I were dead . . ."

He was holding the ice pick in his hand, and he was crying as he drove it into her chest with all the strength he could summon up. He closed his eyes tightly, willing the tears to stop. Willing them both to finally be at peace.

When he opened his eyes again, it was Spencer Randall lying on the bed, soaked in blood. . . .

Spence woke with a start. He sat up in bed, soaked with his own perspiration. *It's been a long time,* he thought. *The ghosts haven't been around for a while.*

They were back now because of his old friend Michael Callahan.

He's got to be stopped, Spence thought. *No matter what it takes, he's got to be stopped.*

Once and for all.

Spencer Randall's one ruthless SOB, no doubt about it.

Michael lay awake, thinking about it. He remembered that day in the bar as clearly as if it had been yesterday, rather than seven years ago. The man had threatened him. It had been a very clear, unmistakable threat.

He's the one who wants blood. Mine.

He turned over to face Maria. He loved her. It had taken him a long time after Janet to fall in love again, but here he was, in love with the only daughter of a powerful, vengeful man who was bent on destroying him.

I couldn't have fallen for one of the salesgirls at Bloomie's, he thought. *That would have been too simple.*

I had to fall for Spencer Randall's daughter.

He'd not only fallen in love with her, he wanted to marry her, but he knew Randall wasn't going to let that happen. *The man would do anything to prevent it—including murder,* Mi-

chael thought with certainty. *He'd kill me before he would
allow me to marry her.*

And this book is only going to make a bad situation worse.

When the sun rose over the East River, Spence was sitting in
the same chair where he'd spent most of the night, staring
out the window without really seeing anything.

Something has to be done, he thought. *Callahan has to be
stopped before it's too late. Before he ruins everything I've
worked for.*

Before he exposes me.

"I'll drive you to the airport," Maria offered.

Michael, facing the mirror over the bureau, knotted his tie.
"I thought you had a meeting scheduled for this morning."

"I do, but I can reschedule it," she said. "Who's going to
reprimand me for it? My father owns the company."

He smiled. "Never heard you talk like that before," he
said casually.

"I've never been in love before," she responded.

He gave a little chuckle. "You still love me after last
night?"

She got off the bed and crossed the room to wrap her arms
around him. "I'd love you no matter what," she said softly,
pressing her mouth to his in a long, lingering kiss.

I must be nuts to go to Boston and leave her now, he
thought, more aroused at the moment than was wise, under
the circumstances.

Finally, she pulled away. "I suppose I'd better get
dressed," she said, pressing a finger to his lips, "if I'm going
to drive you to the airport. I *do* love long good-byes."

"Me, too," Michael agreed. *Unless they're the permanent
kind.*

"It's been a long time, Andy, old pal, but I have a feeling
you've been expecting me."

It was still early, so there weren't many people hanging
around St. Patrick's Cathedral when Spence arrived. He went,
virtually unnoticed by the few people who were there, straight
to the altar of St. Andrew. "I guess you know what's been

going on here." He paused. "If this guy manages to put all the pieces together, it's all over."

He started lighting the candles, slowly, methodically. "I can't let that happen. I have to stop him, no matter what it takes," he went on. "That's why I'm here, Andy, old pal. I need your help. I need you to put in a good word for me with your boss." He put a hundred-dollar bill in the box, then, after a momentary hesitation, put in four more.

It's a small price to pay for my immortal soul, he was thinking.

55

Boston, November 1974.

Michael checked into the Sheraton Boston before noon, and before he even took time to unpack, he started making all the necessary phone calls, setting up appointments with anyone and everyone who knew Spencer Randall. For some reason, it brought back memories of another place—the first time he'd traveled on a story. *Fourteen years ago—New York,* he thought. *Spencer Randall. And today, the man is still news.*

My life would be a hell of a lot easier if he weren't.

Who am I kidding? My life would be a hell of a lot easier if Spencer Randall weren't Spencer Randall. Period.

After the last of the calls had been made and meetings scheduled, Michael turned his attention to unpacking. He hadn't been sure exactly how long he was going to be in Boston, so he'd brought enough clothing for a week. He hung his suits in the closet, put his shaving kit in the bathroom, and everything else went into the bureau drawers. He'd traveled so much over the past fourteen years, done this so many times, it was almost a reflex action, which was fortunate, since at the moment his mind was not on unpacking.

He was thinking about Maria.

It's getting harder and harder to leave her, he thought, remembering how difficult it had been to say good-bye at the airport. *There was a time I hated saying good-bye to Janet, too,* he recalled. *Except toward the end. Then it was a blessing, just to be able to get away from the constant arguing, even for a few days.*

But that was a long time ago. Another woman. Another marriage. And I've been alone far too long. It's time for a fresh start, now that I've found the right woman—even if Spencer Randall is her father.

When I get back to New York, I'm going to ask her to marry me.

New York City.

"I think Michael's going to ask me to marry him."

Maria was alone in her office, talking to her mother on the phone while enjoying the view of the twin towers of the World Trade Center afforded by having a corner office with floor-to-ceiling windows. She leaned back in her red suede executive chair, twisting the telephone cord absently as she talked. "I wouldn't be at all surprised if he proposes when he comes back from Boston."

"Before you say yes, darling, be sure it's what you really want," Anne cautioned.

Maria laughed. "You sound like an overprotective mother," she pointed out, amused.

"I was thinking of your father," Anne explained. "The bitterness Spence feels toward Michael Callahan runs very deep. I just don't like the idea of you being caught in the middle of their private war."

"But Michael isn't at war with anyone, Mother," Maria told her. "He's simply doing his job."

"Your father doesn't see it that way," Anne said, the concern in her voice unconcealed. "He once thought of Michael as a friend—possibly his only friend. He saw the deception as a betrayal of that friendship, and you know your father. He doesn't forgive and he never forgets."

Greenwich.

You screwed the wrong person, pal. Sooner or later, you're going to have to pay a price for it.

Spence sat in an armchair in his study, staring at the photograph on the flyleaf of Michael Callahan's most recent book. *I should stop playing these stupid games with you and put an end to your snooping.*

And get you out of my daughter's life once and for all.

The phone rang then, his private line, the one no one else was permitted to answer. He picked it up on the second ring, knowing before he did who was calling.

"Yeah."

"It's me."

"Big surprise," Spence growled. "So what have you got for me?"

"He's in Boston. Mean anything to you?"

"If it did, it wouldn't be any of your goddamned business," Spence snapped. "You're paid to follow him, not to speculate. Got it?"

"Loud and clear."

"So what's he doing?"

"Nothing that could be considered life-threatening. He went to some residential area, definitely upper class, and talked to some people. Visited a high school. No big deal."

"Call me tomorrow." Without waiting for a response, Spence hung up.

So, Callahan . . . what is it you're looking for?

Boston.

How could I have been so damn stupid?

Why didn't I think of this before? Michael wondered, irritated with himself for not having come up with the idea sooner. He was sitting alone at a table in the student library at the high school Spencer Randall had attended, scanning the photographs in a stack of yearbooks dating from 1932 to 1941. He stopped at 1941 because he knew that Randall had entered the Navy at the beginning of World War II.

He located two photos, one taken when Randall was sixteen and one from a year later. Something about those photographs

bothered Michael. He couldn't quite put his finger on it, but
staring at the lean, lanky kid in the yearbooks brushed him
with a faint sense of unease. *Why?* he asked himself. He could
see the man in the face of the boy, and yet he couldn't. Something was missing, but Michael couldn't pinpoint exactly
what it was. The features, the coloring, it was all there—but
something definitely *wasn't.*

Am I imagining things? he asked himself. *Am I just looking
for something and wanting it so badly that I'm seeing things
that aren't really there? Do I want to bury Randall so badly
that it's come to this? Is Maria right about this feud?*

He stared at the yearbook photos for a long time, recalling
all the conversations he'd had with people from Randall's
past—neighbors, schoolteachers, classmates—the things
they'd had to say about the young Spencer Randall. Things
that had taken Michael by surprise. . . .

*"He was a quiet boy, stayed to himself most of the time
. . . a real mama's boy, that one."*

Michael couldn't imagine Randall ever being the clinging
type, even as a child. Too farfetched. Too much out of character. *Nobody changes that much,* he thought.

*"He was an awkward, clumsy kind of kid. Twelve years
old and still hadn't gotten the hang of riding a bicycle."*

In his mind, Michael saw Spence playing polo—the perfect
coordination, the physical strength and skill, the consummate
athlete. *Nobody changes that much.*

*"He was a good student. Better in some subjects than in
others, of course—never did well in math, though, and that
disappointed his father. He really hoped the boy would follow
in his footsteps."*

Michael frowned. The Randall he knew was a math whiz.
He could crunch numbers in his head with incredible speed,
whether the numbers were stock market reports, bank bal-
ances, or odds on the daily double. *Nobody changes that
much.*

"He was a good boy. Not much of a risk taker, though."

Spencer Randall? Michael almost laughed aloud at the
thought.

He studied the photos again. *The eyes . . . the eyes are different somehow,* he thought. *The mouth, too. The way he
smiles. It's not right.*

In spite of the familiarity, he felt as though he were looking into the face, the eyes of a stranger.

Why? he asked himself again. *Why are all of my instincts telling me something's amiss when most of the physical evidence says otherwise?*

Most. That's the key word.

"*My ship went down in the South Pacific east of the Philippines. We were attacked by a submarine.*"

Michael remembered vividly the night Randall told him about his stint in the Navy, about the night his ship was sunk.

"*When I came around, I was in a military hospital—I'd been pretty badly burned. I had to have extensive plastic surgery.*"

It made sense, yet as he sat there staring at the black-and-white photographs in the yearbooks, he found himself wondering if Randall was telling the truth. *Still,* he thought, *it's easier to swallow than the alternative.*

That the Randall I know isn't the real Randall.

New York City.

"Yeah. Right. No—I don't want you to do anything. Not yet, anyway. Just stay with him. I want to know every move he makes, everyone he talks to. I want every detail, got it?" There was a steadily intensifying irritation in his voice. "I'll expect to hear from you on a daily basis. No, dammit—that's what I'm paying you for!"

Spence slammed down the phone. *Why the hell am I playing games with this bastard?* he asked himself.

Boston.

That's pretty farfetched, Michael thought.

But two days after the notion first occurred to him that Randall might be an imposter, he was still checking out all the possibilities.

He talked to the people he'd spoken with when he'd researched the first book—those who were still around, anyway. A few of them had since taken up residence in the local cemeteries. He also talked to a number of locals he'd missed the first time around. Those who remembered Spencer Randall—the kid didn't seem to have had too many friends, and even fewer knew him well—remembered him as a shy, quiet, even bookish young man who pretty much stayed to himself.

Not the Randall I know. Again, Michael was brushed by a sense of unease. *Randall is reclusive, sure, but shy? Anything but!*

Why would anyone want to pose as Spencer Randall? What reason could there be? It just doesn't make sense. Before the war, he was a quiet, unremarkable kid—it was the man who returned from the South Pacific who became a living legend.

The man who might be an impostor.

If his suspicion was correct, if Randall was an impostor, Michael knew the only way he'd be able to make any sense of it would be to find out his real identity.

What would prompt a man—any man—to assume a new identity? A new life? The possibilities that immediately came to mind were unthinkable.

Washington, D.C.

Anne was worried about her daughter.

She knew only too well what it was like to be caught in the cross fire between Spence and one of his adversaries, and being caught between Spence and Michael Callahan had to be hell. *It's worse since it's Michael,* Anne thought. *He once considered Michael a friend. Now he's a friend who committed the unpardonable sin. Betrayal. I wonder how Spence is dealing with the idea of Maria being in love with the man he considers his worst enemy?*

Probably with his usual ill-tempered lack of reason.

If Maria weren't involved, Anne would have found the situation amusing. *Knowing Spence, he's probably been breathing fire ever since he found out Maria was seeing the man,* Anne suspected.

"Oh, Spence," she said aloud. "I hope you're not going to let that foolish pride of yours come between you and Maria the way you let your stubbornness come between us."

His stubbornness and my foolish pride, she admitted, but only to herself.

In the years since their divorce, Anne's life had been incredibly full, but had been so focused on her career, it had left no time for a social life. Not that she'd minded. She hadn't met anyone she'd *want* to share a so-called social life with. Oh, plenty of attractive, interesting men had passed through her life via the Justice Department, but—

God help me, she thought, *none of them measured up to Spence.*

New York City.

Lately, Spence had been thinking about Anne. A lot.

Even more than was usual.

Maybe it's the feeling of impending doom. The last wish of a condemned man, he thought as he leaned back in his chair, studying the silver-framed photograph of his ex-wife he still kept on his desk. *Of all the mistakes I've made in my life, Anne, letting you go was the worst.*

And the only one I haven't been able to correct.

Washington, D.C.

Anne was roused from a sound sleep by the insistent ringing of the telephone. She rolled over in bed and looked at the alarm clock on the nightstand—then did a double take, certain she'd read it wrong. *Three-thirty? Who on earth would call at this hour, unless—*

Suddenly afraid and fully alert, she grabbed the phone. "Hello?" she gasped into the receiver.

"Hi, doll."

"Spence?"

"Oh—so you *do* still remember my voice!"

"Is something wrong? Is Maria—"

"Maria's fine," he assured her. "Or as fine as she *can* be, given the company she's keeping these days."

She ignored his sarcasm. "If she's all right, then why are you calling—" she began, relieved but confused.

"I just needed to hear your voice, doll."

"Needed to hear my voice? Spencer, do you know what time it is?" she asked, annoyed.

"It's three-thirty-five. Why?"

"Why? Don't you ever sleep?" She was now fully awake. "Or have you discovered a way to do without it so you can work round the clock?"

"I just missed you, doll. That's all."

"Jesus, Spencer—"

"I guess this was a mistake, huh?" He seemed suddenly subdued. "I couldn't get you off my mind. I just wanted to hear your voice. My apologies for having disturbed you—"

She knew he was about to hang up. "Spence—wait!" she stopped him.

"Yeah?"

"I—uh—" The words stuck in her throat. She couldn't tell him what she was feeling. *After all this time, what's the point?* "Nothing. Nothing important," she insisted.

"Right."

The receiver clicked in her ear. She stared at it for a long moment before finally putting it back on its cradle.

"I *do* still love you," she said softly, "I just can't live with you. But I can't very well tell you that, can I?"

Boston.

When he left Boston at the end of the week, having exhausted all possible sources of information there, Michael had compiled a list of others to be checked out:

Washington, D.C.—Department of the Navy

Pearl Harbor Naval Base

Veterans Administration

Private investigators—get recommendations

Michael studied the list he'd scribbled in his pocket-size notebook, as the 727 taxied down the runway and lifted off smoothly. Then he flipped the notebook shut and tucked it into his breast pocket.

I sure as hell can't tell Maria any of this. He couldn't tell anyone. Not yet. It was only a hunch, a gut feeling: he couldn't even explain, exactly, *why* he felt the way he did.

I have no proof yet, he thought, *but if it's there, I'll find it. Somehow.*

His reporter's instinct told him he was onto something big.

56

New York City, November 1974.

It won't be long now.

Maria twisted the gold watch bracelet on her wrist thoughtfully. When Michael called, he said his flight would be arriving at four-thirty. It was three-forty-five now. *Maybe I'll surprise him, pick him up at the airport,* she thought. *He said he wanted to talk to me about something important. It can't be soon enough as far as I'm concerned. Maybe—* On an impulse, she buzzed her secretary.

"Yes, Miss Randall?"

"Christie, I'm going to be leaving momentarily," she told the other woman. "I'll need you to make a reservation for me for dinner."

"Where and what time?"

Maria thought about it. "Lutèce. Eight o'clock," she said finally. "The reservation will be for two."

"I'll take care of it," the secretary assured her.

"Thank you." Then, at the last minute, she reconsidered. "No. Scratch that. No reservation."

"Perhaps somewhere else—"

"No. That's all right, Christie. I'll take care of it myself."

We have to go somewhere special tonight, she thought as she put on her coat. *Somewhere that holds a special meaning for both of us.*

We'll go to Pete's Tavern.

Washington, D.C.

Anne wished she knew what was going on inside her ex-husband's head. *Why did he call me in the middle of the night?* she wondered. *No matter what he said, Spence isn't*

*the kind of man to call me or anyone else in the middle of
the night just to tell me he's been thinking about me. He'd
consider it a sign of weakness.* She recalled what he'd said
the night he called, how he'd sounded.

Are you in some kind of trouble, Spence? she wondered.

New York City.

"If you weren't the boss's daughter you probably would have
gotten a pink slip by now," Michael teased, putting his arm
around Maria as they walked through the busy main terminal
at La Guardia Airport.

"I carry my share of the executive workload," she responded with mock self-righteousness, "even if I do play
hooky from time to time."

"But being a Randall doesn't hurt, does it?"

"Don't press your luck, Callahan, or I won't spring for
dinner."

He raised an eyebrow. "Oh? Where are you taking me?"
he wanted to know. "Lutèce?"

"No."

"Four Seasons?"

"Wrong."

"The Rainbow Room?"

"Guess again."

"Il Mulino?"

"Three strikes. You're out." She gave him a playful peck
on the cheek. "It's just as well. I wasn't going to tell you,
anyway."

"Why not?"

"I want to surprise you."

As they headed for the parking garage, they were so absorbed in each other, neither of them saw the man who'd
approached them at the baggage carousel and had been following them ever since.

Washington, D.C.

I must be out of my mind, Anne thought.

She boarded the plane bound for New York and found her

seat. Once settled in, she attempted to read the copy of *The Washington Post* she'd brought along but found she was too distracted to concentrate. *Why am I doing this?* she asked herself. *He's not my problem anymore. We're divorced. We've been divorced for years.*

The answer was simple, but she didn't like to admit it, even to herself: She still loved him.

I must be out of my mind.

New York City.

"I should have known this was what you had in mind," Michael said, taking a bite of his lasagna. "I'm surprised you remembered."

Maria laughed. "*I'm* surprised *you* remembered," she retorted. "Men are the ones who generally forget things like birthdays and anniversaries and locations of first dates—"

"It wasn't really a date," he pointed out.

"It was as far as I was concerned," she insisted.

"Have it your way," he said with a grin. "I'm still surprised you remembered."

"You said we had something important to discuss tonight," she reminded him. "I thought this would be the appropriate place to do it."

"Very perceptive. How did you know I was going to ask you to marry me?" *Damn!* he thought. *Why did I say that?*

Maria was looking at him, not saying a word, just smiling. Her face seemed to be glowing—or was it just the candlelight?

You idiot! He gave himself a mental wrist slapping. *How could you just blurt it out like that? You were supposed to wait for just the right moment, choose all the right words—*

It made him think of the first time they made love.

"Do you want an answer, or not?"

Maria's words cut through his thoughts. "What?" he asked, flustered.

"You popped the question," she reminded him. "Do you want an answer or not?"

"I had it all figured out. I knew exactly how I was going to ask, what I was going to say," he admitted. "So much for good intentions." He reached across the table and took her hand. "I've really botched things up. I hope you won't hold it against me."

She smiled. "Would I do that?"

"Sure you would. You're—" He stopped himself. If he'd said, *you're Spencer Randall's daughter*, it would have ruined everything. "You're unpredictable," he quickly censored himself.

"Then you couldn't have guessed I'd say yes?" she asked.

He looked at her. "Are you serious?"

She gave a little laugh. "It wasn't much of a proposal, Callahan, but the way I see it, it's probably the best I'm going to get from you," she reasoned. "And since you *are* worth certain concessions—"

"Is that a yes?" he wanted to know.

"That's a yes."

"You're sure?"

"I've always been sure, Michael."

"What about your father?"

"What about him?"

"He's not going to like it."

"You're not marrying my father," she pointed out. "You're marrying me."

"You know he's not going to accept it without a fight," he told her.

Her eyes narrowed suspiciously. "You just proposed, and now you sound like you're trying to talk me out of it."

"Not at all," he said quickly. "But I know how close you are to your father. I know how important he is to you. I'd have to be a fool to think that wouldn't affect our marriage."

She smiled. "Now I know why I fell in love with you."

She didn't seem too concerned about how he's going to take it, Michael thought when she excused herself and went off to the ladies' room. *But then, she has no idea what could happen.* He was thinking of the suspicions that had been aroused during his trip to Boston.

How will she react if my hunch is correct?

57

"Do you want to tell me what's wrong, or do I have to guess?"

Spence gave Anne a halfhearted grin. "You flew all the way up here from D.C. to ask me that? I'm touched."

"I'm serious, Spencer."

"So am I," he insisted. "Better be careful, doll. You could be misunderstood. People might think you actually give a damn."

"I *do* give a damn, as you so colorfully put it," Anne responded in a barely controlled voice.

"You have a peculiar way of showing it." He lit a cigar.

"I've always cared about you," Anne said crossly. "I just couldn't live with you, that's all."

He puffed on the cigar. "Makes sense," he said finally.

"You're avoiding the issue here, Spencer." She folded her arms across her chest and faced him squarely. "What's going on?"

"You're jumping to conclusions, counselor," he told her.

"Remember who you're talking to," she stressed. "I know you—better than you'd like, I suspect. Better than *I'd* like, at times."

Nobody really knows me, he thought grimly. *Not even you, doll.* Aloud he said, "I was under the impression you wished you'd never met me."

She ignored his sarcasm. "Regardless of what I might or might not feel for you at the moment, we *were* married once, and I *did* love you. And since you *are* the father of my child, what affects you is likely to affect her."

"Nice speech, doll." He got to his feet. "But it's getting late. You're welcome to stay if you like. You can have the guest room since I know how you feel about bunking with me.'' He left the room, leaving her staring after him.

Any other time, he would have been glad to see her. But not now.

It's not as if it's something that would have any real impact on our relationship. I wouldn't have to tell her.

Michael lay awake in the darkness, thinking. He was going to marry Maria. Oh, they hadn't set a date yet—he hadn't even bought her a ring—but he'd proposed and she'd accepted. And it had left him with a great deal to think about. *Like whether our relationship can survive total honesty or not.*

His suspicions about her father weren't an issue. At this point, that was nothing more than a hunch, and he had no concrete evidence to support it. There was no reason to say anything to Maria or anyone else until he knew he was right.

I could be wrong.

But I don't think so.

It's ironic, he thought, *that if my hunch turns out to be correct, Randall and I would be in the same boat. Neither of us would be who we claim to be.*

Which brought him to the other problem he had to face: whether or not he was going to tell her the truth about himself, about his background. Whether or not he needed to tell her—or even wanted to.

Spence was also enduring a long, sleepless night. The ghosts were back, and they refused to allow him even a moment's peace. They followed him everywhere, and when he closed his eyes, they haunted his dreams.

It's because of Callahan, he thought, disturbed and angry at once. *Get rid of Callahan and exorcise the demons.*

He would have liked nothing better than to be rid of the man once and for all. Only one thing—or, more accurately, one person—kept him from doing something about it.

Maria.

Spence loved his daughter more than he hated Michael Callahan. He knew that should Callahan meet with a suspicious end, Maria would know he was behind it.

I also know she'd never forgive me, he thought. *So as long as he doesn't go too far, Callahan is safe.*

As long as he's so goddamned important to Maria, I'll have to tolerate him.

But at what price?

What's he hiding?

In the next room, Anne was also wide awake—and just as troubled. *Something is definitely wrong here. He's trying to hide something, and whatever it is, it must be serious. Not much frightens him.*

But he is frightened now. More frightened than he's willing to admit.

Oh, Spence. You haven't changed a bit.

"I can't talk now. Call me later, at the office."

"Thought you should know—your friend's making plans to hit the road again," said the voice on the other end of the line.

"Yeah? What's his destination?"

"Washington, D.C. Mean anything to you?"

"None of your goddamned business!"

And Spence hung up.

"Ready to talk about it yet?"

Spence looked up from his coffee. "I should never have called you," he growled as Anne seated herself across the table. "You were never the type to read such crazy ideas into everything I say and do. You're becoming a pain in the ass, doll."

"And you're wasting your time trying to make me think everything is fine when I can tell it's not," she shot back at him.

"Damn right everything's not fine!" he snapped, slamming his spoon down on the table. "Our daughter's practically living with the lowest form of life on the face of the planet, and there's no telling where it's heading. I'd say things are a hell of a long way from fine!"

"Oh, come on, Spence—you want me to believe the reason for this drastic mood change of yours is Maria's relationship with Michael Callahan?" Anne looked skeptical.

Spence shrugged. "Of all the men she could have ended up with, he's the last one I would have picked for her," he said glumly.

Anne raked her fingers through her pale blond hair absently. "You can't choose for her—whether the man in question is Michael Callahan or anyone else."

He raised an eyebrow questioningly. "Speaking from experience, doll?"

She frowned, sipping her coffee. "My father didn't want me to marry you, no," she admitted.

"He didn't want you to marry Jack McCleary, either," Spence reminded her.

Anne stiffened. "That was a long time ago."

He said nothing in response. *A lot of things happened a long time ago,* he was thinking. *To both of us. You were just more open about your experiences.*

And I've lost track of how many times I came close to telling you about mine. I wanted to be able to tell someone. No—not just someone. You. But I never could take the chance. I didn't know how you'd react, and I couldn't risk losing you. But I ended up losing you anyway, didn't I?

And now here you are, trying to save me from myself.

"You haven't heard a word I've said."

Anne's words cut through his thoughts. His head jerked up. "What?"

She studied him for a moment. "You haven't heard a word I've said," she repeated.

"I've got a lot on my mind," he offered as an excuse.

"Obviously."

Looking at her now, sitting across the breakfast table from him, it was as if the years since their divorce had simply melted away, and he was being given a second chance. In that instant, he made a decision he wasn't sure he wouldn't come to regret.

"Okay, doll," he said, sucking in a deep breath. "You want to know what's really bothering me? You may be sorry you asked . . . "

"I have to fly to Washington for a few days," Michael told Maria.

"The book again?" she asked with a note of disapproval in her voice.

He hesitated momentarily. "Yeah."

"Tell me—are we even going to be able to set a wedding date before this book is finished?" she asked, annoyed. "It seems like almost all of your time these days is spent on the book—"

"I thought we agreed on this."

"I agreed it was your decision to make, Michael," she said. "I didn't agree to *like* it."

He drew her into his arms. "I signed a contract. I can't get out of this deal," he said, kissing her. "But if you haven't changed your mind about marrying me, we'll go shopping for a ring as soon as I get back from D.C."

"Is that a promise?" Maria wanted to know.

"You can take it to the bank," he assured her.

"Good, because I intend to hold you to it." She paused. "Actually, it might be a good idea—you being out of town when I tell Spence we're getting married."

"Yeah?" He gave a low chuckle. "You think D.C. will be far enough to go?"

"Darling, Mars wouldn't be far enough."

Anne stared at Spence in disbelief. "Say something," he urged. "Anything."

She rose to her feet slowly. "I don't know what to say," she admitted, shaking her head. "This is all so—unexpected. Of all the things I've been imagining that could be troubling you . . ." Her voice trailed off.

"What's troubling me now is my old pal Callahan," Spence said quietly.

"No one ever guessed the truth?" Anne asked then. "Not even the people from the real Spencer Randall's past?"

Spence's grin was weak. "I guess I'm a better actor than I thought."

Anne paced the black-and-white tiled kitchen floor nervously. "It's so unbelievable—that you could have actually assumed a dead man's identity and managed to pull it off for—"

"Almost thirty years," he finished.

"Why?" she asked, turning abruptly to face him. "What was so terrible about your own life that you had to assume a new identity? What did Frankie Granelli do that was so terrible?"

He hesitated. *As long as you've come this far,* he thought, *you might as well tell her all of it. You're going to need her if Callahan finds all the bodies.* He raised his head, and his eyes met hers.

"I killed my mother."

58

Washington, D.C., December 1974.

Michael stood at the baggage carousel at National Airport, waiting for his luggage. Across the terminal, there was a commotion at the TWA counter. Something about the last flight to St. Louis being canceled. Irate passengers were being told they could get a flight out of Baltimore, but would have only an hour to reach that airport. Some of the people grabbed their bags and ran for the glass doors at the end of the terminal to commandeer taxis waiting at the cabstand outside. Others continued to voice their displeasure with the airline—very loudly—demanding to be put up in a hotel for the night.

Michael shook his head. The scene was all too familiar. He'd lost track of how many times he'd been stranded in airports in various parts of the country due to canceled flights and overbookings. Not a pleasant experience. But for once, it wasn't him, and he was glad of that. He had too much on his mind right then. He didn't need any more problems.

He collected his bags and headed for the doors, silently hoping he'd be able to get a cab amid all the chaos. It had been a long day, and tomorrow promised to be even longer. But he didn't even want to think about that. Not now. He just wanted to go straight to his hotel and crash.

He ended up waiting over twenty minutes for a taxi. When he finally did get one, the drive to the Hyatt Regency–Capitol Hill, where he was staying, seemed to take forever. Normally, he would have engaged in conversation with the cabbie— over the years, he'd gotten some of his best story ideas from cabbies in various parts of the country—but today, he was too distracted to make conversation. He had too much on his mind.

As the taxi came to a stop at the hotel's entrance on New Jersey Avenue, Michael nodded politely to the uniformed doorman who rushed to open the car door for him. It was almost a reflex action, something he did automatically. By the time he reached his room, he probably wouldn't even remember what the fellow looked like.

He had other things on his mind.

New York City.

"You know somebody at the Pentagon?" the voice on the phone asked.

"Why do you want to know?"

"Because your friend Callahan took a cab from the Hyatt Regency this morning, and that's where he was dropped off."

Spence frowned. "I see."

"What do you want me to do now?"

Idiot—how many times do I have tell you? "Stay with him—and keep me posted."

Spence held the phone for a long moment, then hung up slowly. *You're getting close, Callahan,* he thought. *Too close. Could prove hazardous to your health.*

Washington, D.C.

The plane was in a holding pattern, waiting for clearance to land at National. Anne's impatience grew with each passing minute. Had this airport suddenly become the hub of the universe? Was the entire population of the world suddenly immigrating to the District of Columbia? Why was it taking so long?

She drew in a deep breath, then let it out slowly. No use in worrying about it. Wouldn't make the plane land any faster. Unfortunately. She looked at her watch. She wasn't sure why the time mattered so much to her now. It was already too late. *For a lot of things,* she thought.

She was still having a hard time coming to grips with Spence's confession. *How could I have lived with him all those years, been married to him, had a child with him, and never suspected he was hiding so many things from me?* she asked herself. But now that she thought about it, the answer was really quite simple.

Spence never shared much of himself with anyone. Even me.

Even having been his wife, having known him as well as anyone could—as well as he would allow anyone to know him—it still seemed so incredible, so impossible.

His name isn't really Spencer Randall.

The real Spencer Randall is dead and has been for thirty years. Almost thirty years.

His real name is Frankie Granelli.

Frankie Granelli killed his mother.

She thought about the business rivals who had disappeared under suspicious circumstances, and it made her wonder.

How many others had Frankie Granelli killed?

New York City.

"What the hell is he doing at a VA hospital?" Spence asked irritably.

"I was hoping you'd tell me," said the voice on the other end of the line.

"What the hell am I paying you for if I have to do all the work?" Spence exploded.

Before the other man could respond, he hung up.

Washington, D.C.

None of this is making any sense, Michael thought.

Frankie Granelli—son of the woman *his* father had killed—and Spencer Randall had known each other. They had served together in the Navy. They'd been friends. Good friends, according to what Michael had been able to piece together. The last thing he'd expected to uncover. He'd located a Navy veteran at a VA hospital in Virginia who'd known both of them before they were sent to the South Pacific. He'd spoken to him briefly at the hospital.

"*Real strange, those two.*"

"*Strange? Why strange?*"

"*It never quite fit, the friendship between them.*"

"*Why do you say that?*"

"*They just didn't belong together. Not those two. If ever two people didn't have nothin' in common, it was Frankie and Spence.*"

"*In what way?*"

"*In every way. Frankie was a hell-raiser. Real bad temper. Liked to gamble. Spence was just the opposite. Real quiet, kind of a bookworm. Read a lot. Even-tempered, never said a bad word to anybody. Only thing was, neither one of them ever talked much about their families, where they came from. Except to each other, I guess.*"

Michael frowned as his thoughts returned abruptly to the present. Something wasn't quite right, but he couldn't put his finger on exactly what it was. He replayed that conversation over and over in his mind.

Neither of those men sounded like the Spencer Randall he knew. . . .

New York City.

"When are you coming home?" Maria asked Michael.

"I don't know, but it can't be soon enough for me," he told her. "I'm tired of living out of a suitcase."

"I'm tired of living without my fiancé," she said.

"I wish I'd never started this goddamned book," he admitted.

She sighed heavily. *I've always felt that way, Michael,* she thought. *I've always been afraid this book would eventually come between us.*

Washington, D.C.

Anne's primary concern now was Maria.

She knows nothing of any of this, Anne thought, sitting in the study of her Georgetown apartment, sipping a brandy that might as well have been tap water for all the attention she'd been paying it. *She has no idea just how much her father has been hiding.*

But she will. Soon.

Time is running out, if Spence is right. Michael gets closer to the truth every day. The man is no fool, she thought.

What is all of this going to do to Maria—to not only be faced with the truth about her father, but to have it exposed by the man she's going to marry?

Anne picked up the phone and dialed Spence's number. "Spence—it's Anne," she said when he answered. "We have to talk."

"Really?" he asked with a twinge of sarcasm in his voice. "When you left here, I had the distinct impression that all you wanted was to get as far from me as you could."

"Maria has to be told," she said.

"No."

"If you don't tell her, I will."

"No," he repeated, this time with a savage edge to his voice.

"Spence, she's going to find out anyway. She should hear it from you. If Michael tells her first—"

"He won't."

"How can you know—"

"I know I'll stop him, no matter what it takes," he said gravely.

Anne didn't ask what he meant by that. *I have a feeling I'm better off not knowing.*

New York City.

Spence hung up, staring thoughtfully at the phone. *Anne's right about one thing,* he thought. *If Callahan does find out, he won't hesitate to tell Maria.*

It would destroy my relationship with my daughter.

I can't let that happen.

I won't.

Callahan has to be silenced.
Once and for all.

Washington, D.C.

"Frank Granelli died in the sinking of the *Indianapolis* in 1945."

"Are you absolutely certain?" Michael wasn't convinced.

The man sitting on the other side of the desk in the small, cramped office at the Department of the Navy at the Pentagon merely shrugged. "That's what the records say."

"There couldn't be a mistake?"

"No mistake," the other man said with finality. "There were some survivors—"

"Spencer Randall was one of them," Michael cut in.

The man looked surprised. "If you already knew—"

"Why did I bother to ask?" Michael finished. "I had to be sure."

"May I ask what this is all about?"

"You can ask, but I can't answer," Michael said, getting to his feet. "Let's just call it a military secret."

New York City.

"I've got to go," Maria said, smoothing the front of her skirt as she stood up.

"You can stay here tonight," Spence told her. "It's late. Doesn't make a lot of sense to go now."

She smiled. "I'm only five minutes away, Spence," she reminded him.

"You got something against staying here?"

"No, of course not," she said, then turned to face him. "But I can't help wondering why you're suddenly insisting I stay over."

"We haven't talked in a long time."

She looked at him quizzically. "We talk every day!"

"I mean really talk. And not about business."

Maria drew in her breath. "If you're going to start attacking my relationship with Michael," she began, "I think you should know that we're getting married."

Spence felt as though she'd just punched him in the stomach. "Married?" he asked, his voice tight with anger. "You'd actually marry that son of a bitch?"

She raised a hand to silence him. "I don't want to argue with you, Spence, but I'm not going to stand here and listen to you launch a verbal attack against the man I'm going to marry." She picked up her coat. "I think it's best that I leave now, before we both end up saying things we'll be sorry for later."

He didn't try to stop her, though he knew he should have. *I should have told her,* he thought. *But I can't. Maria's all I have left now. I can't risk losing her.*

Callahan's got to be silenced. Now.

Washington, D.C.

I wonder if he's told her yet.

Anne thought about it as she sat in her car on the bridge over the Potomac, stuck in heavier-than-usual traffic.

He couldn't have.

He would have called if he had.

She would have called.

She'd be upset. Or angry. She's my daughter, and right now, even I'm not sure how she'd react.

And then there's Spence. I should never have left New York, she thought, checking her watch and hoping she didn't miss her flight.

Spence needs me. And here I am, rushing off to him, in spite of everything. I was so sure I'd gotten him out of my system. Anne was confused and more than a little angry with herself. *I guess I was wrong. I guess there's a part of me that always has and always will belong to Spence Randall.*

And she hated herself for feeling that way. Hated him for making her feel that way. The man wasn't good for her and never had been. He wasn't good for *any* woman, not even their daughter. Especially not their daughter. Yet Anne had never been able to stop loving him. Now he was in some kind of trouble—not that it was anything new, trouble had always been a way of life with her ex-husband—and here she was, dropping everything to go to him, just as she always had and always would. She liked to think he needed her, if only for moral support.

But Spence Randall had never really needed anybody. . . .

New York City.

"You involved in some sort of illegal arms deal or something?" the voice on the phone wanted to know.

"Don't ask stupid questions," Spence shot back impatiently. "What have you got for me?"

"He spent one real busy afternoon at the Pentagon."

Spence hung up.

Washington, D.C.

It's the only possible answer, Michael thought. *The only one that makes any sense at all.*

And it was so obvious, he couldn't believe it hadn't occurred to him earlier.

Probably because before, it never occurred to anyone—me or anybody else—to connect Spencer Randall to a Chicago street kid named Frankie Granelli, he told himself. *Okay, so Randall and Granelli were in the Navy together. So they were buddies. A real odd pair, but so what? And why wouldn't they think he was Randall? He had Randall's dog tags—God only knows why, but he had them.*

It didn't surprise Michael that Frankie Granelli would want to trade places with Spencer Randall. It was, after all, a golden opportunity if ever there was one: a kid from a rather seedy world who joined the Navy with nothing but a lot of guts and a real instinct for gambling and a kid with no living relatives.

An upper-class kid, Michael thought, mentally considering the possibilities. *Still . . . was it only the status that made Spence trade places with the real Randall?*

Or was there another reason?

59

Chicago, December 1974.

Michael was beginning to feel as though he'd spent more time in the air than he had on the ground in the past few weeks.

Now, as he disembarked from the plane at O'Hare Airport, he was thinking about the events of those past few weeks, about the incredible story he'd uncovered.

The biggest story of my career, but can I write it? he asked himself as he headed for the baggage carousel to collect his luggage. He ignored the Hare Krishna who'd approached him and continued to follow him with unusual persistence. He was still thinking about what he'd unearthed. It would make one hell of a book. *A best-seller—eighty-seven weeks on the New York Times Book Review list, a made-for-TV movie, Johnny Carson, all the trappings of a major success.*

He was also thinking of Maria. She idolized her father. He wasn't sure what it was going to do to her, learning the truth about her father. He couldn't even imagine how she'd react to a book revealing it. A book *he* had written. Once it was reality, would she be able to handle it? He had doubts. Even now, with the project little more than an idea, it was a sore subject between them.

Only one thing missing—a motive, he thought, turning his attention back to Randall himself. *Otherwise, it all makes sense. It's the only explanation that does.*

Spencer Randall and Frank Granelli . . . two men as different as night and day in looks, personality, and background. They might as well have been from different planets. Yet they had met—not only met, but had become friends—in the Navy. A fluke, a twist of fate, had enabled Granelli to assume his friend's identity and start a new life in New York after the war.

One piece of the puzzle's still missing, though: the moti-

vation, Michael thought. *Why did he do it? Why would he want to?*

Okay, so he was a street kid from Chicago. His roots weren't anything to be proud of. No surprise he wanted to get away. But why the new identity? What was he running away from?

What am I missing here?

A man from the wrong side of the tracks simply looking to start over? Michael didn't buy that. No . . . there had to be more to it than that.

But it looks like Randall's the only one who knows, Michael told himself.

And knowing him, he'll probably take it to his grave.

New York City.

"Should I be saying my prayers?" Spence wanted to know.

Anne stood in the doorway, glaring at him. "Probably," she snapped, "but for now I'll settle for you stepping aside so I can come in."

"By all means." As he did so, he saw the uniformed doorman behind her, carrying her bags. "I should definitely be saying my prayers," he muttered, peeling off a few bills from the roll he'd taken from his pocket to tip the man.

After the doorman was gone, Spence turned to Anne again. "There are supposedly seven signs that signal the beginning of the apocalypse," he said. "I'm sure this must be one of them—but what are the other six?"

"I don't know how you can possibly make jokes, under the circumstances," she responded irritably.

He closed the door. "Who's making jokes?"

"Have someone take these to the guest room," she said, gesturing.

"I'll do it." He started to pick them up.

Anne looked at him oddly. "Where's your staff?"

"I sent them to Disneyland," he answered tonelessly.

Rolling her eyes skyward, she sighed heavily. "Spencer, please—"

"They're all on vacation, all right?" He looked up at her as he collected her luggage. "I needed to be alone."

"I can imagine."

"So why are *you* here?" he asked then.

"I think you already know."

"I'm not telling Maria, so you've wasted your time coming here," he told her.

"She has to be told," Anne argued. "She should hear it from you, but if you won't tell her, I will."

"No!" Luggage in hand, Spence turned and walked away.

Why do I still love him? Anne asked herself once again. *Why?*

Chicago.

"Frankie Granelli?" The policeman punched the name into his computer. "Doesn't show anything here."

Michael paused for a moment. "It probably wouldn't be on your computer," he said. "It was a long time ago."

"Like how long?"

"I'm not sure, exactly. Sometime before World War Two," Michael told him.

The policeman looked as though he were trying not to laugh. "You're right—it wouldn't be in here," he said with a nod.

"Where *would* it be?" Michael asked.

"What type of offenses are we talking about?"

"I'm not sure. Maybe none at all," Michael admitted. "But I need to know where to look if there *were* any charges."

"Well, I do know there are files kept on unsolved murders, but as for anything else that far back—" He shrugged. "You want to leave your name and number? I'll have someone call you."

Michael nodded, scrawling his name and the phone number on the notepad the young officer gave him. "You're new at this," he stated more than asked.

The policeman nodded. "Yeah."

I thought so.

The longer the bodies are buried, the harder they are to dig up, Michael thought as he attempted to hail a taxi outside the police station. *And Randall's—or Granelli's—skeletons have been buried a long, long time.*

He didn't see the man on top of the building across the street, the man with the high-powered rifle who'd been waiting for him. Who would have pulled the trigger had the taxi not pulled up to the curb to pick him up, obstructing the sniper's view.

"I don't understand." Maria sounded bewildered. "Why are you in Chicago? Spence never lived in Chicago."

No, Spencer Randall didn't, but Frankie Granelli did. "I'm interviewing some of his former shipmates—from the war," Michael told her. "Survivors from the *Indianapolis*."

"When will you be coming home?" she asked.

"As soon as I can," he promised. "Probably by the end of the week."

"Good." Her voice took on a more cheerful note. "I'd like to think you're going to be home for Christmas."

"Me, too," he said. And to himself: *I'd just like to know you'll still be waiting for me when this is all over.*

60

My father killed Randall's—Granelli's—mother.

Michael thought about it as the plane taxied down the runway and lifted off smoothly, leaving O'Hare Airport behind as it soared upward into the clear December sky. *It's too bad it's not as easy to leave other things behind,* he thought, still trying to comprehend what he'd discovered within the past forty-eight hours.

He took the photocopied newspaper clippings he'd gotten at the Chicago public library from a large manila envelope and reread them yet again, in search of something he might have overlooked the countless other times he'd read them at the hotel. *There's still something missing,* he thought.

Kathleen Granelli was a prostitute.

Leonard Rogers was one of her regular customers.

Rogers liked to beat up whores. One night he went too far. He killed her. Her son Frankie was the one who found the body. The kid was sent off to a home, but he ran away. Rogers continued to declare his innocence, right up to the day he was executed.

End of story. Or is it?

So the kid didn't come from a model family. So his father was a bootlegger and his mother a hooker. It wasn't anything to be proud of, but it still doesn't explain why he felt he had to run away, assume a new identity. A piece of the puzzle's still missing.

And only Randall—Granelli—knows what it is.

New York City.

"Why don't you just pack your bags and go back to D.C.?" Spence asked, irritated. "I'm sure the Justice Department needs you more than I do."

Anne looked unconvinced. "There was a time you would have wanted me to stay," she reminded him.

"There was a time I didn't want you to leave," he said, lighting a cigar, "but you left anyway."

She paused thoughtfully. "I'm probably a fool for telling you this, and an even bigger fool for feeling it, but in spite of the divorce, in spite of everything that was wrong between us, in spite of all that you've told me, a part of me still loves you and always will."

"Any other time, doll, I'd be glad to hear that," he told her. "Even if it didn't mean you'd be coming home."

"Any other time?" she asked, not sure she understood.

"Right now, doll, I need to be alone."

Anne refused to give up on him.

Why do I bother? she asked herself more than once. *The man has been on self-destruct as long as I've known him.*

But at least now it makes sense.

*   *   *

"He's back in New York," the voice on the phone told Spence.

"What do you mean, he's *back*?" Spence roared. "You were supposed to take care of him, goddamnit!"

"I never got another chance—"

"What the hell have I been paying you for?" Spence demanded.

But he hung up before the other man could answer.

What am I going to tell Maria? Michael asked himself, sitting in the back of a taxi en route to Manhattan from Kennedy Airport. He hadn't let her know he was coming home today because he knew she would have insisted on meeting him at the airport, and he wasn't sure how he was going to answer the questions he knew she was going to ask.

Not until I've talked to her father, anyway.

"Isn't this rather short notice?" Maria asked, taken by surprise by her father's call.

"I never thought the day would come that I'd have to make an appointment to have dinner with my own daughter," he said.

"Oh, now don't pull that injured father routine on me," she replied. "I'm just surprised, that's all."

"Then I'll tell you something that will surprise you even more. Your mother's here. She'll be joining us."

"Mother's in town? Where's she staying?"

"Here."

"Here—as in with you?"

"Yep."

She laughed. "You're right. I *am* surprised," she told him.

"So—are you coming?"

"I suppose there's no reason why I couldn't," she said. "Michael hasn't called, so he's probably not coming home tonight. What time?"

"Why don't you just come whenever you leave the office?" he suggested. "Give us more time together."

"Sure, why not?" She paused. "I'll see you then."

Spence hung up slowly. *Tonight, Callahan,* he thought, *it's just you and me.*

*   *   *

I've decided not to do the book. I'm going to give them back their money and let them cancel the contract. Why? Oh, that's simple. Because if I write the book, I'm under an obligation to tell the whole story. The problem with that? Well, for starters, there's a pretty strong chance that your father's real name is Frankie Granelli and that his mother was a prostitute in Prohibition-era Chicago who was murdered by one of her customers, a man named Leonard Rogers. Why should revealing that bother me? Leonard Rogers was my father, though I didn't know it until a few months ago.

He'd rehearsed it in his head a dozen times, but he still didn't know how he was going to tell Maria the whole story. He didn't even know how he was going to tell his publisher without explaining why he couldn't write the book. *I can't just say, "Well, George, I've just changed my mind. That's all."*

In the first place, they'd probably sue me.

He let himself into his apartment and put his suitcases down next to the door. He wasn't in the mood to sort through junk mail; he'd worry about his mail later. Right now, he had to call Maria.

And I have to figure out how I'm going to tell her, he thought grimly. *If she's tried to reach me at the Drake, she knows I've already checked out.*

The red light on the answering machine was on. He pressed the replay button and listened to his messages while he took off his coat. There was one from Maria: "Hi, darling. If you've been trying to reach me, I'm having dinner with Spence and my mother tonight. Can you believe it? She's not only in town, but she's staying with him!"

I could believe just about anything right now, honey, he thought.

The next message was from Randall himself: "I think it's time you and I had a talk, pal. Face-to-face. St. Patrick's at nine-thirty."

How like you to get right to the point, Michael thought. *Well, St. Patrick's is public enough. Even he wouldn't do anything stupid there.*

He decided to leave a message for Maria. Once this meeting with her father was over, they had to have a talk.

I have to tell her everything.

Spence sat in the back of his limo, en route to St. Patrick's Cathedral, but he wasn't alone. The ghosts were with him. They were always with him, his mother and Spencer and the others, constant reminders of the past, of who he'd been and what he had become.

He fingered the loaded gun in the pocket of his overcoat. *Soon,* he thought, *soon it's all going to be over.*

Soon we'll all be at peace.

Michael had trouble getting a cab.

He stood on the curb, signaling to every taxi he saw, until finally one stopped for him. "I was about to give up," he told the driver as he climbed into the backseat.

"Christmas shoppers," the cabbie offered in explanation. "We're busier than ever this time of year, if that's possible. The lousy weather doesn't help, either."

"The rain feels like it's on the verge of freezing," Michael observed as the cab pulled away from the curb.

"It's supposed to change to snow tonight," the cabbie told him. "Could be we'll have a white Christmas this year."

Michael wasn't listening. He was thinking about what he was going to tell Randall. *He'll be pleased to know he's won,* Michael thought.

That there's not going to be a book after all.

"I can't believe he's actually gone off to a business meeting after insisting I come to dinner," Maria said as she and Anne adjourned to the study for an after-dinner drink.

"He said it couldn't wait," Anne commented as she poured the brandy. "You'd think the fate of the free world was at stake."

"You two are getting along unusually well these days, aren't you?" Maria observed, seating herself at her father's desk.

Anne smiled, handing her daughter a brandy. "You could

say we've achieved an armed truce," she said.

"Seems like a little more than that to me," Maria insisted.

"Don't get your hopes up," Anne cautioned, seating herself. "We've had some unfinished business to take care of, that's all."

Maria sipped her brandy, then put her glass down abruptly and reached for the phone. "I need to check my messages. I haven't talked to Michael all day, and he's probably tried to call me." She dialed her home number, then punched in the code to play back her messages.

"That's odd," she said, looking mildly confused as she put the receiver back on its cradle. "Michael called—he's back."

"I would think you'd be happy about that," Anne said.

"He didn't tell me he was coming."

Anne shrugged. "Maybe he wanted to surprise you."

"He surprised me, all right," Maria said, clearly troubled by the message he'd left. "It would seem he's the one Spence is meeting with tonight."

Anne was suddenly alarmed, remembering what Spence had said before about stopping Michael from exposing him. "That *is* strange," she said slowly.

"It gets even stranger," Maria continued. "They're meeting at St. Patrick's Cathedral."

"Prompt as always, I see."

The cathedral seemed to be deserted. Not at all what Michael had expected. Startled by the sound of Spence's voice, he swung around. Spence was standing in the aisle, maybe ten yards away. "Some things never change, do they, pal?" he asked, glancing at his watch. "Nine-thirty, on the mark. I prefer to be early myself. I like to get the jump on my competition."

"Is that what I am to you?" Michael asked. "Competition?"

Spence laughed. "Hardly," he said, taking a step forward. "Did you enjoy Chicago?"

Michael shrugged. "I can take it or leave it."

"You might have enjoyed it more if you hadn't spent all of your time at the library."

"So," Michael began slowly, "you had me followed. Can't say I'm all that surprised."

Spence grinned. "Then it won't surprise you to know that I had you followed to Boston and Washington, too."

"I hope you got your money's worth."

"Unfortunately, I didn't. He came highly recommended, but he was inept." Spence put his hands in his coat pockets. "Didn't do what I was paying him to do, so now I've got to take care of it myself."

Michael stared at him, saying nothing.

"Good help is so hard to find these days," Spence went on.

"Tell me something," Michael said then. "Am I on the right track? Did the real Spencer Randall die on the *Indianapolis*?"

Spence smiled coldly. "You don't have proof? I'm disappointed."

"Well?" Michael asked.

He seemed to be considering it. "I suppose it doesn't make any difference now," he said finally. "Yeah. Spencer Randall died on the *Indianapolis*."

"And you?"

"I think you already know the answer, pal."

"I don't understand," Maria began as she followed Anne up the steps to the cathedral's Fifth Avenue entrance. "Why are you so worried about this meeting—"

"There's no time to explain now," Anne told her, easing the door open. "Just stay behind me and keep quiet."

Maria gave her a puzzled look.

"Spence has a gun."

Maria's eyes widened in horror. "You think he's planning to *kill* Michael?"

"I don't know what he might or might not do," Anne admitted, "but while he's armed, it's not a good idea to startle him."

Spence didn't see them come in. His back was to the door when they entered, and the two women moved into the shadows where they wouldn't be seen.

Michael, his attention focused on Spence, didn't see them either. "So after the ship went down, everyone thought you were Spencer Randall," he said slowly. "You decided to have plastic surgery and assume his identity."

Spence nodded. "And it worked—until you came along."

"What!" Maria gasped under her breath.

"Ssh!" Anne silenced her.

"One thing still doesn't make sense," Michael was saying. "Why? Why did you have to have a new identity? It doesn't make sense. The man who killed your mother was convicted and executed—"

Spence's laugh was hollow. "Leonard Rogers didn't kill my mother."

Michael froze. "How would you know that?" he wanted to know.

"He was one of her customers, all right," Spence said, ignoring the question. "He liked to beat her up. That night, he really worked her over. I hated it—hated what he did to her, hated knowing she did it because she needed the money, because she had no other way of providing for me."

"*How do you know Rogers didn't kill her*?" Michael demanded.

"Because I did it, because I had to put her out of her misery!" At that moment, he pulled the gun from his pocket and pointed it at Michael. "But knowing that won't do you any good, pal. Like I said, the man I hired was an idiot. Now I've got to finish the job myself."

"No!" Maria screamed, rushing forward. Anne pushed her to the ground just as Spence, startled, swung around and fired once. Anne took the bullet herself.

"No!" Spence roared, realizing what he'd done. As Michael raced to Maria, Spence dropped the gun and sank to the floor, crawling to Anne on all fours.

"Are you all right?" Michael asked, holding Maria close as she sobbed uncontrollably.

"I—I think so." She looked down at her mother. "Dear God . . . don't let her die!"

Spence cradled Anne in his arms, crying like a small child as he begged her not to die. They were both covered with blood when he finally lowered her to the floor and stood up.

"What have I done?" he asked, looking upward.

He didn't run at the sound of police sirens out in front of the cathedral. He just turned and walked out one of the side doors, into the night.

Into oblivion.

61

Spence had no idea how long he'd been walking or where he'd been before he found himself at the hospital. He didn't even clearly recall fleeing the cathedral. *Is this the right one?* he wondered, standing outside the emergency room entrance. *Is this where they took her?*

He went inside, ignoring the attention he was attracting in his wet, bloodstained clothes, and walked to the admitting desk. "Anne Randall—is she here?" he asked.

The woman looked at him oddly for a moment, then nodded. He looked like a bum. No wonder he wasn't recognized. "Uh, let me check." She checked the admissions records for the evening. "Anne Talbott Randall?"

"Yeah."

She nodded again. "She was brought in—and yes, she has been admitted."

"Where is she?"

She gave him the room number. "Sir!" she called after him as he walked away. "You won't be able to see her— she's in intensive care!"

But Spence kept walking.

"What are you doing here?" Maria demanded contemptuously.

My daughter is not happy to see me, he thought, now confronted with an anger she'd never directed at him before. Of all he stood to lose as the result of his thirty-year deception, this was by far the most painful loss he would have to face. *This, and Anne's death.*

He endured her rage because he had to, because he had to tell her everything now. *Even if it is too late,* he thought. *You were right, doll. I should have told her before.*

The truth shall set you free.

I doubt anything can set me free now.

But he told her. He told her the whole story, from the beginning, omitting nothing. Her expression remained unchanged as he spoke. She clung to Michael, her eyes red and swollen from crying.

It was Michael, his arms around her protectively, who looked oddly sympathetic.

But it wasn't Michael Callahan whom Spence was concerned about. He looked at Maria, who continued to avoid his eyes. "I wish you'd say something," he said finally.

"What's left to say now?" she asked tonelessly.

He stared at her for a moment, then shook his head. "Nothing—if that's the way you really feel—" He stopped short as he noticed a slight movement of Anne's left hand.

Maria saw it, too. "She's coming around!"

Michael rang for a nurse. Spence dropped into a chair next to the bed and clutched her hand tightly. "Anne—can you hear me, doll?" he asked.

She blinked twice. "Spence?" she asked weakly.

"Yeah, doll—it's me." He brushed her hair back off her forehead. She opened her eyes and looked at him, smiling faintly.

"Maria—is she—" She stopped short, gripped by pain.

Maria moved to the other side of the bed. "I'm here, Mother," she said softly. "Michael and I have been here with you since you were brought in." She still wouldn't look at Spence.

Sensing the tension between her ex-husband and her daughter, Anne looked at Spence. "Give her time, Spence. She's got so much to deal with now." Anne's voice grew weaker. "She loves you."

Spence glanced at Maria. "Not anymore."

Maria said nothing.

Anne turned to her daughter. "Your father did what he thought was best for you—"

"Please, Mother—don't try to talk now," Maria urged. "You have to save your strength."

"Has to be now . . . not much time left," Anne breathed. "Don't want to leave the two of you like this . . . you're going to need each other—" Suddenly she gasped with pain, then her body went still.

"*Mother!*" Maria screamed.

At that moment, Michael returned with a nurse. No doubt a cop wouldn't be far behind. Spence stood back, looking on while she checked Anne's vital signs. A doctor came in, and after a brief examination, pronounced her dead. Maria collapsed into Michael's arms, sobbing. Spence stood in the doorway for a long moment, saying nothing. *No point in staying now,* he thought numbly, and turned to leave.

"Spence," Michael called after him.

"Go to hell."

Spence turned and walked away.

He had no idea where he was going. *It doesn't matter, not anymore,* he thought as he walked alone through Central Park. Alone—yet not really alone. The ghosts were with him, as they were always with him: his mother and Spencer—and now Anne. *The people I've cared most about in my life. The people I destroyed.*

And I've lost Maria, too.

"*She loves you,*" Anne had said.

"Not anymore, doll. I should have listened to you," Spence said aloud. "It's better this way. I've killed everyone else who cared about me."

"*You didn't kill me, Frankie,*" said Spencer.

"Same thing, pal. I was supposed to relieve you on watch and didn't. It was supposed to be me. You died in my place."

"*It was fate, Frankie. Besides, as far as the world knows, Spencer Randall is still alive.*"

"*I* know the truth."

"*You did what you did because you loved me, Frankie.*" This was his mother. "*Just as I did what I did because I loved you.*"

"What about you, doll?" Spence asked. "You gonna tel me I killed you because I loved you, too?"

"No, but your actions were those of a man protecting his family."

"Sure."

"You wanted to protect Maria and me. You thought you had to kill Michael to do that. Shooting me was an accident Spence."

"I'm not Spence."

"It doesn't matter who you were, darling. It's who you are now that's important."

"One's as bad as the other, doll." The sound of the ap proaching police cars' sirens sent the ghosts away. Spence stopped walking and turned, and when he saw the flashing lights, he felt unexpectedly relieved.

He could finally stop running.